Seeds

Joseph Thomas Willig

ISBN
978-0-6452850-0-0 (Hardback)
978-0-6452850-1-7 (Paperback)
978-0-6452850-2-4 (Digital)

Gnatdagger@gmail.com

SEEDS

For the voice within each of us

INTRODUCTION

This tale takes place on Irfa, a planet closely related to Earth. It is inhabited by human beings that speak the same languages and, in principle, have the same history as Homo sapiens. The physical laws on both planets are congruent. The era is modern, post-industrial, and technologically-advanced.

It is important for the setting to be in a slightly different reality so one doesn't get entangled with the semantics of preconception. The names of people and places mimic how a toddler would speak; a weak tongue and sluggish lung, heirs of nothing but indifference.

It cannot be derived, yet, if we ever make it past this initial stage of understanding in life's cycle. Regardless of time acquired or the saturation of sensibility kept, individually.

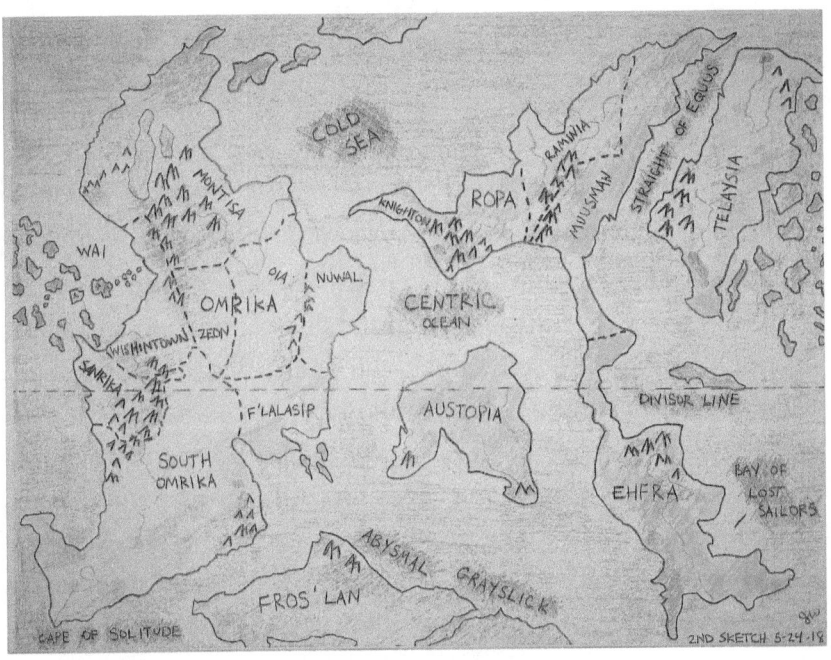

PART A

INCREDULITY

I

The bureaucracy of man has poisoned the Irfa. Not only the mental aptitude of present species, and spirit, but the dirt itself. Gnat is looking over a broad landscape from the peak of the tallest local mountain as the thought passes through his mind like the progeny of a plant, floating on a wind to some unknown destination. Its name is the King of Storms. A long way up with hardly any switchbacks, it has earned this title; not many have succeeded in sitting on this summit. A throne of jagged rock and moss, both living in harmony and disparity concurrently. The clouds are of a cirrus nature. Wisps of ice and water, at such a distance they seem to be only cotton candy. Sharp white, the sky a soft blue, a touch of longing in the shade of it. Across the valley amid the peaks, Lake Kressent. A glacial body formed by maelstrom and the entrapment of water over an unfathomable number of spans. Another double score of shades. Blues, turquoises, and taupes reveal its varying depths. A secret floor unseen. What mysteries does it hide? Things that will never be discovered. Things that will remain long past the expiration date of life. At last, the flicker of a fin seen even from this perch over-looking the wood. Ah, the wood. Pure green amongst coniferous growth strikes inspiration within any onlooker. Trees so old and wise time almost eludes them. The weather can't permeate their herd, their family. Living in unity with all creatures. The watch-men. The shade and protection for the rest. Absorbing whatever is needed, producing only clarity. They challenge each other for the light. Not in fear. Not in anger. Only in competition. Until out in the distance there is a gap. Then another. Cut to shreds, taken by force, leveled for untold distance. What malicious impetus could have done this?

For the jobs, they say. A man needs a job to have purpose. The economy of the state needs it. Children deserve an education. The poor must be fed. The roads demand to be laid, what will carry men to work? How will we transport lumber? It's our destiny to keep the industry local. It's us against the outsiders! They'd do the same to us if they could. No need to discuss, of course that's the answer. Never mind the bird, fox, cat or insect; the lowly animals with no concept of right or wrong, no ideas or opinions in the first place. Forget the cures to ailments that we will never have the chance to find again or an abundance of rich clean air. The future can think about those things. It's about profit. It's about the moment. It's about people.

He's thinking of the generation that came before his parents. An entire age of humans taught how to exist through marketing campaigns. He's heard the slogans from his grandfather many times. *The best thing you can do is pay off your house.* What do you do when you love a woman? *You buy her a diamond.* Why do you drink milk at every meal? *For the calcium. To avoid osteoporosis. Didn't you see the commercial?* The facts of life as told by corporations. Gladly accepted for only a few cents. Isn't it cheap? Yes, it is.

Gnat came to Wishintown in the warm season three spans earlier. A man of twenty-seven, physically, average. Somewhat heavy, but not overweight. A side effect of his affinity for alcohol. Not so much for the fun of it, more to stop his mind from running. To think of only simple things. A round face with round features. Eyes of hazel, sometimes more gray than green depending on whether or not the rain is nearby. Flecks of gold were blown across his irises. A product of the explosions of stars it seems. His long hair has a dark nature bleached by the sun at the tips. Uncut for nearly ten spans, he wears the split ends as if he was a warrior returning from battle, proof of his right to be respected. The slightest of smiles can be seen in his gaze most of the time. A squint in actuality, as if he doesn't believe that anything seen is real or knows something no one else does. A childhood friend once told him he has an angry resting face. In passing people always tell him he looks too serious. However when he does laugh honestly, on occasion, it's infectious. A rolling cackle in a higher pitch than it should be by the look of him.

Clothing is about function, not form. Gnat always wears denim jeans, a black t-shirt, and leather boots. *Practical.* And his brown zip-up hooded sweatshirt. He has done this ever since he left home for the first time so many spans earlier.

There's a purpose in what he wears. A voiding aim or rudimentary statement, perhaps. It's him you meet no matter what the situation. A man naked in the scheme of things, bereft of false pretenses created by a flash of gaudiness.

However he isn't cheap, always spending to make sure everyone is having a favorable time. Gnat pushes people out of their normal level of comfort. This is something constantly questioned. How does he get people to enter into activities they normally wouldn't? His truly nonjudgmental attitude. Some things he's done in his life, no right is owned to throw a stone. The first, or last. Strangers are comfortable around him. Wherever he goes companions are found. Single-use friends, the staple of his social presence. Meet someone, buy them a drink, go on an adventure and never hear from them again. The initial contact is most important. Never a solitary woman, though. Maybe a few girls or guys his age. Locals. People that feel safe with somebody new entering their bubble.

They have someone to reassure them if they doubt what they say or do. Not too much, not too little; the perfect mix of fast and slow. A bit brash, a tiny touch of coyness. Confident yet not completely sure. So many different lives lived. Trying to find common ground with the people he cannot relate to. He enjoys spinning stories to connect with them. Not for the mistruth, it's only a byproduct of an intensely wild imagination and boredom. He's the type to have maybe one or two others close to him at any point. Gnat is not credulous enough to let anybody see him in an unerring sense.

In adolescence his group of friends went into the forest with hallucinogenic mushrooms to find their spirit animals. The real Native Omrikan way. Gnat found a hollow under a group of trees far away by himself. He could no longer hear the sneers of the other teenagers gathered next to the nearby creek. Quietly he waited. The flutters of nauseating euphoria came and went. Up and down, more intensely and quickly as time passed. He glanced at his hands, his totem even then, to calculate the reality he occupied. At the top of this artificial form of transparency Gnat heard a rustle. Slowly his head turned with the creak of neck bones echoing through his brain like ripples on a pond made of gelatin. Thick and penetrating. Powerful. Unable to be ignored. His vision moving in waves, like the static between stations when twisting the dial on a radio. Reaching for coherency.

As his eyes became focused, it was there. Staring back with the same acute curiosity. An owl.

Always watching from afar on some branch, he's still the owl. Not speaking unless he has something important to say, knowing the wisest man listens. No need for glamour, no desire to be the loudest. Although as his grandmother always says, able to be charming when he wants. However, in essence Gnat is melancholy. A perceptible twist of anger, a dash of despondency.

When he was four spans of age, as any other child, he started school. The joy of every university, fresh meat to extort at a later date. As a lion patiently leaves its catch to decompose before eating. The heartbreak of every mother, letting their hatchling flap its wings for the first time. It's unknown how fast they will fall or how far they will fly.

Gnat wore a full suit with suspenders to class, always, a dapper man packed in a miniature space. Extremely shy and unsure of himself, these feelings remained inside him for many grades until he reached adulthood. Although gifted in terms of the educational institution, he felt stupid. When he raised his hand to speak, none of his peers would reply. It was the same in conversation on the playground. Not until he was an adult did he see that his peers did not understand him; his thoughts were over their heads.

In Mrs. Wilumsun's class they raised caterpillars to become butterflies, when the flowers started to bloom. Each child had their own terrarium complete with twigs for the insects to hang a cocoon from. A tiny water dish, and food resembling something between clay and dust. Basic nutrients, they smelled both moldy and healthy. Gnat wanted something magnificent to crawl out of that shell. Whenever teacher wasn't looking he would give his companion extra food and water. His bug needed to be stronger than the rest. How else would *it* reach *his* goal? After some time the bugs started to construct their cocoons, desolation chambers that sent them toward their combined destinies of metamorphosis. Eventually some of the creatures started to emerge, drying their wings. Such fragile things, if touched they become too heavy to fly. The oils from a finger could drown them, trap them on the ground too slow to defend themselves. Gnat's bug remained in evolutionary meditation. Only natural if it was to be the biggest. The release was scheduled for the final class of the term. Gnat woke up and put on his tie with only a clip to secure it, suave nonetheless. Running and laughing toward the building, lunchbox swinging, he and the caterpillar made a deal to win. A bonded duo with similar expectations; to soar, to be recognized. Entering the classroom Mrs. Wilumsun threw a smile that expressed tenderness. Around the corner, he saw it. The cocoon laid on the floor of its cage silent and brown. No butterfly. Had it escaped? Flown to glory without him or the others? *The sign of a genuine winner.*

Mrs. Wilumsun came over and removed the cocoon. Placing it in his hands sharp and knotted, not smooth and natural like he'd imagined. He peeled it open. Inside the caterpillar was dried out like a sponge in the sun. The teacher told him this sometimes happens if the conditions are not right. It wasn't his fault. But he knew then what he had done. Gnat gave the caterpillar too much care. Too much sustenance. Too many thoughts. After a break the children gathered, tiny plastic habitats in their arms. Except Gnat. Those children that had done exactly what they were told without question were reaping the benefits of something they never earned for themselves. It was freely given so they took it. As the seemingly endless flurry of wings flapped to the sky, he watched. What did he see? This exercise, designed as a first introduction to the grace that is life for young budding minds, taught him about the inverse. Death. That the things you put your energy in never give back. That there is only one outcome.

A chilled wind snaps him to the present. The temperature's dropped and the way back to the housing complex isn't short. He is always in his head thinking of the expanses of the universe and this world in it, missing the fleeting details of mundane life. The sun is not visible anymore but the saffron fluorescence remains, encompassing one flank of the sky. The clouds are violet and iron. Completely still. Almost frozen in place. On the other flank rests a young moon, born each night innocent and gentle. It will rise high to the pinnacle then age gracefully out of view by morning. An entire life lived on every cycle. *A sliver off full*, Gnat thinks. This side has the power of a deep, impenetrable sapphire. A few of the brightest stars peek through. *Eventide.* Where the battle between light and dark is authentic, not figurative. Where does moon begin and sun end? You can't quite tell, there is a faint pearl line blurred between these opposing forces. What is that area lacking color? The unknown.

Shivers run down his spine. There's a heaviness, a dumbbell in his pelvis. Cords attached to his shoulders and skull tug at him. It hasn't always been present, or this dramatic. He's tried to feel for something material inside, a parasite or colony of bacteria. However there are no physical symptoms, it's psychological, and separate from other mental instabilities. *There must be an antidote.*

Gnat turns toward the forest. It's too dark to see the details of the ground. He must find the path quickly. There are cougars prowling. A purist of sorts, a light is never carried. He doesn't need it; his own wit and willpower suffice. He likes hiking, but not in the sense that others do. If it's on a trail that is maintained, that's fairly straightforward to define. Walking. When a toddler can skip the track alongside a parent, it isn't a challenge. Gnat always gets a laugh out of the tourists with tailored clothing, poles, water reservoirs, hats, and sunglasses coming out to traverse a perfectly flat circular trail. Everyone is trying to fit into groups, just walk if that's what you feel like doing. He is more about picking a peak and making a way to it through the bush.

The housing complex is a small community that boards employees in the national park. His is a single unit, as a manager he doesn't have to share. This park's name is Orrinpic. Over the last five spans he's worked in many parks. Lifeless Plain, in the desert of Southern Sanrika. The Sirra Niva mountain range. Sisia Key, in

F'lalasip on the gulf of Southern Omrika. Kanoi Outpost, on the boundary between his home state, Oia, Zeon, and Montisa. Sometimes doing maintenance, sometimes cooking, or serving food. Whatever comes onto this drifter's horizon. Last season he got into management. It turns out he is rather efficient with budgets and handling staff. There is a property on the beach of Lake Kressent, Rusty Ranch, that he's spending his first contract running. Now Gnat is close enough to hear the workers having a time, unclear whether it's a fun one or not. A horde of people with no goals to achieve, so they perpetually stay inebriated. Some on normal, legal drugs, some not.

There is a girl waiting for him in his room. Addie. They met the first time he came to the west coast. She is younger, nineteen, but not in temperament. Her route in life has shown Addie a vast deal. She sees things that many people Gnat's age and older have never even thought of. Addie is half Omrikan, half South Omrikan. Soft features and light skin, with the faintest of olive tints. Sporadic brown freckles grace her nose like the spots of a fawn, showing that she's not yet done becoming what she is. Slim figure, still shapely like a woman. Also, the features Gnat finds more attractive than any others. Somber eyes, large and thundering, with the ability to peer straight to the truth of you. Those who look are helpless under their gaze. Thick, sable hair flows to her hips. A gentle touch, she is skeptical of her power as a woman. Addie has a soothing voice, a sharp giggle, and nothing to give but the whole of her person. Innocent with opened eyes, a dangerous combination.

They haven't been together consistently since they met, only when they find themselves in the same places. Gnat and Addie are both broken by opposing circumstances on different levels. Trying to fix each other, secretly from both sides, isn't working. There's another issue, Addie is traveling with her mother, Tia. She is still beautiful, but the pain and partying of the last twenty spans has jaded what she once was physically. Addie's father left them to fend for themselves when she was still an infant. Tia does whatever she has to, with whoever is willing, to make sure that they have what they need. As her prowess fades, so does the quality of the man. Seducing someone had once been easy, not any longer. What was once necessity is now desperation for attention, to the point where Tia will deny Addie to please any new suitor. Not in a conscious, malicious fashion, but in a hope to complete herself. Currently, she fills herself up with cheap drugs and empty sex. She lets Addie pay for it. It gets in the way, Gnat feels like he is dating both women.

Moreover, Gnat is Gnat. Unable to commit to brushing his teeth. Truly phobic of giving out a real piece of himself no matter how hard anyone else tries to convince him. He imagines the first time he spoke to her, under a bridge by a river in Orrinpic. *It was so pure, yet I am weak. I've done nothing but destroy. Unable to admit my feelings for her even to myself.*

Gnat is lost in his totem, his hands. They are dry, steadfast. Addie is laying on his bed casually, holding her head up with an arm, flipping the pages of a magazine with the other. It's a copy of *Outcry*, an independent alternative news magazine run by the kooky neo-leftists on the coast of Sanrika where she grew up.

Addie looks at him, wounded, "What are you doing?"

"I have no idea," Gnat answers with a grin. She makes him do this a lot. "Went up the mountain, nothing special."

She returns to the page. "I've been here since my shift ended, you could have hung out with me. Juun and Libeth are looking for you. Are you going to go with them?" They both know what it means if he says he is. He'll go to the bar, and she isn't old enough to get in.

"Yeah, I think I'm going to. Told them I would, anyway. It's Karaoke night, we do it every time," he states. There's always an excuse to drink, to make it seem like it's for some social obligation.

"So I'm not staying here?"

"Addie, you have a key. You can come and go as you please. Don't start with this again. I won't be late; I have to work in the morning."

She stands up, putting her arms around the top of his stomach, her face sideways against his chest.

"You know that I love you?" she asks. It is apparent that she can't tell if he does or not. *Or maybe you don't want my love*, she thinks.

"Yes, I do know it," Gnat says straight into her eyes. *I know that you believe you do.* She lets go, picking up her (chemical-free) handbag, and steps into the doorway.

"Tia and I can watch a movie. I'll call you tomorrow." Now she's smiling, "You look good."

He replies, "You are beautiful every instant."

She leaves and he misses her a bit already. Not that he'd ever tell her or anyone else.

He doesn't need anything to hit the road, he keeps everything in the same pockets so he can tell immediately if something is missing. His truck is outside, he's been living in and out of it, this prized possession. Omrikan made, four-door, four-wheel drive. A thumping multi-cylinder engine heedlessly burning the remains of creatures long forgotten. Everything the same tones, the only ones he likes on any vehicle, black and chrome. Gnat pulled the rear seat out and replaced it with a battery bank, dry food storage, and a small refrigerator. In the bed, a wooden divider his dad helped him make. On the roof, seven hundred and fifty watt solar panels to power the batteries and keep the chiller going. Many people have camper vans; this is his stealth camper. He parks on streets with expensive sunsets, sleeps, and leaves before anyone realizes.

The truck fires up without hesitation. The bar, First Street Rendezvous, is a long drive past Lake Kressent through the temperate rainforest. It's his favorite place in Wishintown to water himself. He doesn't like clubs or busy places, only secluded rooms with a few other folks keeping to themselves. The bar is situated in a town of about eighteen thousand inhabitants, Port Albany, the nearest settlement to Orrinpic Park. An unhurried town filled mostly with family businesses. You can see Montisa in the clearest of skies by the water. This is a working place, mostly loggers and fisherman, the top industries in this part of the world. The third biggest is seasonal hospitality such as Gnat is doing. No one travels to the upper left coast during off-season, it's too gray and rainy. Which makes it very lonely out here with hardly any reception and only a single road in or out. The fourth biggest industry is drugs. They've taken the dreams and ambitions of many, and at night the streets sometimes resemble a movie about an invasion of the undead.

Juun is the first person Gnat learned to trust here. Five spans a senior to Gnat and on the seasonal job circuit for quite a long time. He's from Sanrika, like Addie, but a much bigger city. Tall and skinny, short brown hair. One of his front teeth rests somewhat over the other. He grew up in action sports and has the stereotypical energy that goes with it. Always ready to go, always ready to party through the night. Juun has never had ambitions of moving up in the world, he accepts things as they come. He and Gnat bonded over two hobbies in the very beginning, drinking and motorcycles. It doesn't help that they are both the belligerent type when they drink too much. Anything goes.

Some time after they met, a girl showed up to work with them. Red hair, blue eyes, too skinny, too loud, completely uncertain of everything. Sincerely, everything: persons, places, opinions, emotions. A city girl, some would say. She smokes like a chimney and can match both Gnat and Juun round after round.

Naturally they became a trinity of disarray. For three seasons it's been like this. She grew up in Wishintown, came to the coast to see what was in the park, and hasn't gone inland since. Her name is Libeth, she's twenty-two. She and Juun started dating within a cycle of meeting. Well, sleeping together. The exclusivity came later on. Passersby always think that Gnat and Libeth are a couple and Juun is the third wheel. Over time Gnat has noticed this creating a rift between them. Understandable, however they've never spoken about it. It's only a secret feeling of Gnat's. He has no interest in Libeth; she's been in his bed many times to talk or watch a movie and nothing's ever happened. Gnat and Libeth are more extroverted in public than Juun, especially when they are drinking. Juun is very quiet, not able to approach new people easily. Which isn't a negative thing, he just doesn't react amicably in social situations.

Gnat glides into the parking space and sees himself in the rearview mirror, another night to regret. Heading to the pub, he sees Juun and Libeth on the other side of the street.

"Ready for Karaoke?" calls Juun.

Libeth says before Gnat can answer, "I know what songs I'm going to do. Will you sing a duet with me? Or all three of us can sing together. I'm so ready for this! I've waited on so many nasty people..."

Gnat shrugs, uncaring, "Anything works. I need liquor. First round is on me," he hollers. The contrasting pair crosses to his side of the street. Libeth hugs him and Juun messes up his hair.

"Let's get rowdy," Juun says with his boyish gleam.

Gnat has already forgotten the doubts he had when he parked the truck. *Forget the cost, let's have a good time and be stupid with each other.*

"I'm down. You up for some pool? Maybe we can make some cash, depending on who's here."

"If you think we can win, we'll win," says Juun.

"I'll be your cheerleader when I'm not singing, anyway," says Libeth.

Quite a few people. He counts thirteen. An older woman singing on stage, her sweetie for the night watching intently. Four loggers, you can tell by the grime on their shirts along with the light dusting of wood chips on their shoulders and hair. Three local girls drinking water, faces heavy with acne and wrinkles courtesy of their primary habit. At the pool tables, two guys probably passing through to see the park and get away from the city. Perfect targets. These are the guys with money. Finally, a bartender and a cook that have just clocked out, winding down, getting ready to do it again tomorrow.

The girl still working the bar knows them, and they know her, neither side by name. Strange, after three spans they've never ever even asked.

"The usual?" she asks.

"Three shots, neat. Three brews on tap," Gnat answers, "You remember."

He knows if he buys the favor will be returned. A great thing about this trio, they always keep it square. Juun will buy the second, then Libeth, and so on. Unlike his school friends in Oia, who expected him to drive, pay, and introduce them to girls. He doesn't miss that. They touch glasses, taking the whole shot, empties neatly stacked on the bar. Being a part of the same industry, they're not going to leave a mess for other restaurant workers to clean up. An unspoken rule.

There are some stools open, down near the pool tables. Gnat raises his eyebrows to Juun, tilting his head toward them.

"After you," Juun says and follows.

"I'm going to sign up for karaoke and go have a smoke," Libeth chimes cheerfully. "Gnat, are you going to sing tonight? I know Juun will."

"Of course I am! That's why we're here, isn't it?" says Gnat. "We'll see if we can drink for free for a little while."

Libeth teases as she glides away, "Okay, then. Don't get in any fights, Juun. Promise me? Gnat, you make sure of it."

"You're giving me the responsibility? Are you sure that's the best idea?" Gnat cackles.

"As long as it's not mine, it's my night off work. And girlfriend duties, I'm not taking care of him while we are here."

Fair enough. He and Juun are watching the game on television as they sip their pints. It's nice to not have reception or the distraction of screens in the park. It's also nice to have a few rounds, and be a vegetable. Juun reminds Gnat of a father in some way. Not the relationship between them, just his physical appearance. He's clean shaven. He always wears khakis. The slight crow's talons on his face, Juun is a smoker too. Gnat has a drag on occasion, but hasn't purchased his own pack in some time. Maybe Juun is just mellow. Yes, that's what it is. Like the dad in the mall with his child constantly pulling on him, asking questions. After a while, he isn't annoyed. He doesn't yell. It is what it is, until it's not any longer.

"You know, we both miss you at the main lodge since you went across the lake to Rusty. It's not the same... It was great with us serving and you running the line in the kitchen. Now it's some ruffian from Nuwal, fresh out of culinary school with no experience. I know you had to take the promotion, who wouldn't? Still, I wish it could be that way again," Juun is trying to be nonchalant but obviously misses working with his friend.

Gnat replies, "Do you want to come to my side? You know I can get you transferred, perk of the job. I'd do it right now if you want. Both of you. I'll give us the same schedule."

"What's the money like over there?" Juun asks, glancing over at him.

"Half what you're making at the main lodge."

He smirks, "Can't do it. You know that."

Smiling, Gnat answers, "Yes."

That moment has passed, that crew and those schedules are memories now.

"Should we try our luck on teams?" Gnat asks, changing the subject.

"They'll go for it. I'll get us another round and meet you. I'm going to have a cigarette first. You go do the talking, you're better at it than me. I'll guarantee you three a game," Juun answers.

Gnat confirms, "Deal."

He approaches the men, they are obviously from a rich urban area, probably in their forties. One is wearing a fake tan. Gnat knows because he has sunglasses on his head and no tan line from the outside corner of his eye to the top of his ear. The other has a sweater tied around his shoulders, like a fraternity brother at an event.

"You want to play doubles against me and my friend, mix it up a little? We had a night off, drove down from Orrinpic. Both of us are out of practice, it's been a while. Up for letting us try to win the table?"

"That sounds alright. Neither of us is a crack shot, but we can hold our own. We're up for some fun," says the man with the tan.

"Want to make it interesting? Loser buys a round."

"Sure thing," says the fraternity brother.

As Gnat turns around, Juun is there, "We're playing for a drink."

"I skipped the cig. Is that all?" He turns to the men. "Are you sure you guys aren't drinking wine?"

Juun laughs, not in a completely cordial way either. They introduce themselves as Beb and Hink. They're up from Nan Friko, the tan man tells them. A big city with lots of funding for technology start-ups. An entire valley fueled by speculation, backed by nothing but the subjective value people give it.

The balls are racked, they give Gnat and Juun the break. As Gnat crouches over, lining up his shot, he says to Juun in a placid voice, "You promised me three."

He hits the cue ball hard, straight, snapping back after impact. Six of the solids and stripes come back onto his side. One of each type goes into a pocket, open table. *Perfect.*

During Gnat's teenage life in Oia, there wasn't a whole lot to do. His neighborhood, Fennytun, is a township of about five thousand enveloped by what is called the grain belt. A place between open farmland and a city full of racial tension. That city, Nata, has a lot of historical significance in the slave trade of the past. Nata was the boundary line between the north and the south of Omrika. The south used slaves, the north didn't. If a slave escaped and made it to Nata, it meant they were free. The hate and energy from hundreds of spans ago still resonate on those streets.

Gnat spent his childhood half as a city-boy, the rest a country-boy. Fishing, camping, bonfires, cliff jumping. On the flipside street smarts, believing nothing, and keeping his mouth shut. There are a pair of bars in the town, more of a pothole than a town, the only place important to Gnat is The Tapped Rune. Although it's not *legal* to drink in Omrika until you are twenty-one, he started going in at seventeen. The Rune is a horseshoe bar that sits twelve at most, bartender included. It's a regulars' bar, the same people are there all the time, including the owner, Kili. Gnat has different bonds with everyone.

In the beginning, he would watch Ri shoot pool. Gnat never played; no friends he knew had a table coming up. Ri would beat anyone, for any amount of money. He never saw Ri lose or take more than three turns to finish the game. Ri was a crotchety old man in his late sixties. Not married, never was, although he had a son. He drank something called a six and six, after playing Gnat would buy him a glass and talk to him. Ri had an interesting life. A mid-level drug dealer in his twenties and thirties with his own truck stop on the freeway for distribution. When he wasn't traveling across the country, he was in jail. He'd spent a third of his adult life behind bars. At some point he was a professional pool player. Then in his twilight, he was unable to play either game anymore. Kili told Gnat once that Ri had been coming in for more than twenty spans. After cycles of talking to Ri, Gnat finally asked him to teach him the game.

A laugh, mixed with a smoker's cough, "Ah, you're too old, it's too late for you. My eyesight is going, I won't be playing but a few more spans myself. Not going to waste it showing you when I already know you'll never be any good."

"Oh, alright," answered Gnat, a touch of sadness. *I thought we were kind of friends, I guess not.* They kept drinking together that night and many others. Sometimes Gnat would shoot a game alone, or with a stranger. He never asked Ri again, only played for fun. Until a night, long after he'd asked Ri to be his teacher, he was about to take a shot on the eight ball.

From the bar he heard Ri, "Hold it, hold it. Damn you. You're holding the stick wrong. I can't stand watching you play like this anymore."

Then, Ri taught. Gnat listened. He became a great shooter. No one else could beat him, except Ri of course. He made a decent amount of money, and started traveling away from home to do it. Never anything official, just in pool halls and bars he passed through in small towns. Sometimes he lost, not very often. When Gnat was twenty-four he went through Fennytun, and stopped in The Rune. Ri was there, they spoke for a while. Gnat asked him for a game. Wouldn't you know, Gnat beat him. Ri missed a shot on the eight that gave him the game. Not purposefully, Ri wasn't like that. Gnat would respect him less if he had, both of them knew it.

"My eyes are bad; they have been for a long time. You finally beat me. Blind, drunk, and crippled is what it took..." said Ri, as sentimentally as possible.

Gnat left town again. Cycles later, he got a message from Kili. Ri passed. Isolated in his house. Gnat, gone. He never got to say goodbye. Gnat thinks of Ri every time he plays a game. The game he couldn't have learned if it wasn't for that misunderstood fellow at the end of the bar.

"That's two beers, boys," Juun tells Hink and Beb, "You matched us to the end! Wasn't expecting that. Try again for some money?" He's feeling it. It's the only time Juun starts to talk this way.

"No way, we aren't falling for this trap," says Hink, "We've got some hiking to do in the morning. Last chance. You enjoy the drinks, maybe a rematch next time we come through."

Gnat replies, "Sounds like a plan. Until then."

The duo leave, get in their rental, and pull out of the lot. The whole front wall of the Rendezvous is glass, Juun and Gnat watch them drive away, drinking their free booze.

Gnat to Juun, "We got a round out of it. Maybe next time, we'll make some money. No one else is playing or waiting to."

"Yeah, let's find my girl. Sing a few."

"What about those guys? Can you believe the things that people spend their paychecks on? A fake tan, a watch that costs as much as my truck? Aren't there clocks on phones now? That's an obsolete piece of technology right there. Save the resources, nobody is impressed."

"Don't read too much into it, they were just a couple of rich guys from the city. I wanted to take some of their pocket cash, though," Juun interjects.

"I can't comprehend."

Juun straightens up and says, "Only the condition perpetuating itself, brother. You can't escape it. You can't question it. People like us have a place in it too."

Gnat sighs, "How did we get to this? The only thing of worth is standards that nobody really understands."

"And Libeth owes us a round, so stop thinking about it and come sing with us, *Gnat*," Juun puts emphasis on his name, "It's not for us to figure out. We can only control what's in front of us at the moment. Which is spending too much, and driving home when we shouldn't."

But that's the whole issue, Gnat thinks. *Everyone accepts it blindly.* Juun is headed outside, he follows, searching the ground for a clue. Maybe he'll ask Libeth for a smoke, he likes her brand better than Juun's. She is kissing Juun with one knee bent, like in those coming home from war posters from the past.

"Ready?" she asks, "What song? What song?"

"I think I'll do something grungy. I want to scream," Gnat jokes. Not completely, though.

They spend the night singing songs apart, together, sometimes well, most of the time horribly. By the end, Juun is sitting cross-legged on the dance floor. In one hand, a partially empty drink. In the other, a microphone. He can hardly keep his eyes open or hold his head up. Somehow he is still knows the lyrics to a power ballad:

"Every dog hides its bone, like every cowboy sleeps alone..."

Then he is asleep, in the middle of the bar. This cowboy doesn't have to be by himself, however. Gnat and Libeth are looking at him drunk and joyful. What comedy.

"It's about that time," Gnat is giggling. His ears are warm. There's that familiar looseness in his eyes, the thing he does this for. He doesn't care about anything, nothing can make him, "I'll drive us, I can bring you to get your car tomorrow."

Libeth studies him, trying to find where his head is at, "Are you good to drive?"

"I'm never okay for anything. But I can get us home, no problem. Once we get on Route Zero, there won't be anyone else driving to the lodge anyway. Help me get him up. I'll carry him to your room when we get there."

"You're right, go slow."

Gnat rolls his eyes, "Not slow, that's too obvious. Just the speed limit. You're on watch for elk, bear, and deer."

She replies, "Got it. I'm in control of the radio though."

With a couple of gentle slaps, they get Juun up and to the truck. Gnat shouldn't be doing this. He got arrested for driving under the influence once in Oia when he was twenty-two. How many nights has he driven home without remembering? Too many. Right now he is only buzzed. Start the truck. *Check.* Seat belts. *Check.* Lights on. *Check.* Radio on, not too loud. *Check.* And they're off. On the way, Juun stirs and asks to stop for burgers. Gnat grabs a deluxe, no cheese, his late night go-to. Juun gets a double with fries. Libeth, chili-cheese nachos with a shake.

When they arrive safely, Gnat carries Juun while Libeth opens the door. She starts taking his shoes off, stops, and turns.

"I miss you working with us, Gnat. You're the closest person to me since I left home. Next season, I'll apply to come to Rusty. If Juun doesn't want to, I still will."

"We'll work it out, don't think about it now. I miss the both of you too. I do think about the last three spans a lot. Especially that first contract when we met, Addie included. That may have been the best season of my life. See you later. Message me about your car."

She nods, and starts tending to Juun again.

Gnat shakes his head, "Goodnight, brother."

It's still relatively early, there's a buffer before he *needs* to sleep. Over at the campfire, which happens nightly, he sees a few of the staff. Since he became a manager, he isn't invited to these gatherings anymore. Whenever he invites himself, others seem to trickle away. Should he go over? *No, forget it.* He enters his cabin. The light has a yellow tint to it, which makes him feel like he isn't in the present but the past. Gnat sits on the edge of his bed, staring at his hands. Again, his totem. *Is this real? Is this it?* He is fixated on his appendages. The minuscule crevices and imperfections not noticeable without scrutiny are an extremely rugged landscape to any passing arthropod. Tiny hairs, a forest, like he was in earlier. The angular geometry of how the cells have formed, he has seen these shapes elsewhere. *In the trees. If you look at the cells on a scale of bark, just as close, it's the same pattern. Everything is built using the same equation. As a bug crosses the jungle that is me, I cross the tangled web of growth that is, what? What is this place? All this expelled energy and evolution, for what?* His mind is starting to run again. He takes a deep breath, adjusting his eyes so that he's more focused on his peripherals than his center. Gnat rubs his stomach; he feels the weight. It's draining, stealing his life force, his ability to think about anything else. *What is the answer? What is the question that needs answering?*

He rolls onto his side, noticing the magazine that Addie was reading. *Outcry.* He's never been a fan of the news. There have been so many arguments about it with his parents in Nata. They watch the local channel nightly, religiously. The same brainwashing as going to church, really. A country banded together by fear. A predetermined script on repeat. Thug kills another thug, people on the street have opinions about it, old man dies, children with inoperable disease. To make you feel content about how horrible everything is they show you a video of rescued puppies. And the thing he dislikes most, the weather. Want to know what it is? *Go outside.* The national meteorological association, here to help you. A government program trying to predict the random, limitless forces guided by an immeasurable power down to the timing of a snap. Gnat has a theory that the news corporations are paying people to commit these crimes just to have something to report on so they can sell advertising space. He doesn't watch news, he doesn't read it, he doesn't want to hear about it. Things happen, that's it. Some are okay, some are not. *Addie, why do you focus on this? Does it make you feel like an informed person? Does it make you feel better about your own life?* He picks up the magazine by the top corner with two fingers, like it is a piece of garbage off the ground.

"What's the Irfa squabbling about this cycle?" he says to himself. Irfa, what a peculiar planet, hovering along. He opens the magazine in the middle somewhere. An interview with a venture capitalist, no thanks. He has some money, why does anybody care about which laws he agrees with? Next page, there's a picture of a woman. Tiria Sika. She's a Chief Operations Officer at a large corporation. There's a group of people protesting around her. They think that a decision she made lost a lot of middle-class people their jobs.

She looks to be about ten spans older than Gnat, he notices the same resting glare as his. She has thick wavy hair of a sandy color growing past her shoulders. She's very unique yet still attractive. *Good luck, Tiria.* He throws the magazine in the trash can. He has never understood why everyone treats big business as evil. The only reason you start a business is to make profit. For your own bene-fit, no one else's. Every hedonistic person trying to get the fanciest car, to have the most wealth. Striving to possess material things, demonizing the people who do it best. The real problem is that you cannot have a free market economy in a country that is privately owned and publicly funded. In recent history the motor manufac-turers of Omrika were fading away, most of them were going to shut down. There are hundreds of thousands of federated men and women working in the industry; believing high wages are deserved for doing simple tasks on an assembly line. These employees also expect the employer to be loyal to them, to give them paid time off, to give them healthcare. Discounts. Pay for their welfare when they can't be bothered to work. These demands drove the prices of the motors up, and the quality has never matched overseas competitors. Why put extra effort in if entitlement is guaranteed beforehand?

In other parts of the world, such as Telaysia, there are devoted employees, not employers. The workers understand that basically anyone can perform these menial jobs. They don't demand high wages. These employees come to work early and set up their station before they start getting paid. The company in turn can put out a superior product for less. Irfa is no longer comprised of isolated markets, it is globalized. Communication is seamless and accessible to everybody. In a truly free market the Omrikan motors would have disappeared. Over time those jobs would filter into new mar-kets. Solar power, wind energy, indoor vertical cultivation. The systems in place through the government, such as unemployment, could then be utilized for those men and women stuck in the middle of the transition. With time the market would balance itself. Yet this is not what was done. The motor corporations pleaded for a bail out. Think of the citizens, of the children, they said. They played the emotions of the country through that tried-and-true platform, news networks. The government obliged, giving the companies billions. They had paid it back, this simple stop-gap. How long until it's needed again? The Omrikan motors will never match the quality or price of Telaysia or Ropa, their business model is diseased. Everyone knows that smoking causes sickness. If you smoke your whole life, then get a respiratory disease as an elder, is it a tragedy?

Gnat gets under the blanket. *Everything seems too easy.* He wonders what he's reaching for. He remembers why he looks at his hands the way he does. There was a girl he used to hang out with as a teenager in Nata. Cu'al, she was four or five spans older. He'd go over her house, they would do drugs. On one occasion they had done hallucinogens and were peaking. She was rubbing his hands, when the thought occurred to him. Hands, it's where your body ends. They are the things you manipulate the tangible world with. There's so much you can tell about a person by their hands. Short, stubby fingers. Hard-nosed, close-minded, stuck in place. Long, skinny fingers, like Gnat's, always reaching, searching for what's next. She asked him that night if he was reincarnated, what would he be? He told her that he would be a rock at the bottom of a crossing in a stream. The mean rock that everyone would step on and he'd cut their feet.

Drugs have always been a part of his life. More in an experiential fashion than in addiction, unlike alcohol. He does it for the passages opened in his mind, and wants to learn how to have these channels appear without help from something he ingests. This place he goes to, it's where he finds the things that make the most sense to him.

It's much less about the high that touches your body. Many of his friends have died from hard drugs. A weak mind gets lost in the feeling, not the sight. People who want the feeling get addicted. Just another way to live in emotion. However, research shows that for a substance to affect your mind, there must be a biological receptor for it to connect to. We would not have these receptors if there was not an advantage from the standpoint of evolution. It takes a mind strong enough to wield the substance and not be destroyed by it. The addicts he has encountered in his life usually say very logical things. They are elevated in the high, mentally, without noticing. The negative, again, could be that humans put a twist on it. A thousand spans ago, the Miyens of South Omrika chewed certain leaves for energy while planting and harvesting. Then man figured out how to turn it into highly addictive powder. Natural plants used to grow wild throughout Irfa flowering with two or three percent mind-altering substance. Now the same species is refined and contains levels up to ninety-five percent, making it too easy to get lost in. If Gnat had a reason to stop doing these things, if he had intent, if he could live on the level these counterfeit teachers take him to naturally he would let them go. *It's cheating, paying the boatman to take you where you shouldn't be yet. How do I earn my way?*

Stop thinking, he tells himself. *Go to sleep.* It's always so hard for him to rest. Insomnia has plagued him since childhood. Always anxious, he's waiting for something to reveal itself. *Work in the morning. You never know what's going to come up.* He turns off the light, closing his eyes. He is imagining a field of freshly cut grass. There are shapes off in the distance. Are they the silhouettes of people? He starts sprinting to catch them, they move also. And, faster than he, the gap between them widens. He stops. His lungs are burning, the air is thin. There is no horizon, simply this endless field. The shapes are gone, his chest is rising and falling more slowly now.

Gnat curls to the ground, standing on his knees. The weight inside pulls his body to the grass, his cheek in the ground cover. Back on Irfa, he sleeps.

II

Kaaa. A scream bellows outside his cabin. Gnat is jolted awake. The sun is up, barely, the radiance on his walls has a hint of pink in it. No call for an alarm here, he's awoken by a bird each morning as the bringer of light shows its face. This is no rooster; he is unsure of what it is called however it looks similar to a crow. The species differ because this bird sounds like a human being howling in agony.

"What a wonderful way to wake up," he mutters, his voice is hoarse. He shouldn't have smoked last night, "Another shift."

He goes through the practice of getting dressed and packing food. Despite his location constantly changing, his routines never do. They are the things that bring him a sense of normalcy. His diet is strict, nothing fried, no dairy. Baby cow growth hormones can't be good for adult humans. He eats only within a certain period, no snacks between meals. Except the occasional late-night burger. Anything is okay in moderation.

In Omrika the big event for many families is going out to a restaurant. The activity everyone anticipates is eating. Three meals. Snacks. Coffee. Where did this come from? The number of calories they are consuming is not equal to the number of calories they are burning. It's a simple formula, eat as much as is needed to live. Food is simply sustenance. A basic need, not a luxury. Not something to be hoarded or kept from others. It doesn't help that food served when dining out isn't wholesome or balanced. It's a bag of trash, the nutrition is burned to oblivion. Hence a country of overweight people with no fitness level to speak of; eating so much sugar and salt their bodies have become diseased. All that's needed is a small amount of self-control and the health problems disintegrate.

His sentient wake-up call yells again as he moves to the parking area. Some employees pass and don't offer any greeting, instead hurrying away quickly. He notices the area for employees covered in plastic bags and cans. Seasonal workers, who pose as free-spirited travelers, come to labor in the last protected majesties of this world only to treat them as landfills. To Gnat, littering is a crime worse than murder. Every human is a murderer, the circumstances that push a person to act is what varies. There is always a reason. *In cold blood* isn't a defensible term. A serial killer, for example, is not evil. This word is subjective. Evil is just something that upsets the sustainability of the status quo. Serial killers are not hardwired the same as the extreme majority of others. It isn't wrong in their mind to kill. It's necessary. Or someone that ends a life for someone's possessions. Their reason is simple: desperation, greed. A spouse that kills their partner. Jealousy, being driven to the limit by verbal or physical abuse. In war. Slaughtering on a massive scale because one culture fears what it doesn't comprehend about another. Littering is different. An absolute disregard for everything and everyone around you. The most careless act, defacing the habitat that fosters your life without reason.

The brightness off the water next to the road and the snow at the climax of the mountains make him relax. He does like his current job. The crew is great, he takes care of them, they never let him down. Gnat has the approach that he is there for his staff, not the other way around. He knows the issues they are dealing with, having held every job you can imagine at a resort. He would never go against an employee in front of a guest. He gives everyone the same schedule so they can make plans to enjoy the park. The only things Gnat asks is that everybody does their job the way he shows them, and if they are going to be so much as a traffic stop late, they let him know. Mutual respect, his business protocol. Gnat is the manager of operations. This means he takes care of personnel and guests, along with ordering and inventory.

His boss, Jin, is the lodge manager. He takes care of the budgets and corporate directives. They are very similar, working together efficiently. Jin is something of a mentor to Gnat, a solid friendship has developed between them. He is thirty-five and grew up in Zeon. He comes from wealth, but you would never know. Jin is tall, burly, carries himself well, and demands your attention. He wears a short beard with shaggy brown hair.

As he arrives, Jin is waiting for him out front of the lodge, a glaze of annoyance on his face.

"Gnat, guess who called? Frink. He quit." Frink is his only cook for breakfast.

Gnat grunts. "Are you serious? You know why? He wants more pay. He knows I won't find anyone else, and there's no way I'm going to do it."

"You can't. You close the lodge every night. He's at thirteen right now," says Jin.

"I'll call and offer fifteen. He has to finish *this* season to the very end, I'm not picking up the slack on his dishes anymore. I'm not hiring him back for the next season if I'm here. He demands too much, he's whiny. Does he know at thirteen he's still making more than the breakfast cooks at Kressent? They are doing plated service over there. Frink only has to keep a buffet line filled for a third as many people."

Jin leans in, "Gnat, maybe you should tell him the same thing. If it takes fifteen to not have to worry whether someone will show up every morning, fine."

"Heard," Gnat replies.

"Also, the propane is going to run out, the valve was opened when I got here. Housekeeping is short on paper towels for the rooms and the vendor is out. Food truck, remember you told Brind he could come in late so he could go to an appointment. So you'll have to stock it yourself. We need to call the plumber for the showers in the campground, there's no water pressure. I pulled straight in to guest complaints this morning. Are you ready for the guests?"

"Every cycle is a cycle."

Jin says, "Can I get a smile? Don't look like you dropped your Ice-cream."

This makes Gnat laugh, he knows exactly why Jin said that, "I don't eat Ice-cream!"

"Maybe you should, it would bring you some joy." Jin is turning to go to his office, "Dinner at the Telaysian place?"

"Jin, we've gone every cycle this season. It's tradition now, no need to ask."

The front door closes behind Jin. The life of a manager. The spans of training, working his way up. Now he cherishes when he gets to wash dishes for a while and not have to figure out an answer to some problem presenting itself. *That's what you call going full circle.*

Into the lodge, which was built more than a hundred spans ago with local timber. It's a giant log cabin, the smell of cedar and spruce fills the air. Almost spicy, soothing to everyone that enters. The cabins on the property are the original homesteads from around the lake, transplanted over time. Moving an old home from its foundation without demolishing it is no easy task. Each example is unique, yet built from the same stone, irfa, and wood. Seventeen in total. Over on the far side of the plot is a campground. More than twenty-five spots, half of them on the waterfront, the others under a canopy of pine. You can see the King of Storms towering behind the opposite shore, on the horizon. The restaurant fills a third of the inside of the lodge. The dining room walls are windows, reminding guests of the current serenity they are part of. Adjacent to the restaurant and kitchen are a gift shop and reception. Jin and Gnat share an office in the center of the building. Jin's desk has stacks of papers, trash, no order whatsoever. Somehow he still knows where everything is. Gnat's desk is perfectly clean. Computer monitor, keyboard, a notepad with pen on top. The first thing he does, same as most office employees in Omrika, is clear his inbox. Here he finds messages from vendors, future visitors, or people inquiring about work. Gnat writes the supplier of cleaning products, finding replacement paper towels that will get them through. A call to the plumber, he's coming out. Next, the gas company, rush delivery is extra, no problem. See them later. *Done.* He goes to the kitchen, checking everything is rotated and dated. There's a whiteboard for Brind, he writes a prep list. As he is finishing, he hears the food truck pull in. The driver brings the items to the kitchen on a dolly, so it isn't hard to stock. *Oh, yes,* Gnat remembers, *I need to call Frink.* In the office he dials his cook. Frink is an older man, in his late fifties. His head and face are completely clean shaven, ritually it seems. In a word, glabrous. A loud and talkative individual, he laughs at everything and is set in his ways. He's tall, lanky, still spry for his age. The phone is ringing.

"Hello, Gnat. I've been waiting for your call," Frink says brightly. This is a game to him.

"Frink, why did you quit? You know how easy you have it on this side of the lake with me. What did I do to deserve you quitting at the end of your shift, when I wasn't here yet?"

"I just feel unappreciated, and lonely in the kitchen there by myself. The chef at Kressent says he might have a spot for me on his team."

Gnat takes a deep breath, "You would rather work for less and do hundreds of separate plates every morning? That crew is five or eight guys in their twenties. It's hot. They do everything from scratch. Frink, let's be honest. You don't have the cooking ability or the energy to keep up over there."

"Are you calling me old?" Frink asks.

Gnat pauses for a moment, choosing his words carefully, "I'm not saying you are old. But you aren't twenty anymore. If I know the difference at my age, you do. We have a good thing going. I keep everything stocked for you. I don't micromanage, as long as you show up and work. So, you really don't have to answer to anyone. I give you the same schedule, they won't do that on the other side. You keep things hot and fresh; you get to talk to the guests in the dining room. Then you clean up and do whatever you want on your time. I don't see how it's not ideal for you, really. We can both count on each other."

Frink answers, "There's something I need, Gnat..."

"What is that?" already knowing what he's going to say.

"More pay. It's the only thing that ever matters, in a situation like this."

It really is, Gnat thinks, *how is it always about money? More understanding or higher sight, these are the things I would ask for if I could.*

"Okay Frink, what's it going to cost me?"

"Gnat, I need a twenty percent raise." A hesitant reply; he knows this is almost an absurd request.

"I'm not going to hassle you. Like I said, it's a two-way street. I'll give you fifteen until the end of your contract. Which, you have to finish with no more changes of loyalty. Also, you need to make sure the dishes are clean and on the racks before you go. I've been doing it for you. See you tomorrow, then?"

"That's affirmative," Frink says. He is a military veteran, after all.

Gnat places the phone on its base. Jin is in the room, Gnat swings his swivel chair around to face him.

"You handled that perfectly," Jin says, "Frink isn't the easiest to talk to. You laid it out there honestly, and didn't give him a chance to get going. I'm sure he appreciated that, being from his generation."

"I like the old guy, when it comes down to it. I'm going to check on our boats."

He gets up, heading down to the beachfront. The boat rental shack is away from the main building. There are about thirty canoes and kayaks locked to the pier that anyone can rent for different amounts of time. There is a cliff jumping and swimming hole a short paddle away. You can also meander there on a trail going around the shore. Yes, the boats are alright. He really comes down here to be by himself and let his mind wander.

The main soda rivals in Omrika are Presto and Zap. When Gnat first started at Rusty, the lodge was using Zap. The driver is, personal opinion aside, not that great at delivering what is ordered. Breakfast is a self-serve buffet, part of that is pitchers of orange and cranberry juice. His first order of the contract, Gnat requested six cases of orange syrup from the driver. He brought two. After three breakfasts, the restaurant was out of juice. Then Jin had to rush to town, not a short drive, and buy expensive juice not from concentrate. They're isolated, therefore it was the only option. Zap only delivers once a cycle. No exceptions. The next order, he called Zap and requested six cases again. Two were delivered. So, Gnat went to the office and dialed Presto. He asked if they could come out and put in their machines, bringing the syrups including six cases of orange. They said of course, by the end of shift it was finished.

When Presto asked where to put Zap's equipment, he replied, "On the curb."

The next morning, Gnat called the Zap driver, telling him to come pick up his stuff quickly, as it might get stolen. An exception was made by Zap, the driver came and got it later.

That whole next cycle, everything went smoothly. Until the district manager came by to speak to Gnat.

He asked Gnat, "Why have you switched from Zap to Presto?"

Gnat explained, "They shorted my orders and left us without beverages for breakfast guests. Jin had to buy juice at retail prices and make the drive to town for them. We both know that people like Presto better than Zap anyway. I'm of the mindset that if you aren't going to provide service, I'll find somebody who will. I need to keep the business running. It's not a friendship, it's a contract. You do something, I pay you for it."

The district manager revealed that the current national manager of the corporation used to be the same for Zap. Therefore the company must use them because part of his bonus for moving laterally is adopting Zap's products in our facilities worldwide. This made it clear to Gnat that moving up isn't about your actual intelligence or skill-set, only how much of your dignity you are willing to sell to get to the top.

So, Gnat rang Presto, who were understandably upset. He told them he was angry also, it was a breach of contract, unbeknownst to him, and he had to settle for a lesser product. Then he called Zap. The driver came, did his duty, not coming to speak to Gnat before he started or after he completed the job. Gnat heard the truck pulling out. He went into the kitchen, and saw six cases of orange syrup. Six more have arrived with every delivery since then.

"Did it really have to be that difficult?" Gnat says to the castle he was titled to protect.

Brind pulls in and heads to the rear entrance, waving as he does. Gnat holds his hand high and pauses briefly, then starts toward his makeshift headquarters. Brind can get to work without direction.

Jin is fiddling with the budget, his least favorite and most performed task, using up a third of his schedule. It's odd, there is a main financial controller for the whole area. Jin predicts the budget, sends it to her, then she advises him on what to change. Again, only speculation to seem more enticing for stockholders, it isn't real. Why the volleying? The controller could predict the budgets and send them off herself.

Gnat sits at his desk, staring at his screensaver, a sailboat. His biggest dream, to live on a boat and sail wherever he wants for the rest of his life. Solo, away from everything. Full keel. Inboard engine. Fiberglass. The blue water, that's where he wants to be.

"What's for lunch, apricots and a banana?" Jin says tauntingly.

"No, apricots and an orange."

"The NRS is coming for inspection tomorrow, so I'll be doing that."

"Again already? How did that woman get her job? She is completely clueless about how any of this works. She must know a really important person," Gnat says.

"She is pretty... horrible..."

The National Resource Service. Hailed as the savior of those things precious in our natural landscape by the government, in actuality the most corrupt institution in their fleet. Gnat has seen it firsthand many times during his tenure in the parks. They are the final say in anything to do with these areas. They always choose profit over protection of animals, plants, natural water tables, fires caused by humans, erosion caused by overuse of trails, clear cutting, or fracking.

The corporation that Gnat works for is the concessionaire that runs the attractions in the parks for the NRS. When they come to inspect, they are actually coming to see how they can squeeze more revenue out of the place. Every price, color of fabric, appliance, placement of display, menu item, name, and description must be approved by them prior to updating. The contract goes to whatever company yields the highest percentage of revenue; regardless of their environmental practices with food, logistics, or procedure.

The water for the property comes from the lake, through a filtration system on site. The NRS then bills the corporation for water use by unit. The water company of the state has a set rate, the NRS charges seven hundred percent more. In the by-laws, the water must be supplied by the NRS in national parks. Jin had a plumber come to install waterless urinals for the campground. To save resources, which saves money and helps out with the shortages across the west coast. When the NRS came to inspect, they cited a complaint that the restroom smelled. In the conversion to urinals that use water again, the NRS sent their own maintenance man, billed at higher rates than any other plumber in the area.

When Gnat was working in Northern Zeon, near the noble passageway, he learned of another NRS victory. Forty spans ago in that park, there was a problem. The compound had over five million visitors a season. The planning required to move that much waste was overwhelming due to the dangerous, twisting mountain roads. So they created their own garbage dump within the park. This attracted local creatures for the easy feeding. The numbers of bears prior to the landfill were estimated at thirty-five hundred specimens. The NRS rangers decided in the interest of safety for the tourists, they would kill the bears that were feeding at the dump and disregard the population in the backcountry. What they didn't realize was that the bears feeding at the dumps *were* the bears that were also traveling the wilds. The rangers started to hunt, by the end only three hundred fifty bears remained. The NRS declared them endangered, and started collecting donations for the conservation of these creatures. The bear population in that area has never recovered. The politics of man, the destruction of balance. Only for the safety of visitors, and the park's stockholders. *Remember the picture we took there?*

Gnat says, "You'll get through it. I like that she comes with her minions. They agree with everything, telling her what inventive ideas she has."

"I don't even want to know what their salaries are compared to ours. How great would we be at doing that? If it's sunny, I'll be okay. I can get out of this chair. We should take the boat out."

There's a skiff with an outboard, a rowboat salvaged from the weeds. It doesn't leak, so it serves as their rescue vehicle. Gnat enjoys speeding around in it, sometimes taking employees home to Kressent.

"Maybe later, I've got to talk to human resources about getting a few overseas visa kids. Another cook and a few housekeepers would be nice. The girls are getting worn out. I want Brind to have help when I'm absent. I cover breaks when I'm here, when I'm not he goes straight from open to close."

Jin asks, "Are the beds available for them at Kressent?"

"Yeah, there have to be fifteen empty. Maybe I can get a group of friends that can bunk by themselves. I don't want to do it. There are no applicants from town that want to come out, though."

This is the biggest disadvantage to seasonal work in remote places, keeping trustworthy employees. The locals from the area don't want to do it, the drive is too far, the pay isn't enough. You have four basic types of workers that are on this circuit of employment. The first is college students. They want to have a fun time and see a bit of the country. These employees arrive late in the season and leave early. Not great workers, more concerned with "experiencing the area." Which equates to getting drunk and having casual sex. None of them have any viable skills, they aren't really worth having because you have to hire a whole new crew and train again to get through the end of the contract. The second are people that just don't know anything else. Juun is an example of this. Bouncing from the big parks in the heat, to a ski resort or beach town opposite. Take the pay while you can, what starts out as going on an adventure becomes the same schedule as somebody with a career living in the city. The third, people that don't fit in any place else. The drifters, the junkies, the thieves. The ones who left home at thirteen and have been figuring out how to survive on their own. Tia fits here. With this group, they never last long before deciding their own fate. Which is leaving on bad terms, every time. It's so hard to find people to try this lifestyle that everyone who applies gets a chance. There is an entire subculture of laborers traveling around the country doing this type of work. It's not a thing that the average person stops to think about when going on vacation to some random roadside attraction or remote area.

The last option is foreigners on a visa, a special working vacation scheme the government uses. Always the best workers, and loyal. Gnat doesn't like to use them because of the lie they are sold on. First, these younger people are at university for hospitality or tourism, and are required by the school in their home country to do a semester abroad in an Omrikan speaking country. To obtain this special visa, the student must get sponsored by a corporation. When this happens, they sign a contract. They have four cycles before and after the job to travel. There's a large fee for this visa, fifty percent goes to the government. Fifty percent is handed to the corporation for giving them the opportunity. The brochures an applicant sees says things such as "Come live in Omrika, see the park, travel, make friends." When they arrive, the schedule shows that they are a dishwasher every shift. Or they come expecting a serving job yet none are available. The only position that remains is in waste management or as a night porter. They can't go to a different corporation because of the contract. If the visa holder quits or gets fired, they must leave the country immediately and will never be issued a visa of any kind again.

"Okay, please make sure that the kids know what they are in for prior to coming out. We have to transport them to and from housing, it might not happen right when their shift ends," Jin insists, "You know it's been an issue."

"Oh, I do?" Gnat says sarcastically. He's been making three or four trips a shift. Another oversight by the men in the top office, not thinking of the tiny acquisitions such as Rusty Ranch.

"Do I get a driving bonus at the end of the span like a trucker?" Gnat asks, knowing the answer is no, joking anyway, "Working for a salary is not what it's cracked up to be. I enjoy signing the checks for the servers making twice as much as I do."

"Go do it again, then," Jin answers plainly.

Gnat's voice gets a touch louder, "I didn't say *that*! I'm still adjusting to it, I'm used to having cash in my pocket after every shift."

"You know the problem with that. You never take the time to give it value when it comes from tips, so you blow it anyway. When you have put in the work first, then wait for the check, you feel you've earned it. It's easier to budget and save money when it comes in predetermined increments."

"Yeah, I don't spend as much when the idea that it will be replenished isn't there," Gnat says, "I'm going to the kitchen. Brind is probably mad because I threw out his clam chowder, I told him it wouldn't sell! It's hot, nobody wants soup."

On his way he watches an eagle swoop down, extend its claws, and catch a fish from the lake. It has to strain to gain altitude again, and reach its aerie on the ridge. *This place is epic.*

He pushes through the swinging door between the dining room and kitchen. Brind is breaking down whole chickens for dinner. He is a large man, extra height along with weight. In his early thirties, he reminds Gnat of a certain donkey in a cartoon from childhood. He speaks passively, lacks confidence, and makes fun of himself. Brind fought in the wars over oil in Muusman on a few different tours. You can tell, he suffers from traumatic stress conditions. He has blonde hair, which is leaving him. Although he is cooking, Gnat lets him chew his tobacco. He can't take away the only thing Brind has to calm his nerves. They've always shared laughs and gotten along. Brind shuffles nervously, "I see you were right. That chowder was a bad idea."

Gnat answers, "It was tasty, I tried it after it was finished. A cycle and we hadn't sold a bowl, we can try again when it cools down."

"Eh, I know how to make it now. I'll try something different. These chicken bones can make a stock for... I'm an idiot," Brind bellows.

Gnat ends the sentence for him, smirking, "For a soup?"

They both start to chuckle, stopping harmoniously. Gnat puts his hands in the front pockets of his jeans, thumbs out.

"You could make a stock, reduce it down. Then add the base to the water every time you make rice."

Brind raises his eyebrows, "Now that's a good idea."

"See, there's a reason I make the big bucks."

Brind peers at him with an unbelieving expression, "Whatever you say boss," he chimes in again, "Have you seen anything about what Lellin said?"

Gnat is completely straight-faced, "No, and I don't want to know. I don't want to see it. I don't want to hear about it. I have zero interest."

Lellin is a businessman in Omrika who has been in the public eye since birth. He comes from a rich family, and has gained a lot more wealth during his career. A master of cashing in just to leave with exorbitant profits right before something tears apart. He has operated this way since his beginning, destroying the economy of small and large towns alike. Gnat doesn't care, it's how the world works. Someone is going to fill that role, and no amount of talk will change it. The part that bothers Gnat is that this man recently won the primary to be on the ballot and lead the country. He still has to campaign and beat the other parties, but he actually made it this far. How bored did Lellin have to be to want to do this? He swayed everyone to vote for him with a simple catchphrase, "Create more jobs for Omrika." The industry in the country is suffering. The average person doesn't understand the idea of a globalized economy. Manufacturing is not coming back. Other countries do it better, and faster. For less.

There is a redeeming fact in this, though. Average people don't want more of the same, useless politics that have raged on for spans in Omrika. They want to change things. They just don't know how. Lellin played the part, and took the prize. Yet he has no eye or experience for the thing that matters most in a connected planet, foreign policy. When it comes down to it, the leader of the country is simply a figurehead. Something for people to focus on while the agenda moves forward. More taxes, no upside for the working class. Personal liberties taken through fear tactics. Every leader in the history of Omrika has been bad, still, they more or less held the office with dignity. Lellin is an embarrassment. Only a leader in the context that he is the first to eat from the plate, not leaving enough for anyone else.

"Would you fight the battle if he was the general?" Gnat asks.

"That's kind of the job of a soldier, you shoot when you're told to in whatever direction the officer tells you." Brind isn't content with his answer, however true it is.

"Why did you sign up?"

"The Muusmani's attacked our civilians on home soil. I was of age. My friends were going. I had to fight next to my brothers."

"Aren't the Muusmani our brothers as well? The people you were fighting against were as much involved in the attack as you or I. Isn't it the same? They are fighting with their brothers against us, who attack them on their home soil. I don't buy that line; it makes men fight because they feel like the nation is questioning their allegiance. What if we just understood that people don't believe in the same things? That there is a possibility that we are wrong, as individuals?"

In his head, Gnat ponders. *War. So, it isn't logical to remove yourself from the equation. It is logical to kill, maim, and rape people who live in different countries because you don't agree with them? War is a symbol of the weakness of men, and an oxymoron. To bring understanding and prosperity through murdering others. To supersede. To force undoubtedly with no rational reason as to why.*

"Hey, I wish I didn't go. They've more or less proven that the Omrikan government was involved in the attack. And every other event that got us to enter a war in modern times. It was about oil, it was about putting people under a thumb," Brind states.

"There are these imaginary lines drawn on the globe, they represent nothing. The carnage they create is real. You can see it, you can feel it," Gnat adds. "Where does this allegiance come from? It's blind. You don't turn eighteen and decide what country to be a citizen of based on your personal beliefs. It's random. And everything we believe about this place was taught to us growing up. It's conditioning, indoctrination."

"Brainwashing," Brind says. "Think of the oath of fealty in school."

Gnat exclaims, "Yes! The original indoctrination of citizens using public schools! Every morning from age five to fourteen, you say it. We're the best, I know it, I defend it, the creator is with us. Over, and over, and over. Until it becomes part of you. Part of your identity."

"People would call us crazy right now, it's completely true..."

"Then what do you get?" Gnat says. "Boys that grow up, giving spans or their lives to this ideal. In their heads it's honorable, correct from a moral standpoint. They have been manufactured into pawns to do the bidding of other men. The ones with hidden accounts, schedules for themselves and the future."

Brind's eyes have more water in them than normal. Not enough to make a tear form or his voice break, but he realizes that he had filled that role in the past. That he had accepted the lie and become a stooge to be misused.

"When you get home, they call you a hero. All I did was murder people because our culture doesn't understand their culture, and it makes Omrikans afraid. They said we were protecting freedom. We were perpetuating hate."

"Well, we need the oil to keep the machine rolling. A self-fulfilling destiny," Gnat is standing next to Brind, his open hand up on the man's shoulder. Brind is studying the ground, blinking rarely. Gnat supposes, *they destroyed this gentle giant. How many men of its own has this country taken decency from? Entire generations. How could you find meaning in anything after taking part in such senselessness?*

Brind stands up straight, he had been leaning on the broiler. "I know what I'm not going to do again."

Gnat is genuinely curious, "What's that?"

"Start a conversation about Lellin with you."

They both sigh. Gnat, simply and politely speaks, "Thank you. Brind. I'll come cover your break. Keep prepping, it won't be busy tonight. We can get that list completed before we go home. I'll make the coleslaw. I know you don't like using the grater."

"We've both cut ourselves on them before. It's brutal."

It really is the worst thing to cut your finger on in a kitchen. Mandolins and knives are bloody, yet clean. When you cut your finger with a grater, you can see the layers of skin in different ovals down to the muscle.

"It sucks," Gnat says, pushing through the door back to the real world. He and Brind always have open conversations. Mutual respect, again.

Jin is at the front desk helping a few campground guests check-in. A pair of older women, they are upset about something. Jin gives Gnat the head nod to help. He can hear one woman saying that she wants site number nineteen, it's empty. It's the site on the corner of the grounds, next to the beach, with more space than the others. Every guest wants it. Whoever requests it first, gets it. If your camper is under a certain length, you can't have it. It was designed for the biggest class of busses.

The woman is a person that thinks being as loud as possible will get her anything she wants.

"It's first come, first serve. Someone else booked that spot for tonight. It's already paid for," says Jin. "There are other spots on the water available."

She balks. "First come, first serve? I'm here first. You aren't giving it to me."

"The booking was made prior, they were first. That family is checking in later," Gnat says.

The woman continues, "Put them in a different spot, they won't know the difference. We're going to take it when we go out there anyway, so it doesn't matter."

The side of Gnat's mouth twists up in a smirk. "That family comes every span and stays in nineteen. It's already been confirmed for them. You can set up there, that's fine. When the people who reserved that spot show up the rangers will be here to escort you out."

"You wouldn't do that," she says.

"I will. I have before. What class are you?" he asks.

"It's a pop-up..."

"You can't stay in that site. It's for the coaches that use more power, we only have three of them. So, you couldn't stay there despite it being open. There are other spots that have great views. Walking in during busy season, you're lucky to get a spot at all."

The women stare at one another. The second persists, "We'll try another lodge around the lake."

Jin enters again. "Every lodge is operated by the same company; the others are booked. We only have some availability because of a recent cancellation. Try if you'd like, however our sites might be gone by the time you check around. Then you'll have to return to Port Albany, where most of the hotels are full and there are no campgrounds."

The women end up booking a site for their pop-up. Both men return to the office.

"Luckily, I saw them come in. I knew they would cause an issue. You know how timid our receptionists are. Livi would have given them the spot and we would have had a fiasco when our locals showed up," Jin says.

"People with campers are the worst," Gnat barks. "It's the most pointless activity on Irfa."

"Pretty ridiculous, I agree."

"You have a house full of stuff. You buy a camper. A model you can drive is a few hundred thousand. A pull-behind maybe thirty to seventy, which needs a truck to pull it, so the same amount again. You pack it full of things from your house, using five times the fuel because of the weight. You go to a place that has concrete pads to park on and level it yourself. Full electric and sewer hook-ups. Satellite. Then pay motel rates to stay and watch movies in the campground."

"Most people don't use the bathroom they have inside, they use our facilities. The kitchen either! They eat in our restaurant," Jin adds.

"Yeah. If you fly first class, stay in five-star hotels, eat out every meal, and rent a car when you get where you're going, it's still the cheaper way to travel."

Jin responds, "Then they're angry when the spot they're given is a few paces away from their desired space."

"Yes, like boaters. Go watch at the ramp. I've never seen a smile or laugh when loading or unloading from the trailer. Recreational vehicles are easily the most gluttonous display of irresponsibility I can think of. A colossal waste of resources. The fuel. The pollution. These monsters clogging up the highways." Gnat is disgusted.

"It's a paradox. Can you believe people buy a camper on a thirty-span term like a house? Like any other road vehicle, it loses fifteen percent of its value for driving off the lot. Imagine what it costs to maintain something like that. It's a racket. Those manufacturers found a niche, and sold people on it hard." Jin shakes his head, rubbing his eyebrow on his shoulder. "What's Brind up to? Is he feeling good? I saw him clocking in."

"He's Brind, the only employee that I consider my friend. We talked about the military earlier. They broke him," says Gnat.

"You shouldn't speak to him about that, you know it messed him up. He's trying to exist again. He doesn't need to relive it," Jin replies.

"He brought it up, talking about Lellin. I dislike so much as putting energy towards thinking politically, much less speaking about it."

"I hear you," sputters Jin.

"Thinking about this word, freedom. We aren't free in this country. You can't do whatever you want. You have to find a place to live. You have to get a job or you go hungry. I can't do what I really want to. Do either of us want to be working hard, so some corporation gets the upside? Because they had the funds to buy it in the beginning? That gives them the right to use me for their purposes?"

"No, it doesn't seem like the rules match the current circumstances. We're too far in to make it different from where we are," Jin suggests.

There it is again, the voice inside his head says. *Just accepting it as the way it is.*

He answers Jin, "In this country, if you shut your mouth and do what you're told, pay your taxes and subscribe to the idiotic institutions, you can live a life that is easier and more comfortable than anywhere else. That's not freedom. Just because you get to choose which fast food restaurant you eat in doesn't make you free. You still have to pick an option that's offered, use the currency, which only has value because you were told it does, and keep producing afterward."

"You don't feel free though? Despite being able to say things like you are right now?"

Gnat widens his eyes, "Freedom of speech doesn't mean any-thing, if the person who tells you to speak freely already knows that you have no power."

"That's something to think about."

"Every entity, legal or not, conforms to the same patterns. It's a matter of perspective. The largest drug cartels, from a personnel and systematic standpoint, are organized exactly the same as the most profitable companies in the world. Including the government institutions we trust!"

"You're going to have to elaborate on that, before I decide you're going too far with it," urges Jin.

"I can do that no problem," Gnat continues. "When you join a gang, you have to pledge your loyalty to the leader. No matter what they tell you to do, you aren't allowed to question it. In whatever way that you are told to do something, you must do it. If you disagree, you are disciplined by the people with a higher standing than you."

"Right," says Jin.

"Then, you are given an area to protect, maybe a few blocks, where you sell the drugs they tell you to sell. You charge a price and you give the cash from the whole of what you sold to the boss. Everyone above you takes their piece, and in the end you get a paltry percentage to live on. The lower your standing, the more work you have to do, the more expendable you are to the people in power. You're paying for yourself to be a pawn."

Jin asks, "Okay everybody knows this is more or less how it works. How is that the same as a business or the government?"

"Let's use the police as an example. So, you want to be an officer? What do you do?"

"Go to the police academy," Jin says.

"Yes, where you're told what you are defending, *the law*. You have no understanding of its purpose for being written by politicians. You can't question it; you simply enforce it. You can't change it; you can only follow protocol as you've been taught."

"That's true. Go on."

"Then, the city gives you a car with a beat to work. Which is a few blocks. You drive around and protect it, issuing fines to those who break the law."

Jin concludes, "Ha! Then that revenue goes to the state, who divides it up to pay the salaries of everyone above you, and a small percentage goes to the officer in the end. He's the same pawn as the low-level drug dealer he arrests. Damn, never thought of it that way."

"You know what happened, the last ticket I got? I was driving to go fishing in F'lalasip. On the highway, right lane, no other cars. I was in my truck, doing the speed limit minding my own business. A trooper in the left lane passes me full throttle, gets in front of me, and slams on his brakes. There was white smoke, seriously. He jumps behind me as I pass him and almost bumps me, again, not being dramatic. I swerved because he was that close. He hits the lights, and writes me a ticket because I didn't have a seat-belt on. After he leaves, I see the price. Over three hundred. The fine for the seat-belt was only twenty-five of it, the rest was administration fees. Each officer writes a single ticket, pays his wage, the rest is profit for the government to use. A perpetuated, self-fulfilling fraud on the Omrikan people."

"If you don't pay it in two cycles, the fine doubles," Jin says.

"Yeah, law was designed to protect you from people trying to hurt you, not from yourself. What about after you get convicted of something? Go to a prison, there are guards and convicts. Who is actually serving the sentence? For the guard, there are strict guidelines to follow. Any issues dealing with the well-being of the inmates, the guard must put the prisoner's life over their own. They have no idea who is actually guilty or innocent. Closed eyes, the same as a soldier. Being obedient to something they don't understand. Like a dog. On the other side, the inmates. Who still get any contraband they need from the outside. Three meals, healthcare, cable, meditation classes. If they don't like another inmate or a guard, they can be as violent as they want. The prisoners have nothing to lose. By breaking the rules, they are separated. By returning themselves to this feral state, somehow these men and women have broken the shackle, not locked it. This is the worst level the state can take them to, yet their basic needs are met, by way of the taxpayer. It's a diluted concept of punishment, the civilians accept the burden."

"Most jails are for-profit now, too. So, the government is putting people away on made up charges to collect the check. It's interesting you said something about a dog. I always see the dog and owner, and wonder who really is in charge. I would never get a pet, too much commitment for nothing except a hassle," says Jin.

"Oh, I know, you pick up after them. They get hair on your clothes and furniture. Bad breath. You can't have a conversation with them. You can't go anywhere you'd like; it has to be dog friendly."

Jin adds, "Have you ever had the friend that always has to leave in the middle of a good time to go and let the dog out?"

"Of course. That could just be the excuse they use though."

Jin retorts, "You're right."

"You know what dogs are like? Living cigarettes," Gnat goes on. "If you are so desperate for affection, hire a prostitute."

They both start chuckling, Jin so hard he holds his stomach. The businessman brings it together from a monetary standpoint, "It is so clean and easy, isn't it? I give you money, you provide a service. Quick, simple, both sides understand what it is. No different than calling a plumber to fix a shower. Speaking of, what's the timeline on that, Gnat?"

"He should be here soon. I'll bet the NRS guy messed something up on purpose, thinking we'd bring him back out."

"At his rates? Not a chance."

"It's time to take the cart around."

Another of Gnat's duties. Go to the sites, talk to guests and give them suggestions for things to do. Be welcoming, if he is capable of that. After his many spans in the industry, he fakes that hospitality smile with the best of them.

"Oh yeah, that's why we're here, to work. That totally slipped my mind for a moment, talking about the flaws of our existence," says Jin.

"It's the only thing that's ever on my mind," Gnat answers, on his way out.

He finds the cart by the housekeeping building and speeds down to the campground. People with campers are usually elderly couples or young families. Gnat acts bubbly, going through the same question and answer session as every other time. Local spots, the best restaurants. Favorite road trips in the past, the men always want to show off their rig and talk about how much they spent. Then, how he got the job, where he's been. Gnat doesn't dislike it, but how is it possible that so many people are so alike when they talk to you? It's almost as if everyone is programmed by the same algorithms. Desiring the same things, it comes out of what they've been shown, not what they've experienced in their own life. If you were born naked with no family, in a world with no definition of right or wrong, what would you end up desiring? A degree from a university, a health insurance plan? Everyone always tells Gnat he's negative and too judgmental. That isn't it. If you see somebody on the street with long hair and a guitar and the thought crosses your mind, *get a job,* that is literal judgment. If you look at a man, seeing the intensity in his eyes, his facial cues, and body language, then come to a conclusion based on your past interactions, that is wisdom. Experiential knowledge. You can't take that away; it can only be earned. Sadly, that's not what is valued on Irfa. What is valued is not thinking or coming to conclusions on your own merit. Humans are simply repeating what they've been told, reaching for goals provided by feckless educators.

As Gnat drives to the lodge under electric power, a veil of caliginosity covers him. He feels an undecided force gestating within him. Uncertain whether it is going to be symbiotic or encumbering. He sighs again, closes his eyes, and realizes how tired he is.

"Hey, I have some good news for you," says Jin.

"Oh yeah, what's that? Everyone at the front desk quit, there's nobody in the pipeline to hire, so that duty becomes ours too?"

Jin answers, "Not quite. I've got a lot of information to put together for the call tomorrow. Budgets, of course. Every lodge manager on the coast will be there. So why don't you take off now. I'll close. Turn your phone off. Rest tonight."

"Really? That'd be great!" Gnat says, surprised. Usually Jin does mornings, Gnat does nights. He has scheduled time off, but managers rarely get it. Maybe a third or half of what they should. Brind closes for him sometimes. Gnat balances the safe the next morning.

"Go, before something comes up," Jin says, turning his chair back to the desk. "See you tomorrow."

"Yes, see you then."

***

Some employees are talking about going to get booze and food in town.

"Pick me up a case?" he says to one of the girls in the car leaving, "Keep the change, I'll be by the water for sunset. Leave it on my stoop?"

"Alright," the girl shrugs her shoulders. "Give us a while."

Gnat goes and changes his clothes, which is really only removing his polo shirt. There's a beach not far away, abandoned except by the occasional employee. A view through the cleavage of the mountains shows the sunset in stunning fashion. He used to go regularly in previous spans, no chance yet this season. He grabs his guitar that isn't played much of late, either. Gnat taught himself when he was eighteen. There was a video game that simulated being in a band. Some girl bought it for him. Eventually he could beat the expert level on every song. He wondered why he didn't learn how to play the real instrument. So, he traded his gaming equipment for an electric guitar and that's where it began. At some point, Gnat thought he would do something with his music. That dream has left him, although he still enjoys playing for others and writing his own songs. It's his outlet. He thinks the only way he can genuinely portray what he feels is through his songs. It never comes out quite right in normal conversation. On the beach, he starts to flat pick with a roll almost like a banjo. His voice is somewhat hoarse, others have said they are drawn to it in the past. Like it traps you in to listening.

Just a box of crayons, falling to the ground.
Can't you see them fall?
Colors down the wall.
All I see is red, white and blue are dead.

Doesn't matter anyway, these hearts have turned to gray.

What colors do you see?

These gray times, must change.
Promises made to a generation of shame.
These gray times must change.
Color outside the lines don't be afraid.

Just a box of crayons, a consolidating cloud.
Can't you see the colors bleed?
It's a puddle at my feet.
The puddle turns to black, seems like no turning back.
Doesn't matter anyway, our times have turned to gray.

What colors do you see?
What colors do you see?

These gray times, must change.
Promises made to a generation of shame.
These gray times must change.
Color outside the lines don't be afraid.
Color outside the lines don't be afraid.

He witnesses the last speck of the sun pass behind the peaks. *Sustenance gone.* Gnat pauses in stillness for a while, absorbing the silence. Almost as if he doesn't want to disturb it. Eventually, he stands up, braving the pitch of night to rejoin the cycle he's stuck in currently. At least he will have a few drinks for later, maybe they will allow him to put up with the people around the fire. More than likely not. The case is on his step. It's surprising they bought it for him, much more of a shock it hasn't been stolen. Gnat takes it, never to the fridge, he enjoys alcohol at room temperature. He writes and plays more guitar. After a while, laughs are heard across the complex. The crew is going to trash the place again. Gnat smirks, stepping to the window. *A few more, and I'll go out.* Shortly following the thought, he puts on his jacket and grabs more cans. Locking his door, he sees Juun and Libeth pulling out of the housing complex. She rolls down her window, slowing.

"Where are you guys off to?" Gnat hopes he might not have to go to the fire after all.

"Date night, dinner and a movie," Libeth answers.

"Oh, don't let me keep you. Who took you to get your car?"

"Caught a ride with the people going on an alcohol run. See you tomorrow. We'll knock and see if you're home after dinner."

Gnat says, "Not likely. We'll catch up. Later."

He starts toward the pit, with unusually high flame. There are probably ten to fifteen people.

"Let's see how this goes," he says to himself.

A few people give him a smile, which is more a movement of their cheek muscles, passing quick glances to each other. There are some people from past contracts. They ignore him and keep talking amongst themselves. In communal living, it isn't impolite to skip the greeting every time you meet. A newly hired couple, Ick and Briti, are present. She left her last boyfriend and hooked up with Ick on the road. She's what some would call a street kid. Greasy hair, always dyed different colors. Homely, quiet, nothing to really add to a conversation. Ick is, in a word, tedious. The guy who always says something as loud as he can trying to be funny, but isn't. No substance in his words. Overweight, unclean, he doesn't know the meaning of the word hygiene. A believer that his opinion holds value, because he has it. The only problem is, it isn't backed by any insight, solely audio snippets collected in his head courtesy of the most advertised media outlets. Gnat sits across the flame from him, hoping this barrier will keep him from having to interact with this unamusing jester.

"Hey there, Gnat," Ick says. *So much for avoiding him tonight.* "I'd tell you a joke about pizza, but it's too cheesy."

The group cackles. Gnat looks at him blankly. Ick is uncomfortable that he can't get a rise out of him.

"Don't you ever laugh?" He speaks in a way in which everyone can hear. "Where's your sense of humor?"

"I know where it is. You haven't found it yet. Keep trying though," Gnat replies.

Ick turns to his girlfriend, and starts talking about some recently released show. Every idea seems to get green-lighted by the on-line channels. It's the same series, they never end. They are like a drug, written in such a way that every episode is a cliffhanger, yet there is never any resolution. Scripts about monsters or the undead. Fantastical ideas, creating robotic viewers through routine conditioning. Always something to watch. Nothing to discover or learn. This story is about a group of children that are entwined in a government conspiracy theory. Gnat watched a few episodes then became uninterested when he knew it was more of the same.

"Now there's a joke," says Gnat, "This politically correct nonsense has finally corrupted every level of the media, science fiction included."

"What are you saying?" Ick protests.

"It's a group of specially selected kids that don't have anything to offer but the color of their skin to make every consumer feel good about being represented. One white Omrikan girl, an Ehfran boy, a pair of orphaned Ropan twins, and a Telaysian boy in a wheelchair. It's ludicrous. Have you noticed commercials on television? Every couple is interracial, then the baby is an ethnicity that doesn't match either parent. How does that work? That's not what they taught me in sex education when I was twelve," Gnat says grinning, his eyebrows scrunched up, taunting Ick.

"That's not very nice," says Ick's girlfriend. "You shouldn't judge people by the color of their skin."

Gnat answers, "I'm not, and I never do. When I meet a person, I may subconsciously notice their skin tone or that they come from a different culture. I don't interpret that as a tell of what to expect from them as an individual. What these writers are doing is just that, completely. Consciously choosing someone because of their complexion *for* a reason is exactly the same as *not* choosing them for something because of it. A double standard, forced on us to make a profit."

"Some people are different from others, we should recognize that," some other boy says, sipping a can of craft brew.

Gnat continues, ignoring the primary-school announcement. "Yes, everyone is living in different circumstances. That's irrelevant. Racism within a race, who's the victor, who's the victim? I've been busted and broken at the bottom. You know what, I picked myself up and got out of it. I didn't look for pity or a handout, or blame where I came from for holding me down. I'm an individual, me and my choices get me wherever I go. Up, or down. This time spent on recognizing differences, what a waste. You know what we should do? I live my life, and do whatever I want. You live your life, and do whatever you want. I'm not worried about it. I'm not going to die for you, I can't try to live for you. You want an abortion? Get it. You don't want an abortion? Don't. You want to be gay, whether by genetics or choice, be what you want. I don't need to hear about it. If we do that, mind our own business, guess what happens. The boundaries disappear."

Another girl, with a jacket on and the face of an innocent, enters and says, "That seems like a frigid way to exist, not treating people with dignity."

"What are you talking about?" Gnat scoffs. "Did you listen to anything I said? I'm proposing complete and utter acceptance of every person through means of understanding that we can't change each other. We need to quit with the victimization of every individual who gets upset. You're offended? Who cares? I'm offended that you expect me to change the definitions of biology and science as I know them so that you can feel better about yourself. It's deranged. It really is. This idea of social justice, it doesn't work. It's individuals recognizing personal insecurities and trying to make others feel isolated as well. That's not equality, that's projecting self-pity."

The same girl asks, "Are you talking about transgender people?"

"Not specifically, but that's an example. There are laws, of nature and biology. They are steadfast, not changeable or malleable. If you want to have the body of a woman and you are a man, or vice versa, fine. It isn't perverse, it's not immoral. It *is* body modification, the same as a piercing or a tattoo. Cosmetic. More extreme, maybe as far as you can take it, but it isn't changing your biology. You are still the same sex as you were born, genetically. Evolution doesn't make mistakes, it's simply a chance. That's not to say that some men are more feminine than others, or women that are more masculine. The issue is the same as I said before. It's a double standard. You want to be accepted as being different, by demanding me to change what I believe. If you were really doing it for yourself, what I think shouldn't be part of the decision-making process. I don't vie for your acceptance for being what I am. Why are you? Is it more about attention than intent?"

Ick yells, "Yeah, says the straight white male."

The people listening to the conversation move to see if this is all it took to make him concede.

"I can't have this conversation with you, if that's the reasoning you're going to use," Gnat says dryly.

"Clearly you can't," Ick answers.

"I *can* tell everybody else why that response only shows how ignorant your thought process is," Gnat goes on, "First, you are assuming that because I am a white man, I am also heterosexual. Which is a paradox pertaining to this conversation, because you are assuming facts based on my physical appearance, which is what you are trying to demonize me for. Also, you're a white guy discounting the opinion of another, for being white. Based on your logic that makes your opinion mean nothing. You're operating from an emotional standpoint, which is fueled by what you see on screens. Not your own experience. That's blind trust in standards given to you, not morality. What race you are born into isn't choice, again. This thing about feeling guilty for being white needs to stop."

"What about the past?" Briti exclaims. "There is so much bad history based on what whites have done! We can never make up for it."

"We can, simply let it go. In the context of history, some things need to be remembered. When a lesson is learned, we move on and try not to repeat it. However, the emotion connected to the original action doesn't need to remain. This only leads to dwelling for generations, while living people have no real understanding of why they feel as they do. This creates misplaced anger, and arbitrary dialogue that resolves in loss of sight. Cause and effect, remember? Social feelings or reactions tied to that point in history, forget them. They were doing what they thought was best, as we do now. What will the future think of us? Would we want them to remain broken due to our inadequacies? We can reach no resolution in this future while it's still tethered to the emotional past. How long do minorities get to use this as a crutch? The opportunities are there, for anybody. At some point, you have to stand on your own and get it for yourself," Gnat says. "Who is it affecting, anyway? Rough numbers. Seven billion people on Irfa. Three hundred fifty million Omrikans. Half that are working age. Two-thirds of that hundred seventy-five million are in the workplace. Ninety percent of that group is in the middle or lower class. What, twenty percent are minorities? Ten percent identify as not straight? That makes about thirty million people out of seven billion? That's... less than ten percent of Omrika, not so much as a single percent of Omrikans against the world population," Gnat answers, "Seems like a lot of talking and legislation for nothing. You're never going to make the minority so powerful that it's equal to the majority. Come on, that's what the words actually mean. Are you going to tell me that semantics need to be redefined?"

Ick interjects, "Things can change. Anything can happen. Anybody can do anything."

Gnat says, "I agree. Although, words can not have any definition that's necessary. Then nothing symbolizes anything. Language loses meaning. It reverts to who can grunt the loudest. If the speed limit is sixty, you can't get a fine for going sixty. If you are going sixty-one, you can. There's a line. You can't always get another chance; you can't always change the proposition. You have to decide, one way or the other, and stick to it. That's what gives a person value. Not the way other people see them. Labeling yourself is an inconsistency, you are separating yourself from the whole and begging to be accepted by it at the same time."

"I think that it's sad to be so negative about everything," the innocent girl says. "Why not live your life? Things just are the way they are."

"It's not negative, it's not about emotion, and it's not about what you think. It's about what you know. And I know that we are getting taken by every system of control on this planet. How to change it? I'm unsure. I will not ignore it, and I won't accept it," Gnat replies.

"There are always things holding us down, we can't change that," she says.

"Not with that level of conditioning and complacency. Where does identity come from? Your color, gender, or religion? Is it internal, mental, unseen? Is it based in the opinion another holds of you? Is it centered in what you were told you are, from the beginning? If that's the case, your identity, your thoughts, were never yours to begin with..."

Gnat rises and notices that the only employees left are this girl, Ick, and Briti. They stare at him with hollow eyes, magnified by the orange glow from the fire, which creates a tango of shadow and phosphorescence across their faces. For only a flash, these eyes seem to be pleading with him to bring them to some place where certainty still exists. A human condition that can hit another pinnacle of understanding. Humans are supposed to be in this together. Basic survival is no longer an issue on Irfa, as a whole. Now, we have only sentimentality as function.

Gnat takes a deep breath of the mountain air outside his door. A touch of ocean, a single wisp of wood smoke mixed with its cleanliness. He enters and rests on his bed. Living in a world doing what everyone else is doing, eating what you are fed. Being cool is being a clone. Gnat is part of the Millennium generation, as the news calls it. The turn of a tide, a leap toward progress. There is no progress. His peers are soft, whiny, bored, and self-important. Complacent was the word he used in the conversation tonight. To live is to be greedy. To be greedy is to take. To take is to be violent. These things are just synonyms for survival instinct. This generation now focuses on the surface level, which is emotional reaction. This is the flaw in the thinking of human's Irfa. The mistake that this generation has made is confusing being progressive with being reactionary. There is no soaring to a higher plane when you have grounded yourself with labels, guilt, and trust in the counsel of simple-minded bureaucrats. Only spouting whatever emotion encompasses you at the moment as righteousness, decency, or tolerance. Take this civilization, this society, that is trying to correct itself. In its rebirth, it loses the things that make it what it is. The thought, the recognition of frailty, superseded by the rights of an individual. The loss of education for standard, the loss of intelligence for ease.

Gnat is lying in bed now, with his palms up. He is warm yet uncomfortable. *Everything in this place is a useless binder full of procedures, trying to provide meaning to the suffering that is survival*, he determines, feeling the living mass within pushing him into the mattress. He closes his eyes. There is a field, again, with the same shapes that he can't catch. Something is different this time, however. The gap is getting smaller as he runs, the forms stop. Gnat still tires, he can't reach them. There is an echo, a sound. It reminds him of a creature under the water. It penetrates his essence. He has the sensation of floating. What are these beings trying to say to him? *It is beginning.* These are the words that stick in his brain.

III

He awakens to a text message from Addie.

Can I see you?

The lodge doesn't close until late, it's his responsibility to lock up. He types to Brind.

Will you close this evening? I'll stay until the last rush is over. Makes us equal for covering and stocking the truck.

Gnat stares at the screen until a reply comes.

Alright.

At least he can count on someone to help him out sometimes.

Okay, Brind is covering for me. See you later.

He shoots the verdict to Addie. A simple smiley face is returned to him.

The same routine as every other shift, some unforeseen issue will arise at the lodge to occupy most of his shift. Exiting his cabin he sees Ick and Briti are standing on the opposite side of the lot talking. It doesn't matter what about. Both see him and disappear behind the building out of sight. Gnat shakes his head. He never feels bad about things he's said, regret *is* felt about putting effort toward trying to explain. Especially when he already knows that they are deaf in one ear, and it goes out the other.

At work, the nearly catastrophic disasters that present themselves are expected. He handles them with a calm seriousness, getting the employees and guests through the shift. Frink finished the morning with a jolly step, dishes complete. It's about six, a quiet night. Very quiet. Stepping into the kitchen, he finds no tickets for food.

"Are you good, I'll go a little early?" Gnats asks Brind, with a hesitant expression.

"Yeah, I should be fine. A bunch of guests went to town together, I don't think any more parties are coming."

"Where's our server?"

"Smoking. I can tell her to go if nobody comes in soon. I'll do both sides if people show up," says Brind.

"All good. Just make sure the stainless steel is wiped. We'll rotate everything and prep tomorrow. Thanks for staying, see you later, Brind."

"Until then."

Dari is a man who does maintenance at the lodge Gnat worked the first season. That place has healing springs, immersed with Native Omrikan tradition. Dari and his wife live in Port Albany. He was the very first person Gnat met when he came to Wishintown. He's in his mid-sixties, there to lend a hand with a gentle grin. Gnat considers him a friend. Addie and Tia live with him, away from the drama of the housing complex. He already knows what Addie is going to want for dinner. There's a pizza place where you build your own pie in-store then cook it at home. His part without cheese, of course...

Addie is sitting on the front lawn next to a garden. The porch light is illuminating the blooming flowers, that seem somehow agitated by this artificial source of radiance interrupting their growing rhythm. Addie watches him approach, not standing up to greet him, only waiting for his affection. He submits, grabbing her hand, smothering it with both of his, kissing her in the middle of her forehead. She demands another on her lips.

"How was it?" she says.

"You know what I'm going to say."

"Every cycle is a cycle?" Her head tilts slightly to the side.

"Yes, better now," replies Gnat.

"Are you hungry?"

"I could eat," he says, playing off the fact that he's starving.

"What do you want to eat?"

"Food."

"What kind of food?" She's giggling.

"Good food."

Slap happy now, he tickles her sides. They have this exact conversation every time meals are mentioned.

"I already know you want pizza," he taunts.

"You don't!"

"I'm fine with it, I really am. I just want to be with you, absorb your body heat and relax," says Gnat, "Come on, I'll drive us."

"Tia is in bed already, she has to work the early morning shift, so we have to be mellow. Shotgun!"

"There's only two of us, you don't have to call it..."

She runs to the passenger door, uncaring. Addie is always so excited to see him. He is as well, however it's harder for him to share his sentiments when it comes to the opposite sex. There's something about a man being strong that's ingrained in him. He never cries in front of others; he never talks too deeply about his feelings. Of course, he has emotions, he just doesn't live in them or let them control his decision-making process.

At the house, they watch an animated movie about a cheery fairy creature. Her favorite, they've watched it many times. She knows every word and Gnat enjoys hearing her re-enact it more than viewing the film itself. Tia wakes up and comes in to ask Addie for a cigarette, then scurries outside in a desultory manner. Returning to her room she mutters something about how they should have saved her a slice.

There was a time last span when Tia didn't get off the couch for an entire cycle. She made Addie get her food and bring it back to her. Along with her smokes, booze, and drugs. Which really meant that Gnat had to drive around town so Addie could pick it all up. Addie paid for everything. These women are more like a pair of codependent lovers than mother and daughter. Tia keeps taking, Addie believes it's her fault. Like she is some sort of horrible burden on her supposed caretaker. Addie tries to mend the relationship by bowing to every whim. Gnat always feels a certain tension when he's around both of them. He can only imagine how deeply this affects Addie. This truly is the biggest obstacle for her and Gnat to get over. Finding balance when the scale is weighted so heavily in favor of Tia. He would leave and travel with her, full time, but Tia is part of the package. Addie doesn't know how to live without her.

Addie is peering up at Gnat as her mother leaves the room. He already knows what she is going to say.

"No, I'm not going to go get her something. She's an adult, with a car, and her own bank account. She can go buy something if she wants," he says.

"We did eat the whole thing, you know? We didn't think about her."

"Ha! That's because we are having a date night. It's already bad enough that your mom is sleeping in the next room. We didn't have to think about her. It's our pizza. When's the last time she bought you food?" he asks.

"Forget it."

Gnat agrees. "Yes, forget it."

The movie has ended. She gets up to go do the dishes, he grabs her wrist. She turns, he is giving her that stare. *Can I have you?* Addie tugs at his arm until he rises, pulling him toward her bedroom. After sharing some demure revelry behind a closed door, they lay parallel, breathing deeply.

"Where do you think you'll go after this season?" she questions him.

"Not sure yet. No way I'll go to ski-land. I don't like the snow, and skiers are much worse than the weather. Remember when I was in Zeon? How can you be so excited to spend money on new gear and an outfit, then wake up to go down the same run twenty-five times? Maybe the desert. Southern Sanrika, they have beaches and mountains. Who knows?"

"Yeah. I don't know yet either," Addie says quietly, waiting for an invitation.

He goes on, "I told you if Tia goes somewhere else you are welcome to come with me. Live in the truck. We can share a room wherever we end up. I'm not going to have a forty-something child in the middle of us. I can't draw *your* line, only *mine*. I couldn't if I wanted to, it's not my place."

"I don't know how."

"Too easy! You say, 'I'm going to a different resort than you. We can meet up after my contract ends.' Don't tell her where we are going."

Addie has sad eyes. "She'll be by herself."

"Either she'll be alone, or I will. That's for you to decide."

She flicks on the light atop a dresser next to them, and rolls over to lay her head against his shoulder.

"Why does it have to be an ultimatum?" she queries.

"It isn't. If you want to risk not seeing me through the next contract and only have a chance of ending up where I do after that, okay. I'm not going to carry the weight of Tia's bad choices for the rest of my life."

"It seems like you are being dramatic," says Addie.

"Look, you have the wherewithal to do anything. Whatever capacity you want me in your life, I accept it. You can have as much of my time as you'd like."

She sighs, "I'll think about it. Troubles woubles for me, as always..."

He gets his boxers from the floor. Then his socks, jeans, t-shirt, and jacket, dressing in that order. Gnat checks that everything is in the correct place by patting each pocket, pauses, a flash of doubt crosses his face.

"Do you find me intelligent or insane?"

"Why do you ask?" she answers.

"I have these specific processes I go through. I'm unsure if it's because I am organized and analytical, or obsessive and compulsive. I don't know if people understand me, or write me off as a space cadet. I think people misread my intentions."

Addie is smirking at him. "Like the conversation you had at the campfire with Ick and Briti?"

No detail of anyone's personal life or interactions with others is sacred on the seasonal circuit. Everybody knows everything you do.

"Yes, like that. There are two ways of seeing things. From the standpoint of being educated, or being intelligent. You can't teach someone to be intelligent. Intelligence is inherent, genetic. There's only one thing that you can teach somebody, or indoctrinate them with, that's societal definition. Which makes you more informed as to how the system operates within these limits, never more intelligent. Intelligence tests are also irrelevant, it's still a gauge of how highly you can function within the bounds of understanding the society is capable of seeing. That's not truth, or vision."

"You don't think that anyone can see the truth except you? That's your sign of being a crazy person. Did a voice in your head tell you what's real?" she taunts.

"Come on. People have been bombarded with an agenda for so long that they don't even know how to speak their minds anymore," he says.

"Ick was pretty passionate about making you seem like a vile person in the mess hall."

Gnat replies, "Exactly! I questioned him in a way that he couldn't debate because he hasn't heard my viewpoint on the news. So what does he do? Deflects it to emotion. Belief is nothing more than infinitesimal opinion. It has no bearing on anything, except the emotional status of the believer. What matters is the truth. What is the genuine truth? Not your individual reality, based on teaching and personal circumstances."

"And you know what it is?"

"No, I do not. I won't settle for the common answer because it's easier and I don't need to explain myself," he says.

"Why do you feel like you have to always get your point across to make others feel lesser?"

Gnat sighs, "See. Misread. I'm not trying to make anyone think *less* of themselves. I'm trying to get them to question every-thing they've ever been told. It's nice when people come up with systematic answers that sound politically correct or culturally ad-vantageous, however what it comes down to is action. A white guy trying to tell everyone that white men are evil isn't going to actually change anything. It may make him feel better about himself personally. Talk is just that."

"And?"

"That's my question. Why are we striving for ignorance as a culture? Every level of politics, education, healthcare, and justice is flawed. Everybody knows it, yet they still give themselves value by ingraining their lives with its blindness."

"You can't change the world!" she says.

"But I could separate myself from it wholly, somehow. Some way..."

She reaches for him to lay next to her, "Where are you going with this?"

"I'm not sure." The force in his stomach hardens. Gnat's voice becomes quieter. He is living with Addie in this moment again, realizing where he's at in a tangible fashion. He continues, "Remember when we went to that carnival? The amusement park on the side of the road? Everything was old, wooden tracks for the coasters, the merry-go-round had those ancient hand-painted horses with full filament double-blown glass light bulbs?"

"Yes, you kissed me on that ride. That was the sweetest kiss you've ever given me. We had so much fun. You were ten again," Addie recalls.

"Remember the shirts the country people were wearing? Save Harlon. I'm a federated pipe-fitter. My kid is an honor student."

"What about them?"

"The only thing I could keep thinking about was 'how many ways can people justify that eating and taking as much as possible until they can't anymore serves some greater purpose?' Can no one see this fantastical façade we are living behind?"

She answers, "I think they can."

"If they can see it, and choose to ignore it, that's worse than not knowing the difference."

"I also think that you care way more about the destiny of us much more than you would ever admit."

He rolls his eyes slightly. "Think, believe, have an opinion. There you go, like everyone else."

Addie slaps his stomach and they stare, taking the time to see how much they really do represent to each other. She puts on a shirt and her underwear.

"Do you want something to drink? I am going to eat the rest of my Ice-cream from last time."

He rests his hands on top of his head, fingers interlocking. "Just water, take your time, I'll be here when you get back. I'm way too tired to go home."

"You're going to let me cuddle you?!"

Usually, he doesn't stay. The drive to the lake in the early morning is treacherous. The men who drive the logging trucks are ridiculous. They don't exercise any caution on the mountain roads, most of them are still tipsy from the night before.

"Yes, it counts as your birth date and End of Span present though," he beams.

"You're such a gentleman." Addie leaves the room.

Lying in the bed, eyes closed, he starts to let his mind wander. *An open mind, or a closed mind? I can't consciously tolerate close-mindedness. Some people may see that as hypocritical. I do not see it as such. I see a closed mind the same way as I do organized religion or the government. In the structure of our makeup, as a race of beings, not individuals, these things are the recessive traits. They will be erased over time. As a collective organism our race should learn from history and evolve. This same process doesn't transfer to the individual, however it should. To me it isn't about peace or compromise, which are fallacies in and of themselves. It's about living by my morals, which come out of my history and circumstantial experiences. As long as some humans try to control the experience of others, we can't reach the next plane of ingenuity.*

A plate falls to the floor, shattering in the kitchen. Then voices are heard, both similar, one clean and bright. The second a tattered version of the other. Tia is awake, and in the mood to sabotage every chance of Addie enjoying herself. As always.

"I told you I needed a pack of cigarettes, and you went out and bought food with Gnat instead. On top of that, you didn't save me any. Now you are eating the last of the Ice-cream. Adin isn't able to give me any money or drive out here until he gets paid. I'm totally screwed. I'm glad you are full and your boy is here. That's what matters," Tia says condescendingly.

"Gnat paid for the food. I bought myself this Ice-cream a while ago. There's only a bite left. We get paid tomorrow! You'll be able to buy whatever you need then. We need to start saving for the end of the season, who knows how far we have to travel," Addie answers.

Tia goes on, raising her voice, "I know he didn't pay for it. You let me be in pain, why not spend your paycheck to make me feel okay? You don't care about me, it's always about you. I heard you and him earlier, you are going to leave me stranded, aren't you? As long as you get what you want, everything is great."

At this point, Gnat is in the doorway of the bedroom, leaning on its frame. He is glaring at Tia, half angry, half confused.

"Which of you is the custodian in this relationship?"

Addie jumps in, "Stop it, Gnat."

"No, if Tia is going to ruin our night with her nonsense, let's at least try to find some reason in it. Because I've never seen her do anything for you, Addie. Not once. How much are you sitting on right now, Tia? Because Addie doesn't have any savings, she's been paying for you. Is that how you keep her trapped? So she has no option but to stay with you? How about I start paying for her, she can come with me. You can't."

Tia replies, "She wouldn't leave me for you."

He snorts, "The same way that you never left her for some random guy? Every time a man gives you attention, you drop your own daughter. You've kicked her out of the house multiple times."

"You've been with other girls since you've met Addie," Tia fires back.

He glances at Addie's face, that comment hurt her. He pauses, as in a moment of silence.

"We aren't talking about Addie and I. We're talking about you and your daughter. Stop trying to make us feel bad. The first sign that somebody doesn't have anything valuable to say is deflecting everything onto the other person. You keep repeating the same things over and over, getting louder. You're emotional right now. You're saying what you think is beneficial to you in the situation. I know what you're doing."

"Come on, Gnat, go to the room." Addie tries to diffuse the conflict.

Tia snaps, "I think it's time for you to leave now, Gnat."

He snorts again, with a chuckle, "This isn't your house, it's not your place to tell me that. It's Dari's. He told me I'm welcome any time I like."

"We pay the rent."

"You're cycles behind, from what he said. So don't go there. Again, use some logic. Addie and I want to find some resolution with you. It has to be real, not what's easiest," he says.

"I can always go with Adin," says Tia, "He said he has a room for me anytime."

"It's not about getting over on us. You already know that guy is going to drop you as soon as he finds someone else to sleep with until he's bored again. He's using you the same way you're using him."

"Gnat, seriously, let's go to sleep!" Addie exclaims. "Please, you are both upsetting me."

He looks down at her, pursing his lips. She doesn't deserve this woman as her guardian. She doesn't deserve any of the bad things that come into her path. Addie has something to say, but for some reason he doesn't think she will ever get to tell anyone or be heard.

"Alright," he whispers, simply.

Tia is watching them, arms crossed, and as she goes to her room tells Addie, "We are leaving early for the lake."

Gnat interjects, "She doesn't work early, I'll take her and be late myself."

Tia's gazes from Gnat, to Addie, to the ground. Wordless, she shuts her door.

"Why did you have to do that?" Addie asks, "Now she's going to be horrible."

"It's better than her making you feel horrible about the missteps she's made. You can stay at the lake with me if it's that bad."

"Really? I'd like that."

"If it comes to it. Come on, do we have enough time for some sleep?"

"It is," she says, checking her phone, "late... or early. Maybe both."

He goes in first, removing his jeans again.

"You know that saying about taking your boots off? It's true. They are such a hassle, when you remove them, it implies you're finished. No chance of putting them on again. If I would have tonight, I'd be driving home. That's the only reason I'm staying, so you know."

Addie shakes her head, "Will you shut up?" She vaults in, getting under the covers. Off goes the light. Her hair smells like the shampoo that she makes herself. *With lavender.* They close their eyes in unison, unknowingly, and off into their dreams they go, separately.

On the drive the next morning, they don't speak much. It's like this between them. Comfortable with the other, there's no need to fill the space with meaningless chatter. Outside the main lodge, she's gathering her things as Gnat notices a couple getting out of their car. He taps Addie on the shoulder to stop and watch along. A man in his fifties would be his guess. Hair dyed blonde, gold chains, a shiny watch. A few rings on his fingers, one looks like it may be from where he was *educated*. The car is a coupe, red with tan leather interior. It has chrome rims and wears a showroom glow on top of its paint, courtesy of an impeccable detailer using wax as his medium.

The woman has the blonde hair to match. The same jewelry on her neck, wrists, fingers, ears. The thing that isn't parallel between them is age. She is younger than Gnat, and has already chosen the parts of her body that weren't good enough. A surgeon fixed them. The man waits for his prize, she comes around the car and he holds out his arm. The young woman gently links her arm with his. She's kept, like a pet. A parade starts in the man's mind as they head into the restaurant, music and applause included. They're having three courses, of course. No expense is spared to show he's the man to be envied.

"What a joke," he says to Addie. "Everything is a joke. How can we take a person that cares about their status and call them intelligent? Or that identifies with a political party? Or someone who values a salary? I can't find purpose in the way things are structured. I try, but can't."

"She's just a gold digger with a lonely old rich guy. He's probably got a family in Sanrika somewhere that thinks he's on a business trip." She shrugs nonchalantly.

"So that's the epitome of what we are jealous of? A lie? That's what we all want? To be fake?"

"I'm going to be late, Gnat. Give me a kiss goodbye."

"I have to drive you to work *and* kiss you?" he says.

Addie taunts him with a straight face. "Kiss me." So, he submits.

She waves, leaving. Gnat nods his head. That gaudy couple put him in a sour mood. There are so many people living with sadness and anxiety because they don't fit that mold. People forced into solitude because of a flaw in the way they appear, an undesirable body shape. This word, value... He can't find it in anything. It's completely lost on him. Whenever he goes to the grocery store, he sees the tabloid magazines in the check-out line. Who do the citizens of Irfa look up to? The girl who got famous for making a sex tape, subsequently showing more of her body in public as time goes on. The athlete that cheats. There is a captain from an Omrikan sports team, a pretty boy, always up for sharing his artificially whitened teeth to the camera. He has won championships, making hundreds of millions in the process. After a few seasons, he was caught cheating for the first time. Then the second, and third. Still, he remains the leader of the team. Still, he collects the paycheck. His trophies should be stripped, he should be banned from the game, he should have to return the salary to the city he scammed. Yet, this is who we let our children idolize. Teaching them that your dignity is something to be bargained, as long as notoriety and net worth replace its footing in your character.

"I can't subscribe. I won't," he says to himself. "Rusty, Rusty, what's in store for me?" Incidents, events, things.

***

Gnat locks the doors of the main lodge with a sigh of relief. *Finished.* He ponders drinking for a moment, then decides against it. He needs a night of actual sleep, not passing out. Healing rest, as it were. Driving around the lake he realizes what he needs to do, create music. Maybe he can throw a new song together. It's been some time; his muse has eluded him. It's also dealing with Rusty. It doesn't allow him to sit and contemplate, work, and rework his music. In the compound, a large group of employees leaves in a caravan. There's a house party in Port Albany he wasn't invited to. Not that he would go anyhow.

The lights are dim. The generator for these cabins must be on the fritz. He can hear ducks on the water and the shriek of a cat acknowledging itself on a catch. A night with a full belly and a dry hole off the edge of some cliff, hidden in the forest. The nature of every living thing, desiring nothing except food and shelter. Thoughts of the couple from the morning cross his mind again. The rat race in the big cities of the first world. South Sanrika, where everything is fictitious. Including the beaches, they bring sand in from other places. The disunity between a place like the city and a place like this. Where you find what really means something to you, only your own mind to keep you company at night. Gnat starts to pick very slowly, almost not noticing the melody, the words come out. Not consciously, his muse has returned with an offering to him for absorbing its discontent.

> *I thought about it, last cycle or so.*
> *Even though I won't sing*
> *Let's play a show.*
> *I thought about it, a while ago*
> *I heard the people*
> *I heard the people say...*

> *Let's go to the river.*
> *Let's go to the sea.*
> *Let's go to the mountains*
> *And speak quietly.*

I thought about it, on a foggy bay
Why live in the city
When you can drive away?
I thought about it, screaming my oh my
I heard the people
I heard the people cry...

Let's go to the river.
Let's sing to the sky.
Let's go to the mountains
Our time is nigh
Nigh, oh, nigh...

I thought about it
Just to say
Even though I left it
It's not far away.

So, let's go to the river.
Let's swim in the sea.
Let's go to the mountains
And be...
Set free...
Free, oh, free.

A perfect symbol to represent the fleeting palpability he has, living on this peninsula. Next season, somewhere else. Another group of people. Another set of procedures. Now, right here, he is at home in the rainforest. He understands this place, the power it gives openly, if you take the time to recognize its presence. More importantly, respect it.

He plays the song again, writing the lyrics in his journal. There's silence around this night, no hoots or hollers from the distance. From humans at least. Maybe he'll get that good night of sleep in the end.

While brushing his teeth and washing the sweat off his face back at his cabin, Gnat stops and studies himself in the mirror. He's noticeably older than last time. *What are you doing?* He wonders. *Not what you want to be.*

He goes into the bedroom, rest is reachable, when…

"Knock, knock! Let me in!" a voice at his door.

"Libeth?" he says, startled.

"Yes, come on. Open the door, let's watch a movie."

"Coming."

Sluggishly he gets to the deadbolt. Before he can turn the knob Libeth pushes her way in, stumbling to the bathroom.

She says, "I need to pee first."

"I can see that." He widens his eyes. "You're wasted. Did you drive from town?"

"Don't worry about it," she affirms. "Turn something on for a while. Juun stayed behind."

"Should I get you something to eat?"

"Some chips or something. Water. I need to come down."

"Action or comedy?" he asks.

"Don't care, anything works. Maybe something we've both seen a million times, I can't pay attention to a story right now."

Gnat finds his portable device for playing movies and plays a comedy that he *has* watched many times. A story about smoker pals trying to evade a kingpin. He only has trail mix, which she declines, so he heats her up leftovers. She gratefully accepts it, the entire plate is empty before she has the chance to taste anything. They watch until he hears the light purr of Libeth snoring. Gnat takes a slow breath, in through the nose, out through the mouth. He didn't want to put up with her tonight, but how could he deny his friend? She would have done the same for him, no question. He moves around the bed, bending down to pick her up and carry her home. As he is lifting her, she turns toward him and grabs the collar of his shirt, pulling him slightly closer.

"No, I'll sleep here tonight."

He let's go, she slumbers once more. He takes the blanket and puts it over her, tucking her in. She'll probably wake up shortly and go to her place. He lays on top of the blanket on his side, fully clothed. He turns to face the wall away from Libeth. Now, he is seriously tired.

"Gnat! Hey, Gnat!" An aggressive shout from outside his door, followed by banging. Not moving, he opens his eyes and grumbles, "The single time I try to rest." It's bound to happen this way, how many times has he been the one to keep everybody up?

"Hey!" The banging continues. "Open up."

"Hold up, give me a break," Gnat calls.

As he undoes the lock, Juun pushes his way in, "Is Libeth here?"

"Yeah, she..."

Before he can finish the sentence, Juun punches him in the eye and pushes Gnat to the ground. Gnat stands up and deflects the next swing while Juun stumbles. Gnat grabs hold of him from behind, putting him in a headlock. By the smell of him, Juun shouldn't be able to speak right now. Gnat won't hit his friend in this condition, it's not in him.

"Why do you think this is okay?" Juun is trying to grab Gnat over his head. Gnat squeezes harder. Libeth wakes, jumps up, and starts screaming at Juun. Almost immediately she is crying.

"Stop it, Juun, stop, you're out of control. Nothing happened, I swear!"

Juun yells, "The light was off! You were both in bed and the light was off! I was gone and you did this to me, I knew you'd been talking about it behind my back..."

Gnat interjects, "Juun, you are the best friends I've got, I wouldn't do this to you, be serious." He has Juun on his knees, still holding him, "You're drunk, cut it out, man."

"You slept with her, I know you did! Admit it!" he roars.

Gnat is searching Juun's face, trying to figure out where this is coming from. He, Libeth, and Juun have a friendship that isn't caustic. The three of them have a bond, how could Juun be doubting that? Doubting him? There's a rustle at the door, everyone freezes and turns to see what's moving. Not a mountain lion, an elk, or the monster out of a children's story. For Gnat, any of these things would be better. It's Addie. He had asked for her to come, if Tia was being unbearable. Addie glances at Libeth, she's never liked her, and switches to Gnat.

She asks, "Did you do it?"

"He did, the light was off when I got here, he just won't say it," Juun answers.

Gnat let's go of Juun, the betrayal of their friendship is complete. "No, I didn't sleep with her, Addie. Never."

"Was the light off when Juun got here?"

Libeth starts to say something, but Addie simply holds up a finger to her without looking to stop the phrase from exiting her mouth.

"Gnat, was the light off?"

"Yes," he answers.

Addie's eyes are locked onto Gnat's as he breathes deeply, then she leaves. He's speechless for once. His gaze blazes at the people in his room bitingly. Putting his hands in his pockets, he heads to the bathroom.

"You guys should go," he mumbles. "Go."

In the mirror, his face has changed, despite the quick timing since his last appearance. He has a fresh black eye. *That will be lovely to explain to my staff, Jin, and the guests.* He washes his face again. After, he stands leaning on his arms over the sink, staring at the ground. His mind is blank. After counting the freckles on his cheeks, he returns to the bedroom. It's empty of life, only the remnants of battle remain. *This is what it must be like to stumble upon a crime scene.* Pulling the blanket over him, lights on, he says, "Can I sleep now?"

Not for long, another noise at his door. The luminescence is coming from the window, at least a new sun rises. The knock sounds official.

"Gnat, human resources. We need to go over a few things with you," says a woman's voice. Niti, he recognizes it.

"On the way," he answers.

As he blinks, recognizing the sting of the shiner, he knows he isn't going to get out of this one. He opens the door, it's Niti with her assistant, a girl whose name isn't really worth remembering. Niti studies Gnat and looks taken back.

"Are you alright? What happened to your eye?" she asks, " We heard you had a party here last night, your neighbors complained."

"They are up partying every night, the first time there's a noise out of my cabin, I'll bet the fools were waiting in line at your door when you came in this morning," he says, agitated.

"So, you did have a party?"

He sighs, "No, that's not what happened."

Gnat goes on to tell them, line for line. Truth for truth. He would just take the write up for breaking the rules on their curfew, but with the evidence surrounding his eye there is no way out of explaining it. When he finishes, Niti asks the most important question from her position.

"Do you feel unsafe with Juun on property? Do you think that he will try something like this again?"

"No, I don't feel unsafe. I didn't hit him, he got it out of his system. He was drunk. It's over."

Niti frowns, "Juun assaulted a manager, that's a pretty serious offense. I'm not sure he can stay."

"Listen, don't think of it that way. He and I have known each other since we both started the same contract. You hired us. I don't want him to lose his job, I really don't. Libeth will probably leave too. They're your best servers. It will be hard to replace them. It was an argument between friends. We are close, tempers flared. It's bound to happen at some point, in any type of relationship," says Gnat.

"What if other employees feel like he is a liability? You know how a single person can change the atmosphere of the entire operation. Living and working together is a delicate balance," the assistant recites.

"So, who makes the final decision?" he asks.

Niti explains, "Well, we need to talk to Juun and Libeth separately now. We will get back to you soon. The higher-ups may need to make the call since you are a salaried employee and he isn't. If you worked at the same lodge, there's no question he would be terminated. Is it okay for us to come to you at Rusty when we know more, or should we wait until you're off to contact you?"

"Anytime works, what do I tell my staff about my eye? Word gets around, they'll know anyway. I don't want to lie to them."

"Say there was an altercation. Don't give them any details yet."

"Alright, I hear you," he says flatly.

"That's it for now. We'll see you, Gnat," Niti says.

"Until then."

They get in their car and drive away, not talking to each other during their stroll out of the cabin. What a weird pair. Forced to be partners, the younger one waits for her superior to leave or mess up. The other gives menial jobs to her subordinate with the exact same training, only a lesser label.

Gnat pulls his phone off the charger. *If I could go back to when I plugged this in and know not to open the door for Libeth.* No reason to mess around with this, he scrolls to the district manager and hits send. The dial tone gives him a touch of anxiety.

"Hey Gnat, what can I do for you?" he asks.

"Do you have time to talk about an interpersonal dispute that happened between an employee and myself last night?"

"I'm in the car on the way to a meeting, go for it."

Gnat tells him what went on, about the conversation he had with Niti. When he's finished, his superior speaks plainly.

"That doesn't sound like something I would respond to kindly, staff assaulting a manager. Some of it is personal, yes. I may not know what feelings are involved between the three of you. However, it's the principle of it."

"I agree, that's the only thing that matters," says Gnat.

"It's not a safe situation, or straightforward. I know you don't feel that it's going to happen again, but can you guarantee it?"

"There's nothing that you can guarantee..."

"Gnat, can you be sure that it won't happen again?

"I..." he trails off.

"Can't say more than likely it won't, can you?"

"I never thought it would happen in the first place, really. So, I can't say that he won't be aggressive toward me again, even disregarding the physical aspect," Gnat answers.

"That's something for me to consider. And the others living at Kressent? I don't need people to be on edge when they come home. I'm at the convention center, I need to go. I'll talk to Niti once she's gathered every fact. Take care of yourself." *Click.*

Gnat peers at the wall blankly, then goes to change clothes. Maybe the world around him will get cleaner, in a transparent sense. He will have to explain again to Jin. Third time's a charm, they say. What does that even hint at? Does telling people about empty emotional confrontation somehow bring enchantment to everyone's lives? Or is it more like a talisman, will he receive it in the mail? Will it stop people's idiocy from getting in his way? *No,* he determines. *Just another slogan for humans, rationalizing and hoping that things will change for the better without any input from them personally.* His phone starts ringing again. It's funny how when there's a bit of theater in your life, everyone starts lining up to get the details of your current calamity. Gnat hasn't talked to this many different people so quickly since he's come to Wishintown. It's Tia, calling to somehow make her and Addie martyrs, he's sure. If not that, then to be holier-than-thou and make him feel bad. He picks up the cellular, and greets his mistress in misery.

"Hello Tia, how are you?"

"How could you do that to my daughter? You think she deserves to feel this way? Because of some guy that is despicable and not good enough for her? Who do you think you are?" she questions.

"I don't understand why you are coming at me right now, when you never so much as asked me what happened. You believe every-thing the other burnout employees say to each other. It's like the telephone game, snippet after snippet of underhanded information becomes what happened."

"You slept with Libeth and you got caught in the act by your so-called best friend and your girlfriend when you feel like being around her. It serves you right. You think you live above the rules. Now you can be alone in them," Tia says.

"I did not sleep with Libeth. Juun was drunk and made a scene. I've never even kissed Libeth. I've never thought of her that way," he responds.

"That's not what they are saying at the lodge. She said you've slept with her and a lot of other girls on the peninsula. Juun told Addie and I that it's true, he knows better than anyone else. Why would he lie? He said he doesn't want to see Addie get hurt and we should move on from you."

"Oh, is that what he said?"

Tia keeps silent for a moment, "That's what he said, Gnat. Addie doesn't want to talk to you or see you again."

"I get no chance to try to explain to her what happened?"

"No, she's done. She saw what she saw."

Gnat interjects, "She saw Juun and I fighting, Juun saying things he didn't understand yet, and Libeth sitting on my bed. The rest is speculation."

"Addie is so embarrassed. Everybody knows what you did to her. She doesn't want to feel that way ever again."

"I'll let her cool down. Tell her she can let me know when she wants to talk. She can come to Rusty, call me, text me, or come to housing. It's up to her. I won't force her to do anything."

"I'm telling you, she's not going to talk to you again. It's over. If you see her in passing, act like she isn't there."

"Don't be so dramatic, Tia."

"Goodbye Gnat, best of luck in the future."

He pushes the END button on the screen. *Maybe as much figuratively and literally.* Gnat sends a text to Jin telling him that he will be later than usual. There's another dialogue he needs to have with Juun and Libeth. There's something not quite coming to sums for him with everything that has gone down. Tia said that the two of them were relaying that he had not been loyal to Addie, which is just not a fact. Gnat heads down to the lodge at Kressent, eyes are darting away from him faster than normal. He doesn't actually care what any of these people think or believe, they don't know what the circumstances of the situation really are. They didn't see it. They believe what they've been told by other people who also weren't there. He enters the dining hall, scanning, the place holds hundreds of people, until he sees the pair. And they *are* a pair, talking and laughing like nothing happened. Libeth sees him first. She faces him spoon in hand, it hangs toward the table.

"Hey Gnat," she says, with no stress in her voice. They have had many nights where crazy things happen that none of them quite remember. Juun doesn't acknowledge him.

"Hey guys, what are you doing?" he asks.

"Eating some breakfast, we..."

He stops her by clearing his throat, "No, what are you doing? You told Tia and Addie that we did sleep together? Juun, you told them I have been hooking up with different girls? What is that? Why would you do that?"

Libeth says, "I didn't tell her we slept together, I told her we've slept in the same bed before..."

"Juun? Care to tell me why you told Addie that? That you should move on from me? Does it have anything to do with the fact that Libeth and I are closer than you are with her?"

"I don't know why you think it's okay to sleep in the same bed with my girlfriend, really. That's all," Juun answers.

"And rather than talk to me about it, you doubt my loyalty and start rumors?"

Juun says, "Something happened at that house party last night. That's what drove me to come over your place like that. Libeth broke up with me."

Gnat's stomach drops, now he understands exactly who is to blame, who manipulated him to get what they needed. To feel in control of the situation and her boyfriend again. He turns to Libeth.

"You used me against Juun, didn't you? To make him feel like he's lesser in the relationship, so he caves to every request you make of him, right? To feel secure?"

"No, it wasn't that..."

He speaks to Juun, "You doubted me. You sold me down the river for this girl. I would have been your friend for the rest of your life, how long are you two going to last? I would and have given you anything, any help you needed. I thought I could trust you."

"I was drunk and angry, I can't tell you why I did it," Juun says.

Gnat replies, "Because you are insecure. Because you are weak-minded. Because you need the approval of the people around you to feel complete. You know what? You guys can have it. You want the empty friendships in seasonal, the people that hang around each other to not be alone when they get drunk, go for it. Nobody has anything to offer, they are treading water to keep their breath. It's fake. The people, the mindset. You know I was on a call with the district manager this morning to save your jobs so you wouldn't have to separate while you are down here smearing my name in the mud. Keep it, keep all of it. I'll leave now."

Juun starts to say something about how he doesn't want Gnat to go, and Libeth stands up to try and make him sit next to her.

"Save it, both of you. No more lies, Juun. Me leaving is exactly what you want. I'm going. The both of you are dead to me," he says, in finality.

Neither says anything as he leaves. Right before he exits, he hears Libeth's giggle. *Like it never even happened.*

Gnat takes a deep breath, holds it until his face gets warm, then lets it out. What is their relationship? It's people taking what's in front of them because it's easy. There isn't any growth, no team-work, no addition of substance to either of their lives. Gnat always gives everything he can to others. It never comes back. Isn't that what love should be? Like they say, unconditional. It's not about what you are getting, but about what you are willing to give. Every-thing, despite it destroying you personally. Like so many others, *love* is just a word, it seems.

There's a flaw in him, at least according to the rules generally accepted by the unimportant. Some people would use the phrase 'I don't care.' However, this indicates that on some level they actually do. Whatever issue is affecting their personal equilibrium some way. By verbalizing it to the world, to themselves, it somehow displaces whatever anxiety or embarrassment that's inherent. Gnat, however, doesn't care. Not by action or conduct. It's not something that he strives for. It's his essence. There is no boundary to cross with him, no line. Nothing offends him. Either take him the way he is, or do not. What he sees, what he feels, is not in tune with the opinion or beliefs of others whatsoever. He doesn't put energy into the actions or convictions of others, it's simply a waste of time. Why would he limit himself with a label or an image?

His essence, however, does have an effect on the people he comes in contact with. Because other people do have boundaries, Gnat forgets this. He isn't conniving or being malicious, it's sincerely lost on him. He is honest with himself and everyone he comes across, only wanting the same in return. Everything else is secondary.

How many times has he lived this? Made this drive? How is this any different than an office job? Because the view is a giant rock with trees on it, not a concrete spire with weeds and graffiti? As he enters the building, to say goodbye to Jin, Gnat knows that he has gotten what he could from this place. From these people. *Maybe all people.* Jin is outside, trying to tell some Telaysian tourists they can't keep the fish they caught as they filet carcasses on the beach. A common problem, the language barrier with guests. Gnat always wonders to what level everyone plays their ability to understand Omrikan. There was a guy his first span from Muusman, who laughed at the shows on television every night. His shift started early in the morning. He would wake up, sign in, and go back to sleep. When they woke him up after the breakfast break, he would hold his hands in the air and act scared, pretending not to understand them. The boss would shake his head and return to his office. Himed was his name, a composer of confusion, a master in his own lazy way.

Jin sees Gnat and immediately holds his hands up to the tourists. He drifts over to his protégé, looking him up and down.

"I heard what happened, Niti called me. You called the district manager? Bold move, not that I would expect anything less from you. So, you should probably be fine, it's obviously not your fault in terms of policy. Choice of company, on the other hand..."

Gnat cuts him off, "Jin, I'm leaving. I came to say goodbye to you. I saw them this morning, they were laughing with each other like nothing happened. I've gotten what I can from this place, this lifestyle. I'm sick of putting everything out there and it never coming back around. The highway is calling me, I want to see what else is being offered."

"What about Rusty? What about me?"

"You know the controls we've put in place will hold everything together without either of us being here. Like I said, I give a hundred percent, or nothing. None of the upside comes back to me. I can't do it anymore; I need to consider myself first."

Jin, distraught, says, "Sounds like a cop out. You have a future with this place. I'm not just saying that, either, Gnat. I consider you my friend…"

"I consider you a great friend and teacher. It's not a future I can't build any other place, if I wanted to. I'll keep in touch with you, I really will. It's not a discussion, I can't be persuaded. I'm simply telling you. I'm packing my stuff and leaving. I'm sorry if this is me letting you down."

Jin reaches out his hand, Gnat shakes it. They lock eyes. They have both been in this type of work for many seasons and know the chances of them actually keeping in touch are very slim. It's an unspoken thing, in this world. You may or may not meet again, yet the ones who you connect with stay present forever. Whether for the strange quirks in their demeanor, recognizing negatives you don't want to portray also, or the life lessons given as between them. Jin points towards the shed, the tiniest quiver enters the businessman's voice as he speaks.

"I better be the guy to check on the boats from now on, not that I can do it like you. That's your armada of plastic and paddles over there. Think of the joy and memories your work on that has and will create when you are long gone. It's not for nothing, I hope you see that later on."

"See you on the flip, Jin."

He nods, "Yeah, see you then. Be good in the meantime."

Jin starts off to the boats, pausing to talk to some guests on the way about the history of the lake. Gnat knows, because the burly man has a booming, confident voice that carries. If that wasn't the case, he would still know the speech almost word for word. He has heard it many times. How do so many people work like this for so long? An infinite loop of false, kind greetings and stories, only to make them comfortable to spend more. Why should Gnat care about the joy that it brings these people? Through *his* efforts, visitors get what they want. Gnat is left empty.

He arrives at the cabin which *was* his. Transitory surety, provided along with a pitiful wage and menial job. Talk about living on the edge. He doesn't need the known, however. A thing Gnat has always enjoyed about living so light and organized, he can be gone in a flash. He cleans his room, no reason to be spiteful. His covert living quarters are packed and idling. As he throws a garbage bag in the dumpster, he glances at his hands. A little dirt, or dust, from wiping the window sills down. What are these appendages driven to do? *Call Addie.* He selects her from his contact list, holding the phone up. Before it rings, there is a beep. The robotic voice from the provider comes on. "There seems to be an issue, the number you have dialed is no longer in service or reachable by the device you are currently using..."

He hangs up, unfocused.

"Blocked," he whispers. *Addie's gone.*

He notices the mountain ridge while getting in the driver's seat, with a bit of a frown. The gear selector slides down to the 'D,' Gnat pushes on the gas. Up to the first stoplight at the entrance. No one coming, only going. As he turns onto Route Zero, he speaks to himself, "If the world were a grave, I'd piss on it."

IV

This peninsula, outside of work, meant so much to Gnat these past seasons. It's been the only place he's ever felt at home. Sincerely, basically, he appreciates the way people operate in this part of the Irfa. Of course, it's eclectic. You can't always get what's wanted, mostly only what's needed. Neighbors must help each other, no one outside of the community is coming to the rescue. It's still personal, unlike the rat race of most of Omrika. However, at the same time everybody's private. Secluded. Spread out. Sometimes a solitary drive of vast distance separates you from another. The first time he saw these trees, it calmed the eternal spinning of his mind to the point of imperturbability. The lucidity in the air jolts you to life each morning, with a damp crispness to be experienced, not explained. Living life step by step, a joy that most never get the chance to uncover.

Port Albany, PA, comes into view through the windscreen. Rolling past the shops, he knows many of the owners by name. There's a cargo container on the docks. Some older women are selling their wares alongside the fisherman peddling crabs to passersby. A few sailboats sway across the horizon behind drunken surfers noticed with only a lazy glance. Both are chasing that next rush, fueled with forces controlled by the movement of planets. Finally, the mountains loom, a constant reminder to the beings below of the ephemeral plight of their lives.

He takes a left, at the Rendezvous, and parks. It may be a long stretch before he returns. As Gnat enters the bar, the person he wants to see is there.

"Where are your friends?" the bartender asks. It's the nameless girl that he has ordered from for spans. No longer.

"They are back at camp. I'm taking off early this season, I won't be in anymore," he says dryly.

"Oh, man. That's too bad, off to another job?"

"Something will come up. There's a bad taste in my mouth. I guess I'll trust my instincts and head south."

She hesitates, undisturbed, and replies with a question.

"A couple of drinks?"

Gnat grins and snorts out of his nose, "Skip the strong stuff, I'm driving. What's your name, anyway?"

"It's Charlyn. Yours?" She seems genuinely interested. The hurt expression she always seems to have has lifted already. He's recognized her as a person, finally.

"Gnat, with a G," he teases, "Nice to finally meet you, Char."

She laughs, "Most people say Lyn!"

"Good for them. I like Char. It suits you."

"Enjoy your drink. I'll see you next contract, won't I?"

"Anything can happen, you know. I'll catch you somewhere, we are both wanderers, right?" he winks.

"That's true, be safe out there, Gnat," she says, and steps into the kitchen.

He sips away, alone. How did he make the mistake of trusting *another* person? Every time someone's been trusted, he's gotten crushed in the end. Through his entire life, no exception. Now Juun and Libeth, too.

Doubt and betrayal. The thought, energy, and time he has given them. Road trips to see them on opposite borders. All those great adventures. Trivial. Unimportant. To top it off and feel like they have won, telling Addie things that are untrue to cost him more. To make him feel he got the worst of it, like he's evil, so the same old habits can continue unchanged. If you can't see it, it isn't happening, right? What's the saying about insanity? Doing the same thing over and over while expecting a different result. How do you give anybody a chance without opening yourself up to trust them?

An empty drink. He takes a spin around the Rendezvous, thinking about the nights he's spent here. *Where to?* The sun is almost down, you can't see the hills or the sea, everything is devoid of color. A few stars peek through the cloud cover.

The engine fires to the end of Route Zero, the conclusion of the path, hence its number. The sign shows an arrow pointing in each direction, one with the word MONTISA, the other says SOUTH OMRIKA. For a moment, he considers Montisa, something pushes him that way. *Sometime soon.* He takes the right, making a run for the warmer border, at least that's how he feels. A bandit with no home. *I told Char south. Let's see what comes up.*

Over the next cycles, things did. After driving halfway through Sanrika, Gnat picked up a job in the Sirra Niva mountains. The lodge needed a server. The tips were good, the crew was way off. The dishwasher snorted powder on his breaks, always dressing as a swashbuckler. His hair was buzzed on top, down back it reached to his waist. He was a nice man, really. His trailer was nearby, he kept to himself. The cook, Peej, was a totally different animal. Fully tweaked-out, he could barely stand still. He was a very aged forty, tall, fat, with dark hair. The first time Gnat met him, he stuck his hand into a pot of boiling water.

"You see that, I can do that because I'm a cook. I wouldn't recommend you try it."

Another time, someone ordered a glass of red wine. As Gnat opened the new bottle, Peej asked him to fill up a paper cup so he could drink on the line. Gnat poured him part of a glass; it's not uncommon in the restaurant business. He took the tray out to serve. By the time he returned, the freshly opened bottle was bone dry. Peej had chugged the whole thing. When Gnat did inventory on the wine later on, more than thirty-five bottles were missing.

The place held some remote charm. Two of the five biggest trees in the world were in his backyard. The other employees were older, it was pretty mellow outside of work. Never that busy, he had time to play guitar and sit alone in the wilderness. On a large boulder, overlooking the valley between ranges, a song came to him, a gift from mother Sirra Niva. No one could hear him, except the birds. Open notes and octaves, at a fast pace.

I wander the path
That you lay
For me to stay.

I swallow the sun
Just for fun
Just for fun.

I lie in the grass.
Let the time pass.
Peace at last.
In the grass.

I fall for you, too
Like the rain
In a monsoon
In a monsoon...

There was some trouble with his truck. Over the last season, he had gone up and down the mountains many times across rough terrain. His brakes were beginning to fail, he could feel it. No time to fix them, or parts. Or tools. On a particular trip down the mountain, he pressed the brake pedal around a turn and it went to the floor. The calipers literally crushed what was left of the rotors, they collapsed. He had no choice but to let the truck glide downhill. If a car had been coming the other way, disaster would have been spelled. They twisted down, Gnat and his truck, like spiders trapped in the vortex of a draining tub. Until the road flattened; he shifted to third, second, first. In a calculated fashion. When he could, he pulled a U-turn and returned. He couldn't go to town, there was no way to stop at the signals.

The postman picked up parts for Gnat's truck on his run. Gnat did the rotors, calipers, pads, and brake lines with nothing but a rock, a bottle jack, and an adjustable wrench. As soon as the truck was functional again, he said farewell.

He headed east, landing in Zeon. A woman had bought a small motel and didn't have a clue how to operate it. So, he told her he'd get it running properly for her. Gnat did what he did best. Fixed things. However, another woman turned up. Sil was South Ehfran, recently divorced. Her ex-husband and his second wife were in a different city, the man had the gall to ask her to be guardian of his newly adopted children from the other partner. Sil had nothing. So, he fronted her a room, and gave her some work around the place to bring the rent down. She didn't show up to help him the entire first cycle because she was high. He got her a paid job in town, through another tenant, but when they wouldn't give her a smoke break on her trial shift, she told them it wasn't going to work out. A man came through town with a car for sale. Gnat called Sil, she came out and made arrangements to make payments with him. A cycle later, she sold it without ever giving the man anything. Then, her friend and his son showed up, along with their dog. Which bit another guest. Gnat told her the dog had to go, that her friend needed to pay rent if he was going to stay. On top of that, she was far behind on hers. He asked her after what he'd done, why she was forcing him to be the bad guy on both sides? The next morning, she was gone. The room which he had painted and carpeted for her was trashed and the business got hit for the cost of repairs. He questioned himself. *Why? Why did you do that for her, when you knew she would hurt you? Everyone is taking whatever they can. Somebody will prove me wrong, won't they?*

He kept moving south within Zeon. From the low elevation on the outskirts of frozen ridge-lines to the plains. He passed through the town of Siin. There was a hunting lodge in the cowboy town. They needed a bartender; Gnat was available. Never in his life had he felt so secluded. Cowboys and Gnat did not mix, they didn't understand each other. He did get along with the general manager, an old guide that drank wine and spoke about politics with him. They had about fifty horses to pack gear in and out for the hunters. Guests that didn't hunt could ride them. Every morning, Gnat went to the horse stables. He waited until one came to give him a greeting, large and white. Sixteen hands, the manager told him. Strong, sure-footed, steady. This was the horse that Gnat rode, no other. It was the horse of the absentee owner in F'lalasip, he never got ridden, he never liked people, excluding Gnat. His name? Traveler.

On a free night, the other employees asked him if he wanted to go to town with them. He agreed. Maybe they'd find some common ground off the ranch. He arrived at the bar, wearing his usual jeans and black t-shirt. When he stepped in, every person was wearing outfits that reminded him of a gay bar in Nan Friko. The men had leather boots and chaps, collared shirts with tassels, bolo ties, wide-brimmed hats, the felt of which was brushed into patterns. The same style hats and boots adorned the women, along with short black dresses. Everyone in their best attire for what big event this night? Line-dancing. Gnat drank in the corner, nobody asked him to dance, of course. *Different strokes*, he giggled.

A coworker, a member of the very close-minded cowgirls approached him. She's studying animal science, always speaking about how much she loves horses with a voice that comes mostly through her nose. It makes her seem arrogant, like she's talking from above you.

"You don't want to dance?" she asked.

"No, I'm fine right here. Not really my thing, you know," Gnat answered.

"What's your problem? You never talk, don't you think we notice you avoiding us?"

"I'm not avoiding you. I'm just consciously not putting energy toward you. Inconsistencies in logic and lifestyle leads to disagreements. I don't want to argue. I'm here to make some cash and move on."

She snapped, "What inconsistencies?"

"You say you love horses. You spend most of your time with them, caring for them."

"Yes, I do," she said.

"Yet you take people on trophy hunts for elk to make your money. What's the difference between a horse and an elk? What percentage of their DNA do they share?"

"I don't know, they are different species. It's negligible really."

Gnat replied, "Well, not really. Just a guess, let's say thirty percent, for the sake of this conversation. Can we agree on that?"

"Okay. Thirty percent."

"So, thirty percent of the whole is a negligible number. I heard you talking about how people don't recognize the plight of the physically disabled at the lodge, the things your brother has to go through, others don't understand."

"How are these connected?"

"In principle, and genetics. What if a single ethnicity in the country makes up thirty percent? Should their voice be heard, or not? Based on your principles, which aren't actually yours, it's no more than what someone told you at university, that group is negligible."

"That's totally different, that doesn't make sense. It's humans versus animals. Of course, human lives matter," she answered.

"Humans *are* animals. It does make sense, you can't have things both ways. It's okay to deflect your own morality on one hand, because you profit from it. Then it's fine for you to stand by that moral again, on the other hand. Not because it indicates anything to you, but because what you think might hurt somebody's feelings. Are the few negligible to the many, or not? Is the elk equal to the horse, or not? Is life valuable as an entity, or as a function of how we decide to define it?"

"As an entity, I think," said the girl.

Gnat sneered, "If life is valuable as an entity, you are living as a hypocrite. A life is, a life. From insect to primate."

"I don't see it that way. A human's life is more valuable than an elk's."

"Why? Because we are conscious of the life we hold? If we are actually aware of how precious life is, why would we ever think the value of deciding which lives continue and which perish is something we could comprehend?" Gnat questioned.

"We try to hold the balance, that's what I'm studying now," she said, less confident than at the start.

"What would it be to every other thing on this planet if humans were to disappear, but an advantage? Balance? Everything was balanced in the beginning. We bicker about skin color and sex, when it has no practical application to anything but individual circumstances and feelings."

"That's not true, it means something to people!"

"Exactly. To people, personally. Not to peers, the country, the government, or Irfa. On our level, or the sea creatures. Seriously, animal science? Environmental science? These are patches, trying to find out how to stretch things so we don't ever have to change the way we consume, systematically. Measuring the levels of toxicity in fish faster doesn't solve anything, except for right now. Soon, all fish will be inedible. Knowing that we can't eat them anymore isn't going to feed anyone. We destroy everything we touch in the natural world. You are studying the death of a planet through globally organized destruction of its beating heart, the lives and resources," Gnat concluded.

"You're so strange. This isn't your place. What made you come out here?"

He raised his glass, and nodded his head slightly, "Waiting for something to prove me wrong, better keep searching."

"I'm going back to dancing."

"You approached me, not the opposite..."

Those were the last words they ever had.

There was another girl from the big city, Cyan. She would listen to him play guitar at night, asking him about his life. This was her first time away from home, he enjoyed her sense of naïve confidence. Once, they stole the company truck and went to see a blues show in town. When he left she gave him a note saying that she hoped when he told his stories in the future, that she meant enough to be included. To Gnat, she is. Always there for a poor soul trying to find his way. She was the redeeming quality of Siin. The thing he always waits for in these places he goes. Not that these qualities make it any more worth it, in the end.

Finally, the location that called his name when he first left Wishintown. Montisa, on the boundary waters with his home country, Omrika. This place has a similar thread to Orrinpic in its eerie silence. The long, vast fields covered in snow, barren season has set in. Fishermen are on the ice, with their flannel shirts and earmuffs. Gnat is their bartender most nights, they treat him splendidly. He's been eating like a king, fresh fish every meal. It's a basic operation, he's the only barman, the owner covers his time off. He doesn't go anywhere, too much snow for him to explore. He's delaying the inevitable here. That's going back to Oia.

Montisa is a relaxing place, however. The songs of loons take you off to dreams, and Gnat surprisingly caught the glimpse of a lynx at dawn one morning. A magnificent creature, as rare as it is mysterious. Not many have seen them in the wild, they hide themselves from others.

An unforeseen person has entered his story line, she is as rare as she is beautiful also. Her name is Hipslyn. She is from Raminia, north of Muusman on the eastern border of Ropa. Carrying herself on a petite frame, she has a somewhat frail quality about her, which makes Gnat feel like he has to protect her from being preyed upon. She has black hair, right past her shoulders, and giant black eyes. These eyes hold the shape of almonds, a clue to the ancestry her people share with Telaysia. They follow you around the room, you know she's watching even if you are facing the opposite direction. Her skin is smooth and pale. Unblemished. Her voice holds your attention, it has passion in it. Hipslyn and Gnat have spent many instances speaking, him behind the bar after she's finished cleaning rooms. He makes her laugh; she scrunches her nose up every time it happens. She makes him think about her, which is where her rarity comes from, among other things. By a lake, they shared a kiss, nothing more. Not that time or any other. It was soft, Hipslyn completely unsure of herself or the situation as he leaned toward her. Right before they touched, she focused on him. Gnat could feel the electricity passing through her lips to his, heart fluttering. They held still, made of stone, then she moved away. She beamed, touched his face with her hand and left. When visiting Gnat in the bar after her next shift, they didn't speak of it. She still comes to see him when he's working. She is with Gnat now, the guests are in their rooms. Hipslyn is drinking her staffie, the free drink staff receive every shift. White wine, always.

"Gnat," she says coyly, "what are you doing tonight?"

"I was going to go to the water, think for a while."

"You are always reflecting in reflections, that's why the workers say you are one of the loons from the lake." She giggles.

"Oh, you're so funny. Hehe. Make fun of the stupid Omrikan boy. I get it," he taunts.

"It's okay, you can't help what you are. I'll let you go and think, I know it's important to you." She rolls the 'r' in important, the same way they do South Omrika. He likes it. Too much, maybe.

"Yeah, I'm off soon. What about you? Let's take the truck to town and get a square meal, none of this pig slop they serve us here."

She bats her eyes, retreating in her shyness, "I'll think about it. If you are nice to me."

His mouth opens, jaw dropped. "I'm not nice to you?"

Both blush in unison. A guide enters the bar, he's from F'lalasip, about fifty. You could say he's a know-it-all, and like so often with this type, it can be deduced after a short while he knows very little. Also, he has been working at this particular place for many spans, believing it wouldn't operate without him. He's a legend in his own mind. The door stays open behind him, the temperature is below freezing.

"You shouldn't be messing around when you are still on the clock, you know. The bar needs to be shut by now," the guide says.

"Oh, I'll finish," says Gnat dryly, "I don't want to be here any later than I have to."

The guide continues, "I'll have to say something to the owner..."

Gnat stops. "I thought you worked outside the lodge, the bar has nothing to do with you."

"Well, I've been here a long time, I like to look after the place when I can," he says.

"Go do that somewhere else. I'm in the middle of a conversation."

"You're going after the knee-high? She's not from this country, does she speak our language? She looks like a raccoon with those big dark eyes on such a tiny body," he bullies.

Hipslyn has hunched to the floor. A literal pout is on her face, she is completely red with embarrassment. The guide, this passing carnivore, is unsure who his competitor is yet.

"Don't you talk to someone you're below like that," Gnat answers.

He stands up taller. "What are you hinting at, below me? This is my country. She can leave if she doesn't like it. I've been here for fifteen spans..."

"Yeah, yeah, you've been here forever. I know. With the same job, never looking outside of it. Am I supposed to be impressed? Impressed that you've never tried to grow? Disgraceful. You're speaking to a young woman that spent her entire life studying our language to come over here for an opportunity. And feast your eyes, she's already on the same level as you. An employee at some no-star lodge in Montisa. So yes, you are below her. She risked everything to be here, left her family and everything she knows. You took the first job you got, and drink in your trailer by yourself. I bet your mom lives close, doesn't she? Ingrate. You're so stupid, you can't so much as comprehend how stupid you are."

"I'm going to get you fired for talking to me like that, you watch. I have seniority here..." he says.

"Seniority over the nine people that work seasonally and would never come back because it sucks that much? Get me fired, it's the only thing you have control over in your life. You should exercise it every once in a while."

Hipslyn let's a laugh out, better than the tears that were welling up in those incredible eyes earlier. That's what Gnat wanted to do, protect this gentle being. The guide is stomping toward the door, spinning to get the final word.

"Pack your bags and say your goodbyes. You'll be leaving to-morrow."

Too simple, Gnat can't let that be the end.

"You know how they say that beauty is in the eye of the be-holder?" Gnat questions the guide.

"Yeah," he answers.

"So is competence."

The man storms out, slamming the door.

"He was letting the cold in for too long, seems like a paradox to me when his head is filled with so much hot air. I had to say something to make him leave," Gnat explains.

"Thank you for this." She reaches out and puts her hand on top of his, which is holding a glass while his right hand is drying it. He stops, she's passing him current again.

"Let me know what time we are leaving for dinner. I want to go with you. I want a cheeseburger, a real Omrikan cheeseburger and fries. Not chips, fries."

"Okay Hipslyn, I'll get you however many you want." Gnat is smitten. Hipslyn drinks the last sip out of her glass. She doesn't just stand up; she is more graceful in her movements. She always seems like she is floating about, her feet slightly above the ground.

"See you tomorrow..."

"Same time?" he questions playfully.

"Yes, you loon. Don't fall in the lake. Goodnight."

He's already bundled up and starts for a spot he frequents with a rotting log next to the water. The Montisan lights are visible, some sort of magnetic anomaly that creates a dancing rainbow in the sky. The tree trunk is a perfect perch to ponder along with the rhythm of this magnetism. As he clambers over the terrain, he thinks of the guide. A man steeped in idiocy. An entire country full of them. No wonder Lellin is now the leader of Omrika. He won the election, believe it or not. *What's the word I used with the guide? Disgraceful.*

Absolutely alone, Gnat could hear the approach of anything by crunches in the snow. He can also see his breath, the raw air in his lungs invigorates him. The Montisan lights are beautiful albeit distracting. Like the entertainment industry of the sky. Blocking what's real from being perceived. The stars, what are they, to humans? The literal translation of everything we are capable of knowing or learning. All that can be discovered is out there, anything that can be known. Whenever a light source is too bright, it dims the stars. It makes it less possible to see these celestial bodies from which every living thing originates. These bright lights block us from truth. What is light, in a figurative sense? Hope. Goodness. Positive emotion. The representation of things we desire as beings. Yet the light blocks us from what's real. What is there for the taking, understanding itself. Like life, an entity. *Distracted by desires, we are. At the cost of knowing what's true, we grasp on to how we feel.* Just as he has this thought, he hears a splash on the lake. In the glaze-eyed daze of meditation, it takes his sight a moment to catch up with his ears. In his stomach, a familiar feeling. The weight forces him to grab his side, a muscle cramp. His eyes strain out over the panorama. It's too dark to see, he can feel something close to him. A pain strikes the middle of his forehead, brain freeze. A word stuck in between his eye sockets, voiceless. *Soon.*

"HOW SOON?!" he screams toward the wilderness. Silence answers him. It has been cycles since this feeling has shown itself. Gnat has been moving constantly, however. Only here with Hipslyn has he started to reflect, to remember how everything seems out of place. He is patient until the pain in his side recedes, then heads in the direction of the lodge.

"How soon?" he repeats to himself, in a whisper. He notices the guide's trailer light. There he goes, a twelve pack to consume. Gnat isn't judging, he's done it before. He wanted to make him feel insecure, since that was his intention with Hipslyn. In his room, he rubs his hands over his face. The taste of metal consumes his mouth, it won't go away after brushing twice. Maybe from the robotic movements of his life lately. Wake up, work, go to room, sleep. Or maybe it's from the cybernetic hard-lined message he received by the shore. There's a smell, tinged plastic and metal, if a circuit overheats. Something similar is drowning his tongue. An uneasy twilight, not an unusual occurrence.

After sunrise, Gnat heads to the kitchen for something to nibble on. The moment he enters the door passing the office, the owner says his name.

"Gnat, I need a word with you."

He stops in the hall and leans in reverse, so his head is in the doorway.

"Yes?"

"Woggin came in here upset. Seems you were pretty rude to him," says the owner, a man in his mid-thirties. He has a very calm demeanor.

Gnat replies, "Woggin?"

"The guide, he came into the bar last night when you were closing?"

"Oh, that's his name. Yeah, he came in and tried to belittle Hipslyn, I wasn't going to let him do that. Especially in the bar, which was closed, and he has nothing to do with," he says coolly.

The owner leans back in his office chair, crossing his arms above his stomach, fingers interlocking. The same way you see in a movie.

"Woggin says either you go or him. You are great behind the bar, but he's been with me for spans. There are only a few cycles left in the season, and I'm sure you aren't going to return. He will. I hate to say it, but I've got to ask you to go. I'll say you resigned if you want to use me as a reference, this is the best option and the way it's got to be. I'm sorry. He's a bit thin sometimes, I know. He's part of the business, the regulars expect him."

"No reason to explain, no hard feelings. I'll be going to see family sooner than expected, I'll go now." Gnat answers.

"That quick? I could give you the rest of the cycle, it's not a big deal," the owner says, surprised.

Gnat continues on, waving his hand "No, no. Better to just cut ties than linger." He winks. "Can I trust you to pay what you owe me?"

The owner chuckles, "I'll pay you right now."

He gives the bills to Gnat from his wallet. Gnat wishes him a good season. The owner turns to his desk as he exits. Gnat knows, he's an item off the owner's checklist. Onto the next, he's already forgotten about me. He only has to throw his bag in the truck, and roll on. *Done.*

Storing the last of his things, he sees Hipslyn.

"What is this?" she asks.

"They *did* let me go."

She gasps, "Because you stood up for me? Oh, Gnat, I'm so sorry. Let me go and talk to them, maybe you can stay..."

"No need to say anything. Finish your contract and save your checks. I'll go see my family in Oia. It's been a while. They'll be glad I'm home for the Start of Span, for a change."

Her shoulders sag, "What about my Omrikan cheeseburger?"

"It's not in the cards, sweetheart. I'm sorry. I wanted to spend time with you outside of this place. I really did. Here, let me see your phone."

She hands it to him, and he saves his current number, and email.

"This is my number. I don't know how long I'll keep it. My email, on the other hand, is the only thing that doesn't change. It's been mine forever. Send me your information, I'll buy you that dinner. That's a promise."

She slants up with puppy dog eyes. "You promise me?"

"Hipslyn, I promise. If you want me to, I will."

"Raminians don't take promises lightly, I'm warning you..."

"I don't take beautiful women wanting my time lightly, either," he says. "Now give me a hug. Don't say goodbye. It's until next time."

She squeezes him, a touch harder right before letting go.

"Until next time, Gnat."

With amorousness surrounding her, she glides away. He is poised, already yearning. His hands are in his pockets, frozen breaths escape unconcealed to the atmosphere.

"I *will* see you again, Hipslyn," he says, assuring himself and the universe.

***

Montisa, check. He's always enjoyed long treks by himself. Music on, in his head. Most of the highways crossing the country are barren except for a few trucks carrying cargo and other drifters like him. Rubber tramper, vagabond by tire. Leather tramper, on foot. An easy drive, through flat places where the majority of food for the world is grown. No mountains, no ocean, yet there's a certain beauty in what is called the heart of Omrika. Long rolling grasslands, the deciduous forests changing color throughout the span. The powerful curving rivers, dirtied by humans over time. Still, the steamboats cruise at a leisurely pace, which describes the people and the way they think almost to the letter. A place where tradition carries more weight than anything else when deciding how to live. If you were to ask someone here why something happened, the most common response would resemble *that's just the way it is, honey.* Simple minds in complex times.

Gnat's lost in the flow of clouds, when the beast shuts off full stop, no warning signs. He slams on the brakes and skids to a halt, not gracefully but tactfully. He parks and turns the key off. Then he tries to turn it on, nothing, not a click. *What's wrong, truck?* Dropping underneath, nothing's noticeably out of place. Axles, driveshaft, transmission. Maybe something to do with his brake job on the mountain? Nope. He then pops the hood, and opens the fuse box. Relays? *Fine.* Fuses? *All good.* Radiator? *Full.* It went into park, so can't be the transmission. And it rolled afterward. The engine stopped. *There's only one thing it could be.* He takes a deep breath, opens the oil cover pulling out the dipstick. It resembles a silver mine in the sunlight. It's completely saturated with metal shavings. The worst possible outcome for any vehicle. Like cholesterol in an animal's aorta, the truck's heart is dead. For some reason, he checks the battery voltage. *Normal.* The oil level is in order as well.

He could get it towed. Get the engine rebuilt. For what? Little things have been going wrong, hints that it is beyond its prime. It has lived a hard life with Gnat, these past few spans. *A sign of the end of an age.* He grabs his bag, he has some light left. He pats the truck on the hood, leaving his hand on it.

"Sorry it has to be this way. It's time for us to part. I'll never forget the trails we laid together, the amazing places we've been. You gave me the ability to create those memories, truck."

He goes to the driver side, pulls the registration papers out, signs them, and writes a note:

This truck doesn't deserve to fade away yet, but I'm not the man to put the work in. If you want to take the burden and reap the reward, it's yours. Gnat.

He places the papers under the key on the seat, and shuts the door. Taking a last snapshot of his stealth camper, he starts down the road. A man, a bag, a guitar.

The wind is starting to work its way through his clothes, which is telling. He's going to get cold. Actually, frozen to the bone. *You'd better get moving. The sun is going to bed.* After another jolt of air, he calls it. There's a grove of trees off the highway on someone's land. The trees have no leaves, but they'll break up the gusts moving across the open prairie better than nothing. He drops down off the embankment, finds a hole in the center, they are oaks. His small gas stove is used to heat up a can of beans. A cowboy fire burns. Gnat placed some stones on top to let the embers heat them. They will be buried in the dirt beneath his tent to keep him warm through-out the night. Thoughts of Addie cross his mind, he wonders what word she uses to describe him. Hate? Betrayal? Maybe she doesn't think of him at all. Then, the thought of Hipslyn. What is she doing? Drinking a glass of white wine, talking to whoever is behind the bar instead of him? He can only tell himself no, she isn't. It isn't that empty. It represented something. Things can mean something, can't they? A feeling of apprehension attaches itself to this thought as the trio of them drift off to a frozen slumber in his imaginings.

Gnat, rustling, can still feel some warmth coming from the ground beneath the tent. The very first light creeps over the horizon. *Rise with the sun.* A natural alarm clock, any person who has spent time in the wilderness knows this. He can see no smoke rising from a building on the horizon. Not a good sign, life not within sight. *Keep moving, something will come up.* After a hot meal again, warmth penetrates through his body bringing a spell of mild comfort. An old farm truck cruises up, slowing. A woman with more than a few teeth missing rolls the window down. If gray hair and wrinkles reveal wisdom, this woman may be the wisest being on Irfa.

"You walkin' by design?" she asks, checking him over thoroughly. She's determining if there's any trustworthiness in him.

"No, my truck broke down last night. Slept in the trees. Trying to get to a town. Really, a bus stop."

"That black truck a while back?"

"Yes," he answers, "Not worth fixing it, to me anyway. Just trying to get home to family. I thought the sign said not far to town? I haven't seen anything."

"Oh my, that sign is wrong, it hasn't been redone in spans. You got a gun?"

He grins, "No ma'am, no gun."

"I do, don't fool with me. I'm headed to town. You can come along. Throw your stuff in, let's go," she says inside the window, rolling it up.

"Much appreciated miss, that's a long way to go in the cold. Can't say I had enough food to make it."

"You an Oia boy? You sound it." She pats him on the leg. "Let's get you to your kin."

"Sounds good."

They don't talk much. Her name is Mig. She tells him about her family farm, which once was profitable. Now, they work the entire span just to break even. Can't get out of it either, not enough land to be attractive to the farming conglomerates taking over agriculture. You have to sell as a group, and neighboring families won't. Too much pride out in the country, he knows, it's where he came from. Mig pulls into a gas station, and tells him he can buy a ticket at the counter. He gets out some money to give her for gas, she squints her eyes.

"I don't want that, boy. Spend it on your girlfriend. You'll pass it on when you can, won't you?"

"Of course I will, I always do."

"Go on. I've got some people to meet uptown. Get home."

"Thank you for this. I couldn't have gotten here without you."

She smiles, her wrinkles get wrinkles. She accelerates, not hurriedly, but with purpose. Gnat asks the clerk for a ticket to Nata. Some luck, there's a bus coming soon. He pays for the pass to return to his least favorite destination. *Should be free, if you have to go but don't want to.* Outside, his mind is a brick wall. He doesn't want to think about going home. He stares across the road at the water vapor floating upward, coming off the snow being melted by the sun. The trees form a barren wasteland against the skyline. A mass of screaming creatures, begging for the warmth and nutrients of the rainy season. They will survive, no matter how far the cold pushes them. There is a return to glory in the cycle of seasons. The ebb and flow. The balance. *Is there one in my life, as well? Is that what being joyous amounts to? Knowing the most devoid, low existence and not being in it at the present time?* The pain of thought drills to the center of his skull, it has come again. His left hand becomes a fist, and is tapping a spot on his forehead. The voiceless words are trapped in his vision, although his eyes are crushed shut in agony. *Soon. Closer now. You will see...*

It's gone. Gently, eyes remain closed. *What is this madness?* He leans his head against the wall of the station.

The sudden hiss of the buses air brakes scare him and he jumps. The hinged door opens, the driver yells out, "Waiting on me?"

"Yes, I am," Gnat answers.

"Final destination?"

"Nata."

"Let's go, put your stuff in the first bin."

The door pops open and Gnat lifts it up, tossing his things inside. Not too many people. To be expected this time of span, nobody moves in the frigid weather unless there's no possibility of *anything* better.

"We're behind schedule already, let's get a move on young man," the driver says. There's an old man in the seat across the aisle from him. A few rows ahead, a group of boys around his age. A man in the rear seat is asleep, minding his own business. A girl in her twenties, by Gnat's guess, recently out of prison.

"Where you coming from, where you headed?" the old man near him asks.

"Left Siin, going to family in Nata. Truck died on me, still have places to be, however. You know how it goes."

"Yep, I've been on the move most of my life. Cars, trains, motor-cycles, planes, boats. Somehow the bus is... simpler," he says. "I'm headed to Nuwal, I've got part of the ride with you before I transfer. Upstate, not the city. Completely different worlds. Oh, you've been to both. Oh, I see. I've got a new venture now, as a rancher. No, not cattle or pigs. Rabbits. Yes, rabbits. To sell for their furs, for meat, and as pets, if someone wants..."

So it begins. The man tells Gnat the particulars of the rabbit ranching business. The breeds, how long they take to raise, what to feed them, how to shade them from the sun, how to keep sheltered from inclement weather. What age to kill them for meat, what age to kill them for grade-A fur. Gnat listens intently, this man has a soothing voice. His skin is leathery, like the furs he tans. He's worked hard, you can see it on his knuckles and in the corners of his eyes. His hair is long, salt and pepper, still thick. The old man never lost his hairline. Bushy eyebrows, a long beard. If Gnat had to bet, it's been spans since he's cut it. His age is hard to guess, because he seems so young and vibrant while speaking. Rabbits truly are his current passion. You can tell. After the sun's moved to an undisrupted position above the tree line, there isn't anything else to say. Gnat did enjoy this, not just to pass the time. If he wanted to start a rabbit ranch right now, he probably could. The silence at the end of a conversation rests between them.

"What's your name, sir?" Gnat asks.

"Don't call me sir, my father was sir. Call me Wudy. That's been my nickname so long I don't remember my full name. Ha!" He laughs once, and rests his hands on his belly.

The bus has stopped a few times, the girl just out of the clink has latched on to a boy. She has his cellular, and he already promised to buy her a meal at the next stop. *There are so many levels of fox and hen in this existence.* Gnat, the owl, is watching from afar, studying the tactics of this predator. He has a feeling that her and Tia would get by fine in the wild west of Omrika's past. A middle-aged couple has joined the passengers, sitting in front of Wudy. They are talking politics. Gnat is listening somewhat, from afar. It sounds like they get their information from the television.

"So, what's your plan, young man? You need work?" Wudy asks.

"Eh, I don't think so. I'm going to relax and catch up with my family. I haven't been the best son or brother, only been home a few cycles against spans."

"There's a place at the ranch in Nuwal, if you want. I can always use a dependable person. I've got a place for you to stay, an extra room in the barn, too."

Gnat considers the offer. "You know what, that might just be a good idea. I could do upstate Nuwal. I'll give you my contact information."

As Gnat writes, the woman from the couple in front of Wudy faces him.

"You're from Nuwal? Is your family safe? Did you hear about the school shooting? What a tragedy."

"Nah, I've been on my own for a long time. No family to speak of..." Wudy says.

"They want to arm the teachers now. They say the kid listened to metal music and wore black clothes," the woman explains.

Her partner chimes in, "Yeah, I wouldn't want my kid to be around somebody troubled like that. They should arm the teachers, it's only sensible..."

Gnat joins, "So what happens when a teacher kills a student, and they need a scapegoat so they say the child is innocent, the teacher has mental issues?"

"Typically, there's always a reason things like this happen. If the educators are trained and informed, I think it could work out," the man says.

"So, teachers are police now too?" Wudy asks.

"Not police, protectors," answers the woman. "They already are protectors. It's taking it to another level. We need these disasters to stop happening."

Gnat snorts. "We are going to fight fire with fire? That's so cliché. The only thing that happens when you do that is everyone gets burnt."

Wudy adds, "Yes, sir, seen it myself many times."

Gnat nods his way. "How about we fight fire with water?"

The woman pipes up, "What do you mean?"

"I mean the inescapable liquidity of logic," he continues. "The reason our children are going to schools and shooting each other is because that's what we show them."

"No, it is not!" the woman protests sternly.

"Yes, it is. Every problem with the environment, war, and trade can be traced to Omrika. We are the most ignorant, consuming mass of people on the planet. Our government has a force of assassins that protect and guide the flow of the natural resources. Anyone who disagrees with us, we kill. Anybody who thinks differently than us, we kill. Any country that opposes us, we destroy. We glorify the men who do this as heroes, we say it's for the cause. Furthering freedom..."

"How does this create school shootings?" the man wonders blankly.

"That's what we teach. If someone is different than you, fear them. Isolate them. Demonize them, and in the end, kill them. You kill me, what does that do? It doesn't solve your ignorance; it only removes my opposition and allows you to keep living in disillusion. Buying your fast food, feeling informed by the biased media, consuming endlessly."

"The fight for freedom doesn't create violence in schools," the woman says, "and it isn't right that you talk badly about our soldiers."

"That's the whole point, there is no fight for freedom. This is the lie you've been convinced of, to feel content living the way you do. It's the lie those boys buy when they join up. It's a noble idea, a sacrifice they're willing to make. And, they are brave. It's still living a lie. It isn't their fault they didn't see it beforehand, they're only trusting the hand that feeds them. The only fight is for control of the planet. What you can't change, what you can't control, you destroy," says Wudy.

"Yeah, and it's acceptable for kids to watch the news and see people die overseas, play games full of gore, and binge on shows where people get blown up by the busload, but it's abominable for them to see a naked body..." Gnat replies, and Wudy starts to laugh.

"What are we, animals?" Wudy bellows. Gnat gasps, and covers his mouth with an open hand. The couple recoil disgusted. People don't like when their beliefs are questioned. Too bad their beliefs were given to them, not earned through experience.

"It's people like you that, that perpetuate..." the man starts.

"Common sense?" Gnat finishes the sentence flatly, "In all seriousness, every man is a murderer, it is just a matter of what drives him to it. It's our essence, as Wudy said. We are animals, nothing more. Violence and greed are synonyms for survival instinct. The circumstances of survival only matter to society, not reality."

"Society is what defines reality," the woman retorts. "You can't escape reality, or society. They are one in the same."

"Yes, if you never question anything, that's true. If you accept what you see and hear on the news, which is controlled by the same people waging war, it's simple black and white. Right or wrong. Good versus evil. You're still ignoring the truth to be comfortable. Justify. Deflect. Smile. Die. The modern Omrikan way. What are the things we spend the most money on? Weapons and cosmetics. Annihilate the stranger, look good doing it," he answers.

"I'm finished talking about this," the woman says.

"Yes, me too," says the man.

"I'm sure you are," says Gnat.

The couple retreat, murmuring to themselves. Wudy gives Gnat a shining grin.

"You sure you don't want to come up to Nuwal now? We'd have a mighty fine time talking. Especially when we drive to the center of the craziness, the big city."

"It's tempting, I have people to see first. You've got the out, you transfer. I'm stuck with the progressives on my own, probably to Nata with my luck."

The woman scolds him, "We're going to Nuwal city, leaving this line soon."

"I could have guessed," says Wudy. They both chuckle again.

Everyone keeps to themselves for the next interval. Gnat is peering out the window, trying to focus on objects as they speed past. A light post, a farm animal, a mailbox, a tractor. Before he knows it, the bus starts to slow, and the driver announces the switch is coming. Wudy touches his shoulder, "I've got your information. I'll call you when the season picks up."

Gnat shakes his hand, "You do that. Be good until then. Don't have all the fun without me."

Wudy allows the couple to exit in front of him, no hard feelings. On his side, at least. The ex-con is getting off with the boy. *Don't do it.* He will figure it out on his own. Or, he won't. Into the slaughterhouse, glad as can be. Gnat thinks of a cartoon from his childhood, with a walrus inviting the oyster babies to a party. They are eaten alive while clinging to the promise of something nice. *Maybe most people never figure it out, or they do, only a smidgen too late.*

He wonders who else will come along during the ride. Gnat does enjoy the bus, always has. So many characters in the world, all subjected to a bus ride at some point. You are only on the bus if there's a reason, never by choice. A broken-down truck, a missed flight, leaving your life in an instant because you can't take it any longer. The first step to change your footing is jumping onto an overnight bus to anywhere.

This group of people bonded in nothing but disunity and indecision are moving down the freeway. It remains silent, Gnat relishes in it. He's deciding what his path will be. No promise of a job, no transportation, no prospects. *That's untrue, I could be a rabbit rancher's apprentice.* He smiles to himself. A pleasing thought. Like most things, it will never happen. There's a sound behind Gnat. The sleeping man now grunts, and proceeds into the tiny restroom in the rear. This man is middle-aged and dressed like a biker. Long hair, beard cut into an anchor shape, at minimum three earrings on each side. He wears jeans and boots, similar to Gnat except his footwear is black leather and comes to a point at the toe. He wears a black vest and jacket, also leather to match. Tied to the jacket's collar on each side hang halves of a coyote's jawbone. Gnat is simply watching the world, until he hears the voice.

"Hey partner, where you headed?" the fashion biker says.

Gnat, casually, "Nata. Yourself?"

"Oh, I'm going to F'lalasip, to stay with my brother and find work. I'll be going through Nata with you, though. Come talk, there's a ways to go. Might as well have some company."

Gnat stands up. "Alright. Whether I'm good company or not is another question." He moves to the seat across from the biker. "I'm really digging those jawbones on the jacket."

The man straightens. "Like those? Killed the scoundrel myself. He was menacing, kept on killing my chickens. Those birds are family. Jix Spire is my name, pleased to meet you."

"Gnat, my name is Gnat Dagger."

"Say, hold on, let me find something. Saving it for a special occasion..." Jix continues. "Here, fancy to split it on a bus ride with a new friend?" He holds a fifth of liquor, made in F'lalasip, the best in the country.

Gnat takes a deep breath, chuckling once while exhaling. "Like you said, it's a long ride…"

Jix nods his head. "That's my boy."

They speak of Oia and F'lalasip, of which there are many similarities. Jix asks what genre of music Gnat likes. He says many, though his favorite is metal.

Gnat describes Dil Curl, a man who started a band named *Irfa*. He doesn't have more respect for any musician he's ever heard. The music is instrumental, beyond that it is an exploration of melody in its slowest, heaviest state. This band is exploring sound on its most basic level, vibration. Intonation. Many of his thoughts came out of meditating while listening to Irfa for cycles on end. The things he writes couldn't have possibly happened without the alternate senses of life their music give him within the crevices of his mind. Dreaming while awake, in control of your subconscious, he tells Jix.

Jix replies, "Sounds like something on a deeper level than listening."

"It is," Gnat answers, "Genius unappreciated."

They continue to chat and smoke cigarettes during breaks. Gnat is on the way to Oia, and two-thirds through the bottle shared with Jix. Smoking is the furthest worry from him. Eventually, both men fade off. The freeway continues to roll on, unseen by these drunken drifters. Until the light creeps up again, and the bus driver comes on the speaker.

"Okay, passengers, we are coming into Nata shortly. If this is your stop, please remember to get your things. Check under and above the seats. If you are continuing on, we will stay in Nata for a short break and then head to Mim, F'lalasip. Thanks for your attention and traveling with us."

"I'm still drunk, Gnat. Always remember to answer with 'might as well.' Back to sleep for me." Jix rolls over and covers himself with the jacket. *Farewell, traveler.*

He can see the skyline which he doesn't adore getting close. His stomach gurgles. Maybe from the booze. Maybe from the anxiety of being in this place. He closes his eyes until the bus idles, the brakes hiss again. The bus has stopped. In Oia. In Nata. He grabs his gear, trudging into the terminal. Sullenly out the main entrance, he finds a cab.

"Fennytun, if you please." He gives the driver a more specific place.

Up the hill and away from the river, past government housing, the rust-stained buildings built over dishearteningly unmaintained pavement. The driver stops at the address, Gnat thanks him as he pays. Here it is, his family home.

V

The structure was built before his grandfather first drew breath, a time when craftsmanship still garnered admiration. When people did things by hand and stood by their work. This dwelling has endured many storms and heatwaves, unshakably protecting different occupants along the way. His parents purchased it when Gnat held five spans in his grasp. They moved in on the span's first cycle, symbolic in some way, of course. It has a basement, the sign of quality in this part of the country. A place to hide from tornadoes. Plaster over brick, with two stories above the cellar and hardwood floors of pine. The planks are not equal width or evenly sanded down, but laid out as they grew, gnarled and inexact. Beauty comes out of imperfection, his mother says. The driveway wraps around the rear leading toward garage bays. A shed his father built stands solitary at the boundary line with the neighbor, white plastic star affront. His mother and father have spent a few dozen spans of their lives wearying over the details of this property. The grass shows the neurotic attention given to it, cut in three directions like the inside of a sports stadium. An Omrikan flag as old as the house hangs in front of the door. Gnat recalls when he helped center it as a child. He was only off by the width of a finger against the entire entryway.

"Good eye," his father told him.

He knocks in an offbeat pattern. Shortly after, footsteps within. They aren't expecting their son, not in the slightest. It's his father, Ju, gaping at Gnat, not knowing if he's still dreaming.

"Gnat?" he says, coming to his senses. "Son! What are you doing home? Come on, come in, say hi to your mother. I didn't hear your truck, is it on the street?"

"Long story, Dad. I'll tell you everything, don't worry. I caught a bus here."

"Oh, alright, I'm sure it's wild, whatever it is. You are mine, you know. Su! Su... oh wait, she's not here. I got excited and forgot. Put your bags down," Ju says. They absorb each other for an instant in reverence.

Ju stands slightly shorter than Gnat, carrying a lot more strength in his stockiness. Gnat's face is almost the same as his dad's, like Ju's is similar to *his* dad's. Once they compared pictures of the three generations at the same age. You couldn't tell which was which, except for the style of paper the photos were printed on. The amount of respect Gnat has for his father is almost inexplicable. He knows that if he could be a third of the man his father is, things might turn out. Ju has lived his life thoroughly, completely, for his wife and children. Gnat didn't know until he got older, but his family was part of the lower-middle class. The reason he never noticed is he never wanted for anything.

Growing up, Gnat would show his father something in passing, a new gadget or toy. His dad would nod. At the next special occasion, birth date, or if he had a little to spare after paying bills, Ju would get the item for Gnat or his sister Ima. Gnat played every sport possible. His dad not only came to games, but coached the teams. This wasn't the easiest for him either. For most of the span, he left and returned home in the dark. His job was in a factory with no windows. The floor, walls, and ceiling were made of concrete. The only peace Ju found was to sneak away to the dock door, catching a glimpse of the world racing so quickly around him. He never clocked out for breaks; he wouldn't call in sick. He had paid vacation every span. Ju would take the check, and still work to get the extra pay. On the twentieth anniversary of their marriage, Su told him she didn't want a gift. She simply wanted him to take his vacation and spend the time with her. He did. After Gnat and Ima were grown, he was able to retire from his job. He does landscaping for the local school district now, in the sun and wind. He sports a uniform tan.

Ju didn't have the most nurturing adolescence. If he had the opportunities most people do, he could have been anything he wanted. A caring, kind, intuitive man. He can read the intentions of others with only a glance, and is never wrong. Gnat has never seen Ju misjudge another person. In essence, he's an artist. He brings beauty to the world with everything he does, because he executes things with honesty and passion. Like the grass, he not only cuts his lawn, but his elderly neighbors' lawns on both sides of him. Not for money, he'd never take it. Just to bring joy to their lives. To let them know that someone cares, to make the street a touch more tranquil for those who live on it or quietly pass by.

When Gnat was growing up, Ju worked every moment he could to take care of his family and responsibilities, yet somehow found a way to stay present in his children's lives. By the time he left work during the school span, Gnat and Ima had already been through the rigmarole of practices and homework. They'd eaten and were in bed. Ju would come to each of their rooms, separately, for a short time. He would talk with them, imparting lessons for life and asking what they believed in. Ju would kiss them and tell them to sleep well. Then he would go downstairs and pack lunches, something he did until Gnat graduated at eighteen. The same thing every time, Gnat liked roast beef on white. Ima liked turkey and cheese with mayonnaise. He made Su's lunch also. She's a teacher. Each in a brown paper bag. At school, Gnat would grab the sack from his backpack and head to the cafeteria. There it would be, a cartoon drawn on the bag, portraying some part of the things they had talked about the night before.

It wasn't until spans later Gnat realized the significance of this ritual. Ju had drawn the cartoon, knowing Gnat would think of him in that moment. The same way he was thinking about Gnat, in that concrete box so far away. Irony and pride colliding, knowing he was trapped there for Gnat. For Ima. For Su. He was doing his duty as a father and husband.

Yes, a third. Gnat can truthfully say Ju is the best man he's come across, anywhere. Not out of genetic obligation, like the gimmicky coffee mugs. Ju holds a spot in the temple of Gnat's mind that is unattainable by any other.

"Turn on the TV, when's the last time you watched something?" Ju asks Gnat, who is lounging on the couch. Boots off, wearing them inside is a violation.

"Oh, snippets when I'm in town or sitting at the bar, I'm not big on it anyway, you know that."

"Yeah, you want a drink?"

Gnat folds his hands on top of his head. "You have alcohol in this house?"

"No, no. A pop or juice or something." Ju shakes his head. "You know your mother doesn't allow that."

"Ah, I know, I only drink water outside of booze."

"Yeah, you should only drink water," Ju replies, going into the kitchen. "I'll get you some."

"Thanks, Dad," He somehow feels transported back to preschool age. He hears the sound of tires squealing over the blacktop.

"Su's here. She's going to cry, make sure you hug her," Ju says from the kitchen.

"Come on now, I know this!" Gnat exclaims, closing the recliner. "I can be a son when I need to."

"You always are, you can't turn it off. Show her."

The garage door burrs open, you can feel it through the walls. He moves into the kitchen with his father. Her footsteps boom up each step. Again, you can feel the vibrations of her feet diffusing body weight through the floor. *Everything is connected here. Maybe on every level.*

A clenched hand lightly touches her collarbone. Her purse hangs from the fulcrum that is an elbow. She reaches the top of the stairs and finds Gnat's eyes straight away. Without hesitation, she inadvertently drops the bag on the ground, hugging him tightly. She does start to cry, not quickly, deep sobs coming out of her core.

"You're home," she says, her hand cradles the side of his face. "I've missed you. You seem so confident, not like when you left. How long are you staying?"

He considers his words carefully. "No plans as of yet," he adds coyly. "If you want me to get a motel, I will. Don't let me burden your life."

She wipes her eyes. "I miss talking to you. Don't be silly. Your room is the same as it's always been. You'll stay with us. You're skinny, you need to eat. What do you want?"

"Whatever dad wants."

Ju interjects, "No, no, you pick."

Gnat sees Su in the corner of his eye and hides his grin. "I did. I pick whatever you want."

"Just tell us! You know your dad can't make a decision." Su rolls her eyes, "How about chili? You can't get our chili anywhere else, have you thought about it?"

"I have. Dad, chili?" questions Gnat.

"If that's what you want," Ju answers. "I'd rather have something else."

"Alright, so pick! I told you to in the first place."

"Chili is fine," he says.

Su sounds exasperated. "It never ends. I've been trying to get him to say what he wants since I met him. He can't do it."

Gnat puts his hands in his pockets. "Things never change, do they? Come on, let's get in the car. Here's something different, I'm buying."

Ju brightens up. "Oh, in that case, we're getting steak."

Su ends the debate. "Get in the car, your son wants chili. Be glad you get to see him."

"Right." Ju opens the door.

Su pats Gnat on the shoulder. "I am glad you are here, bug. My Gnat, buzzing around. It's okay to buzz home now and again. You always remember your mother, don't you?"

"Yes, of course," Gnat says.

Su holds herself with a certain sense of dignity which brings no question or strife from those around her, publicly or privately. She has a thin build and isn't too lanky, or the opposite. Everything about her sort of... fits. She has red hair, once bright and explosive in its tint, now faded to more of a pale orange mixed with blonde. She has a few grays coming through, somehow it only makes her more beautiful. Her skin is pale, holding many freckles. Almost as if it is possessive of them. *Beauty comes out of imperfection.* A simper creeps up on Gnat's face.

His parents are complete opposites, he doesn't know how they ever made it this far. Su spends freely, lives in the moment, and cannot be swayed from her path regardless of what you throw at her. Another person's malice, greed, or pure lack of intelligence will not affect her. You can't bring her down.

Ju is frugal, a hoarder on some level, and let's everyone's feelings or opinions create self-doubt on a crippling scale. On the other hand, both grew up in Nata. Both were poor. Both were in the right place at the right time, making choices within chances to get what they wanted. Outside the differences in personalities and personal proclivities, they both wanted children and wanted to grow old with somebody.

The gestation period of a human woman is forty cycles. Gnat was born a span into their relationship, thirty-two cycles after being married.

Traffic is non-existent in this region of the country when compared to a place like Nuwal City in the east, or Nan Friko out west. The chili parlor is cozy, dark, and warm. The smell of cinnamon and chocolate waft through the old ventilation ducts. They occupy a booth. The cheap vinyl of the seats is ripped and cracked then repaired with duct tape. Which is ripped, cracked, and repaired again. The plastic cups aren't dirty or clear. They have been run through the heat of a dishwasher too many times, the molecules have been altered, giving the containers a foggy appearance.

Gnat orders a favorite, which he *has* thought about many times on a bleak night in the mountains. Su and Ju get hot dogs on a bun with chili. They are, in a word, magnificent.

The parlor isn't crowded, the service station is an island in the center of the room creating an atmosphere of discretion. Perfect for a small restaurant. On the way here they got the casual conversations sorted. Now is the time for serious things. A silence sits on the table top, more in anticipation than tension. They aren't uncomfortable with each other; his parents want him to settle nearby and live a simple life. Neither parent quite understands his lifestyle, which is normal, no individual in his circle does. The fact that they are related doesn't give their opinions on the subject more weight, however.

His mother clears her throat and tries to sound interested. "So, how was it out in Wishintown this past season? What's there that you can't get here?"

"Mom, you don't need to be condescending. It is the same country, that's about it. Out west, in the mountains, life is different. The flow, the landscape, everything. It suits me better than Oia, it's too close-minded in this city."

She sounds hurt. "This is home, Gnat."

"No, you are my family, this is where I was born. I never felt at home in this place, only like an outsider. I never thought anyone was hearing what I was saying as a child. Now I know they just weren't comprehending, because they accept what they are told by the church or their parents and never question anything. You marry the first girl you sleep with. You work the first job you get until you retire. You buy a house, and never leave it. Pay it off, have kids. There's food on the table. Why would you want anything else? It isn't me. You know this. I found the place I want to be; I wish you could be there. It's not about leaving you, it's about being me."

"People know, they comprehend you. Don't think you are the only one that understands some things aren't completely right." Ju says.

"Dad, which is worse, if you actually can't understand, or if you do understand and ignore it? Don't be a politician, reading the cue card. Every human is only doing things that are fed to them as trendy or socially acceptable. Can't dress yourself? Pay us, we'll send you fashions that are with the times! Oh, you want to be a chef but don't want to put any effort into learning the art? Pay us! We'll put the meals in separate bags and you can heat them up on your own and post it online! *Your* opinion that *we* gave to you matters! No thought needed? How easy!"

Ju glances around to see if anyone else has noticed. "Stop, Gnat. You are being crazy. Just calm down. Here comes our stuff."

The waitress puts the first plate in front of Gnat. The server is a girl he has known since he could speak. She started this job when she was sixteen, her first one. She fails to recognize him.

Su continues, "When you are past this lifestyle, you can move back with us and finish your degree. After having these experiences, you'll know what you want to do."

"I do know what I want to do, it's this. See as many places as I possibly can, the work in between is a means to an end for travel. I find no joy in working. That doesn't imply I don't try my best or take pride in the task, but it doesn't give me purpose. Finding the things I don't want is the goal. Completely immersing myself in discomfort, testing myself. I haven't started on the world. That's next. I've just been moving around Omrika and Montisa so far..."

"Eat your food. You have plenty of time to think about that decision," Su says, subconsciously swatting the idea of him doing this away with her hand as she speaks. "Spend time with us, we are getting older, you know. There's a lot of family you need to see."

"I'm going to see you two and Ima. Outside of that, it doesn't matter to me. They just sweep anything outside of sports games and restaurants under a rug like it doesn't exist. It's exactly what I said..."

Su interrupts him, "Let's not talk about this now." Her face is neutral; he gets his resting expression from her.

"Just eat. We'll get Ice-cream before we go home." Ju raises his chin to Gnat, the sign to let things be.

Gnat sighs, submitting. "I sure have missed this chili. It was the first thing I wanted to eat when I got to your place..."

"Your place, too," his mother says, before taking another bite.

They ask questions about what he's doing, in a robotic way, out of obligation. It isn't something his mother processes, she only wants him home. When it comes to his stories of the world, she is tone deaf. This is the most important lesson he's learned from his family, from the people in this part of the world. They are masters in avoiding anomalies. It doesn't matter how much fact, scientific proof, or pure logic you set before these individuals. Through personal beliefs founded in nothing except empty conversation, they are able to normalize and justify anything into something that fits their life as needed. To make sense of anything, according to the predetermined notions handed to them. Or worse, as his father had brought up, they see that they are too weak to break out of the mold and force themselves to settle after realizing getting what they want is difficult. Someone else may get upset by choices made, and *that* price is too high. Complete acceptance by your family and peers is what's comfortable. In this place, the only merit to consider is ease.

Coming home, feeling less than because I make my own choices, through my own morals that I've earned. Why do I subject myself to this place? Something will come from it. Something will come...

As he pays, his schoolmate asks him straight to his face how everything was. He's beginning to think she knows who he is. This job has taught her how to fake everything like a professional. Which she is, with spans of experience selling kindness for tips.

He smirks, "That's the second time I've been asked that question tonight. Let's not go too far. I'm an Oia boy, I can say great. It was great, it always is and always will be."

"I think you're right." She tries to hand him the change from the register.

"Keep it, enjoy the night after you leave."

"Oh, thank you," she says.

"See you around," Gnat returns, cordially.

"Hopefully. Be good until then." She leaves to seat another party. *She knows me.*

At the table, Gnat confesses. "My salary isn't great, the bank is broken after that. I'll get something without dairy, it's on Dad."

Su is waiting for him to get out of the booth and nudges Ju with her shoulder, "Come on stinky, buy me Ice-cream, act like you like me."

Ju is surprised. "How do I get stuck paying?"

Gnat answers, "It was your idea!"

"Chili was your idea!" rebutting his son.

"And who paid for it?" Su asks him. The three of them start giggling. She always gets the last word with her husband. It never gets old. Not ever.

Su pats Gnat again. Ju has gone to open the door for her. "Don't you want to be able to do this with us all the time?" she asks.

"I do, move to Wishintown," he answers.

"The plane ride is long. I can't leave my mother, either."

"Yes, you can. You can do anything you want. You just have to do it. Being in the air is a deal breaker for you? Come on Mom, don't be silly. Change is great. You've lived your whole life in this town. I always think about what you say, think about what I say. Don't throw it out. You'd enjoy Wishintown. I know you would. I do. What do I come from?"

"Okay, I'll think about it. Your dad is waiting."

"The world is waiting for the both of you," Gnat concludes.

Gnat thinks about how fun they were to be around when he was younger. For a flash he feels his emotions. He is privileged to have his parents. After all, they might not have made him what he is, consciously. But what *they* are gave him the tools to see things the way he does. The dichotomy between his parents. *The balance.*

On the way home, they stop at an Ice-cream parlor. At a business with the word 'cream' in its name, the need for something without dairy is somewhat satirical. His parents share a banana split, he watches calmly as they take turns and speak about what's going on with other family members. He is only pretending to listen; he has no interest. The truth is his mind is occupied by something else. It doesn't take long before they finish and head to the house.

Su says, "Come upstairs, we can see if there's a movie on."

"Okay," answers Gnat, "Maybe rent something? I can't stand commercials. You know there's a fact somewhere about how much of your life you spend watching them if you make it to seventy?"

"I like commercials, some are funny," Ju says.

"Maybe the first time, but watching it hundreds of times? Like a sports game that's four periods, do you know how long they actually compete?"

Ju stares at him. "Four periods, Gnat."

"No, the clock runs in between plays. It's only about one full period by the end," Gnat replies, "A television slot is triple the length of a full game, so the match itself is an advertisement."

His dad replies, "People like their teams."

Yes, because they are told to.

There's a show about killing alligators in F'lalasip. Ju starts watching, he's locked in. His hands are resting on top of his head, away from the remote. A sign that he won't be needing it for a while.

"What kind of nonsense is this?" Gnat asks.

"They are trying to tag out on alligator season," Su says, from the chair. "They only have four cycles a span to make their money."

"So, this is a nature channel with a show about killing animals? There isn't a reason to hunt them, except for menial specialty items no person actually needs."

"It's just a show," Ju hums dismissively.

"It's also a reality show not based in reality? Does this actually happen?"

Ju says, "They really kill the alligators and sell them. It's probably scripted."

"What a waste. Did you hear about the fires in Austopia that destroyed a third of the koala population?"

"Oh yeah, that's horrible," Su answers.

"Since they are cuddly creatures, their deaths are a tragedy. It's alright to senselessly kill reptiles because we can't pet them and we need trinkets to sell in gas stations?"

"Well, those fires..."

"Were caused by man," Gnat completes the sentence.

"And a lot of people lost everything they had during that," adds Ju.

"How unthinkable!" he continues. "A house built in a forest has the ability to burn down, a suburb lower than sea level next to an ocean might be at risk of flooding."

"Have sympathy for those people and what they worked for." Su pleads.

"I have sympathy, so much of it," Gnat says dryly, "especially for the person who loses their house in an inevitable act of nature, then builds the house again in the same spot. It's not a matter of *if* it will come again, only *when*. How can reasoning so basic be overlooked in lieu of personal want?"

"Time for the news, Ju," Su interjects. "Turn it on."

This is why, the local news. Brainwashing of the masses with propaganda, fear, and hate.

"Please no. Really. Please," begs Gnat.

"I want to know what's going on," says Su.

"I'll tell you. Child has cancer. Black man murdered someone. Terrorists. Old man dies. At the end, here. A puppy. Joy. The same thing every broadcast. How can you watch it? It's so apparent they want you to be afraid of everything."

"Stop! Let me watch," she calls.

Gnat leaves to get a drink. Of water. He hears a voice speaking about a group of nationalists from Ropa and how they were evil, brutal in their madness and murder. Some group of neo-nationalists was found in a rural town in the center of the country. The script flips to a piece about the border patrol agents, watching the line between Omrika and South Omrika. No person in or out, under any circumstances. Gnat plops down again. "What happened to a movie?"

Neither of his parents answer.

"Are they making a comparison between the Ropan nationalists and Omrikans?"

"No. There is no comparison," Ju states, mesmerized by the screen.

"We're pretty much the same as they were a few generations ago. We hate whomever is different than us. Illegals, Muusmani citizens, anyone that doesn't support our military. Anyone who won't give us their natural resources. Our borders are closed, yet we feel the need to define and control everybody else's. Yes, there are radical groups everywhere in the world. As part of every faith, including here in Omrika. We don't define ourselves because of that, yet we judge that entire part of the world based on a paramilitary group that isn't associated with their lawmakers. There's only a single group of real terrorists on the planet. That's the Omrikan government."

Su fires at him, "Don't say that. A lot of men have died for what we have."

"That were indoctrinated with ideals at a young age and gave up their lives willingly without questioning it. Sounds a little like a man who straps a bomb to his chest protecting what he believes, or uses his plane as a missile in battle to sink a ship, right?"

"It's not the same, Gnat. They are extremists!" she says.

"Because of the ideal or the weapon being used? Why don't you like Muusman? Have you been there?"

"You know I haven't."

"Right, so why do you have an opinion? It's mindless hate, based on hearsay. You adamantly hold belief in things you have no knowledge of, on either side. It's empty, and zealous. Sorry to say, that's the literal definition of extremism."

"Glad you are home, son," Ju contributes. "Always a pleasure to be lectured by you."

"It's not a lecture, Dad. I'm simply questioning what you hold dear. That's obviously something you haven't tried. If your opinion comes out of what you've heard, it holds no value whatsoever. It's fine to drink coffee because it makes you more productive and alert within the system, but white powder isn't because it makes you feel glad while doing the same thing? Which drug is more addictive? Which is worse? Why?"

His mother rises. "I've had enough. I'm going to sleep. See you tomorrow. We can go to lunch, Gnat. Just you and I. I do like when you are here, you make me think of things in a different way."

"I'll be up. I'll sleep out here if it's too late to move around, so I don't wake you." *Ignore and deflect.*

"Okay, bug." She smiles. "Our extremist family in Oia, turning in for the night. We don't even know what we are."

She leaves the room. His dad looks at him, quietly. "You haven't been to Muusman, either, Gnat. Remember?"

"I *will* go, and I won't make an opinion of it until then. That's the point I'm trying to make. My beliefs will always be created by my experience, not what someone tells me. Why is this such a hard thing for you to accept? You want me to be a carbon copy that discovers nothing new? That walks the line drawn for me?"

"If you feel like you need to see things, that's fine. At some point you have to settle down," his father says.

"Settle for what? Less than I want?"

"What are you getting from this lifestyle, bouncing around constantly?"

"I'm not just bouncing around, I'm earning knowledge. I have a set of rules I live by, and I don't deviate from them. I'm a traveler, not a tourist. There's a difference," Gnat says.

"I don't see it, son."

"If you buy a round-trip ticket, it's not traveling. That's vacation. There's no sense of losing time, or going with what comes up. You know where you have to be and when. You know how long your funds have to last; you have a specific amount of time. If you go with someone else, there's always a fallback. A safety net. Somebody to share the burdens of uncertainty and keep ties to home. Same as having a cell phone or social media. It defeats the purpose, taking your comfort bubble with you. Booking a room, tour, or rental car beforehand. Going to the local attractions. That's not traveling! It's being a tourist..."

"What's traveling, then?"

"Only buying a one-way ticket. One person. One bag. No room before you go, no idea where you are going. Letting things happen. I don't want to go to the peak with a paved parking lot and a viewpoint where millions of other people take the same picture. It holds no vigor. I want to find a rental room off the beaten track, spend my time immersing in the routines of the locals. Eating food I don't know, understanding what it's like to be from wherever I am. That's earning the knowledge for yourself. Not from a tour guide and a pamphlet. That's experiencing, not paying for a packaged experience."

"Huh, I do see the difference, actually. You know, I saw a lot of Irfa when I was in the military. Austopia, Telaysia, Ropa, Ehfra,"

Ju replies. "There's a lot of things out there to find, they aren't always good."

"Simply settling and existing is not fulfilling to me, Dad. This isn't a phase, only a stepping stone. It's me figuring out how to be sustainable anywhere."

"I know you are going to do what you want to do. Why does it have to be so far from us? What did we do to deserve you leaving? You know it hurts your mother."

"It's a waste of energy to try and make you browse outside this life, in the Oia mindset. To see how nonsensical it is. I don't want it, not any part. It's too simple, too empty. It's not real. Despite touring in the military, you paraded in the false pretense that you were better, they were lesser. They needed you, you were right. That's not immersing, that's suppressing," says Gnat.

"How can you tell me that my life isn't real, that it's nonsense? I've lived it."

"Lived what? The Omrikan dream? You try to define everything according to your reality, which is based on how you feel in the moment. Or what you hear from someone else, who heard it from someone else. It's not factual or of substance. I challenge you to not have a conversation for a cycle dealing with what somebody did, said, or what happened to you. Do you think you could do that?"

Ju leans back on the couch. "People talk about themselves, it's all we have. What we are! How can you think that?"

"See, that's not what we are. No matter if you create or solve every problem within humanity, someone will agree and someone will disagree. It's irrelevant and immaterial to any type of growth. Every cycle, is a cycle. What's the aim of your routine? Where is it ultimately going to take you? Things won't always come around to the way you do it, like you believe..."

"What's your *aim*? To not live like us?"

Gnat sighs. "I feel like you hear my words, but don't process them. Same as Mom, when I question her and she says 'I like it' or 'that's the way everybody does it.' She's patronizing because she doesn't know why she's doing it either. There's no backing, just joy. No thought of who or what it's affecting outside of what is best for her. No, it's not what most people do. Omrika is only five percent of the world's population. The majority of people do things completely differently. We are the vast *minority* of humans living. Your capacity to see, or *want* to understand, is nonexistent. How do you know that you like it? You've never tried anything else. This is why I left, this is the reason I don't talk to you that often. The family, this state, this country exists in some sort of meaningless, endless emotional loop. No matter what I say or how logical it is, all you do is deflect and justify whatever side you are on. When I say that something doesn't equate in your existence, you get angry. You, and this *you* is generalized, don't want to think about the fact that nothing holds any weight. People want to keep living in ignorance, on repeat. Your life is only what you've been told it is. Yes, this is your house, right now. When you're done, it will be someone else's burden. Some other kids will grow up here and won't know anything about us. It's like we never happened."

"If you spend your whole life seeing the world, in the end it will be the same for you," says Ju. "So how is it any different? What's your goal? You didn't tell me."

"I'm only learning as much as I can right now. What that becomes later, I can't say. I know that I don't want what's been offered to me, so far. That's it."

His father sounds weathered by a storm, somehow. "I'm sorry you don't find any meaning in the things I did for you, growing up. Time for me to sleep, too, I think..."

"Dad, don't be like that. I'm not saying that I don't have anything but the deepest admiration for you and what you've given me. I just don't value the same things as you. I think you should be glad I want to define things for myself."

"I am glad that you are your own man. You figure it out as you go. You've always had to learn things the hard way, it's your nature. Remember your mother and I are not against you. Not now, not ever. You don't have to treat us so harshly. See you tomorrow."

"When you ask me something, I answer honestly. It doesn't have to be amicable, it's not an argument either. Only what I see. Goodnight, Dad."

Ju leaves him alone with the lights low. Every picture placed in a spot, cleaned habitually. The same with the rug laying on the hardwood floor. The drink coasters, the table they nest on. The couch with its cushions. The lamp in the corner has a stained glass shade with roses in red, pots in green. Kept up for appearances, yet no one from the outside ever peers at this room's perfection. No guest is entertained. It's done, because it needs to be, in his parent's minds.

Parents. In certain ways they know you better than you know yourself. However, as you get older, you don't age in their eyes. They defend the image of you as a child until the end. When you are older, they ignore your faults. Or don't see them. They are unwilling to entertain the idea that their kids might not be what they wanted them to be. It could be because they subconsciously see it as a personal downfall, it could be because they are simply jaded by expectation.

The same goes the other way. When Gnat was a child, if his father told him he could lift a tree out of the ground, Gnat believed him. Now, he's aging. *I see him as a human, yet still somehow above everything.*

"I'm not five anymore," Gnat says to himself. " I'm not sure that's a positive thing, either."

In the basement he unpacks his guitar. A capo is on the third fret, he plays without a pick, touching the strings as lightly as possible so as not to wake the household. Like the pattern of steps down a straight line, bouncing back and forth between the same chords, nothing more. Muses don't keep time, only appearing when they feel it's right. Now is the time, the words flow freely out of him.

I'm a third the man I want to be, you see.
A spirit trapped in normalcy.
I walk, down the narrow hall.
Insanity, my name it calls.
Mr. Maccaferri, what can you tell me?
Tell me?
Mr. Maccaferri, what does your wisdom tell me?
I cannot see.

(He whistles the melody, as lightly as he can)

I'm a third the man I want to be-e-e, e-e-e-e
A spirit trapped in normalcy-y-y, y-y-y-y
Whoa, whoa, whoa...

He creeps up the steps, skipping the plank that creaks.

Five percent. Omrikans make up five percent of the human population of Irfa, yet use thirty percent of the resources. Every person uses six times as much as they need to survive. Half of the food produced gets thrown away when it doesn't sell or isn't exactly the correct shape or color. There are two vacant buildings for every homeless person in the country. Literally, people die in the street and others let them, government included, because they don't have good credit. Because they've slipped through the cracks of a broken system. If everyone on this planet lived like Omrikans, humans would already be extinct. Producing at the highest level possible, there isn't a physical way to allow every human to live in such incapacitating disregard and excess.

"Ugh," Gnat murmurs, eyes closed on the couch. "Breathe. Sleep, go to sleep. You can make them see. Just, not, now…"

Dreams don't come this night, too many things are on his mind to focus on an idea and personify it.

***

The nervous cleaning of his mother wakes him. She's incessant, it's an addiction. All people have a vice, acceptable only if it can be marketed and taxed. He stretches. *Lucky me.*

"Are you awake, bug?" his mother asks from another room. "I'm starting to get hungry, get ready. We can go to the diner you like. They have the honey mustard that's your favorite…"

Gnat hasn't thought about it for a long time, getting excited he says, "Oh, yeah! That's the one, I can't wait."

On the drive to the diner, Su plays an album they've enjoyed together his whole life, by a girl that's been gone for fifty spans, a soul singer from Nan Friko. They sing along, the sun blinding them with yellow light. Through town he sees many things that have never changed, and never will. A drug deal at the gas station, where the dealer works. Perfect cover for people constantly coming and going. A friend from school in the pizzeria, he started working there at seventeen. Gnat can see him through the window. The Tapped Rune, with cars that belong to Kili and Beb. He's glad he escaped, it's so rare to do so when born into this life. His mom turns down the radio and slaps him on the knee.

"What's going on with you and women? Any special girl in your life? Where is Addie?" She awaits an answer.

"Addie disappeared, moved on to some place I'm not aware of. I won't hear from her again, I don't think."

"There's no one new?"

He thinks, answering slowly, "There's a girl I met in Montisa. She lives a long way from here. I think I may see her again. I left it open so that she can contact me if she'd like to," he says.

She digs in. "What's her name? Where is she from? Tell me about her..."

"Ha! Come on, Mom. Her name is Hipslyn, from Raminia. She's very intelligent and graceful. I told her she can have as much of me as she wants, however that looks. You know that it's hard to build something when you are constantly moving around."

"If she pulls you that much, you'll have to make the decision to stop moving. Are you ready for that?"

He stutters, "That's, um, unclear."

"Then you aren't," she confirms. "I don't think you're ready to commit to someone, or compromise for them. That's not to say that you can't or won't, but not right now. You still have too many things you want to do on your own, don't you think?"

"Yes, maybe," Gnat agrees.

"It isn't fair," she explains, "especially with distance. You can't expect her to wait for you if you plan on leaving anyway."

"I agree, you're right. If she sends me a message from home, I'll go see her, no doubt. She's worth the chance, to find out, at least. I know that."

Driving into the diner, she stops midway through the turn, wide-eyed. "Isn't that near Muusman? I don't know if that's a good idea, Gnat..."

"Why, because you saw it on the news? Can we not go through this again, please?" he says.

She defers. "I don't want to either. Let's enjoy lunch. I may not get to do this with you again for spans..."

"Don't think about it, I'm here now. Don't waste it being sad about the unknown, Mom," he confides. "Come on, let's eat. Remember the song we sang, *Take It When It's There.*"

Su parks, locking the doors twice. Something done at every stop for as long as he can remember, although they will be able to see the car while they eat through the window. It's ingrained. *Fear it, the uncertainty.*

They are shown to a table, actually, a booth. Always a booth, no matter where they go. Gnat continues on about relationships.

"You know how you said I'm not ready? I don't know. I have this thing that I always think, friends are just placeholders until you find what you are really looking for," he says.

"That's true. After I met your father, I never really hung out with my friends after that. Not even my close friends from before we met."

Gnat takes a moment. "Right, because you found everything, the mental and physical. We place so much value in people when it comes to the physical. Really, isn't affection a need? If someone isn't giving it to you, you will just find it somewhere else. That's simple. I think people confuse reactionary responses to impulses as meaningful and certifiable emotions."

Su's already finished her first drink. *Better be quick, if you want a tip!*

"On some level, but you make a commitment. If you go out and get sick, or get your partner sick, or get someone else pregnant or something..." his mother trails off quickly, "then somebody has to deal with your mistakes, too. That's not any good."

"Yeah, yeah, I agree. That's not the point I'm trying to make. We never think about the *mental* part of a relationship. So, you're married and have a friend that is also a man, like Dad."

"Right."

"Dad isn't giving you what you need, in some intellectual capacity. Challenging you to think about things differently or deep conversation about the universe, for example. Instead, you meet up with this other guy friend because he's really great at these things your partner is lacking. Isn't that cheating? Seeking out something you aren't getting from your so-called other half? Going outside of the bond you've made to take care of each other?"

"I don't know, maybe to some degree. You have to understand that people are different. That doesn't indicate you don't fit, just because they are lacking something."

"Shouldn't you both be willing to put the energy into getting these things from each other, rather than take the easy way out and getting it somewhere else? That's what I'm saying, it's the same as the physical. You are still nourishing a part of you with the care from another."

"It's about finding a place where both people are comfortable with the lives they live separately, as well as together," Su answers.

"It's about forcing yourself into the easiest situation you can find? People aren't *made* for another. If they were, you would get absolutely everything from them without having to try or talk about it. You tell yourself you want a spouse, so you find some person that you feel like you can put up with on a mundane basis, living in comfort. When you are over it, you leave. Because you are still doing what's best for you, not the partnership."

She considers what her son has said as their food arrives. "You have to live a life you can stand waking up to, in the end. That has to make sense to even *you*."

Gnat swallows. "Yes. You take the best option at the time. You settle, you try to be comfortable with it."

"Maybe, you'll have to let me think about it and ask me again." She continues, "Some gossip. Remember Ris, from your class? He has a new boyfriend; I saw them kissing while I was shopping. Can you believe it? He's gay. I remember him coming to the house when you were young."

He recalls the interactions he's had with Ris over the spans. "He always was pretty feminine, growing up. I don't mind it, if it's what he wants, you know? Or what he is, doesn't matter. Not for me to know. It's his life."

Su responds, "Oh, I'm completely fine with it. It's so strange to me that coming out is so socially acceptable now. You used to get arrested or killed for doing things like that!"

"I know! It's crazy what people will do when somebody else does something they don't understand, huh? We just came full circle from what we were talking about last night, somehow, didn't we?" He smirks at her.

Her face is straight. "Don't get wise with me about it."

"I read something about a scientist who wrote an algorithm that could predict your sexual orientation by analyzing your bone structure. The program is right almost a hundred percent of the time. He thinks he could tell you everything programmed into you. Beliefs, emotional response. What makes you angry, or glad, or what you believe. He is trying to prove that stereotypes were created for a reason, because they're straightforward and true," Gnat says.

"I believe a lot of them are. I have a student this span, he's five. You're right. His features, they're soft. He has big, long eyelashes. He talks about princesses and gravitates toward the other girls. He's obviously gay, though he doesn't know it. Which isn't an issue. I think of the beautiful things in his life likely to be destroyed because being a man is described in a certain way," Su answers.

Gnat says, "The truth is, none of it matters. He will always have to hold back his true personality in some way to make it through. Yet, we all do, don't you think?"

"Of course."

He continues, "However, when you buy in and label yourself, you are feeding part of your own demise. Something I've said before, just do what you do. So will I. Then boundaries disappear. There's no reason to find a place in something only short lived."

"What do you mean?"

He smirks again. "Human existence!"

"Oh, stop it. We've barely touched our food, it's getting cold."

"My burger bun is so saturated with mayonnaise it's falling apart..."

Su pays, handing the server money when he returns. A job well done, he kept her drink topped up.

Driving, his mother starts to talk about his family. He starts to imagine Hipslyn's face. Working the bar in Montisa. That frozen highway, the woman who gave him a ride to the bus when the sign was wrong. What was her name? He can't recall. There's a divot in the road, a pothole. So much for road taxes around here. The main roads are like a minefield that's been completely detonated.

"Do you want to see her, Gnat?" she asks. He has no idea who she is talking about.

"Sorry, who?"

"Ima, your sister," Su says plainly.

"Of course, why would you ask?"

"She'll be over tomorrow, so you know."

"Alright," he answers.

He does want to see her. They were best friends as children. No one understands him, or the deep-seated reasoning in his mind better than her. They both ended up wanting different things later in life, however.

"That was perfect," she adds, "I'm glad we got to share that."

Gnat glances over. "Me too, I'll remember next time I start to miss you."

As they pass down the main drag in Fennytun, he sees The Tapped Rune. Kili is there, and maybe others he'd like to see.

"Hey mom, leave me out here, yeah?" he says.

"You are going to the bar this early?"

"What else am I going to do? Sit at the house staring at the wall? I'm not an upstanding member of society, it's my place," Gnat answers.

Su stops, "Don't go too far, I'm not picking you up from jail."

"Come on, don't be dramatic," he says, lowering his head. It isn't that operatic, she's had to do it before. "I'll find a way home, don't wait up."

'Okay bug, be safe."

How many cycles of my life have I forgotten here?

The front door is propped open, Kili sees him and perks up. "Hey, Gnat, we didn't know you were coming home! How have you been?" She beams.

She's a bigger woman, with black hair and lots of jewelry on her fingers. She moves slowly, with purpose. Kili knows the secrets of every patron that comes to this place, having seen them at their worst. Never would she break the trust people put in her. It's the job of a bartender, the poor man's psychologist.

"Hey Gnat, great to see you!" says Beb, a man that comes to the bar to avoid his life and responsibilities.

Gnat takes his old seat. "Hey there, guys. Yeah, unexpected for me too. Things went bad on the road, I had to leave the truck behind…"

"The one you spent all that time building?" asks Kili.

Gnat clicks his tongue. "Yes, that one. Left it on the side of the highway up north. Forget it, things happen. You adapt, or you don't, right?"

"That's right," says Beb. "Couldn't put it more plainly myself."

Beb has been a friend for spans. A kind man, he runs his own business. In his fifties, an old musician type. Slicked back hair, a perfectly groomed goatee.

"Kili, can I get a drink?" Gnat calls over the bar. "Whatever Beb wants too."

"You got it," Kili answers, "Beb?"

"Oh, just a tonic and lime will do me," he replies.

A duo comes into the Rune, his childhood friends, Kiiv and Sheg.

"Gnat!" Sheg yells. "What's new? We are off work, going to get drunk and go to the casino."

"Hey, I'm in for whatever," Gnat answers, hugging both at the same time. "Kili, more shots for us three, please!"

"You never change, do you?" asks Kiiv.

"Not in some ways," Gnat answers, laughing. "No reason to stop having a good time, is there?"

He and his friends get lit quick. It's like they were never apart. Gnat and Kiiv had the same first class at school. He was there when the butterflies were let loose. Sheg showed up a few spans later from Nuwal city, when his parents divorced.

After a few games of pool won by Gnat, they are perched on the bar. The TV is on in the background. Gnat starts to drift off, the layer of fuzz provided by the alcohol not allowing him to quite formulate the words he searches for. He's in a corridor of tall vines, thick as a concrete wall. Blocking his vision. He rests his head in his hand, on top of the wooden horseshoe that serves as a drinking surface. How many spans of spills and conversations has this old slab of stained wood absorbed? Trees, he misses those old trees in Wishintown. He wants to know what they know. He wants to speak to them, to be a part of them. Running within their grains, amongst the twisted knots. Always with, never against.

What had Sheg said? *You never change.* He has, though. So many nights like these, forgotten. *There's no reason to stop having a good time,* he had told Sheg. He doesn't think that you should. But just a good time that only leaves you after, forgotten to the emptiness of how much it meant in the first place outside of emotion, is ignorant. *Right?* It's having a good time in the pursuit of a goal, reaching for something that leaves positive energy as you take it in turn, that hints at something. Doesn't it? *No, that's silly. The person who has the most fun wins...*

He's refocused by a punch on the shoulder from Kiiv. "What a surprise, Gnat!"

His girlfriend from high school, Ezlie, has shown up. He hasn't seen her since things went bad between them, spans ago. She has wavy red hair that cascades over her shoulders like a waterfall made of feathers and molasses. She sees him. He hurt her; the circumstances are no longer clear to either side. He doesn't know she's forgotten. They were only children then, anyhow.

"Hey, Ez," Gnat says, with a calm gaze. He doesn't know what to expect from this interaction. "Good to see you."

"Gnat, call me Ezlie. Everything is fine. I have a job, an apartment. I'm here with my friends. We'll have a round and go."

He replies, "Don't leave on my account. Let me buy this round."

"No, don't. This always has been your spot, hasn't it? I heard you are doing great on the west coast. I'm glad for that. I always knew this wasn't your place, you needed to go and see things for yourself."

"I can't say you're wrong."

"We'll sit outside. Just let us be, please. Don't feel bad, I don't. I hope you've gotten what you wanted. I have, or at least I'm trying for it. It's worked out for the better, I think."

He beams, trying to be charming. "We could have three kids and a mortgage by now..."

Ezlie studies him, he can tell she still thinks about him. In her eyes, there's an attraction. "Neither of us would like that, would we?"

"I don't think we'd know the difference, if we were in it," he says. "You're radiant, as always. Be good, Ezlie."

"You too, Gnat. Take care of yourself. Don't force it. Things will come." Ezlie turns to her friends.

He remembers the good times with her, she was very sweet. He can't remember where his mind was, then. What he was pursuing, if what he believed was correct. They are fond memories. Being carefree, a teenager, partying. Every benefit of adulthood, no accountability for mistakes made. Some classmates weren't allowed to be around him or drive with him. He was searching then, too, misunderstood. He wouldn't eat what was being prepared back then, either. Gnat knows that taking any of those standards seriously is a waste of time, that makes others nervous. *Afraid.*

"That wasn't so bad," Sheg says. "Considering you slept with her best friend."

"Is that what I did? Seems like so many spans ago, a different life," Gnat answers. "More drinks."

Someone goes up to the jukebox and puts on hip-hop music. Kiiv and Sheg go outside to smoke, he leans on the bar by himself. As the music punches on he starts to listen to the lyrics. He's lost to the liquid, a thought arrives...

Every hip hop song mentions the difference between being white and black, that there's a line between. Songs written in other genres don't mention race, not in this generation or any other. It's like the industry is instilling a predisposition to victimization and racism subconsciously into listeners. Perpetuating and creating the stereotypes.

"Indoctrination through the media," he whispers to himself. "Another example. How do people not pick up on these things?"

During the cold, sun dissipates early, taking sustenance with it. Leaving only shivers in lifelessness. He sees the national news rolling over the TV screen. Then he hears a name, Tiria Sika. Where is that from? How does he know that? Her face appears on screen, the sandy blonde hair. It's the woman, from the corporation. *From Addie's Outcry magazine.* It seems that she's making many people angry, about something, he doesn't know. They already explained that part of the story. *It was a decision she made, that cost a lot of people their jobs. Wasn't she given the power to make the choices?*

"Take one away, another comes," he mutters to himself.

Kiiv and Sheg ask him if he wants to go gamble. Usually he would, however he declines, says goodbye, and starts the trek home. He starts to wonder why he's spent so many nights of his life in that place. Listening to the same bar stories. Standing by himself, fuzzy vision, pockets lighter and no closer to finding remedies for his ailments. *I have changed. I used to wake up for this. Waking up to forget. It doesn't hold meaning for me any longer. Ezlie was right. I was meant to be somewhere else. Why am I here?*

Gnat arrives at his parent's house. Theirs, not his. He sneaks to the basement.

"I haven't written this much since the last time I was here," he whispers. *I only write when I'm dark. That's always in Oia.* He starts to play quickly and quietly, however not as politely as the first night. Variations of the same chord on different octaves, strumming in triplets.

There's a line,
There's a line.
That separates, night from light.
Never will you cross my line.

There's a line,
There's a line,
Between you and I.
Never will,
Never will it end.

Only one thing you can do.
It's inside you.
It points you toward the north and the south.

Use the compass,
Compass in your eye,
Compass in your eye.

There's a line,
There's a line,
So thick.
So black.
So angry.
Between...

Use the compass,
Compass in your eye.
To divine...

"They try to draw the lines between us, don't they?" he says, lying on the floor. He's drunk and can't hold his eyelids open any longer. He crosses his hands over his chest.

"So we keep fighting over nothing, the agenda moves forward unhindered..."

Gnat is passing out, thinking of the time he's wasted being wasted, when a sudden burn comes to the middle of his forehead. His stomach turns into a ball, a familiar feeling to him, still uncomfortable. *You can go now, see for yourself. You are ready.*

That voice. So calm this time, no sense of urgency. A vision of those shapes, a man. He can see now, older than he. A woman, with long hair. What color, he cannot tell.

***

"Gnat," his mother calls, "Gnat, bug, wake up. Your sister is here."

He blinks his way back to consciousness, as the Irfa comes into focus, "I'll be there."

Up the steps, still hazy, he sees her. Ima, his younger sister. Physically, in a word, beautiful. They appear alike in many ways, her features are smaller however. Softer, and more delicate. She's tiny, yet holds the same distinction as her mother, someone not to be trifled with. Her hair is like Gnat's. Her skin is a bit brighter; they have both inherited the same number of freckles from their mother. They possess a similar process of deduction, mostly coming to opposite conclusions. Ima uses her beauty to get what she wants. Men that she meets are seduced, spent, then cast aside before they recognize what happened. She makes the mistake of picking the same type of companion over and over, expecting it to be different. Growing up, Ima had watched what Gnat was doing and avoided it. She doesn't drink, she doesn't do drugs. She went to school, then university and got the grades. She followed the path as it was laid out for her.

The only thing that she ever wanted to do was travel to Ehfra on a humanitarian visa once she finished her degree. Teaching others to adapt in an evolving world. She was accepted. At the same time, she got test results confirming a disease which requires medication in perpetuity. Prescriptions that she couldn't receive in Ehfra, so Ima couldn't go. She had done everything she had been told and in the end was still subject to chance. Since that twist of fate, when she understood that you never actually get what you work for, Ima hasn't been the same.

"Hey, buggy," she says to him, resting against the counter in the kitchen.

"Hey, sissy," Gnat replies. "What's new?"

"We didn't think we'd see you. Things didn't go to plan? Did your drinking get in the way of things?"

"No, it didn't. Truck troubles. Woman troubles. You know how it goes."

"I have a friend, Illin. He's a life coach," Ima presents to him. "Maybe he can give you some advice about the next step."

"No, I'm alright. Life coach? What has he accomplished in his life that warrants me listening?"

"He has his degree with honors. He works at a corporation now. He has a giant house, out in seven hills."

Gnat cuts her off. "So, he's a master of subscribing to standard, and he wants to bring everyone else toward it?"

She rolls her eyes. "He's helping empower people, it's a good thing."

"What is empowerment, to you?" he asks her.

"Enabling somebody..."

"Similar to an addict?"

"No, not like an addict. To be a valuable member of society..." she answers.

"What is valuable, now? Being a slave?"

"No!" she exclaims. "Anyone can be anything!"

He gazes at the floor, its tiles. Every piece in its place, it only works and creates a surface to stand on if nothing ever moves. If each tile is glued to its spot. Aligned and defined.

"You know, there are periods of specified time throughout human history," he states.

Ima speaks over him, "Like the mid-ages?"

"Yes. Do you know which we live in now? Neo-slavery, disguised as privilege."

"What do you mean? People are empowered now. To do anything they want," she responds.

"Empowerment is simply coming to terms with your shortcomings and wanting others to be lesser for it. People now only find value in themselves, if other people find value in them. In the title. Empowerment? If you do what you are told, you can operate within the whole. It's not objective. You are told what means something. A degree. A job, a house. You can decide how to get these things, not whether you want them in the first place. You have to label yourself within the whole, only to try and be accepted by it."

"I don't think that's it," she says.

"It's not about thinking, it's about knowing. Seeing."

She pushes herself up off the counter. "We are trying to come together with some kind of understanding."

"By doing what we are told and not going outside of it?"

"No, not that, Gnat. You don't want to create any conflict within the circle you operate."

"Yes you do, sis. You want to create as much conflict as possible. You want to question everything you see. Question the questions, constantly. Never accept what's been given to you. That's what being free is, the choice to break out of the mold to discover for yourself. People bow to 'that's just the way it is' instead of what they have seen for themselves."

"People have to find value in things to keep going, though." Ima says.

"It's just substantiating what's best for them as meaning?"

"No, it's..." She is searching for the words.

"It's drawing the lines in a different way within the same game. So, the federal government starts to fund the hospitals in the country. Great, right? Then what do they do on the back end? Write the medical policy. Say who gets treated and who doesn't. They package it as empowerment, it's really creating complacent people. They won't vote against the funding, ever. They want the money, and willingly give up their rights to keep it. A politician knows what's best for sick people? I seriously doubt that. Do they know how to get something from citizens, somehow? Definitely."

Ima is sitting in a chair now. "Everything isn't a conspiracy. You take it too far."

"No, I don't. They give you choices within the system they've laid out for you. You must have a house, you must get a degree, you must get a job, you must have insurance. They profit from each decision you make within the guidelines. The individual decides where they will live, what job they will pursue, not how to get there. Not what they really want to spend their time pursuing, just their position within what is already there. That's not choice," Gnat says, solemnly.

"What is it?" Ima questions.

"It's empowerment. Empowerment into subjection," he says. "The only way that things will change is if we stop driving cars. Stop building houses. Stop going to work and paying taxes. Not talk about it, not half measures. All together, at once."

Ima snorts. "That's not going to happen, is it?"

"It could! They keep *us* focused on how we feel about ourselves, that distracts from what *they* are really doing. Think about the guy trying to support his family, putting cinnamon rolls on a conveyor every cycle for thirty spans. Is that a life? He is told it's honorable, it's paying the bills. Making circumstances better for his children. Anyone could do it, just as well. However, he doesn't question. He has submitted, unwilling, unable to change it."

"He's doing the job he was given, though."

"Exactly. Eating what he's been fed. No more. The supervisor on the floor, who's got the title only because he's been there longer than anyone else, he thrives in that position. It defines him. It's what he is. He feels appreciated. Alas, he is unknowing. The job is only his *because* he is the most submissive. The one that memorized the checklists before anybody else, endlessly doing the task without a second thought. He doesn't know he is the type of person they search for, the individual described in the handbook of the manager. The meek. The compliant. The strong build the standards around the pitfalls of human intelligence. If you feel appreciated, you keep producing. It's like getting a participation medal as an adult."

"Come on, Gnat. It doesn't go that deep."

"Of course it does, the fact that you truly believe it doesn't only shows that you've been duped too. What's the thing most talked about now? What's the thing that is demonized most in the media?"

"I don't know, what?"

"Freedom of speech. It's being manipulated by these news agencies. There's an agenda to keep people occupied with their feelings and definitions of themselves. What happens when some person goes against these feel-good messages with logic? They are deemed evil. Insensitive, offensive. There is always litigation served on those with opinions. So, what do people do on social media? Their opinion, their belief is whatever is popular at the time. To avoid *conflict* as you call it, to avoid being outside the bubble, people simply stay quiet to not be ostracized. Opinions are the new rock n' roll music..."

"Good to see you, always. Can I go now?" Ima says.

"I'm not spouting nonsense about emotion, I know that's what you are used to. Give me a logical rebuttal. Come on, Ima!"

"I am done talking about this, I'm going. Mom, can I have some money to go out with my friends?"

"Sure, Ima," Su says. She has been listening to her children this whole time from the sideline.

Gnat starts laughing, "Are you serious? Aren't you a modern, empowered Omrikan woman with a degree? You don't have lunch money? Still playing both sides whenever you can, huh?"

As Su hands her a bill she puts it in her pocket and turns to him. "Best of luck with whatever you do next, buggy. See you again in another few spans..."

"Okay, Ima. Be good. Don't leave too many hopeless guys without any pennies."

They hug briefly. She is out the door and up the driveway before he can say anything more.

"Why do you always have to take it that far?" his mother asks. "You could have asked her what's going on in her life."

"I already know what's going on, she's a clone. The circumstances don't matter. The worst part is that I know she sees the same things as I do, and ignores them," Gnat says.

"You could be right, but it's her choice."

"To live in ignorance, because it is easier than making a decision on her own? Yes, it's my choice to not accept it."

"Don't be angry at your sister, bug..." she trails off.

"Why is it always about emotion? I'm not mad."

He remembers why he hasn't spoken to her in such a long time.

If you can see the things that are oxymora, yet you still operate in the systems that support them, you are worse off than the person who is too unintelligent to see the abstraction in the first place.

"Ugh, what's the point?" he murmurs.

That intentions never get anything done.

"This is Oia. This is the amount of time it takes to realize why I left," he continues the conversation alone, sitting down by his guitar in the basement. "My parents, Ima, Omrikans. This false sense of security everyone clings to. From baby products, to the banking institutions, to the military. It's a façade. False security, so people feel good about themselves and keep consuming. It's empty, this thing humans do, rationalizing their individual relevancy. Clinging onto ideals, how to make the system better, how to grow. No one is willing to live with a choice, it's always about having a backup. No individual is ready to change the way that they live in order to make things better. It's about ease, nothing else."

This time, he doesn't want to play. It's too frustrating, that someone made of the same things he is could be so... uninsightful. *Then again, every human is made of the same things, aren't they?* He starts to write about her, his sister. His Ima.

> *She knows how to read, and learn*
> *But she, refused to see*
> *Above the weeds.*
> *How they grow, so fast*
> *And strong.*
> *Why can't she, be free*
> *Of their grasp?*
> *They've got thorns*
> *And she, only green horns.*

She shall rule the world.
Even though plans unfurl.

Ships are meant to sail
The trees, have roots
So let them grow into your mind.
The songbird finds those notes
To let him flow
Above the clouds
But she, refused
To see above the weeds.

She shall rule the world.
Even though plans unfurl.

How did it get this way between them? Is it his fault, for wanting more? Or hers, for accepting less? Somehow, he knows it will never be the same as it was, swimming and laughing with not a care to be had. No understanding, either. *Is it better to be blissfully ignorant, or ignorantly blissful?*

"I want neither," he says.

He thinks of his friends, Kiiv and Sheg, other classmates. The circle of this tiny town. They were friends, yes. Out of choice or necessity? Some kids liked sports, some liked video games. You had to go along with the few that did the same thing you did. There weren't many options. This goes along with the married people from here, like his mother's parents. They met in adolescence, and are still together fifty spans later. They have never been very affectionate, compatible, or friendly. Within the circle they grew up in, the options were few. *Think of all the couples who have been miserable their whole lives because no one ever leaves or thinks outside of it.*

Gnat wakes again to an empty house. Work has started, his mom and dad are at their jobs. On the porch, the birds sing along with him. There's a tulip tree, registered as the biggest in the county. During the rains, the flowers bloom, pale yellow, the same diameter as a dinner plate. In the center, each flower holds a stained ring of blood orange. Fleeting beauty. Now, it stands as a bare trunk, branches swept upward reaching for the sky, for the light that doesn't show itself this time of span. It will wait going through the pain of darkness to present its best. To tempt the bees, which spread its pollen and life into the future. He enjoys the quiet, resting on the porch. The song is complete. *The thought.* As he goes inside, an email comes through. Maybe from the corporation he left, asking him to return. *Not an option.*

It's from Hipslyn. She's back in Raminia at her apartment in Curesti. She's starting to study again, after break. She asks how his family is, where he is. As soon as he finishes reading, he checks one-way tickets to Curesti. There's an immediate option at a steal of a price. It isn't close enough to the End of Span to fill seats, a last moment deal. Curesti really isn't a destination any Omrikans are heading toward, anyway. Without thinking, he buys it. Forget the money, the opportunity has presented itself. Take it, or not? That's the only thing to decide. He writes her back.

Hipslyn,

I bought a ticket. I'll be there in Curesti soon. If I can stay with you, I will. If that's not okay, I'll get my own place. I hope it's fine that I'm coming. See you. I'll send you details of when my flight arrives, you can meet me at the airport or not. It's up to you. Here I come, I told you I would. Gnat.

He gets a response, listening to his heartbeat.

Gnat,

I can't believe you are coming, of course you can stay with me. Yes, I will pick you up. I have so much to show you. Tell me when to get you!

He packs his bag, still mostly untouched since his arrival. He runs to town and buys a few odds and ends. He passes his grandparents' house. The car is in the driveway. He pauses, then continues. *What do I have to say to them that they can relate to?* As he turns into the driveway of his parents' house, both of their cars are parked.

"Hey son," Ju says as he enters.

"Bug, where'd you go?" Su asks with an interested face.

"To buy some things I needed. Personal hygiene, you know how I am totally into that stuff."

"Ha! When's the last time you showered?" his dad jokes.

"The last time it rained," he teases. "I need a ride to the airport early tomorrow, before you work. If you can't, I can get a taxi."

"New job? Where you going?" asks Ju.

Gnat knows what's coming. "No, no job. I'm flying to Raminia, Curesti."

"What?! That's by Muusman. Why would you do that? Come on, you're joking," his father says.

"You are going to see that girl. She sent you a message," Su responds with certainty.

"Yes."

"Girl? What girl?" Ju is confused.

"He met a girl up in Montisa from there, Hipslyn." Su explains, "You'll be away for the End of Span again, then, Gnat?"

Gnat squints his eyes, he doesn't like to upset her. "More than likely. After she starts studying, I am going to bounce around. See what comes up."

"To where?" asks Ju.

"Not sure yet. We'll see, Dad."

Ju gazes at Su, then at Gnat. "How long will you be?"

"I can't say, really. Can you drive me in the morning? Either way is fine, I just have to know."

"We'll take you," Su answers.

"Thanks, Mom."

Ju gets up. "Last dinner, you call it, son. I'll go and get it."

Gnat raises his eyebrows. "Whatever you want, Dad."

Su laughs along. "So... we aren't eating tonight?"

"Burgers!" Ju exclaims. "You need a good burger to fly on. They don't exist outside Omrika, you can trust me on that."

"You're the boss," Gnat says, falling to the couch, "I'll finish packing later."

Gnat doesn't complain about what's on or the commercials once. When life gets ambiguous, certainty comes with what you know. He's completely content traveling on his own, and needs it again. He may not see them for another span or more. They go to their room shortly after finishing food, he puts things in his pack and goes to sit outside. The wind is asleep also. The air here has its own tinge. Something like industry mixed with farming. Gasoline and soil. Fire and corn. At the very end of a breath, if a smell existed for it, simplicity. He looks at his hands, understanding something. Maybe putting words to it for the first time. This isn't his house, no. This isn't his place, never. However, it's where he came from. These are his roots no matter what understanding or definition he discovers. He's a simple Midwestern boy when it comes down to it. In bed, his eyes are closed, however his mind races. *What's coming?*

What will happen? With Hipslyn, with me? He isn't nervous, or scared. Just ready.

The alarm goes off.

Away to the airport, a big hub here in Nata. This city was the heart of everything moving west in the past. On the scale of this country's history, so long ago. In the scale of time, a blink. Maybe half of a blink. *A wink.* He's outside the terminal with his bag before he knows it.

"Bug, be good," says his mother, tears in her eyes. "You can take care of yourself, I know it. I'm not worried. I'll miss you. I wish we had more time together."

"I'm not worried either," he says, kissing her cheek. "I'll stay in touch. Maybe not as often as I should, but I always do, don't I?"

"Yes, bug, you do."

"Remember, don't get taken by any of those terror groups. Don't trust any women in dark places," Ju says. "Could be a trap."

"Unlikely, Dad, but I'll keep my eye out," he hugs his father. "See you when I see you."

They lock eyes, like when he first got home.

"Be smart, son."

A few more goodbyes, then they hop in the car and zoom away. He checks in and ponders. He's people watching, very tired. He thinks of his friends, his sister, his parents, then himself. What is the difference? How did he end up being the one to live this life? To leave Oia behind, when nobody else did? It's not just intelligence, his mother is as smart as him.

I'm riding the wave. It's a function of forces I can't control, things out of my hands. I go where it takes me. Sometimes roughly. Sometimes I can't breathe. Other times I'm on top. I see the view that no one else has. I'm in a series of things that will never happen exactly the same way. If it's time to go, I'll ride it to that end. Whatever or wherever it takes me. There's no reason to fight against it. What did Ezlie say? Things will come. What are they doing? Riding the train. It's safe, predetermined. Speed, course, and the number of seats are quantified. You pay to get on, you get off when you are supposed to. Too easy, and you never get anything that anyone else can't take the exact same way.

A voice comes over the intercom announcing that boarding has begun for passengers traveling to Raminia. Gnat feels dazed, almost in a dream. He hands the attendant his ticket. She smiles, saying welcome. *To what?* The voice answers without pain. *The next plateau. Go.* He walks down that suspended hallway into the unknown. The line between sand and water. Where he thrives.

VI

The flight allows time for gazing over Irfa, like the bus. The endless daze of corn is replaced by a vast spell of ocean separating Omrika from Ropa. He wonders about the original men who set out across it, unsure what they would find. Maybe certain death, maybe immortality, or lessons of why we exist. Most were focused on treasures, though, the type you can sell. Not that take you to higher levels of understanding.

When the plane stops and connects to the terminal, every passenger jumps into the aisle immediately. Even the last row. Gnat remains seated. *Why are you in a rush? We're going to the same place, there's only one way to get there...*

Ultimately, an escape through customs. Many families and friends are reunited after unknown lengths of absence, some by choice. Some by necessity. Gnat scans the rows, remembering how petite she is. He hears his name, coming from a speaker without the power to enter overdrive. Hipslyn.

"Gnat!"

He locates the source, its absolute perfection. That face. She's waving to him.

"You're here, you are actually here!" The roll of the 'r' sends a tickle through his spine.

"You didn't think I would show up?"

She throws her arms around his neck, kissing him. A suspended link, like the first time. Deeper, more familiar. The connection between them is solidified and real now. She knows that he really does care for her.

Gnat ducks under the railing, Hipslyn takes his hand while they proceed into the briskness that is a bitter evening in Raminia. The car is silver with retro Ropan styling, just as one would imagine.

"Who's is this?" he asks.

"My father's. They don't need it. He told me we could keep it while you are here."

"That's unexpected. We can go wherever we want now!"

"When I told them you were Omrikan, they got excited. They cannot wait to meet you," she explains. "First, we'll stay at my apartment, through the mountains."

"Can you make the whole drive? If not, we can get a room or I can do it."

"No, you flew your part of the journey. Now, I will drive you the rest of the way to me."

"Thanks," he says, pecking her forehead. "Let's go."

The car reminds him of a toy. It's almost impossible for him to find room. Manipulating his body, forcing it, he makes enough. He has never been in a vehicle with Hipslyn. Her driving is the opposite of the way she moves across Irfa with her feet. She's erratic, forceful, and never quite straight. Always wobbly between throttle and brake. Like she can't find her center. She's too elegant for a task so dirty as driving. Gnat doesn't say anything, it doesn't make him nervous, climbing. Descending from elevation, she goes much too fast on the ice through the curvy roads unguarded on the edges. He says something about her speed in the snow.

She replies, "This is my country, I know how to drive the passes."

He rubs his thumb across the top of her cheek. *Okay then, Hipslyn.* The current turn in the highway opens up to more lanes, the city has consumed the valley. Speed limits drop, and drop, and drop. Traffic gets thicker, heavier, groggier. Finally, they turn onto a short lane. She parks in a lot with too few spaces, the car barely fits.

This country had its own extreme socially motivated government, which still existed after Gnat was born. You can tell by the converted building Hipslyn lives in. All gray, in concrete. Every angle is ninety degrees, windows dark. No extravagance, no excess. The outside walls are stained with time, not cleaned since they were erected. An imposing structure, something between a prison and a barracks. Brutalist, in every sense of the word.

The entrance is opened with a key. A second door, a second lock. Up four flights of steps, no elevator. A third key opens her apartment. It's a tight, tidy space. The same angles, the same mute colors. A functional kitchen and bathroom. A window, no porch to relax. Hipslyn doesn't know what to expect, and seems shy. Maybe embarrassed.

"What do you think of this?" she asks.

He lowers his bag to the floor. "I think I've never been so excited in my life to see someone or be somewhere new. Thank you for letting me come."

"Gnat, you can stay as long as you want. I didn't know if you'd dislike it, because…"

"It's different from Omrika? No way. That's what makes it so great, we aren't there. We are here. Together, now," he answers. "I'm ready. For you, for this place. To make memories together."

"Me too, Gnat. I want to know what we can be," she says, moving over to him, holding the sides of his jacket. "Kiss me."

He very much enjoys waking up to her arm across him, her face nuzzled on his shoulder the next morning. She beams at him. While getting ready, he washes himself in a way he's never experienced. A bathtub, with a nozzle on a handle and no curtain. You must sit in the tub and rinse, not spilling on the floor.

First, to the mall. It's the same as any big shopping center in Omrika, busy for the vacation season. There are many stores familiar to him, with different names than those he's used to. Hipslyn buys some things for traveling to her parent's house. Gnat exchanges some currency at the bank. Then, the food court. Whatever ethnic greasy food you desire. Most counters are moderately occupied by guests, some have none whatsoever. At the far end, a crowd of at least fifty people huddles.

"What's that?" he wonders.

She starts to laugh. "You might know, let's go see…"

He deciphers the sign. The most famous chicken franchise from the Midwest, here in Raminia.

"No way! I don't want that! I can get it at home!" he exclaims.

"Read the menu, it isn't like yours. It's better," she protests. "It's what I want."

The offerings are much different. He nods to her, in self-assurance.

"Spicy wings? I'm in."

After they begin to eat, he stops. "This is better here than in Omrika, how is that possible?"

"I told you. No matter when you come here, the line is always long. We enjoy your chicken, that we do better. Most people don't know, I do. I've had it on both continents," she gloats.

"Now I've had it both places, I can agree. People in Oia won't believe me, though."

She giggles. "Omrikans will never admit to being second place, will they?"

"Ugh, no! The sad part is they don't understand we are much lower than second in the scheme of things," Gnat answers.

"We are going to a hookah bar later. Tomorrow night, you'll meet my best friend Ta'it and her boyfriend Divi for dinner and drinks. Are you still tired?"

"Jetlag," he says, annoyed. "I'll be fine."

She's telling him about places they can visit. It's past mealtime and getting more crowded, so they throw the trash out and head to the car. The parking garage is a madhouse. After a silent shuffle through traffic, liberation is reached. They're on their way. Hipslyn and Gnat. Together. He notices a big difference, almost immediately, in the architecture. This place has a much more expansive history than his country. The socialist, somber buildings are plentiful. Also, there are many new structures. Futuristic, trying to rocket above the fog of the recent past into the modern world. On the other side, things built a thousand spans ago, some with nothing but a trinket shop for tourists or a fast-food chain on the ground floor. There are many statues cast in bronze or carved from marble. Passing through the center of the city, a group of people stands protesting outside what seems to be a palace.

"What's that?" he asks her, again.

She responds, "Something like the city hall, to you. They are protesting a recently passed law."

"Which is?"

"Any politician is now allowed to embezzle a certain amount of funds and not be arrested. Our government is very corrupt. Maybe the worst in the world."

"What is protesting going to do? Did the people elect these officials?"

"Yes," she answers.

"The people gave them the power and expected them to do right with it? Haven't we learned through history that never happens?"

"What can you do? The system is there, you can't escape it."

"You can decide not to subscribe, to live outside of it," says Gnat.

"These people are standing up for what they believe. I think that's okay. You can't judge them for that."

He thinks for a moment. He doesn't want to fight with her. "So you vote to give somebody the power to do what they want, then turn around and protest them for using that power whatever way they see fit?"

Hipslyn presses the accelerator. "You vote in the people you think will represent you the way you want them to."

"And that opinion you have of them is based on what they say to the media, right? None of these politicians are legally held to any promises they make?"

"No. But the people can show that they aren't okay with it, hence the protest," she says.

Gnat replies, "They are already in office, there's nothing they can do until the next election. They made the choice; they can't be mad about it now. The people have to live with it."

"And just be taken advantage of? You have to stand up for yourself!"

"Isn't standing for nothing, something, Hipslyn?"

"What?"

"I mean," he continues, "not registering. Not consenting, or pitching in. Letting the policies burn out. Governments don't nourish themselves. Their only power comes from input. What happens if nobody votes? If nobody pays taxes? What if every person said, 'no, we aren't doing this anymore,' and goes to live quietly on their own? Standing up for nothing."

The car rests at a stop light. She responds, "That's never going to happen, is it?"

"No, I don't believe so. People are too concerned with petty differences to put energy toward making things different. It is possible, conceptually, though. Human emotion is what makes it impossible."

"Gnat, you can't say do nothing and things will get better."

"I'm not. Think of being a rebel without a cause, because you don't see and don't care how to see. That's something. What about being a rebel *with* a cause? That *cause* being not engaging, ever, based on your knowledge and understanding of human nature?"

"Come on, that doesn't make any sense," Hipslyn argues.

"Sure, it does. The first implies nothing. The second is a conscious choice," he answers.

The pair sits in the lot at the apartment. "Okay, I'm cold. I'm going inside. Are you coming?"

He smirks. "Of course, why wouldn't I? Did I upset you?"

"You came to spend time with me, not debate politics. We should be warm in my bed watching a movie, not this, Gnat."

He fades away, then replies to her, "I get lost in my head, you know this. In my own realizations, where I live, up in here." He points at his brain.

"I know, live here with me, while I have you, please..."

"It's always half-moons and half-certainties, with me, isn't it?" He winks at her. "You pick the movie."

"Thank you." She gets out of the car, he moves to hold her hand. Up the steps with three separate keys to a science fiction movie about wars on other planets. When it is over, he drifts off, soon after she brings him back.

"Are you ready to go to have a smoke and get some tea?"

Hipslyn is wearing a green parka with fake fur and jeans. She has suede boots to match the color of the fur around the inside of her hood, which is up.

"You resemble a dog musher, a pretty one. Let's go," he replies.

"What flavor do you like?" she asks.

"Hookah?" Gnat recalls the times he went with his friends during his teenage spans, "Grape mint."

"Oh, never had that."

"Probably pairs nicely with green tea," he says.

It's an old establishment, turned into something of a den. An upscale crack house, more or less. It's dim, each room is decorated in a different fashion, the ambience altered as you pass through the spaces. They end up in a room with paper stars of blue or purple hanging from the ceiling and walls. They're alone. It turns out that the combination of grape, mint, and green tea does work.

"Why did you come, Gnat?" The hookah's handle is hanging from the corner of Hipslyn's lip.

"The timing was right. We are both in between things."

"Just that?"

"Hmm..." He pulls the tip of his nose with his first finger and thumb. "No, I've thought about you a lot. I didn't want to miss seeing what happens. I couldn't let a plane ride be the thing that kept us from doing that."

"I have to finish studying, you know. That's another two spans," Hipslyn says. "There are Omrikan speaking universities here that you could attend for free..."

"It's something to think about. Let's see how this visit goes, first. I want to enjoy you with no pressure for it to be anything now. I'm here, aren't I? That should show you enough."

She nods. "It does."

Following tea and the demise of the smoking octopus on the table, they exit slowly, arms interlocking.

"I'm glad you are here, Gnat. I was sorry our time got cut short in Montisa. That man wouldn't speak to me the rest of the season."

"Who, that hillbilly guide?" he asks.

"Yes. I laughed in my head every time he went past. He showed his real colors. Is that how you say it?"

"True colors," he replies, "Don't think about him. He's not worth the thought. There are millions of dragoons exactly the same as him across that country of mine."

"All over Irfa," she concludes. "Can we watch the next movie in the series before sleeping?"

"We can. No promises I'll make it to the end."

"I hope that you like Ta'it. She has been my best friend since I was a child."

"I'm sure I will," he assures her.

They watch the movie. She curls up in the same spot that she had the night before. Gnat sleeps hard. The upside is that when they wake the next morning, he's on the correct schedule. At the mall again, he tries the burger. His father was right; they aren't the same outside of Omrika. She calls Ta'it to make plans, while he sits patiently, watching people. Another difference, in the humans here. He's unsure what to call it, until a realization hits him. They're unmotivated. Moving along because that's the expectation, not the desire. She finishes the call, more excited than usual.

She explains, "We need to get ready to meet them. We'll take the bus so we don't have to drive."

"Sounds like a plan."

The sun is going down. He's clothed no differently than normal. She wears a dress with thick leggings underneath. Her hair is down, straightened. They jump through the rear door of the bus to avoid paying.

"Only four stops," she justifies.

Gnat and Hipslyn hop off, head down an alley, and across a park. It's his kind of place, a brick dive at the end of a street by itself. Entering, the smell of stale alcohol hits them. Maybe fifteen tables are strewn about the place, plus twenty or so seats at the bar.

"There they are." She points.

Ta'it has blonde hair, dyed different colors on the tips. She is much taller than Hipslyn, and heavier. Not in a sloppy way, just on a bigger frame. Divi is overweight and bald, with an enormous brown beard. They both gleam and wave.

"Hey Hipslyn," Divi stands to shake Gnat's hand. "Gnat, so good to meet you. Please join us."

"Thank you," Gnat says. "I'm glad to be here."

"Gnat, what do you drink?" Ta'it asks. "We got our first without you, sorry."

"It's fine, no worries," Gnat answers. "I like anything with alcohol."

Hipslyn nudges him with her arm. "Stop it, be serious, Gnat."

"Ha! I'll probably drink dark liquor if they have it. And something local. Divi can recommend."

"I surely can, follow me. I know what Hipslyn wants already," Divi says.

"White wine," Gnat says, both men chuckle conspiratorially.

They squeeze their way through everyone to a line. On the television above the bar, a game is being played. One in which touching with the ball your hands is against the rules. Players must use their legs and feet.

"Do you fancy this sport, Gnat?" Divi asks.

"It's new to Omrika. The first organized teams didn't start in my town until I was in school already."

"You played?"

"I did, not for long. Maybe until I was twelve or thirteen," he replies.

Divi responds, "I played through high school, it's the biggest game around here, you know."

"Oh, I know. When the Irfa cup came through Oia in my teenage spans, my mother took us to watch. She's a big fan."

"You like to watch professional then, who's your team? Mine is Knighton," he perks up.

"I watch when it's on, occasionally. I don't follow any specific team. I have a problem with the way the game is played, now..."

"Oh, what's that? Not enough points scored? I know you Om-rikans like high scoring games, it keeps things exciting."

"No, not that. The gameplay itself."

Divi cringes. "What about it?"

"I see a correlation between the way players try to manipulate the rules and the way people find loopholes in the law to get away with things. Half the game is acting to draw a foul, to get a penalty kick or better ball placement. That's not talent, it's con-artistry."

"Well!" he exclaims. "Anything you can do to get ahead, you should."

Gnat replies, "That's the point. In a game, it's your best against the other man's best. The rules are there to keep it equal, so no one has an advantage outside of ability. The same way the law was originally written to protect you from the worst in others. Now it's written to protect you from yourself, and the rich from the poor. The rules keep changing to make it easier for the weaker player to be equal to the better. That's not something I care to watch, impassioned influence over objective principle. It's a study through sport of how the rules in society have become nothing but a straitjacket on the people."

"It's a game, you shouldn't read into it so deeply, Gnat."

"Things filter from the top to the bottom and permeate all levels of existence with time, once introduced. I don't think recognition is a bad thing," Gnat answers.

The bartender comes, Divi orders. "First round is on me, you traveled a long way to see us. We'll speak more later. Let's have fun with the girls first."

"Alright, thank you."

They return to the table. The girls are laughing. The old friends didn't even notice the boys were away. Another lesson Gnat learns, Raminians can drink. Round after round, even Hipslyn keeps up.

He stays behind as they go outside for cigarettes. Peering into the glass he holds, swirling it slowly, Gnat tries to find something within. The answer in the bottle, so many quests to find it through the spans. None have succeeded. None will. *That in itself may be the answer.* Someone drops into a seat at the table. Divi. They are beyond drunk, enough to cross lines that shouldn't be crossed at a first meeting.

"It seems that Hipslyn really likes you, from what she's told Ta'it," says Divi, slurring. "Where did you meet again?"

"At a place we were both working in Montisa this past tourist season. She was doing housekeeping; I was the bartender. She would come in and have her staff drink with me every night."

"An Omrikan bartender? Why would she go for that?"

"I'm not a bartender, Divi, I was tending bar at the time. What's *that?*" Gnat furrows his brow in amusement.

"You're Omrikan! The evil of Irfa, the scourge! The rapists of everything else! You think you're better, that it's all for you..." Divi hiccups.

"Would you think that, after meeting me? Or is it what you saw on television?"

"Everyone knows it already. Nobody needs to tell us, Gnat."

"You think I'm evil? Me, personally? The people in Omrika think Raminia and Muusman are dangerous war-zones filled with scam artists, illegal weapons, and terrorists. Would you agree with that?" Gnat asks him.

"No, that's not true. You know this!"

"Right, because I am here to see it for myself. Have you been to Omrika?"

"No, I don't want to go there. Why would I want to?"

"I came here to let the people and culture show me what it really is, outside of what anyone says. Yet you want to judge me based on what you've heard and not seen. The same way Omrika does. If one of us is acting Omrikan, it's you. You're being close-minded and afraid of what you don't understand."

"That's not true, everybody knows..." he trails off as the girls return, then continues, "An Omrikan, Hipslyn? Really? Montisa must have warped your mind."

A conversation goes on between the three Raminians in their native tongue, which Gnat understands none of. He silently finishes his drink, holding back a grin the best he can. After quite a long discussion, Ta'it pulls Divi up.

"I'm so sorry, Gnat. He's had too much. He doesn't want you to be uncomfortable, he gets like this sometimes." she says.

"No worries, Ta'it. Really, don't feel bad. I'm sure he didn't mean it. Like you said, he's had too much."

Hipslyn joins in. "Get him home safe. We'll see you later, for a real party. With dancing. That way we don't have to speak about cultural differences."

"Yeah, alright. Goodnight, try to enjoy it. I feel bad we ruined some of it."

"Stop, it was still great to meet you. We'll see you again before I leave, I'm sure," Gnat calls over the noise of the bar, as Ta'it and Divi go out the door.

"Gnat, I didn't know he was going to be that way. I apologize if he made you feel out of place." Hipslyn says, holding his arm, sitting on her knees beside him on the bench.

"Foreign guys get emasculated when they meet a man that comes from the best place on Irfa," he teases, nudging her as she did to him earlier.

She hits his arm, grinning. "Quit it. Are you fine, really? I hope you don't dislike them now."

"No way, I'm perfect. I'm in a bar with the most beautiful woman present," he answers.

"Gnat!" She nuzzles his cheek, drunkenly.

"You know," he continues, "it's nothing to get mad about. It always comes down to the same thing."

"What's that, Zen master?" she jokes.

"There are two types of people in the world. Those who talk too much, and those who don't know they talk too much."

"Which are you?"

"I haven't decided yet. But I don't think I talk too much."

"Gnat, you're silly. Get me to my apartment safely. You are the man, it's your job."

"Let's get out of here."

He navigates his way to the bus stop the best he can, then realizes that it has stopped running.

"Should we camp in the phone booth?" Gnat asks her facetiously. She giggles. He hails a cab and Hipslyn gives the driver the address.

In her room, they both fall on the bed in their clothes and are out for the night. He stirs later on. They weren't sleeping, just in an alcohol-fueled hibernation. He takes off her shoes and jacket, putting her under the covers and a pillow under her head. He does the same for himself, bringing her close to him. Now he sleeps peacefully. No dreams. No voices. Gnat and Hipslyn. Drunk and infatuated with one another.

The trip to her parents in Sav is tomorrow, they've been bumming around Curesti for more cycles than needed. He can tell that Hipslyn is nervous about him meeting her parents, she is getting shorter and shorter with Gnat every moment.

"You need to trim your beard before we go," she scolds, "You need to look nice when we show up. We need to go and get you some clothes, you always wear the same thing."

"No, I'm fine wearing my clothes. Take me or leave me, I'm not putting on heirs for your family. That's false advertising," he retorts, eyebrows raised. "They will like me for the same reasons you do, I'm myself. Stop worrying, Hipslyn."

She stomps into the kitchen as he lays on the bed. An answer isn't received, so Gnat rolls over and starts to write in his journal. It's not a mundane account of what he has done. More realizations that come out of his experiences. Raminia has many of its own intricacies. The people, their culture. The government, their oppression. Hipslyn returns after a long while, saying nothing. She's on the bed next to him.

"Are you ready for the drive to Sav? It's quite a long one," she finally asks. The argument about his appearance that had almost started has been vanquished.

"I wish I could drive. I feel bad that you have to, but my license isn't valid here. I could just do it anyway, you know."

"No, I'll do it. Everything is opposite to Omrika. Just talk to me so the trip passes quickly. We'll be there with enough time to walk around after we check in somewhere," says Hipslyn. "Sav is the most historical city in Raminia, almost untouched for a thousand spans. There are many things to see. The snow makes everything more beautiful in the glow of the gas streetlights."

"I can't wait," Gnat assures her. "An End of Span season to remember, I'm sure. I've never seen anything like this country before."

She rubs his hair, almost like petting a dog. "I am glad you're here for it."

The trip to Sav is on a highway with a single lane in each direction. Out of the city, the land is soft hills of blue, dusted with white. Ice crystals atop the scrub and blades reflect the world, a pathway drawn for the blasts of frozen air to follow. The ruins of fortresses from the important conflicts of this continent are planted sparingly through Gnat's passing focus. Men lost, their choices and beliefs forgotten, imaginary lines redrawn at dozens of occasions since their deaths at the hands of one another. The road flows alongside a river, the latter has a history that will far supersede the life of this man-made pass. They stop and visit an ancient barracks to stretch their muscles, climbing to the peak of the mountain it sits upon. An outlook of desolate, barren land encapsulated in frost. She looks at him, and he back, blankly. Wordlessly, in silence they watch each other's breath try to heat the environment around them, only to be condensed as everything else.

Sav comes into view after another trio of turns along the river, the blueprint to the fastest route across the land for the men who built this route. Tall spires in black rise out of the dirt, reaching for the sky with delicate fingers carved from stone. Steeples, reaching for the thing they promise those who enter. Eternal existence exempted from damnation. He can see the lights, more dirty than pure. The outcome of the combustion of gasses in the antique glass globes, not the artificiality of electricity. A haze wraps itself around the town, people are burning wood and coal inside to keep warm.

"There it is," Hipslyn says. She seems dazed from the drive. "Almost done."

"I could use a blanket, pillow, and a girl keeping me warm after we get our room," he replies.

"Deal. I'm sleepy, a quick nap won't hurt. We don't have to see my parents until tomorrow, anyway."

After rolling into town, the task of finding accommodation is over before he has to think about it. The room is cozy, warm, and clean; exactly what they need for solid rest. Waking time will be busy and spent outside or with Hipslyn's parents.

They are without an automobile, on foot. She takes him to a bakery within a cobblestone corridor. It isn't big enough for vehicles, only people or bicycles. Ribbons, bells, statues of creatures, boughs of evergreen, and the natural snow of Irfa adorn everything in view. They eat while strolling and arrive at the biggest spire in town. The Black Shrine, as it's called. A man is selling steamed chocolate and spiced tea in front of a bonfire on the main square. Others are releasing miniature hot air balloons to the atmosphere, powered by candles and wishes. Gnat buys her a tea, himself a balloon. He opens it, places the candle inside and releases it to the sky. He puts his arm around her, as they watch it float away to some undiscovered magical place. This is his desire for the gliding lamp, to escape the existence he is caught in, somehow.

"What did you wish for?" she asks.

He answers, "No wishes. I told it that I'm grateful to be here with you."

After returning to their room, he undresses down to his shirt and boxers getting under the covers. Hipslyn is brushing her teeth, he already completed that chore. He feels decompressed. Not comfortable, far from that. However, the thought of Omrika isn't soothing either. Actually, it isn't present. He rolls onto his side, the sounds of Hipslyn escaping him as she lies down taking her half of the blankets along with some of his.

"Are you ready to meet them?" she whispers.

Gnat doesn't answer, he's already asleep.

As Hipslyn exits her morning shower, Gnat enters. It will most assuredly take Hipslyn longer to get ready than him. The sunrise was spent watching snow fall out the window of a local pub. He'd had a few drinks with no food. Hipslyn's mother has been preparing dinner for a cycle. Gnat thought it'd be best to arrive on an empty stomach. By the time he's dried and dressed, Hipslyn is doing her make-up.

"Are you anxious, Gnat?"

He grins. "No, are you?"

"I was before we drove here, but not anymore. They are *my* parents, after all. They will see the same things in you that I do."

"And you're bringing an Omrikan boy to their home for the End of Span." He snickers.

"I'll bet they never thought this would happen." She laughs. "A loon I met in the wilderness, in Raminia with me."

She's tying her shoes.

"Are we off, now? Finally?" he jokes again.

"Be on your best behavior. No debates. Just normal things about home, things you like to do, okay?"

"Things I like to do?" he questions.

"Yes, your hobbies."

"I only really have one, though."

"That's enough," she replies.

"It's debate, Hipslyn. Don't worry, parents never dislike me. I've got this."

She sighs. "Be nice. Come on."

A quick jaunt through the main square of town, and over a field of mossy dirt. More of the concrete buildings of the past repurposed to house the members of a new generation. Hipslyn rings the buzzer to her parent's flat, a count to three and the front door shocks itself open. They live on the fifth floor. Up the steps, no elevators here.

Her mother and father are waiting in the hallway as their daughter and the foreigner approach.

"Hipslyn, you're early. The food is not ready yet," her father says. His job required him to learn the language of business, Omrikan.

"It's alright, it doesn't have to be perfect. You can give Gnat a tour of the apartment," she replies.

Her mother hugs her, repeating the greeting with him. She speaks some Omrikan, just enough to hold a basic conversation.

Hipslyn gets her looks from her mother; they are the same person in different stages of the life cycle.

"Greetings, Gnat. I am Mikla. We are glad to have you here." She beams. "I cooked for you."

"I hear you are quite the chef," Gnat answers humbly. "I am so flattered you have done this for me. I can't wait for you to tell me what everything is."

He turns to the father, a shorter man with broad shoulders. He carries himself with dignity, a man that seems he would stand by his word no matter what the cost. *He's already earned my respect.*

"I am Hipslyn's father, Julyen. She has told us many things of you. I hope to discuss your culture and government," he says, shaking Gnat's hand. "Come in. Welcome. Make yourself comfortable, please."

The flat is simple and quaint. It seems that everything has a place, no excess exists in this home. If something doesn't serve a purpose, it is removed. The kitchen is aglow with the heat from simmering cook fires. The aromas of ambrosian spices and delicacies unknown to Gnat waft through the entire place. The living room has a large table on one side, presumably where they will eat. The side nearer to him has a couch and some chairs next to a television. A guitar rests against the table in the corner. On the walls, paintings hang. One is of a girl that looks suspiciously like Hipslyn.

"Who did the paintings?" Gnat asks the room.

"I did, it's a hobby of mine," replies Julyen. "I wish it could have been my job, this is what I enjoy doing most."

"You are very talented, really," Gnat says in honesty. He is inspecting each of them. Landscapes; one of the city, one of the same plains Gnat and Hipslyn traveled through to get here. A self-portrait, the study of flowers in a vase. Then, a canvas completed in dots. A bright sun in a clear sky, a sailboat, moving windward next to a beach.

"You know, this is my favorite. My biggest dream is living on a sailboat, going wherever the wind takes me," Gnat says to the artist. "You too, Julyen?"

"It is always the desire of a man to go places he cannot see yet. I wanted to drift away, on that exact boat. It's what I was imagining when I painted it. In some way, I did."

"Yes, I know what you mean," Gnat says, riding the swell in his own mind, for a flash. Julyen has taken him there with the stroke of his brush.

"It's yours," Julyen decides.

"What?!" cries Hipslyn.

"This painting is Gnat's now. He understands where it takes you. Now he can go whenever he likes."

"Dad, you've never given anybody a painting before!" Hipslyn exclaims.

"You don't have to give me the painting, Julyen," Gnat interjects, softly.

"I already have, it's done. I will send it to you, in Omrika. Give me the address. I insist, that's final," Julyen responds, not angrily, forcefully.

"I'm honored. It will always hang on the wall wherever I go. Thank you for this," Gnat responds.

In almost perfect timing, Mikla enters and places the first dish on the table.

"Time to eat," she says, then says something in Raminian to Hipslyn.

"She says I have to serve you first," she tells Gnat.

It turns out that Mikla is also an artist, through and through. What follows is the best meal that Gnat has ever eaten. There are three different types of roe, sausages handmade with intestine in the old way. Dried meats and cheeses are paired on a plate with olives. Some things are aged, some are mixed with lava ash. The center-piece, a turkey. Cooked to perfection in mirepoix and its own fat.

Julyen also makes his own traditional Raminian spirits, by dessert Gnat has four different types of booze in front of him. *When in Raminia...*

Of course, they speak of nationalism, the decline of these beliefs. Omrika, the opportunity there. The private economy, the freedom to do whatever you wish. At some point Hipslyn hands Gnat the guitar. He plays, they listen. Julyen pulls the painting of the sailboat off the wall, and writes a message on the back. A final salute to the acceptance of Gnat in his daughter's life. Laughing, understanding, mutual respect. A beautiful affair. As the younger pair prepare to depart, more goodbyes are had. Everyone has a full stomach and the warmth of alcohol running through their veins. This always leads to favorable outcomes from parents to their children. They will meet again soon. This isn't the last goodbye.

Strolling across the square, Gnat and Hipslyn hold hands. The temperature is low, they are too joyous to notice.

"I can't believe he gave you a painting," she says. "He's never given one to me or my mother! He hoards them, they are his prized possessions."

"He wants one to hang on the wall of a house on the other side of the planet. That makes sense," Gnat says, nonchalantly.

"Gnat, when we get back, I want you," she says.

"You've already got me!"

"No, I want you to take me. I want to be together in the way that we haven't yet."

He considers her proposal. "Are you positive? This drunken boy is who you choose?"

"Yes," she says, continuing on.

Later, they are lying naked under the blankets. Both stare at the ceiling, his right hand holds her left above the covers. Her hair is down, bedraggled, it doesn't seem natural for such a graceful being. He notices this, their eyes lock. The darkness in hers isn't reflecting the light behind him clearly. The daze of drinks is gone again, for the second time. Her gaze wanders again. They are both doubtlessly serene in the company of the other.

"I was thinking of the painting," Gnat says. "Imagine a man living on a sailboat. It's his existence. His universe, you could say. He's out at sea, separate. What of the flies born on this boat, way out there? They live, they die, the cycle continues onward. The boat is their planet. Their Irfa. Their truth, their understanding. Unaware other insects exist. Other boats. Other currents. Continents. Yet, if you asked these flies how to live, they would tell you without question, how to do it. The best way. The *right* way. With no comprehension or wonder about things outside of themselves. I see humans much this way. Drifting on a rock. Through nothing. Self-important bacteria, growing. For this purpose and no other."

The air stays still between them while she thinks about what he has said, about what he means to her.

She responds, "Your mind is amazing to me, Gnat. I can see what you're saying, I've done it myself. I didn't know that any Omrikan would think the way that you do, not ever. Although I hadn't been there yet, like you were saying to Divi. I can't believe that you are here, still. That a Raminian girl like me would be enough for you. That I would be anything at all. But now I do, and I know you are also. To me."

"What's to come is unknown," he says. "I feel this thing between us. Let's keep feeling it, not trying to define it. We still have time together. Now is the moment for sleeping."

"I'll see you tomorrow, Gnat."

"Yes," he answers, nodding, "you will."

He listens to her breathing slow, and level out to give her the oxygen needed for rest and rejuvenating muscles. It's pitch black, he stares in the direction of the ceiling, which he cannot see.

Is this what I want? Remembering what his mother had said, that he isn't ready.

Isn't there a saying? The grass is always greener on the other side. People always want what they don't have. When I go home, friends and family sometimes say they are jealous of the life I live. They don't understand that stress is simply stress. It's all the same. Some people worry about how they are going to pay their mortgage, others worry about where the next meal is coming from. The circumstances of the anxiety don't make a difference. Do I want to be with someone forever? The same always? Or am I living exactly the life I want to be living?

There are only two women that have ever meant anything to me. There's Addie. The problem was I tried to fix her, when I am broken myself. The other is Hipslyn, who understands me on a level that no one else has. In essence, she knows me. She knows that I'm broken, she knows that I'm searching. Is this enough for me? If there's any doubt, which I have, does that make it not correct? Or is it like my mother said, you have to work through the differences and doubts? Is this something that I am willing to try? With Addie, it wasn't; I hurt her. I changed her in a way that she can't change back. With Hipslyn, maybe I am willing. But at the risk of destroying some part of her innocence?

He turns in her direction, next to him. Again, he can't see her, but feel her. He can hear her breath, steadily. The word he thinks of most often with her. *Graceful.*

"We shall see," Gnat whispers to himself, ending such an enlightening happening.

"Wake up," Hipslyn demands, in underwear and nothing else. They have crossed a line that cannot be uncrossed.

"Good morning, wonderful," he returns. *She truly is.* "What's the plan? I'm at your mercy."

"We are going to a rave when it gets dark."

Gnat perks up. "A real Raminian rave?"

"Yes, can you handle it?"

"What? Why haven't you told me about this? Of course, I can," he replies, almost giddy.

"They have to be spontaneous, so the authorities don't find out. Ta'it sent me a message, her and Divi drove to Sav."

"Do I have to be lectured about how evil I am again? Or can we have fun?"

"There will be hundreds of people, probably. The DJ is famous here. We may not even see them."

"These Raminian raves are almost like a myth in Omrika. A legendary undertaking." Gnat shoots up. "I'll get ready, we need to get our energy up! We may be awake until morning."

"That's not a question, we will be up until tomorrow." Eyebrows raised. "I have to go meet Ta'it to pick up some... substances. It's best that you stay here."

Gnat lays his head back onto the pillow. "I understand. You go. I'll be here."

***

It's evening, the time has come. Hipslyn wears a black dress, cut halfway between her waist and knees with no straps. She uses black eye liner to create swooping lines from the corners of her eyes, coating them with golden sparkles. Like a warrior ready for battle, showered in mysticism.

"Ready?" the fete-fairy asks.

"Always. Won't you be chilly?"

"No, I'm calling a taxi. Here, take these." She hands him pills, imprinted with silhouettes of naked women. "Wash them down with this," she says, handing him a drink, and doing the same.

"I've never seen you so excited, Hipslyn."

She gives him a playful nudge. "Tell me that again after we've danced our way into a new cycle."

Hipslyn guides him through the maze of a manufacturing block, into the stinging dusk. His hands feel light. There's a man playing security guard at a door. She gives him some cash and he lets them pass into a hallway barely wide enough for one. The lights are almost nonexistent, only enough to see outlines. Then he hears it. The thump of bass through massive unseen speakers. It's in his head, the beat becomes his pulse, the flow of blood through his veins is driven by it. Holding Hipslyn's hand, she pulls him along. Her pupils are wider and darker than normal. She stops and leans up to kiss him, putting her face against his. It feels as if she is melting into him, they become a single being. She starts to giggle, Hipslyn feels it too. They are both in it now. The beat is still prevalent, low and overpowering. A blockade of metal stands in front of them.

"If we get separated, don't forget your phone, text me. We won't be able to hear," she says, "Ready?"

"Let's go," he replies, unsure in his mind.

Hipslyn pushes the bar of the door down and as it opens, a tornado of sound comes through. The lights are blinding, swirling. The bass is at the bottom of many layers of mid and treble tracks which were not audible outside the room. He steps forward, seeing the pedestal with the wizard creating this cacophony of brilliance. What seems like an innumerable amount of people bounce in harmony. He's taken aback. His hearing is drowned out. In actuality, every sense is frazzled. The vibration is in his literal consciousness, controlling him. Hipslyn pushes into the crowd, as he follows, someone hands him a drink and he sculls it to empty. *Safe? Who cares?*

The next span is a blur in the quest for release. Dancing, touching, everyone is together. Everybody is open. Lost to the music. Lost within themselves, found again in the glance of a stranger. His hand is taken again by his partner, guiding him off the floor and outside. A group of other ravers is smoking cigarettes. Some tobacco, some from dreamland.

"Can I have one?" Gnat asks.

"Of course," she gives him a cigarette, withholding the lighter, "Take these first."

Hipslyn hands him another duo of pills. He takes them without a word then lights the tobacco. He needs to stabilize himself with it. To focus. *To balance.* It's futile, it seems, as he takes a long drag. Hipslyn brings a flask out of her waistline.

"Where did this come from? I didn't know you were like this!" he exclaims.

"You can't reveal everything at once, you know."

"Isn't that the truth," Gnat states, mostly to himself. "Go back in?"

"We shall."

He flicks the butt against the wall, ashes flying off trace themselves to nothing. A second wave of joy and coherence so deep you can't remember the feeling afterward. It has ended, her hand his guide to the mundane level of reality in which they are forced to exist. No words, only movement. The first rays of light can be seen if you study closely. They're in the apartment after what seems like the single frame of a film, frozen in vision.

They shower together, she leaves him under the nozzle. Water falls on his face numbing the nerves of his nose. What a happening.

Why is this criticized by everyone? Or is it society? Gnat's eyes open as he leans away.

It is society. Partying is demeaned because it's realizing and acting on your animal instincts. Gluttony, sex, drugs. Always looking for the next high. The system can't gain from you if you don't suppress your wild self and become a robot...

The flow stops suddenly and Gnat sharply focuses on Hipslyn.

"I know you. Don't let your mind run. I'd not like to see the places it goes. You think too much. We are high. Come to bed," she says, "Hurry up."

He's exposed, wet, isolated. He dries himself. In bed, he puts his arm around her.

"What am I going to do with you, Hipslyn? A girl that I can take home *and* take to an underground party. You babysat me. Usually I do that. Thanks for these memories."

Her only reply is, "Say you'll take me home again."

They start to melt into one another, giggling...

"Any more big adventures for us while I'm here?" he prods. He has a headache focused between his eyebrows. The brightness of morning doesn't help.

"A few. Start of Span is coming. Another excuse for a party. Why?"

"Just wondering. I haven't experienced anything like that in a long time. Trying to recover is brutal."

She speaks quietly, "Maybe you're getting old, did you think about that?"

"Whoa, hold on. I'm seventeen in my head. That's never going to change."

"Your mind and body are separate things. They don't always keep up with each other, sadly."

"Maybe I'll find a way," he interjects. "Cognitively being the wisest seventeen spans-old, dissolving the concept of physical time."

She giggles. "You are dreaming. Always in your head, aren't you?"

"Things make sense in here," he says, pressing the epicenter of the ache currently held within his skull.

"Have you thought about the future, with school or job or whatever?" She changes the subject.

"What would you have me do, Hipslyn?" Gnat questions, eyes low. A gentle stare with a hint of teasing. Or longing. Which, he's unsure.

"I have university to finish, I can't leave Raminia until then."

"You want me to be a part of your future?"

She takes a gulp of caffeine. "Is this something you've thought of?"

"I would have to learn Raminian. I could do that," he trails off. Giving himself up to the will of another is not a welcome feeling.

She replies quickly, "You could."

"Maybe pay rent for us upfront while you do your last span. I could teach Omrikan online or something. Play my music. Learn the language. When you graduate, we can go over to Omrika."

"You said a span, I have twice that almost before I'm done…" She trails off, sharing the same feelings as Gnat.

"You start school again fairly soon. I can go bum around some other countries while you do, find a job for another season. Save money, then come over when you start school next session. If I do that, we won't have to ever worry about anything. The exchange rate is in my extreme favor living here."

Hipslyn hesitates, considering. "You know why my parents were so good to you?"

"I'm a nice guy?" he says, eyebrows raised, bracing for the coming insult. "What else could it be?"

"You're Omrikan. You can give me things that no one else can, by taking me there."

"If it's something you want when the time comes, I'll gladly do it. If you want to stay here, I'll learn the language. I have no ties. I can do anything that I feel like," he answers.

"I would be a tie," she says plainly.

"If I thought of you that way, I wouldn't be having this conversation. It's that easy."

She sighs. "It's not a deal, yet. I know what you are thinking. The same as me. I could see something happening when I am able to be that person. When school is over, and I have the time to grow with somebody else."

His stomach drops, mother's words crossing in front of his migraine. *You aren't ready.* Gnat starts to think about growing with someone else. Into somebody else. Like the sensation of the pills, but statically. Forever. It scares him. He pushes the thoughts out and away. Then he sees her. She's beautiful. *Beautiful.* So much his equal, in so many ways.

"I agree, it's there to pick up when it's right," he answers.

With this, empty glasses are left on a vacant table. They're closer now, after this conversation in a café. Closer is the incorrect word, possibly. Transparent. They each know what the other wants, this may not be a fling. There is an end in sight which only leads to another beginning. The *last* beginning, as both have been told since birth, the only time it matters.

They travel to a castle that belonged to a certain ruler who became legend; an undead seducer of the night. A food festival on the streets of Sav. Gnat sleeps very heavily after gorging the delicacies of the region. His diet forgotten throughout the entire experience, not regrettably. Hipslyn is taking him to a special place created half by humans, half by millions of spans of heat and pressure from inside the planet. An abandoned salt mine, converted into a mix of museum and amusement park.

She drives in the lot and parks. They set off to explore these mysterious caverns. After a few dozen steps, Hipslyn starts to run to the car.

"Gnat! Get in the car! Hurry!" She's frightened. He has never heard the sound of fear in her voice. Now he knows its tone.

Without saying anything, he runs and closes the door right after she secures the driver's side.

"What is it?" he asks prematurely, then catches movement coming across the front of the mine.

Dogs. Mangy, scruffy, wild dogs. In a pack of a dozen domesticated breeds. Some large, some not. They are barking, growling. Searching for food.

"Hipslyn, what is it?" he repeats. He sees the dogs, but doesn't understand.

"Stray dogs. They're a huge issue. People can't afford to feed their pets, so they drive them out to the country and let them fend for themselves. They form packs. They attack people, they've eaten some children. It doesn't happen in the city. Just out here in the grassland."

"No way. That's wild. No pun intended," Gnat says, staring in bewilderment as the mob moves opposite from where they appeared. No food is to be had here, interest lost.

"Man inbreeds wolves for thousands of spans to create the family dog, trying to control forces they don't understand. Creating mutants and what *seems* like submissive genes throughout an entire species. At some point man loses control, casts the animals to the field, and what happens? They revert straight to what they are. Predators, pack hunters. That stuff about man's best friend is a farce. The dog is there to get an easy meal. Take that away, it turns *you* into the meal."

"Silly humans," she adds, "You don't have this problem in Omrika?"

"No way. Omrikans care more about dogs than their fellow man starving on the street."

"I'm tiny. I have to watch out, they could get me," she says. "I've been chased a few times. Luckily dogs can't climb trees."

"A group like that would get me too, I think," says Gnat. "Don't feel bad about it."

The ticket seller throws a passing comment about how glad she was they made it to the car... a friend lost a young child to wild dogs... the government should do something... it isn't right...

The flight of steps downward is narrow, the space between planks too wide. No sense of safety or comfort is offered by this path. These stairs were cut purposefully with the thought of using less material. To save on the budget, not resources. The void underground is enormous. It's almost unfathomable to the brain that an air bubble this large could lay underground. Thoughts of how many of these pockets exist and how massive the Irfa is run across the imagination as you take it in. The air is wet, not just damp. You almost feel as if you are breathing water, yet it's warm. The way you feel in a living room on a cold night blanketed in front of a fire. The color brown, never favored. Here, however, magnificent. At the bottom, a pool fed by what appears to be innumerable rock turrets hanging from the ceiling. The water is pure, dark, untouched by chemical or animal. Rings of gold and orange line its edges. On the far side some carnival games are laid out.

"I'll beat you in all of them," she says, continuing down.

"Yeah, probably. If I let you," he throws back.

She does beat him at everything, except one. Throwing a ball through the hole on a piece of plywood, painted like some sort of cave monster. He knocks its teeth out.

They start the long climb to where life thrives. While driving temperatures are low enough for frost crystals to form on the windshield, reflections of their existences glimmer as they cling to the glass under speed. His hand is resting on hers the entire ride, while hers grasps the shift knob. He asks if she ever considered something like this would happen, him being here, before leaving for Montisa to work.

"No, never," she answers.

***

Ta'it's friend works at the hostel where everyone is meeting for the Start of Span party later. Events are planned on the city square, they'll drink beforehand. He nodded as Hipslyn explained all of this at an Omrikan diner. *I'm just along for the ride.* The diner, however, isn't anything near authentic.

"Maybe I should open a restaurant here, it would be successful. I could do justice to the food from my country. This is a disgrace. Ketchup on ribs? No, just... no," he says to her as she eats a burger that has beetroot and kale on it.

"It still tastes okay," Hipslyn retorts. "We'll go to the liquor store after this. Then I need to get ready. It's going to be mostly a quiet night, I think."

"We need a bottle of bubbly for the count down too, obviously."

"Obviously!" she agrees.

Hipslyn dressed more utilitarian than she had for the previous party, still in black, however. Only a blouse for this occasion. Jeans cover her legs, along with boots.

"I wanted to match you," she tells him as they arrive, fashionably late.

"I was going to say, your taste is better than ever before." He winks. "You've got to stay warm on a night like this."

"*You* need to keep me warm on a night like this." She jibes, "I'll be bouncing around with Ta'it. You meet new people. When we go to the square, we can be close again."

"Okay," he agrees. "I'll try to make some friends."

The accommodation is in a very old stone building. On the second floor, a balcony borders a central courtyard on the ground. About forty people are floating around the halls. He's offered best wishes for the coming span. He returns the greeting and tries to find his in. He sees a man in the garden below, surrounded by others at a picnic table. It seems they are having a decent conversation, judging by their body language. He sees Ta'it with Hipslyn talking to another girl. *That must be the other friend.* Some guys are hovering around the trio, watching the women as unassumingly as possible. He isn't jealous and doesn't hold a second thought about it.

As he steps onto the grass one of the people at the table glances at Gnat. He holds his drink in front of him, the same with the others. Gnat listens to their voices, to try and gauge how far they've descended into drunkenness. Sober, or close.

"Can I join you?"

The man closest to him slides over, creating a seat. "Please, do," he says in an Eastern Ropan accent. He's young, not more than twenty. As is the couple sitting across from him. The other man is older, maybe by ten spans.

"Thank you," Gnat accepts.

"No problem, I am Stifin, these are my friends, Dini'l and Ina. We are from Raminia, celebrating. And you?"

"I'm Omrikan. Gnat. Nice to meet you. I'm here with a girl, she's Raminian, around somewhere."

"Ah, that's delightful," Ina says with a grin.

The older male chimes in, "I'm Met, Montisan. Hey neighbor! I'm here attending seminary school. We were speaking about the ultimate goal of religion. Do you know what that is, Gnat?"

"Mind control?"

"Funny! No, it's peace. Within yourself and with others," Met answers, calmly.

Gnat smirks. "These institutions of *peace* aren't doing a very good job, are they? Isn't it bad manners to speak about religion when you first meet someone? Feelings get hurt…"

"I welcome debate. It's what I study," says Met. "Why do you think religion is failing at peace?"

"Religion created war. Before religion, tribes fought over food and territory, which is only natural and animalistic. Not until the creation of religion did wide scale death on Irfa exist. Manifest destiny, thinking it was created for you and your group."

"I think we must let the past go and focus on what's happening now," says Dini'l.

"I do too," agrees Gnat. "Not in the context of religion, however. If we let the past go, the story, doesn't that negate everything? You can't pick and choose which parts mean something, that's interference with the divine, which we are not."

Met starts, "In the quest for practicality and meaning…"

"Practicality?" Gnat retorts. "If you're arguing ambiguity for unseeing eyes to ignore. A baby's step in the *quest* to find a reason for it all. This doesn't get far, because men in rooms throughout history thought it up. Man is nothing but flaw, growing on a globe. A pebble, really. Important to the pebble, unnoticed in terms of the whole. Unable to understand the complexity, just lost in his abject definitions."

"The war, death, and famine of history are outcomes of human emotion, not god. That isn't what it wants," Met adds.

"The whole thing is based in human emotion! A man wrote down the words. There's flaw in that."

"I've never heard this word before," says Stifin. "What is *flaw*?"

"Imperfection. Like I said, you can't pick which parts mean something. It's all or nothing. Which parts conveyed to him did he translate in his own way? The part about it being legal to sell your daughters as slaves? What about eternal punishment? Did he add that part to strike fear into the masses and make ruling them easier? What about this man, that spoke directly to god? Why isn't he the final prophet? It must have taken a long time to write these things down, the relationship between them wasn't documented?"

"Don't make jokes, it is a serious conversation," Met says dryly.

"I'm not making jokes. Maybe the prophet was a normal person, and wrote these stories to solidify his place in history. We have no idea where it came from," answers Gnat. "The point is that any law, of religion or government, is touched by man, who is an unknowing being. Any rule humans make would therefore be errant. You write the beliefs you want, get one other person to believe, then the avalanche starts. Manipulation of mankind."

"That's what faith would be, you know. Confidence, trust in what you've read. What you've been told," says Met.

Gnat interrogates, motioning with his hands. "Told, or given? Any human who has read a spiritual text with any sort of intellectual grit can see it's at most describing the political situation of the time with parables."

"It does have a lot of world history in it," Dini'l pipes up. "I have read some of these books before. Lots of tiny differences to create so much destruction and hate. I think I agree, culture stems mostly from religion. It's central to what creates meaning for a people. I can see how every conflict comes from this."

Stifin adds, "I read, somewhere, in Raminian. I'll try to make a correct translation. Something like 'Once we know how all things operate in our habitat, religion dies'."

Ina is interested as well. "Yes, like Native Omrikans, Gnat. They believed weather events were gods. Ancient Ropans thought people were warring in the sky. In South Omrika, stars were living beings. It was trying to make sense of things they couldn't understand."

"Yes," says Dini'l. "Science eventually erased these beliefs."

"It keeps doing the same thing now," smiles Gnat.

"The true god had not revealed itself to those groups of people at that point, it took missionaries hundreds of spans to reach them," Met argues. "Many men gave their lives in pursuit of bringing light to the darkness."

"Along with blankets poisoned and diseased. What of the billions of people that existed before this god decided to show itself? Are they in purgatory or being punished somewhere for not being good enough for their creator to say hello?" asks Gnat.

The Raminians laugh. They hand a can of beer to their new friend; he sets the bottle on the table to share. He sees Hipslyn. As their eyes meet, he waves. She does also, mouthing the phrase 'Be nice' and shakes a finger. He mouths 'I am' and at the same time in his head he says *always*.

"God invented everything, including science and logic, you have to remember," jingles Met after a drink.

Gnat replies, "So, it invented the things that will ultimately undo belief in it? The idea of god is the absolute absence of logic and science. It's fear and false hope. Organized religion was another attempt at answering 'What's the point?' and 'Are we accountable for anything that we do?'. They recognized the pointlessness of themselves, and a god is the most primitive way to feel they had a function. 'We are being watched. We are the playthings of some bigger creature'."

"What happens when you get to the end, and you find that god is there? What will you do?" Met questions.

"You believe because it's a safe bet? Because you are afraid of wrath? That's proving my point. Fear is the power of this force. False hope is a powerful tool against a simple-minded being. At no time has there ever been a manifestation of physical evidence from another dimension to prove that any of these beings exist. Not once. Ever," Gnat states.

"Faith!" Met exclaims.

"I'll believe what I can see." Gnat goes on, "The only way to take something seriously, literally, is to experience it firsthand. You said you know what god wants, Met. How? Did you speak to it? What did it say, word for word?"

"It speaks through the world around me. You must be in tune and be able to recognize what means something and what doesn't."

"Your religion helps you to an end, then. Your faith allows you to not think about how unimportant you are. Anything can be a sign in your life, positive or negative. That way you are able to find purpose in the suffering and menial tasks of your fleeting life," says Gnat. "You are just the early man trying to figure out why, producing signs from the hereafter along the way."

"Oh," Ina interrupts, "I've thought of another. The Great Northern Ehfrans, from thousands of spans ago, their main god was the eye of the sun, because they lived in the desert!"

"That's true!" laughs Stifin, taking a swig.

"What image were we created in, then?" Met inquires the group, "How can you explain our knowledge?"

"Chaos and physics," Gnat says tonelessly, taking his turn with the bottle. "Knowledge? Or basic awareness? Again, wanting to know the reason why we're here was the motivation. Thinking we are special. By deflecting the only truth, our ignorance, and trying to justify a reason for the dismal lives we exist in. Instead of finding balance within it, we tried to control it, and in turn have destroyed it. I mean, come on, we were created in the image of an omnipotent being? Does god trip and break its arm? Stub its toe? Feel pain? Does god make us feel despair and sorrow to prove something to ourselves? Or, does this being make us feel this way to show we aren't as powerful as it? That's not very godly."

"Sounds like a bully to me," adds Ina.

"Yes, a bully," Gnat concurs. "The idea that some being created us to watch us make choices in desolation and shame is ridiculous."

"What is *this* for, then? I don't believe it's right that you question my faith like this. It can't be for nothing," Met cries, dejectedly.

"Faith is inherently unbreakable. It should help to find a road to the end of suffering, which is deflection. It's submission into what you've been told. What exactly is *this*? Indentured servitude. By deflecting that you mean nothing, and finding purpose in the systems defined for you, you can now perceive value in yourself. This allows you to find substance in things around you and work for the institution blindly until you die. Faith is deflection. Deflection is ignorance. Ignorance is bliss. Bliss is virtue. The circle cycles onward."

"Prayer is the tool we use to guide us when we doubt our faith or convictions. It's a direct link to the holy. God answers. I told you, not with a voice, with a sign," explains Met.

"You determine where the sign is and what it indicates?" Stifin questions sarcastically. "Pray to the good lord, hope for the best. Can't control it."

"There you go," says Gnat. "Reduce, reuse, recycle. The three Rs of every religious and political campaign, I think they mixed that up in school."

With this, everyone but Met starts to laugh unhindered. Their old friend, intoxication, has shown its face more tangibly than any god ever has on Irfa. Met has opened his phone, he turns the screen off again.

"What are your thoughts on prayer, Gnat? I'm curious."

"Prayer is just thinking of another person or situation. It's more of the same, leading back to right or wrong, imposing your will subconsciously into or onto the world, finding an emotional connection with something you can't conceive. You have no power to control anything but your reaction while something is happening. Prayer is reaching for understanding, a sense of connectedness. A hope that everything isn't just random. A cry to not be alone, if only for your own sanity in nothingness. The thought of being part of something larger that you have an effect on makes it easier to deal with ramifications."

Stifin interrupts, "We must go now, there are friends to meet. Good luck to both of you, it was nice to practice Omrikan."

"Goodbye, best wishes!" Ina and Dini'l wave from behind Stifin.

"Have fun, be safe," Gnat calls cordially.

"Thanks for the company, enjoy Start of Span and the party!" Met says. Turning to Gnat again, he continues, "I'd like to talk about more, if you are up for it."

Gnat finds Hipslyn in the crowd. She's dancing with Ta'it. The same guys are watching them from afar. One of them has gotten the courage to dance next to them. Not rhythmically, but that doesn't matter. *Good for you, man. Live life.*

"Yeah, for a while longer, I think," he says to his single-use seminarian acquaintance. "Where were we?"

"You told me your thoughts on prayer, that it's a cry to feel like you can impart change on something which you mean nothing to."

"Karma is the same, really. Justifying actions and choices, imagining consequences for past regrets. The thought of carrying some kind of weight for the whole is calming to people, I guess…" his ears are warm. He isn't drunk, just carefree.

"You don't think we answer for our choices in any way? There has to be a consequence, somewhere, surely."

"Why would there be? I never agreed to this. I was forced to exist. You give me the ability to choose, then punish me if I don't do what you tell me to? That's a trap."

"I don't know that it's if you don't do what you are told. If your intention is to be malicious…" says Met.

"If you are the kindest person on Irfa, and you don't believe in god, can you still get through the gate in the clouds? I've been told it isn't possible by every religious person I've asked."

Met says the same thing to him, "Belief in god is the most important attribute a person must have to be with their god. That makes sense, doesn't it?"

"You know what doesn't make sense? This idea of eternal punishment and how it's used. If you don't believe in any of it, don't subscribe to it, you are still held accountable for what you've done by this god you didn't live for. That's what I'm saying, there is no freedom in religion. On the other side, if you do believe, there's no possible way for you to understand the effects your decisions have had on others. It's the original idea to hold people to account. There is no actual *right* or *wrong*. Just personal confirmation of what makes life easier for the individual doing the choosing."

Met's brow furrows, "I'm not sure what you mean, can you give me an example?"

"Is it right or wrong to wear shoes made by a slave in an underground shop somewhere in rural Ehfra?"

"People don't buy the shoes to perpetuate slavery of children, though," Met answers.

"No, they buy them because they're cheap. By doing what's easy and comfortable for them, others suffer. They know where the shoes are coming from. It's a conscious choice. What if you decide to run a red light and by doing so someone else gets harmed?"

"This is silly, Gnat. You can't be judged for that."

"If there is some being that knows every possible outcome and presents you with a choice, then you decide to break the rule, you are punished. It doesn't matter to what degree. Right is right. Wrong is wrong. In religion, as you believe it."

"There are different levels of sin. You won't be punished after death for beating a red light."

"What if you being selfish causes the death of somebody else? How is that different than shooting them for their wallet? God wasn't being circumstantial, it made a rule. We chose what the different levels are. It's a lie."

"Do you try to be a good person, without religion?"

Gnat shakes his head slightly. "You aren't listening. Being *good* is still personal perception. It's an emotional response to the random happenstance."

"So, you don't think that you are good?"

"I don't think I'm good, no. I take what I need and try not to get in the way. There's no emotional link. I'm existing. Let's return to this idea of burning in the afterlife, it can't exist according to the rules within your belief system."

Met is focused intensely. "What do you mean?"

"It would only exist through god's hate and spite for its own creation. God gives people disabilities that cause them to harm others, then makes them suffer for it after they die?"

"God gives you the choice to do anything you want, that's what you are judged on."

"After giving you schizophrenia with violent tendencies?" Gnat prods. "How is it an open choice if the options are predetermined? Let's say that there is a married couple, the man kills his wife. He gets caught, convicted, and receives life in prison."

"Yes..."

"Then the family of the murdered woman say they want him to 'rot for eternity'."

"Keep going..." Met spins his hand in a circle.

"Aren't you supposed to forgive anyone for anything? Within the bounds of scripture, wishing bad on somebody is the same as acting on those thoughts. In the eyes of a completely just being, both parties would be the same. The idea of redemption is that you feel sorry for the acts you've committed, you are forgiven, then you still get through the gates in the clouds." Gnat feels a sudden urgency to conclude the anticlimax of this discussion. "If there's an infinite soul within us, what's the difference between getting sentenced to a cycle in jail or a lifetime, here on Irfa? Against infinity, the difference is still mathematically zero. If we truly believe in an afterlife, why imprison people during their lives? They'll answer when they go to meet this god. Why not kill them and save the resources?"

"There must be a system of guidelines while we are living the life we have in this shell. Otherwise, everything would be in turmoil!"

"You don't believe people are good, either? Religion is a way to control their actions with fear of eternal damnation?"

"No, that's not what I said."

Gnat tilts his head. "It's what you implied!"

A boy runs by in only his boxers, with a case of unopened alcohol in his arms. Another empty box is on his head, with holes cut to wear as a mask. He screams like a banshee as he blurs past.

The men at the table pause for a moment, sharing a revelation. *We are getting too old for hostels.*

"I wasn't implying that people aren't good. But we have the commandments, ten of them, to help determine those guidelines. They are the bridge between the lives we live on Irfa and after, that is the purpose of them, Gnat."

"Met, if you consider it logically. Really. You can see that there is no way it is a valid path of reasoning. It's based in human emotion, which lacks any understanding outside thought of itself. There's nothing celestial in these concepts, they're too weak to be from something considered supreme."

"The commandments were not written by man, they were given to us..."

"How were they not? Don't steal my wife? Those commandments are the first rejection of instinct. Worries became rules, which became forced, then widely believed. It was only man trying to separate from the animals," Gnat remarks. "Religion is a synonym for blanket control, being so indoctrinated that before every decision you doubt and never investigate or change."

"There's a correlation between what we see, think, and choose to do with our intentions along with faith that has a point. I know it." Met sounds as if he is reciting something from a card.

"I see a correlation between the human condition as it moves along and the institution of theology trying to twist the rules to stay relevant. In the peace generation after the last Telaysian war, when drugs and sex became commonplace, religion said it was acceptable to use birth control. The leader of religion now is the first non-Ropan in a thousand spans. I wonder why? Because most people in the religion are not Ropan anymore, but South Omrikan, as he is. When they elect the leader, it's in absolute secrecy. Remember when people were trying to use lasers on the windows to convert vibrations into words? They were arrested, because they were talking about how to more easily manipulate the world's population!"

"You can't possibly think that's true..."

Gnat responds, "Why not? If these men are literally speaking to god, why would they ask it who should sit in the bulletproof box? It's so mundane and holds no power to change our species for the better in any meaningful way. They are evolving the same way everything else is, even though they don't believe in evolution. Theology is like the Omrikan language, full of exceptions. A rule is made, when it doesn't fit any longer, it's simply changed. They've got to stay in control of Irfa's weak-minded!"

"Fine, so let's say the institution is corrupt. Outside of that, just the divine... What's the point of existence? What are we here for?"

"I knew a girl, she was born on the Omrikan observance of independence, the celebration is a festival of fireworks. Growing up she thought it was for her, that the Irfa was having a party for her birth date. She didn't have the scope or knowledge to think outside of herself. This principle can be extrapolated to our entire race. We think that it was created for us. Because of this we've destroyed everything in such a short time. There is no plan, there is no purpose. Nothing we do will echo in eternity. We are self-absorbed, all-consuming. Living in our moment. We'll disappear."

Met, in a melancholy voice, gives a reply. "I think it's so bleak. Why would you want to think this way?"

Gnat perks up, "It's not about belief or opinion, want or need. It's plainly what *is*. It doesn't matter if you accept or not, it's happening regardless. So, you agree? Religion is simply trying to find meaning in nothing? It's the way you want to think, so it's easier, that's all?"

"You have no beliefs?"

"I understand reality around me, why must I label myself? Atheism is the same as religious belief, being based in absolutes and personal conviction. It might be the opposite, it's still ignorant. Nothing is absolute, except the emptiness of an individual human life and our misunderstanding of existence."

Now, Met gets excited. "You're trying to tell me that you aren't atheist, after everything you've said?"

"I know that no definition within the creation stories of theology we have now could be close to real. We see in three dimensions, the same as other living things. We are not meant to know. Yes, there could be some other realm that we can't see. There could be some force of creation we can't comprehend. The fact of the matter is, we are just a product of evolution here. It isn't for us to see. We are monkeys in the mud."

"You do believe!" Met jumps up.

"No, not in any explanation man has for it. Reincarnation as a scientific principle, yes. It happens. Not based on how well you've lived or not. It's only energy, here. Within this system. You die, you decompose. Your elements feed the plants, which feed the insects, which feed the animals, and so on. Balance. We are not separate, we are a part of it," states the Omrikan.

"You see there is a force greater than us out there, don't you?"

"The laws of physics, chaos, and chance. See? Maybe, maybe not. It isn't important. I'm not arrogant enough to believe I know either way. We aren't ready or able to understand. We never will be."

Met smiles. "You aren't a nihilist."

Gnat laughs, "A true nihilist would never call himself a nihilist. That's giving meaning to something. I don't think anything means anything, on any level, if that's what you are wondering. Knowing or not frankly isn't important..."

With this Met crushes his can and throws it away.

"I've got to get going. Thank you for talking to me. You've given me things to question. My hope for you this span is to find purpose in something. If you have to, sell out somewhat and take what's easy to find joy. Some of what you said may go in my thesis, do I need to give you credit?"

Gnat puts a hand in his jacket pocket, the other holds an almost empty bottle.

"No, you can have it. If it makes anything, you can buy the next bottle."

"I'll remember that. Take care," Met says, going. As he does, Gnat has to get the last word.

"Hey Met! You know over a hundred billion humans have lived on Irfa in total?"

"Now I do."

Gnat squints his eyes. "How do they grow enough food in the afterlife?"

The Montisans head drops as he rounds the corner into the corridor, wordless.

Hipslyn never checked on him, the balcony is empty. He pulls out his phone, a message:

Ran to Ta'it's room for more supplies. Be back before the clock turns. I saw you in a deep conversation so I didn't interrupt. See you soon. It's the Start of Span, yay! xxx

"That conversation could have been worse," Gnat tells himself. The stars are out in full force. The hostel is quiet, everyone went to the square early. The last bit of the bottle goes down his throat. He drifts off toward the sky.

He wasn't your typical religious fanatic; you question them and they claim harassment. They question you and it's spreading the word. Still, he just wanted to hear me say I believe in something. He didn't care how illogical his rules are. I don't believe anything, I know things. Based on what I've seen. There is only one thing that I cannot condone. Ignorance. Three things represent ignorance on its most basic level. Organized religion, bad grammar, and higher education. Religion is a fundamental flaw of mankind. A juvenile experiment trying to understand. The flies on the boat. The bacteria on the pebble. Religion as we know it is an adverse outcome of self-awareness. The idea that it was created for us is what made humans weak, what made us destroy everything. A species wide failure that now permeates every facet of what we are. In the movies now, the ancient gods are portrayed as myth. We know better, like Ina said tonight. Will we survive long enough for this religion, this god we have now to be accepted as imagined? As childish? As a fairy tale? Will we exist long enough for this to happen? Imagine a time in the future with the present god in the movies, people laughing and saying 'they actually thought this was real? Look how far we've come.' The same way we do now with those gods of ancient time. Evolution, reincarnation, energy, balance, truth. Why are people afraid to die if they truly believe in god? Truth is the only thing that matters, religion contains none.

Shoulders are on the table, he's snug in his jacket. There they are, two words in the voice of his mind's throat. *THIS SPAN.* He doesn't move, only his eyes open. It takes a moment to focus, before they can there is a familiar snicker coming from the hallway Met left through. Hipslyn.

"This span, huh?" he says in a low voice, shifting to greet the trio.

"Gnat, we're back! With more alcohol for the square! Where's your friend?" she bellows as if he were across an amphitheater, not a terrace.

"He had to go meet up with some others somewhere. Everyone went out already. Hey Ta'it, Divi. How have you been?"

Divi immediately comes forward and puts his hand on Gnat. "I apologize for the first time we had drinks. I don't know what got into me..."

"Too much liquor, seems like," Gnat jokes. "Don't mention it, I haven't even thought of it. Let's enjoy the night!"

"Yes, yes," he replies. "We can do this."

"There's a band playing Omrikan music on a big stage. Fireworks. We can drink on the way, it's legal in public this night every span," Ta'it explains.

"I'm in," Gnat replies as Hipslyn joins him at his side.

The trip is short. Everyone else from the hostel is in a group at the back of the crowd. Gnat sighs. *Lazy backpackers, shortest distance to a free concert and they stop.*

A cover band plays classic rock from Omrika, bad accents included. To the right, a castle. Something straight out of the animated children's movies Gnat grew up with. Stone, with three watchtowers, the one in the center higher than the pair set on the outer walls. It is silhouetted, completely black in the night. The sky is a rich, fathomless blue that allows you to see the difference between the spires and the atmosphere in the absences of luminosity.

He absorbs what's going on. Hipslyn is speaking Raminian with Ta'it and Divi, he doesn't mind being the owl, modestly watching the time being had. He has a drink in his hand and backups in his pockets, nothing to worry about. A blonde girl approaches him, obviously drunk.

She inquires, "I hear you are Omrikan, me too! Where from?"

"I grew up in Oia, you?"

"I'm from F'lalasip. I don't have a kiss for the change of the span, will you be mine?"

Hipslyn is to the left of this girl's face. He sees her stop talking, waiting for his response.

"No, sorry, I'm here with somebody. I hope she gives me a kiss when the time comes."

"Oh, don't worry about it," she says as she stumbles off.

Hipslyn approaches him, with a face neither angry, nor the opposite.

"You didn't think I was going to give you a kiss, Gnat?"

"I did, I just didn't want to be unkind to her."

"Because I am. I've been waiting for this. I didn't have a midnight kiss last time, or the one before that."

"Hipslyn, there's nothing I want more than to give you that kiss..."

Hipslyn puts her arms around him as he gazes over the setting. So different to his home, this place. Ahead of his family overseas, he'll be living in a different span than they are. The performer counts down, everyone screams with him. At zero fireworks blaze in the sky behind the castle in brilliant white. Again, like those movies he knows from so long ago. He leans down to kiss her, exactly the same as the first time by the lake, but the electricity is gone. They know one another now; excitement doesn't enter the equation any longer. There are no more boundaries to cross. No more secrets. As it ends, her expression tells him she is thinking the same thing. *Verbatim.*

Everyone starts to filter down the street, they follow, holding hands and not saying anything. He gives himself to her once they're back at home and in bed, it's routine now. *This span, huh? What will it bring to me, when will it come?* He ponders these thoughts on repeat feeling empty and alone, more than ever before.

Somewhere in the witching moments, he visits the side of a road, surrounded by endless green grass. Acres, thousands of them, until a range of low mountains crosses from one end of vision to the other. He's enveloped in a vast, flat valley. He tries to turn and peer behind himself but cannot. Suddenly, focus converges on the opposite side of the highway. A pair of bus stops side by side, identical, so close they almost touch. *Bizarre. They should be on opposite sides of the road.* A sign rests atop each, with arrows pointing in either direction following the pavement.

He brings his sight closer. Under the stop on the left, a man. No detail, only an outline. A backpack held in his hand, hanging by his legs. Under the other, the outline of a woman, no features. She holds a suitcase the same way the man holds the backpack.

Gnat tries to step forward, again, yet cannot move. A slight rumble starts through his feet, the tremors of a quake. It is followed by a tone, coming from the distance. Random notes, up and down, something of a wail mixed within. Rising, rising, he wants to cover his ears. No luck. No movement whatsoever has been allowed to him. The figures across the way stand perfectly still, unaffected. The sound is now so loud he can't think. It pierces through his subconscious with the might of a broadsword wielded by a vicious giant, who pushes it through the chest of some foreign invader. He grits his teeth, cheek muscles tremble while locking his eyes shut. He tries to copy the scream, but he isn't breathing. Suddenly, silence. He counts to five, thinking something is there to undo him. The thought of courage makes him relax. Peeking out, a voice. *The* voice. *Choose both.*

Another public break follows, which should be called the national time of recovery because every adult in the country is hungover. The cycles after repeat themselves, Gnat and Hipslyn enjoy going everywhere together, taking their time to arrive. With passion and attention on the world. Each other. She starts school soon, they leave for Curesti. Her father has taken the car, she's gotten them train tickets. They visit a park nearby which overlooks the city. Which is, right now, his favorite place in the world. He can see the churches, the people rushing around trying to get back onto schedules. The sun is fading quickly, as the lights start to turn on around town, he has something to say.

"I bought a ticket to Telaysia. Since you are studying again, you know, and I'm not ready to go home yet."

"When do you leave?" Drops of water are already welling up on the face he always wants to protect.

"You start school soon, I'll fly out just before," he states.

"Why didn't you say anything before you bought it?"

"It was a good deal. I have to leave some time. I don't want to get in the way of your goals..."

The next words, she can barely get out, a dumbbell rests on her vocal chords. "You're one of my goals."

"There's a deal on the table. We talked about this. You know what I will do, it hasn't changed."

"I know," she replies, hugging him. He holds her for what seems like an eternity. "We need to get to the train, Gnat. It's already paid for..."

The train ride is dark and uninspiring. No view, no concessions. A standard identification check. Hipslyn sleeps the entire ride, resting against him. Gnat does not. He has the feeling he won't see her again after he flies away. That Start of Span kiss, the blandness of accepting it, has been weighing on him. *Is that what having a partner feels like? Nothing special, something safe? Never new, just expected?*

As the engine slows for their final stop, he nudges her awake gently. The station is only steps from her apartment, he carries the bags as they go. She makes him a cup of tea before going to bed. He follows shortly after, absorbing her presence of being. There's an early note, which is reflected in gray, carried out by passing rain clouds. She has gone to pick up books, stores are not always open.

The next blur of existence is composed of, actually, nothing. Sex, food, and cuddling. Promises made, are they empty? Are they grasping for acceptance, whichever way it comes? From whomever?

In the airport, the final line to get through security is Hipslyn's boundary, this is where they separate. He kisses her. She rubs his face.

"What will happen in the future, Gnat?" she asks.

"I have no idea. Between you and I, whatever you decide. I've left it in your hands."

"I'll miss you. Talk to me whenever you can?"

"Of course, Hipslyn," he replies. "Time for the flight, this isn't goodbye."

"See you soon, loon..." She smiles. Some mixture of a laugh and a sob comes out. *Back to the beginning. Full circle again. Damn.*

He stands at the checkpoint, Hipslyn waves, he lifts his chin up. Someone bumps his arm, he checks quickly, the person apologizes. He spins around. She isn't there, the spot is void of her.

"One man, one bag, one guitar," he says aloud with a straight face.

***

During a transfer he lands in Witz, an absurd location in its collective moral standing. An independent district in the towering peaks that create a natural border between Raminia and Muusman, they've declared complete severance from any involvement in world politics. They possess no military. They won't help, they don't want help. Nonetheless, this place has become a tax haven for the Irfa's war criminals, arms dealers, drug dealers, and white-collar scam-artists. Witz profits immensely, directly, from the systems they deny being part of. He buys no food; he would rather go hungry.

Another short hop across Muusman and the Straight of Equus to Southern Telaysia. He's grown used to the chilly weather in

Raminia. As he steps out of the airport a wave of humidity steals his energy. A ride to a nearby island, Pi'Kit, is taken by scooter. Thousands of them occupy the roads, two lanes wide, motorbikes sometimes six across between the painted lines. People race past shoeless, shirtless, clutching babies, passengers holding ladders, or bushels of vegetables strapped to the brim. Controlled chaos, he appreciates this immediately. Don't get in my way, I won't get in yours, the rules of the byway. He's dropped off in the city center of Pi'Kit. Gnat needs to find a room and get his bearings. The town is small, yet busy. Many bars line the streets on both sides. *Score.*

He starts toward a beach in the distance. A realization; food must be had, his stomach screams. At a restaurant and coffee shop, a girl serves him the best curried beef of his life and he relaxes with a drink. Beer comes in glass bottles double the size of Omrika's. *Score, again.*

A man in the later stages of life comes out of the kitchen. It's hard to tell exactly how many spans are under his tan. He shoots Gnat a glance, double takes, then greets him.

"Hello there, where are you from?"

"I'm Omrikan," says Gnat.

"Oh, so am I. Oia?" The man is interested.

"Yes... how did you know?"

"Same here, what a coincidence. Where are you staying?"

"Oh, I haven't found a place yet." Gnat shrugs. "I got here just now, actually."

"How long are you here?"

"Who knows, no plans as of yet."

The man puts on his salesman's voice. "Let me show you my private rooms here. You don't have to go to a hostel."

"That sounds awesome!" Gnat exclaims. "I'm sold."

The place has a large bed, a bathroom. Laundry upstairs, along with a patio overlooking town. They agree on a price, not much more than a hostel. As Gnat pays, the man says to his new tenant, "It's about the people you know!"

"Yes, it is. Always nice to meet an Oia boy," Gnat retorts. *That's done, no problem. Why do people have to plan everything beforehand?*

In his room, the sound of his breathing comes to the front of his senses. How long has it been since he's recognized his internal rhythm? How long since he's been alone? When was the last time he stopped moving, not rushing toward something? Physically or in his imagination? Out comes his guitar. He lays down with the body of the instrument pressing on his stomach, arms holding it in place. A yellow pick is resting in the corner of his mouth. No movement comes from him for some time, unthinking. Heavy eyes at first, soon they become lighter. He rises and the words start to flow as he plays, thinking of her.

Every cycle is a cycle
Every cycle has its way
Every way has its own sensibility
So I ascertain.

All these things they say
Are just needles in the hay.
All the hay got ate;
Clear your plate.

My Zen is a 'B' no way
No 'A,' okay.

Finesse of essence
In your presence.
Inherent adolescence
Makes things hectic.

All these things I've said
Put ideas in your head.
Went to sleep instead
Away you went.

Finesse of essence
In your presence.
Inherit adolescence
Makes things hectic.

His eyelids don't only become heavy, his entire being does. Partly jetlag, mostly life-lag, he's lost to the place where humans spend half their lives. A dream state. What tense is this undefined place attached to? The present? The future? The past? Or some mutation of them we know nothing of, yet? A night passes unstirred, untouched, unchanged. The world swirls around him, Gnat separate from its combined tension and fervent intentions. Somewhere Jin is working too hard for a boss he's never met. Julyen is painting a masterpiece in the darkness of which his genius will be contained to, never seen or understood by the masses. Wudy tends his herd of rabbits in Nuwal, the sole supporter of a seemingly subjacent race of creatures. Do they not have their own language, rituals, and understanding? One word or many, a definition is only such if every piece is completing the puzzle for the same capability of vision. Childhood friends cling to any sense of the regular found, geographical location unimportant. Addie cries, Tia feels in control. Gnat hibernates. Until the warmth of the sun returns, and slumber is once again postponed.

A rustle, a stir, a growl. A wild animal, this man. He leaves his dwelling covered in nothing but a swimsuit. The beach wasn't reached before, it will be now. Along the way he stops for a drink. Then a few more, until...

The edge of the continent is lined in glassy white sand along the sweeping crescent of a majestic bay. Towers of vegetation project fiercely out of the ocean fathoms away offshore. Steady, grounded, they will not be moved. The asymmetrical shapes of these lava domes only add to the character of their outright visual dominance amongst the forces engulfing them. To his right, a shaded area under low slung trees, mangroves if he has to guess. A field of rocks are piled next to the arboretum, boulders to a man, an impassable range of peaks to the crabs scurrying across them. Gnat is drunk. He lays in the sand, completing the cycle of swimming and drying a dozen times before the tide recedes with the heat. His skin is burned, just what he wanted, to get the scars of the radiance entwisted with him. Who says the thing without hue is the most beautiful, like the sand on this beach? A dab of blood, a drop of dirt thrown in the mix makes existence real. Purity is satire.

Gnat climbs the nearest rock. A tide pool below, the shoebox diorama of the beach he currently inhabits except humans are replaced by crabs. Some big, slower to scamper. However powerful claws make up for this. The smaller crabs are quick, passing by to nip the legs of their larger counterparts, trying to force them off the warmest spot on the rock. Any way they can, a sneak attack, moving like a herd, or a bum-rush straight from the front. Nothing works, they go unnoticed. The big crab is on the highest rock with the warmest and driest spot. The only way that's going to change is if the king crab dies, another ruler will emerge. An endless circle, facilitated by the weaker members in lieu of the stronger, giving themselves an unearned boost to the top. There's a show he recalls from when he was younger, about a certain fish. The species is taking over the sea, destroying all others without care. The presenter called the fish a nuisance, invasive, a disaster. *How is that any different than what humans are doing on the land? Or the crabs on the rocks?* He watches them, *what foolish creatures*, and has the same thought again. Dusk approaches, the owl's most opportune time to hunt.

Stumbling to his room he passes the same bars and restaurants as before. However, they have transformed into something primal. Something most older men from Ropa and Austopia come here for. The restaurants have become brothels. Not the reason that Gnat is visiting, but he's heard about it before. A bit of currency, a turn with a young woman, sometimes too young, the law says. Everybody on both sides keeps quiet or no one gets what they want. The standard business practice on Irfa. The thought of it being too easy crosses his mind, he remembers talking about it with Jin at Rusty. Maybe it is the perfect business deal.

Cycles later, he's acquired a bronze glow. Gnat is thinner, a benefit of Telaysian food. You can eat as much as you desire and still lose weight. He's had more or less no conversation except ordering things to consume. Nobody at home, not Hipslyn, not an acquaintance anywhere. A clear mind, there have been no thoughts of the rotting infrastructure enveloping him. He only wants the sun on his skin and a drink in his hand.

Something he's noticed, a statue far above him on a hill outside town. An idol, a giant deity carved in rock. He rents a motorbike. Flying to the city center and going through the main roundabout, Gnat sees a hand-painted sign showing the way to the statue; he takes it into the jungle. It's dense, blocking out much of the light. Suddenly the blacktop vanishes, only dirt remains. Uneven and bumpy, the destruction of his transport is imminent. He navigates slowly, refusing to turn around. At the peak of the path, he stops. The bike is quiet. A tremor shakes the ground.

A very large eye peers at him from the forest, floating. Gnat is frozen, not believing what's happening, until he catches a glimpse of movement around the levitating pupil. An elephant, here, with friends. All hesitant of him, this Gnat buzzing around wanting to get to the top of the hill. For what, he knows not. There's a long pause before the massive creatures decide he isn't a threat and cross the road. More gently than some would imagine, frankly, and gone again they are into the tropical wood. Farther up the pavement begins again. He turns the climbing way.

It is a temple. Roaming through, there are many gardens. He sees a door. Entering, others traipse around. A man sits in a robe on a stage of sorts, peaceful. Another hallway leads to a place of faces and figurines, carved into the walls throughout history. He stares, waiting for their gaze to turn and stare back. None do. The faces are abandoned to the prisons which they've been engraved.

A patio stands opposite to where he came in. As he searches for an exit and the bike, a voice says "Come."

Gnat peaks around, the man in the robe is staring at him.

"Come." He repeats. Gnat approaches, he orders, "Kneel."

The man grasps his hand, tying a ribbon of gold and orange around his wrist. The robed mystic says something in a language he can't understand, pulling Gnat.

"You will receive the answer you desire. It will seek you out, when it is ready. Go, be easy and mindful of this until then."

Gnat bows his head and says nothing as he steps out onto the terrace once more. The sunshine cleanses him. Some kind of benumbing mystery hangs inside that place. On your face, in your breath.

Soon, he remembers, riding the bike onto the paved road. *Choose both.* The ride starts to reconnect him to the destination he wants to reach. Not in Telaysia. Possibly not on Irfa.

He returns his rented iron steed and goes to the cool conditioned air of his hideaway behind the diner. After another dinner of rice and fish, he decides it is time, he is ready. A brothel is his destination. *That doesn't mean I'll partake,* he tells himself. *Who am I kidding?* He has avoided dusk thus far, not because he feels unsafe, but the women trying to sell themselves and their friends are overwhelming. He's had his genitals grabbed by men and women more than once. As he strolls, mentions of short-time and long-time drift to his ears. Ladies and ladyboys of the night. Scrambling to give ecstasy for a little coin. Maybe find some acceptance within as a bonus. He sees a wooden bar, under the cover of an awning from the street. Many of the men are older, overweight, and lonely. They wear this final adjective in their odor. A regular bar, it seems. As *regular* as it can be. Every female in the place is a hooker. The bartenders, the dates of men already present, the ones floating around. Hunting the hunters.

Some of the foreigners glance up at him, not impressed. A handsome younger man has appeared. The type of men that fly around the world for sex tourism are *not* very secure with themselves. That's why they're here; they've always been in second place. Unable to win because of some lesser trait that isn't completely obvious except with time.

"Can I have a panther in the big bottle?" Gnat asks the girl behind the bar.

"Sure. Play pool? I win, you buy me a shot. You win, I buy," the Telaysian woman says.

"Deal," Gnat snickers. *Too bad for you.*

He racks the table. She breaks, putting three balls down. She's petite, with an amazing figure. An ocean of hair. Resplendent skin. Like a princess in a graphic novel. Most of the women here are almost too gorgeous to be real. The first game is quick, he loses. Suddenly, he's been beaten three out of three. Hustled by a tiny Telaysian girl in a bar. Or brothel. Whatever the official title is on paper. He leans on the wall holding the stick with both hands. She laughs, and it's hard to recognize whether it's with or at him. At the bar he buys her three shots.

"Double the order, make it six," he demands. It isn't polite to make a woman drink alone.

The drinks are taken successively then she prances over to the new guy that just meandered up. After he orders something, she starts to say, "Sure. Play pool? I win, you buy me..."

Gnat isn't upset that he lost, it happens. The fact that he fell for it, however, is disheartening. *Everyone is trying to get something from everyone else.*

The next place is about the same, it has an Omrikan name not remembered, he has a round and leaves. *If I wanted to be in an Omrikan bar with Omrikan people, and Omrikan food, where should I do it?*

As he continues away from the main drag, there are less and less foreigners, he stands out. The third stop is a club, an employee is giving out drinks to people entering the cue.

"Don't mind if I do," Gnat says, taking one and standing at the end.

Inside there are so many girls in fishnet stockings moving around is impossible. Mixed in are more of these men he's seen around town. He can't hear anything; the music is too loud. The line is crazy at the bar. The thought of breathing the air is off-putting.

Noxious fumes, it smells of sweat and venereal disease. Quickly, an exit is found.

Retracing his steps, he sees the place where he was humiliated in pool. The same girl is behind the bar, at the far end. Another woman has joined her, a couple spans older. He gets a drink, no tricks this time. There's an unoccupied table. He stretches, twisting his head to see if his neck will pop. The thought of work and home, or worrying about anything is so distant right now. Gnat almost can't recall what the stresses of normal life feel like. It's only been twelve moons since he said goodbye to Hipslyn in the airport, it seems like cycles ago. The thought of her, as a passing gust of breeze, tells him he's still drawn to her. Is she still drawn to him? Or is it just the idea of her, of having something to cling onto when he doubts himself? He only wants to get to the bottom, not only of the next bottle, but of what means enough for him to put his focus toward. Mindful considerations are interrupted when a man stumbles to *his* table, in *his* empty chair across from him.

"Where are you from, young man?" he bellows in a thick Eastern Ropan accent. A place where the analytical and mathematical are praised, not the artist or the philosopher. This man is fat, stomach pouring out the top of his pants and splashing against his legs as he squats. He reeks of booze, the thing that has most likely sustained his metabolism throughout his stay. No judgments, except his self-presentation and the ruination of the state of mind he was in.

"I'm Omrikan, you're Eastern Ropan, aren't you?"

"Yes, how could you tell?"

"Your smell," Gnat answers caustically.

"I heard your voice when you ordered," the man continues. "You strut and talk with such arrogance. I could tell right away. What are you doing here? See my table over there, see the women? Where are yours?"

"Tell those women you've run out of money and see who stays. I'm not impressed with your pocketbook or what you do with it. I've *rejected* twice what you've *had* in your life."

The man studies the hoard of prostitutes, then Gnat. "You think you're so smart. With a leader like Lellin, how could you claim any intelligence? This would never happen where I am from. It shows you are weak as a nation."

"I might agree with you. There's a reason I'm not there. I don't want to talk about it, really."

"You don't believe that Omrika is the best country in the world?"

"No," Gnat states, "it isn't. Not in the least."

"Ah, so what is it then?" the drunken fool calms, forgetting the verbal arm-wrestling match that was building.

"Remember your history? Those nationalist Ropans started in the east, where you're from."

"Of course, the shame of our people."

"I see Omrikans as the same thing in the digital age. Hating immigrants, other cultures, anything outside of what their government tells them. At the same time, we are the creator of every plight on Irfa, it all stems from us. Why do we fight wars endlessly? Death makes more money and we get to further the pursuit of controlling the resources, while programming our rule into every facet of life."

"I am still called a nationalist when I go places, Omrika was the worst. They're stuck in the past, not seeing what's going on. Not able to. Your news and internet are censored from what other countries are reporting. Like Northern Telaysia, the so-called nemesis your Omrikan media defames!" the man exclaims.

"It comes down to who writes history; the winner."

"What of the loser, after the initial effects dissipate and stigmas remain?"

Gnat continues, "History is written in a way that best fits the status quo. The loser becomes the enemy. The generals that championed Omrika's beginnings owned slaves. Fighting for freedom, taking it away at the same time to benefit themselves. One of our most famous island musicians that promoted love was a racist and beat his wives. After his death his memory was changed to sell merchandise. Everything we believe is a lie."

"How do you change it? How will *your* country make things right? Everyone bows to you."

"Because we have the heaviest stick?" Gnat laughs, then answers, "Remember the 'occupy Nuwal City' movement? The Muusmani blossom? Ehfran lives matter? Or the 'March for Our Life' recently?"

"I've read things, whatever happened?"

"Exactly. Nothing happened. The celebrities who donated to these *causes* got some exposure and can write it off at the end of the span. You can't beat the top by trying to make them feel horrible about what they've done, or use something as trivial as hope to get people to act."

"How does Omrika get away with it? These things you do, unimaginable atrocities, they're forgotten after a short time. Yet you hold things over others from hundreds of spans ago."

"I guess it's another benefit of the largest military. At some point we won't be at the top. I know we aren't now, like any Omrikan who's being honest. The viewpoint of the rest of Irfa hasn't changed. It will. When that happens, the country will answer. If it means its destruction, so be it. It won't do anything but help. Until some other Omrika comes to power."

"Hmm... I think you could be right about a change of hands. Not pace. That's what it's always been, since *our* beginning." He drinks. "When we think of these rulers of the past; the man who ruled the nationalist Ropans in my country, the Telaysians now, or the conquerors of the wall they built so long ago, we say they are evil. What are they, but consequences of the system they lived in?"

"They are men. And what are men? Weak and flawed. Trying to climb the ladder higher, while stepping over whatever is needed to get there. A system that concedes power to a single man, or millions in the same mindset, will always lose," Gnat finalizes. "The biggest flaw of ethics within our species is *we* created them. Our demise will derive from our own arrogance."

The man is staring somewhere off above Gnat, thinking deeply. "Young man, you have given me things to think about, if I remember them tomorrow," he bellows again, laughing deeply. So much power comes from that stomach of his.

"I must go to my table now. I paid for them, so I should enjoy them, no? I apologize for being rude at first."

"Apology accepted," says Gnat.

The man rises, artificial greetings come from his harem along with cheers.

Omrika isn't what it was, once. The idea that any person could go to a place and try anything they wanted. The guarantee of success wasn't there. The equal chance between everyone was. Some succeeded, most didn't. That's where survival of the most fit and balance met, during the founding of the country. That has been lost and won't return. Somewhere along the line, things changed. Now people see equality as everybody being guaranteed the same amount of material possessions. It isn't sustainable. We are fading out at this point, nothing more...

Gnat heads to the bar, the girl who bested him comes over.

"Another game?" she asks, "This round's on me, no bets."

"What game are you really playing, then?"

"Just shoot for fun. Come and talk to me."

"Okay, then."

While racking she asks him which girl he likes in the place.

"Am I supposed to say you, and take you home? Is that the game?" Gnat asks, rolling his eyes teasingly.

"No, I am the house mom. I drink for free, play pool, and help men find women, that's how I make my money. No pay-sex from me... who do you like?"

"Hmm, who says I need help?"

"No girl in this town wants a boyfriend, just coin. Now show me," she demands.

He breaks. "The girl behind the bar with you seems nice."

"Very nice, and new. I will tell her after the game. You pay me so she can leave, you pay her after. She makes her own price."

The house mother clears the table before Gnat gets to shoot again. She could make a lot more if she entered tournaments. Anxious to get her girl out, she shot perfectly. He meets his single-use girlfriend, the three agree on prices, and off they go to his room...

The next sunrise, he wakes by himself, becoming alert immediately. His clothes are taken out of his bag, folded nicely without wrinkles. Also, his wallet on the table. Inside, everything remains minus the exact amount of cash they agreed on.

"Huh," he says, scratching his scalp. "That wasn't what I expected."

After bumming around the beaches, he finds himself out in the night searching for the same thing. From a different woman, of course. It isn't hard, seeing that all you have to do is be from another country and go into an open bar. It *is* too easy, like he thought when he arrived.

The next forgotten daze is nothing but a whirlwind, spiraling faster and faster without him noticing. The eye of the storm is nowhere to be seen, not thought of or even considered. This front of hot and cold air mixing is fueled by nothing but animal need, which could only be called desire. Gnat finds himself at a bar, which goes unrecognized. A Telaysian walks up gleaming at him very suspiciously.

"Can I have..." he starts.

The girl sets a bottle on the table, "A big Panther?"

"...Yes. Thank you."

"Wait for me to be off, and take me home again?" she queries.

"Uh, we'll see. How long is that?" He plays along.

"Maybe after dinner. You come back if you leave, okay?"

"Oh, alright. We'll talk later, don't let me keep you from working."

"See you!" she says, going into the kitchen.

It seems Gnat has become lost in the dream that is Telaysia. He sets the bottle on the bar without drinking anything. As he heads out he studies his hands. They have nothing on them, visibly. However, they feel dirty, clammy. *This is where the older men I've seen here began. Where I am right now. They were pulled in, and became tangled in temptation. I have lost my way, what am I doing? I am unbalanced.*

The drinks he had have been erased by power of thought in his head. He is sober. *Sobered.*

Gnat's head rests against the wall of his room, he's in disbelief of what he's been seduced by. His guitar lays on the floor with clothes on top of it, not played or cared about as of late. There's a song on the tip of his tongue, which comes out the instant he starts to pick.

Walking down a lonesome road
Trying to find the afterglow.
There you are
My shooting star.

Waking up with you too soon

We got drunk and watched cartoons.
But I never meant
To get you upset.

You're stuck inside my mind.
Why do I waste my time?
To tell you...

I miss you, baby
You're crazy, darling.
Forget me.
I need you.
You're lazy, honey
I'm feeble without you.
I can't stand you.
Please don't leave me.

Baby, honey, darling.

Well I'm leaving town once again
In my mind it never ends.
And all you said
Is love from Pi'Kit.

You're stuck inside my mind.
Why do I waste my time?
To tell you...

I miss you, baby

You're crazy, darling.
Forget me.
I need you.
You're lazy, honey
I'm feeble without you.
I can't stand you.
Please don't leave me.

Baby honey, darling,
Crazy, my crazy baby.

This place isn't good for him. He doesn't want to simply exist in pursuing his primitive needs through emotion. This experience has only solidified everything for him. It isn't negative in his mind; he's done it and now he knows. There's no reason to keep on proving the same thing to himself.

He goes for a last authentic curry. His Oian friend that owns the place asks him where he'll go when he sees Gnat with his bag.

"I don't know yet, wherever I can."

He takes a scooter to the airport terminal. The front of it has a wide overhang made of corrugated steel. Complete with the rust of missed maintenance. Here in the shade, he gazes out from whence he came. He blinks once and holds it, taking a snapshot for himself to produce later. *Over four cycles in Pi'Kit.*

The man working the ticket counter asks him his destination.

"Wherever is cheapest," he answers.

"Let me check on that for you, sir." He starts clicking on his keyboard behind the stand. "A flight to Knighton leaves shortly. The cheapest fare by far, if that's what you need."

"I'll take it, thank you." He nods.

The clerk prints the ticket, hands it to him and directs where to go. Airports are such large places, endless hallways filled with people in limbo.

This is the single place on Irfa where it's acceptable to get a drink no matter what, because nobody knows where you're coming from. He finishes quickly, boarding has started. He stops in the lavatory. Another thing that airports could do without, bathroom attendants. *Enough said.*

On the flight, he watches the screen showing how fast they're moving and at what altitude. This commonplace form of transportation was the thing of science fiction throughout human history. To be able to fly as a bird, how implausible it was believed to be a thousand spans ago! What's been done with this magnificent achievement of man? The same as every other, packaged for a profit. We could reach the stars, but never will for lack of investors.

VII

The weather outside is dreary, which clashes with the pastel-colored houses lining the oceanfront. It's been a while since he arrived, here in the town of Bry. Lynd, the capital of Knighton, has an appeal that comes in the form of scenic spots for photos, nightlife, and drugs; the same as any other giant urban sprawl. If you've been to one, you've been to them all. He took the train to Bry from Lynd and rented a room on the top floor of a row house much like the ones in Nan Friko that are painted in pinks, yellows, and blues. The lawns are kept up diligently, owners trying to outdo neighbors. A fairly old woman owns the house, it's purple, the only example he's seen. Her husband passed spans ago and rental income keeps her going. Gnat cooks almost every night, different dishes from the places he knows. He helps with the lifting, cleaning, and gardening. The latter is coming back to life with their combined attention, it has been neglected for a spell.

"I lost interest in gold stars from the community," the woman told him. They've been a somewhat odd couple since.

Routine is paramount for Gnat's sense of self, right now it's at a peak. Drinking hasn't been on the schedule; interest is currently away. His immersion into town is thorough. Early alarms are set to watch the sun rise across the beach, trips to get things for cooking, he buys only a single meal each visit. Reading and writing in the park while observing runners lap him and playful children living carefree, too distracted with infancy to know stress. Mothers hover above showering affection. After lunch at the same place, he returns to the house. Every time he plays a different set of albums, from the band *Irfa* and others that came later from their influence. Instrumentals, melodic, repeating. Language in art only creates filth.

Lucid dreaming has become a new hobby to supplement meditation. You must be still until your body starts to move toward the first stages of sleep, and learn to stay in this place. Gnat is able to recognize the dream state, and higher plateaus. His dreams are starting to mix with his memories, he's unsure sometimes if conversations are in the reality of Irfa or his mind. He must reprocess events and place them in a tense. One of six, now, in two variations. Past, present, future, alternate past, alternate present, alternate future. Then waking, or sleeping? Much like the music, he operates in murky vibrations, losing himself in what has been and what he wants to come to fruition. He isn't naïve enough to think he can see the future as it will be. However, possibly as he wants it to be. He isn't sure how, but his consciousness is evolving. He was simply floating without any mode of locomotion. Now his muscles are contracting, he's learning to tread. In the alternate plane, he searches for the shapes of the man and woman from his previous visions. They remain unseen. Maybe he isn't strong enough. Also, the holder of the voice, where is this being?

On a separate level, outside of controlling dreams and memories, he spends evenings in a rocking chair with the old woman. The ultimate sign of comfort, when no words must be spoken. She makes tea, an alien concept to an Omrikan. As the star that brings light takes it away from this continent, they watch. She thinks of a life lived, the family lost, beginning alone and ending alone. Is she bitter or grateful? An onlooker wouldn't surmise it matters either way as she sways back and forth. No expression on her face reveals held emotions, she just accepts what's in front of her.

Gnat envisions. He journeys past the sun to the far reaches of emptiness. He has become jaded. The desire of his life is to make people see what he does. The waste of energy everyone puts in definition. In Omrika, the thought of going to the destinations of Irfa was inspiring. He was convinced he would find something to challenge his morals, his understanding of what is. This hasn't happened, concepts he knew at home remain. They have only been solidified, in an outright fashion. On any level, in any situation, everyone is only doing for themselves with whatever reason necessary; justifying it as purpose in the meantime.

Darkness has fallen and his companion tells him that tomorrow she may need help mending the fence before the ivy attaches to it.

"Anything you need," Gnat answers.

"Sleep soundly." He hears in a voice that is frail, quiet, broken, and sure of itself.

Gnat tries to pull a splinter out of his hand from a broken fence board on his way to the diner. The ivy now has a sturdy structure to grow as tall as it likes.

Approaching, he notices a group of people in pink shirts with clipboards. They are collecting for something. He isn't sure what, however there's a distinct possibility he'll find out.

The voice of a boy stops him. "Excuse me, sir, do you have a moment to talk about diseased patients in poor countries with no access to medical care?"

Gnat, brusquely, "How much do you want?"

"The cost of a coffee on your way to work," he tries to persuade.

"I don't drink coffee, I don't work," says Gnat. "Let me ask you, are you volunteering your time or getting paid?"

Another member of the group answers, "We do get paid minimum wage, we live simply to try and help."

"Which is?"

"The same as Omrika," the original questioner replies.

"And the average wage in these countries you speak for?"

"Cents per cycle!" a different pair of them exclaim in unison.

Gnat starts laughing. "Based on your wages alone, the five of you have to sign up forty people per shift solely to sustain you being here. On top of that I could send the money straight to the person in the desolate country and that covers them for a season?"

"It isn't that easy. The red tape of bureaucracy is navigated by our employer..."

"No thank you," Gnat declares.

He's in his regular booth, visited enough to rationalize calling it *his spot*. The cook salutes through the window, calling, "The usual?"

"You've got it," Gnat chimes.

Glancing around, there's a girl at a nearby table from Knighton more than likely. She has pale skin from a lack of sun and streaming blonde hair. He's struck, recognizing the name of her magazine. *Outcry*. That independent liberal publication from Omrika. *I can't escape that place.*

"Hey there, how are you?" he asks politely.

She examines him from her peripherals, immediately spinning the other direction acting as if he doesn't exist.

"You can't say hello?"

"I'm a feminist, I'm not interested," she remarks, staring at the page, which goes unread.

"That means that you can't speak to me?"

She stops. "I know what you want, it isn't going to happen."

"What, for you to be kind to me?"

"Don't be facetious," she says.

Gnat is suspended in a solution of sludge, dumbfounded. "Talk about a double standard. You judge me and assume my intentions, demeaning me based on my sex. The same thing you don't want me to do. What's that supposed to mean, anyway, being a feminist?"

"I want women to be equal to men," she affirms.

"Women are equal to men, though. A woman could be the leader of Omrika or a multinational company."

"I want to be able to assert my beliefs without being put in a box because of my gender."

"It's alright to put yourself in a box with the label of your choosing, though? You only make yourself lesser with the title. You're a human, you make choices. You need to be applauded for that? The social justice generation, acknowledging personal insecurities while making other people feel bad about it. That's not equality, that's self-pity," asserts Gnat.

She sets her magazine down. "Everyone has a responsibility to stand up for what they believe in."

"You are going to do what you do. I'm not sure if that's responsibility or just survival. You have the right to do whatever you want. I have the right to not accept it. In these times, if you disagree with the status quo, you're treated as a scourge. Another double standard. Do I have to accept the story of god so a religious person has the ability to believe in it? Why do I have to agree with your definitions of gender so that you feel good about them?"

The girl comes back, "If we are going to stop creating lines then yes, you must accept."

"So, your lines mean something, mine don't?" He poses. "Let me ask you this, what's the difference between a supremacist rally and a gay pride parade?"

"Ah!" She's appalled. "One is full of negativity, one is full of positivity! One is about separating, one is about coming together!"

"You're stuck in emotion. Every person on both sides of that scenario is simply being supportive of what they believe. Is stupidity not a genetic trait the same as sexual orientation? Which means more? A person in a thong and apron at a bar, or one in a mask at a bonfire in the woods? People are what they are, it's not going to change. Both of these groups exist for the destruction of the other, and cannot exist in the system without each other. The lines will never blur on a worldwide scale, you can only be yourself and not bother with opinion. If either side succeeds, the lines of separation *will* disappear. The same. Positive or negative, it's moot."

"That's ridiculous." No further explanation is given.

"This idea of coming together, we always make it about what's important to the individual. Women's issues, black lives, why isn't it *humans*? I saw an article somewhere about how women moved across Ropa when men originally settled it. That it was a process that took spans to complete, maybe hundreds of them. I'm pretty sure women are half of what's needed to perpetuate the human race. Obviously, there were women. When did females get so emasculated? The *two* sexes have different names because they are different. Genetically, emotionally, socially. We are predisposed to be skilled in different things. We are never going to be *equal*, it's not possible, biologically. We already have the same social possibilities. Making men feel guilty about being men won't create anything but more discord. It's genetics, nothing more."

"Women are oppressed in this world still, that can go away if we keep striving for a higher standard. You can't tell me it's the same for both sexes, honestly, can you?" she pleads.

"What can I do as a man, right now, that you can't as a woman? Every individual is oppressed and abused. Maybe the highest paid female entertainers don't make the same as their male counterparts. The vast majority of people on Irfa live in extreme poverty, men and women. They know nothing of the top five-percent," Gnat says.

"Right, if we start at the top…"

He interjects, "This current victimhood, women don't want to be equal, they want to be the dominant sex. They may get that, then men will have an uprising and call themselves the victims of a matriarchy. Forget human men and women, in competition; *something* has to be dominant. Absolute unquestioned equality means there's no reason for progress. If everyone is comfortable and the outcome is guaranteed, why try? Being passive kills intellect and invention. If you only have to do what you're told and agree so it's easy, what's the reason for living? What's the reason to discover? Indoctrinated clones arguing over labels, that's what this fight is."

"You agree then, men are the dominant sex?"

"That's what you heard me say? Physically, absolutely. Emotionally, I know that the only object driving any man to act is the potential of a partner. You can't tell me you haven't gotten things for free because of your sex."

She giggles. "Of course I have. But something is always expected."

"Nothing's free, don't accept if you aren't willing to pay the price. You can't have things both ways," he says flatly. "If you want true equality, let's wear black outfits with our faces covered. No more favorites, the end of favors. No promotions based on gender. You will be paid and qualified strictly on ability alone, nothing else. The individual that possesses the best skill set moves up. There are many more man-to-woman transgender patients, is that because men know women have it easier? That they thrive in the manipulation of their male counterparts and victimizing themselves? The weak can't be strong. It's not feminism, it's *misandrism*."

"Haven't you seen the level of abuse in the media? Women are being more or less raped to get parts on screen!"

"We are animals. Males try to mate with females, that's how nature works. It's only genetics, remember? A woman can use her physical features and flirt to get a job, a part in a movie, or a rich man. When it's to her personal benefit, nobody cares. When she puts herself out there and somebody bites that can't give her whatever advantage she wants, she becomes a martyr. Women and men are equal, yet men are pigs for following their instincts. It's one way or the other, take the dirty with the clean or take nothing. Advance against harassment, there's a difference," explains Gnat.

"You aren't changing my mind, only annoying me..."

"Feelings have never gotten anyone anywhere but broken. I'll return to my meal."

"You do that," she says with finality.

Soggy food on a plate due to his neglect. A worthy sacrifice, if he could have passed on a smidge of enlightenment. Clouds have rolled over the sea and Bry, a gentle rain falls. The gloom matches his brooding as he eats.

In nature, sexes play roles. The males get the food, protect, and spread the strongest variations of the genes. Females rear children, assess which members deserve sustenance, and contribute half their genes to the best candidates. If the roles were mixed up and the women bore children while hunting, eventually the species would become extinct. The genes, through reproduction, would always be in a state of unrest. Unprotected in the elements. The outcome? Less births, weaker traits, and failure as a species. The offspring born would more likely come from weaker hunters, less apt to be in a dangerous situation that puts the next generation at risk. The roles as defined by genes are the most important job to accomplish.

Then we get to humans and their nature. Which isn't defined by genes any longer, only selfishness. We believe anyone can be anything. Which leaves offspring at a disadvantage. Not basic survival, per say, but consciously. Socially. A child with only a mother doesn't receive guidance by the male, which leads to no respect for others or authority. No concept of responsibility or sacrifice. If the child is with a working mother, it is left to state care through development and education. This leads to no creativity, standardization, and lack of empathy. In turn humans become weaker through time. Less intellectual. Less in tune with one another, along with their habitat. Disconnection. Dissociation. Through selfish emotion, we become less than optimal again, on the level of survival. Neglect of roles and definition within genders will lead to our peril, at some point. We have become weak-minded.

The plate is empty except of crumbs. He drinks the entire glass of water like a camel getting ready for a trek through dry sands.

"Thanks, see you again," he yells to the line.

"Okay, brother!" the cook says, unseen.

He pauses near the girl. "Simply saying everyone is equal makes us weaker as a whole. We must recognize and use our differences advantageously. Take care."

Traveling in the rain is always enjoyed, it's cleansing and purifying on a very fundamental level. The canvassers from earlier have moved to a different corner. He considers the girl in the diner.

"Gentrification is the death of synthesis. I've seen it in Oia, Wishintown, and Knighton. The rich and righteous are destroying folkways with every sip of craft alcohol and political correctness," he mumbles, putting his hands in his pockets and shoulders up, facing the precipitousness. A foreboding pace is held, until chanting voices are heard. In front of an office building a group of maybe thirty people stands with signs. The leader holds a megaphone, the group repeats what is said through the loudspeaker. It isn't completely audible from this distance; Gnat starts toward them.

"What are these clowns doing?" He glares.

The rain is steady, not heavy. The drops are strung out, thin, minuscule enough to be only a petty nuisance. They won't completely soak anything caught outside. The clouds are a light gray, consequence of the intense radiation trying to break through their backsides. The fluorescence from the interiors of buildings surrounding doesn't have enough power to be noticed yet, it will still be a while until night prevails. The wind is nonexistent. The town is still, almost locked in this specific frame of time. It is eerie. He takes a mental snapshot of his location and state of mind. The current that's usually present within him, driving him, is missing. In that brief lapse between thoughts, when all command of sense is absent, a sudden gust of wind blows across town. He looks toward the protesters. Flopping over itself down the street is a crumpled piece of paper soaked through, almost returning to individual fibers as he picks it up. It's from the gathering of angry people shouting in the streets of a reserved and detached town, acting as if any human here cares for goings on in political offices that never touch them personally. He flips the sheet over, at the top is a name. He is familiar with it. Tiria Sika.

It explains what she's done, something untold to him so far. There's a corporation employing thousands that takes a valuable fuel source out of the ground in the form of rock. This rock is fragile, forming in dense layers. Men have known the capability of using this special rock as power for many hundreds of spans. However, the process hasn't become profitable until recently. In the past, it took more energy to create the fuel than the rock gave in return. Now it's plausible to use it as a fuel source. Tiria bought a company ten spans ago, although it has been around for much longer. She filed for bankruptcy last span, about the time Gnat saw her in Addie's *Outcry*. After that claim went through, she reopened the same facility under a different name and is ready to go to market as the first supplier of this new cheap form of fuel for industry. The problem people have is that the bankruptcy made void the pensions of the men that worked for the original corporation. These men were promised retirement checks, more than they ever made while working. She used a loophole and it isn't sitting right with the working class. Tiria played by the rules laid out for her and beat the game. *You can't get ahead, no matter what team you play for. Only the person writing the rules wins anything.*

The voices are still unintelligible, which is fine, he doesn't want to hear whatever rhyming quips they preach.

At the purple house he takes his guitar out under the covered front porch. He plays a few old songs. He's never tried anything with them publicly, what's the point? A feeling which has eluded him in Knighton comes on. His calluses have vanished, the frets hurt his fingertips as he pushes against them. The strings are flat and rusty. His tuner is forgotten along the way, he twists the pegs and lines the notes up by sound the best he can. Something comes out, as he thinks of the sting he feels in his throat.

> *Packing my bag, to get on the road*
> *Starting to think, trying to unload.*
> *Shirt with a stain*
> *Sock with a hole*
> *Put them away, don't tell a soul.*
>
> *Busing again, to the west end.*
> *Seeking a vision, nothing pretend.*
> *Frost on the glass*
> *Pain on the wall*
> *An unknown destination, trying to recall.*
>
> *Living in the moment, lasts forever*
> *Now it's gone, can't remember.*
>
> *Tuning flat strings, playing a show.*

Somebody laughs, feeling too old.

Scratch near my eye

Crack in my bone

Oh yeah, I remember, I'm sleeping alone.

The tattoo fades away, will wisdom find its place?

Loss of self-expression

A sudden bitter taste.

A sudden bitter taste.

A sudden bitter taste.

Gnat absorbs the melancholy and sorrow, and returns it to the atmosphere with his voice and strumming. The old woman isn't home, she must have gone to see a friend since she couldn't be outside due to the weather.

He selects an album on the desktop computer to meditate with. Just in case he logs in to the server to check his mail. His dad may have sent something, no reason for Gnat to worry him unnecessarily. There is a message from Hipslyn, as he reads, his stomach drops.

Gnat,

I am glad that you have had the chance to see the places and experience the things you've wanted to. Our time together was wonderful, I got to show you the best parts of Raminia. Our ideas of the lives we want to live are very different. I have met someone here, he is close to me. I have decided to be with him, and let you go. Please don't answer this email, or show up here. I know you are the type to do something like this.

Goodbye, and good luck.

Hipslyn

"She took what's there, what's easy, safe, and comfortable. She never wanted me, only a body," he says, so softly his lips don't move. It's almost a thought caught in his mouth, not quite escaping to the room. His head spins, he doesn't know where it wants to go.

Every person has at least one redeeming quality; that doesn't make them any more worth the time. Humans are not inherently good or bad, those words are only subject to standard and opinion. People are doing what's best for themselves in the current situation, always! If you are aligned with that you may get some benefits. They may call you a friend or companion. As soon as you differ or the timing is wrong, you don't matter and aren't important anymore. There are so many things like this in my life. Places I've been, people I've met. I can't explain the epiphanies I've had, even for an instant. I keep them for myself. These are the lessons. People see and understand things, but still live in them. I will not. I will not settle. I will not bow. I live in what I know, not what I feel. I'm here, in this house. Soon, I'll be out there finding those things again. In one form or another. On my own, the way I thrive.

"Forget meditating, I need a drink." His voice has returned. He puts his damp brown jacket on. Damp, yes. Also trustworthy, the only thing that has done what it was supposed to do. Follow him wherever, through whatever. Keep him warm, keep him dry.

Out into the weather, *he* is weathered. He doesn't think of his family, he doesn't think of Hipslyn. He only wants a drink; he only wants to forget. Through the ooze of moisture and wind he travels undeterred. If the air was a color, it would be light blue. Thin enough to move through quickly, sharp enough to turn skin red on contact. It also cuts through his worn old jacket, sending a shiver over his chest. *Nothing lasts forever.*

The bar is on the fifth floor of a hotel, a rooftop venue with a patio enclosed on three sides by glass. He hasn't been here until now, riding the elevator like a rocket ship, taking him to another place.

He orders a shot, then another. The buzz of alcohol is in his hands, the totem which is disregarded. They say nothing to him, no signs of where he is inside as Gnat heads onto the patio. The rain has subsided, although the temperature is still frigid. The clouds are turning from blue-gray to black-gray, the light fades. As he watches the skyline he focuses. The drinks were meant to help him dismiss everything; they've always served this purpose. Currently, the opposite has happened. He has intensified, the things in his thoughts will not be suppressed. Gnat considers how he remembers and wonders about everyone he meets. They don't think of him. *They are thinking of themselves.*

*Deflect and justify your own actions, the way of things. No one sees we are baboons running around looking for the next form of entertainment. Nothing is done unless it benefits the individual, which is why the system fails. That's what humans are, monkeys. It's our condition. We barbarically worked our way out of the slime to become agriculturalists. We fought disease, other animals, nature. We became religious, fought wars, defined emotion and what we see as **right** or **wrong**. In the mid-ages, everything was for sin or for glory. After we got past this, surviving was no longer a large scale issue. Now we only have ourselves to think about, creating reasons for why we act. We are sliding into the muck again, only with fabricated reasons this time.*

People are constantly trying to suppress their animal instincts. They smother reason with emotion. They change their physical appearance to separate further from the wild. Everything is useless institutions trying to provide a point to the misery of existence. Some people put their energy in things, some put their energy in thoughts. Only to grow up, live, work, *suffer, and be forgotten. All the strife is only for you. Personal progress is irrational. No one stands **alone** in the general population, chasing a dream you were told to hold close. Issues, fashion, art, and health are fed through screens to the masses. The companies that own the screens fix trends to make more profit. Everyone settles for it. In Oia, it's the same cycle for a lifetime and everybody expects to be taken care of simply because they were born. Then in old age, the hoard moves to F'lalasip and waits to die. Go out to eat, laugh. Some person does something, consequences follow. It's so drab. School for twenty spans, work for thirty spans, slowly rot for the rest. If you are **lucky**. Luck, what a subjective concept.*

He steps to the bar. He thanks the man serving him, maybe he's working to pay for his kid to go to school. Maybe he had something to give, but no entity wanted to take it, so here he is. No chance of moving up, existing for a paycheck.

Gnat sees the crippling effects of delegation, and man's capacity to further the negative circumstances it has always protected.

Life is nothing but entrapment. You can't escape the torture. Like a raindrop falling to freedom, racing toward a destination, only to crash and be washed back to the sea. The randomness of the descent and speed are irrelevant. It's the purpose in the first place. The drop serves to feed life. The location, the feeling, the details pale in comparison to why the drop came to being through the process of evaporation and physics. The condition serving itself. Nothing more, nothing less.

All we've accomplished, the problems we've solved and surpassed, what is the outcome? We've used definitions to become a self-important, self-absorbed race. We've done nothing but help our instinctual desires. And at the same time, destroyed everything around us. A virus. A bacteria, consuming. The human condition is only important to humans. The sum of knowledge throughout our history only pertains to us, here and now.

We have not, will not, and are not meant to find the answer to anything of significance. The response 'I don't want to think about it' fits the notion perfectly. It shows the true ignorance we live in. Seeing things the way we want, not the way they are. Opinion? Belief? Emotion? Not valid against the way it is, what's happening. Your life is just a series of chances and statistics. You are not original, but quantifiable.

The concept of currency, another example of stupidity. A pinnacle of convention, universal on Irfa. It has no actual purpose or quality except that we say it does. It isn't backed by anything; we can print more whenever we feel. However, all thought, art, time, and success are somehow correlated to appraisals of monetary value. It has become the most important thing driving lives to their ends. Wasted energy and false assessment by hairless apes that can't view anything other than what is right in front of them. In spite of death, money is the most important thing that someone can leave behind for their family. Not memories, experience, or wisdom. Their possessions pawned off for cash to go on vacation or whatever else is desired at the time. The explanation? 'That's what they would have wanted.'

Who was the richest man in Ancient Ehfra? Who was the leader five generations ago? What were their foreign and domestic policies? What scandals took place? Who agreed or disagreed? Who won which event at the world games ten spans ago? No one knows now, what happened in those times is history. Literally. It makes no difference except to the people there living it. In all those situations, humans were only worried about what personal effect it would have on them. Not the future or lives of others. They were selfish, the same as every other living thing. All these issues are a way to place your plight onto something you can't control. It comes down to a point. As soon as the emotion is gone, people forget. Legacy is generational, and therefore unimportant.

Gnat's life starts to run on repeat before his eyes. He questions himself, "What can I do?"

He's above the clutter, the ground is so far away as he bends over the edge of the roof.

"I've been going against the submissive, the thoughtless, the goons I encounter. I'm a ghost in a crowded courtyard, speaking but no other hears. Do they not hear me because they don't want to?" He speaks assuredly to the Irfa. "Or because they can't grasp the concepts? Either way, I am mute. I can't possibly forget my morals gained through what I've witnessed and acquired my whole life. I can't redefine my outlook, my predispositions, to only become part of this society I despise so much. I won't subscribe. Not to this." He finishes the drink. "I haven't lost the things I enjoy, things that pass the time, things that are logical. I've somehow lost the thing that meant more to me than I could ever explain in words, there is no *return*. No going forward, either. Just existing..."

The people around Gnat get stuck in the notion that he is crazy or in a phase because he sees things differently. People are defending their own plight, their own way of living. Anything outside normal is tossed away. Like a psychiatrist, taking people and squeezing them into a box through a man-made filter. Limiting the evolution of the mind. Which is, of course, the point. Ease and normalcy being accepted is more important than understanding. Nobody speaks of the metaphysical any longer. Only the finite, the material.

Gnat, however, is a true seeker. A lost piece in a vast and complicated game. He stands in the same spot, still. A statue.

I no longer see value in anything. Not eating, conversation, breathing, laughing. It's just noise. The reason everything falls apart, from marriage to the constructs that invented it. It's about yourself. The past is forgotten, the future isn't considered. You can never influence anything, except your immediate predicament. What's the point of law? The actions that brought these things to fruition are already over. It's people trying to find a reason or pin an action on something. Why suffer with no objective? Or is suffering only living? Isn't living evolving? Isn't evolution chance? Isn't chance random? There is no aspect of human life that means anything. We are the product of animals that came before us. Every murderer, every leader. The entirety within every person, instinct. The collective we've created is solely a means to an end. Our end.

"My end," Gnat states.

The reason being, I have clarity. I can see through the stained glass with perfect vision. It's artificially-produced nonsense, trying to scrape purpose out of nothing. You live, you die. The details in the middle have no bearing on this fact. I've seen the things I wanted to do. The jobs, the possessions, thoughts of wasting time on these things disgusts me. Not physically, worse. Mentally. I'm at the point I've always known I would come to. Feeling like and becoming aware I am nothing but dirt. A temporary growth that has no capability but to take, while given resources are exhausted. Individually and exponentially. Multiply nothing over and over, you come up with the same thing. Zero. Meaning, legacy, or substance, for me or anyone else. However you try to define it, this is the outcome. Obliteration of consciousness and tangibility...

Everyone is committing suicide. It can be quick and absolute or take spans based on the air you breathe, what you eat, what drugs you take. It's only perception.

It's dark, the bulbs from the offices shine out, ships can spot them over the celestial horizon. Citizens are moving below. Like ants, running around. Trying to find something to eat.

"I don't want to do this for another fifty spans or even double what I have now. I don't want to do any of it for one more blink.

We've abandoned reason to sift through tribulation and know it. Cursed by awareness, of the self and of emptiness," he whispers.

Not a single person is present, they've been driven indoors by a bit of chill. Suddenly a pain burns in the center of his chest. He makes a move to the edge of the patio. Here it is, the voice, hidden in the planes of his mind's reality. He has searched but cannot find the source. It has returned and gives him a syllable. *Now.*

Gnat takes a deep breath, contracts the muscles of his face as tightly as he can, restoring aim. Dropping the empty glass from his hand, he hears it shatter on the deck as he falls from the edge into open air. He isn't flying, as a mother might wish for her child, but descending, her biggest fear. The hardened weight that has been in his stomach releases its defined edges, exploding throughout him with the force of a flattened paddle smacking water. It was a marker it seems, waiting for him to come to the correct conclusion. *The only virtue.* Gnat knows its job is complete. He's done what he needed to. There is a certain specific awareness, a genuine smile creeps over his face. *Peace. Pardon. Absolution.*

His body hits the ground. A woman screams. Gnat doesn't process the impact although it happens. He understands, it isn't about what he feels, only what is real. Irfa. Goes. Black.

PART B

DELINEATION

I

The void and vacuum. Negative space. Baseless, blank, immaterial. Null. Nothing can be heard or felt. No gravity, no weight. No air to breathe. No movement, there isn't anything to move. It's not a dream, not a memory. Time doesn't have power, a dimension unimagined. Waiting. The only virtue in this place. To wait.

Something tenuous comes. A ripple, a reverberation strikes. Barely tactile, it's gone. Another, somewhat stronger, on a different wavelength. A pulse of energy, from where? Does this place carry on endlessly, eternally, or does it have a boundary? The pace of these waves hastens to a pounding. Something audible. Not quite a sound, but a change in pressure. Is it imagined? What being is doing the imagining? The twangs of pressure have a pattern of randomness. They must mean something. This place isn't empty. *I am not alone. I. Who is "I?"*

There is a river, suddenly. Running in view as far as each end of this plane goes. Or was it not noticed before? The source, the mouth, are invisible. It twists around rocks and land which don't occur, flowing downhill in a place without grade, encumbrance, or direction. A landscape of frivolity.

The entire body of water starts to flip, turning vertical, its width is becoming its height. This river has no depth, only two dimensions.

In its reflection, no greetings come from entities holding shape or form. It keeps turning, until a face appears on the surface of the river. Its features aren't perfectly clear. A neck, a body. The body is draped in something, what's the word? *Clothes.* All energy is put on the face by "I." Complete attention, fixated. Until the irises start to show, they are hazel. Freckled skin appears, then the grizzled face covered in hair from every direction comes in to focus. *Gnat. This is Gnat. I am Gnat.*

He's in control of himself again. He lifts his hands, they're covered in perspiration, the top layers of skin transparent. Tiny arteries dart across the muscle fibers underneath. He can feel his pulse as he glares at himself in the river. He tries to scream, but there's nothing to power his lungs. This doesn't deter him. He stretches his shoulders back, and tries to force the sound out, again to no avail. His face is purple and blue, blood vessels expanding without oxygen, the veins in his neck are protruding. He drops to his knees, his whole body contracting, trying to make a sound. To be heard, seen, felt. Anything. Gnat is in agony, eyeballs bleeding water. He's hot, red hot, burning up. The air, the escape will be found. The river starts to rumble and shake, then becomes rigid. A mirror. His face has become pale and clammy, the entirety of his strength is almost spent. He struggles to his feet, toward the river turned imager and at a run punches it. The pane shatters in violence, the shards flying in three dimensions. Striking him, they shred his physical body. Before the pain of this is processed...

His eyes burst wide, alive, flicking from side to side. Head locked in place. He's in a bed. In a chamber, bent upward at an angle to see everything. The walls are empty. It is white. Sterilized, supposedly clean. He's isolated. The door to the room is open, no one occupies the hall. However, there are voices. Something familiar as he recalls. The random pattern of words. The same as the pounding in the place he just was. They were coming through to him, these expressions. *Am I alive or dead? Am I in purgatory? Was I wrong, am I waiting to be judged? If so, I'll tell whoever is doing so to keep their judgment. I made the best choice I could with whatever was presented to me. I never got in anyone's way. I ended things the same as I did anything in my life, on my terms. So, kick rocks.*

He begins to sit up yelling in defeat. There *is* air here, and he has a roar. But he has become aware. His entire body feels as if it was dipped into a deep fryer. The pain is searing. He wears a gown. On his feet, socks with buttons of grip on the soles to stop him from slipping. He wiggles toes, the sting of life returns. He can't move his core, it's too much. His left arm is propped up in the air, wrapped. The fingers of this hand are so swollen, they're touching. Movement at the door. What seems to be a nurse comes in, holding a clipboard. She glances at him, and double takes.

"Oh, you're awake! Can you hear me?" she asks.

"Am I alive or dead?" Gnat returns.

"You are alive, barely. Your body fought hard, you must have some things that you still want to do," she answers, gently.

"Why did you treat me, did I give consent?"

"You've been in a coma, darling. We couldn't ask you. Many of the surgeries you need still have to be completed. We have only done what was necessary to keep you alive so far," she answers, "Would you have given consent?"

"What's wrong with me?" he replies, and coughs. She brings him a glass, tilting it over his lip so he can have a drink. To this point in his life, nothing has ever been so refreshing or invigorating as this singular mouth full of water.

"It's here in the paperwork, should I go through it?"

"Please," says Gnat.

"You punctured your liver, a kidney, and a lung. The tube coming out of your chest is for the latter. We are having trouble keeping it open. Every rib is broken, along with two vertebrae, both shoulders, your right foot, and left wrist. Your left arm is broken in nineteen places, it needs to be reconstructed. Your pelvis sheered completely in half. It already has pins holding it together, that will take more than a span to heal fully. The front of your skull was crushed, there are pins and a plate above your eye holding it in the right spot to heal so your face isn't flat. You have severe brain contusions, which are like bruises. They will heal, but it will take some time. You won't stand for quite a while either, it will be hard work for you," she concludes.

"Anything else?" he laughs, which is a mistake, the wounds come back as new.

"Everything that isn't broken thoroughly is fractured, basically. A small percentage of people would survive a fall from that height, you know."

Gnat gets serious. "I do know, that was the point. Is my family aware?"

"Your father's on his way to take you home. He'll be here soon, tomorrow. I have the rest of my rounds, I'll be back later. Here you go," she says, placing the remote in his usable, non-dominant hand.

"Great. Here I am. Can't escape Omrika, can't escape Irfa," he grumbles. Speaking is also painful. He doesn't turn the screen on, flicking the remote away with his fingers. It crashes to the floor popping open, batteries rolling out. *Lucky remote. See, it isn't that hard to break yourself.*

An orderly stops by Gnat's room, noticing he's awake. He comes in, moves the rolling table above Gnat, and places a tray of liquid foods there.

"That'll do the trick. Have something to eat," he tells him. "Glad to see you're awake."

"That makes one of us," Gnat retorts.

He doesn't touch the tray, but finds a button next to him that releases medication, something that will enable him to ignore discomfort. He presses it again and again, the pain he feels both inside and out doesn't subside. After a while he drops this button also, resting his eyes, dreams from this slumber are indescribable.

A team of doctors with their aides enter his room.

"We're going to fix your arm," a younger man says. "The only problem is we can't put you under. You're too unstable, your lung keeps collapsing. We can give you a local anesthetic, you won't feel anything. But you will be conscious for the procedure."

"Alright," Gnat answers, absently.

In the operating room they hold him up in a type of chair and strap him down. His left arm is also braced in three places on a table. He can't move, positioned in full view of his shattered appendage. They inject needles, waiting for the drugs to take effect.

The doctor bonds to his stool, going to work. The young man was correct, he can't feel anything. He *can* see it. His forearm is sliced apart to the bone, which is crushed to pieces. The surgeon pokes and prods, placing everything in its correct place or as close as he can. It will never be the same.

"Will I play guitar again?" Gnat asks as the man works.

"Yes. Maybe not as accurately as you have before." He brings out the titanium plates and screws. "These won't go off in the airport, a bonus for a traveler like you, isn't it?" he says lightly.

Out comes the drill, to put pilot holes in the shards. The smell of bone being burnt is not easily forgotten. The power tool is too strong for such tiny pieces, he's told. It must be constructed by hand. A mental snapshot is taken, regrettably, of the mad scientist twisting the threads into their new homes with a screwdriver. When finished, his muscle isn't stitched together but stapled. The same type of gun used to build a house is wielded against his flesh. As he's wheeled into his whitewashed holding cell someone is waiting for him. Ju, his father.

"Last thing for now," the nurse says. "We need to pull the bandages out of your nasal cavity. It will be nice to breathe through your nose again, won't it?"

A mouth-breather. I hadn't noticed. She takes giant tweezers, grabs the end, wrenching it in circles as she pulls to break it loose. It was connected to a scab on his brain, it seems. His eyes pour tears and he gags involuntarily.

"Why did that hurt so bad?!" Gnat yells.

"And the other side." She grabs the glob of gauze, not paying attention to him. After it's out, he is left by himself. *With company.*

"The orderly said he brought you that tray, you haven't touched it," Ju states, breaking the tension. "Aren't you hungry?"

"I don't want to be alive, why would I want a sandwich?" he spits.

"You should eat. You won't heal if you don't have any fuel in you."

His eyes roll to Ju, gently. He isn't sure what expression will be on his father's face, then he knows. Solemness. He stares at his son, silent. If you go out by your own hand, that's what you are, separated. The repercussions aren't there, you don't know what happens to everyone you left behind. Gnat hasn't been granted this luxury. He tried to leave and failed. Now he must meet these people, both sides knowing he was going to let go. The thought of them didn't hold enough to change his mind. Starting with his father, the most important person in his life. His sister, he was going to leave her to fend for herself. No backup after their mother and father pass. An emotion he allows himself, something he has never consciously recognized or felt before. Shame. He erases it. He won't live in his feelings. He made the choice for a reason. Those reasons haven't changed. If his family doesn't grasp that, then this is the line between them.

"You can turn the TV on if you want," Gnat says. "I'm going to bomb out on pain pills."

The time is filled with nothing, he absorbs the hurt, it's self-imposed, how could he complain? His father watches whatever is on passively, goes to get food when he's hungry, and is available for his son. In whatever capacity he's needed, he accepts. A great man in any situation he finds himself. Every visit, they make Gnat sit up multiple times, the feeling in his pelvis is excruciating. Even with the medication to push it away, the torment is still so bad he blacks out. News comes from the financial office. He doesn't have insurance, they've given him enough treatment to save his life, he will be discharged. However, he won't be cleared to fly for a while. Ju books a hotel outside the city, the ambulance takes them to the countryside.

The whole stay, he doesn't shower. He doesn't eat. He lays in bed, high on pills, watching a show about a veterinarian working on farm animals.

"Can we watch something else?" Ju asks.

"There is nothing else."

The trip to the airport is a fiasco. Gnat is in a wheelchair, so the taxi is a van with the seats removed. He's rolled up and buckled in. Like a car on a flatbed truck, down to the straps.

A toddler jumps around and kicks Gnat's chair after takeoff, not stopping the entire trip home. The kid's parents don't notice, too busy with the touchscreen and movies watched half a dozen times. *My reasons were sound.*

They land in Nuwal city, the largest accumulation of absurdity on the eastern seaboard of Omrika. So-called intellectuals relishing in the fact they don't need to speak for themselves, platitudes say everything for them. Anyone lesser or excommunicated rots, never to be heard from again.

As they exit the terminal, the men see the women at the same time, Su and Ima. Both envelope Gnat with their bodies, trying to smother out everything happening on Irfa. The ride to Oia is forgotten in a very uncomfortable daze of medication. His father carries him to the room they've readied for him on the first floor to avoid any steps. The sun rises, Gnat doesn't. His parents lay out pill bottles, water, and money to order food before leaving for work.

"The front door is unlocked, tell them to bring it in if you call. The phone is on the table here," his dad tells him. "You should eat something, have something, come on now."

He doesn't get anything. The following cycles into the future are like this, he has to be lifted up and taken to the bathroom, to the shower. He won't stoop as low to let his parents clean him, so he suffers through to keep some dignity. Eventually he starts to eat, he tells his mother what to buy. The stash of cash notes he left behind before Raminia is spent, used up to send his dad to come get him.

"You need another opinion by an Omrikan surgeon," Su tells him. "I made an appointment, your dad will take you tomorrow. After, you have to get evaluated for disability. Who knows how long you'll be out of work."

"Whatever you say," Gnat accepts, away in the patterns of brush-strokes on the ceiling. He sees an island, a mountain on it. Maybe it's a volcano? No, definitely a volcano, how else would the island have gotten there? Is it large enough to sustain a human? I could fish, take some seedlings with me. I'm sure there are pineapples or coconuts. Passing birds bring many types of diversified plant life in their droppings...

The subsequent morning, he meets the surgeon, Dr. Pati. A man that holds himself calmly, and speaks plainly. Gnat appreciates this.

"I don't want to tell you, after everything you've just done, but the doctors didn't fix your arm correctly. I need to redo it. Those Ropan physicians are tenured differently, they start in the emergency room to gain experience. You were possibly a first attempt for whomever tried it. It isn't healing, and it won't. I need to take grafts from your pelvis to complete the structure of your forearm."

"Let's do it, no reason to wait, is there? You're telling me that this whole time, I've been living with a broken arm not protected in a cast?"

Dr. Pati smirks, "That's the gist of it. How did you fall anyway?"

"I slipped on a banana peel," says Gnat.

"Those fruit peels can be a doozy. We'll get you back to it, be ready for the strain and hard work. I'll make an appointment as soon as I can."

In the car as they drive onto the highway, Ju says something about the medical care in socially run countries.

"Now to the disability doctor, you think you'll need it? You're strong. You'll work again, when you want to. I know it."

"You know it?" Gnat questions his dad.

"Oh yes."

"I've been living with a sheered pelvis and a broken arm out in the elements this entire time. I know something, too. Going through this process of pain, I've learned that the average person has no idea what being hurt or at a disadvantage really is. You see the commercials for diabetes, fibromyalgia, restless leg syndrome. People act like these insignificant inconveniences are a big drain on their lives. It's a personal scapegoat to not get things finished, while also not having to feel bad about it," he explains.

"You are tougher than the average person," Ju chimes. "Don't forget that."

The disability office is run by the state and therefore can more or less be chocked up to a joke manifested within a building, unkempt, in the poorest neighborhood of Nata. Streaks of brown run from the corners of the windowsills to the ground, where planter boxes are filled with nothing but thorny weeds. The pavement is loose gravel, once solid, the painted lines of individual spots are reminiscent of boundaries drawn on the yard of a prison. Done initially, never to be touched up again. His dad wheels him to the office, where they sit. Yet, no other person is waiting with them. The most up to date magazine is from the span he turned twenty-one.

Gnat's name is called, he tells his dad to stay as the receptionist rolls him away.

This man's office is slate, *misery*, if such a shade exists. The walls are carpeted in a material that looks like suede. A desk made of pressed wood, an examination chair. Nothing else except his diploma. He is a medical doctor, yes. He graduated from the college of the peninsula, lower Nuwal state. The exam is a farce. He checks Gnat's reflexes with a plastic hammer, bends his joints, and tells him he'll be alright. No history, no mention of the accident or his mental state. A precaution to avoid liability for the federal government. Denied by a quack. Not that he'll need the money or the parking sticker, but what if he did? A runaround for people that can't run. This man is recognized because he paid for the title. Most definitely less than some other doctors, the principle is the subject. Why is this man able to decide the fate of others so certainly without question?

Ju buys him dinner on the way to *his* house.

"Eat it now or save it for later, you'll want it."

"Thanks," says Gnat.

In his bed he starts to drift. *General practitioners, doctors. They're revered as intelligent people. Some are, yet most aren't. Doctors don't treat symptoms, they treat standards. Based on what a random researcher testing hypotheses at some prior point concluded. The conclusions of a trial become what is taught. That's not knowledge, it's trial and error. We can't be sure if the result perceived is complete. Consider colony count in an infection. Before a railroad crossed Omrika, a study found twelve individual people with unrelated infections had a bacteria count of a hundred thousand organisms per sample. So, since then, no infection has been treated unless the colony count is found to be the same or greater. If you have symptoms and a count of twenty thousand, that's considered colonization, you aren't treated. Twelve people determined a course of action for millions. It's a field using stop-gaps to make humans feel better while possible. What will the consequences of some of these drugs be for future generations? What does a doctor do? Practices. That's habitual action based on teaching, not progression or insight.*

He remembers a conversation with a man on the road, who was studying biology. When a foreign cell enters an animal's body and the immune system wants to fight the invader off, what does it do? It creates antibodies, which have specific receptors to attach to the stowaway, the virus or bacteria. The receptors on these cells hold an infinite number of sizes and shapes. How does the immune system find the correct one? Indefinitely, it creates antibodies in every possible iteration, releasing them to the bloodstream preventatively. This is why some viruses are beaten internally and some aren't able to be cured. It's not a miracle, only a thing. Chance. The body is giving itself the best option it can without any inherent knowledge attached.

He starts a movie on his mother's laptop, picking up the bag of food from Ju. By the time he stops watching films, he has a realization. *I tried to kill myself, and lived. What am I going to do with it? Sit in a bed, eat fast-food, live off the government, and be in Oia? No, this end is worse than death. If I'm going to keep going, I need to find a way to reach people and share what I have. But, how? How? First, I have to get up on my own.*

He lifts himself to a sitting position with his good arm. Not easy, considering his core can't be used either. The chair is next to the bed. He swings his legs over its side with the help of his arm, the release of a wince hides the ineffable burn throughout his lower body. He's ready to try, a fluid spin on the balls of his feet to the seat of his chair. His dad left the wheels locked, it won't roll away. *Check.* He can't put the full weight of himself on his hips, it may reinjure his bones.

"Okay, on three... THREE!" He yelps, trying to forget what his nerves are telling him. He grasps the arm of the wheelchair, swings up and around a hundred and eighty degrees, and down. He's made it.

"That's the beauty of centrifugal force for you. Don't fight it, work with it," says Gnat, triumphantly.

He releases the brakes, lifts his legs up into the stirrups, and turns the wheelchair around. Which is easy with just his right arm, moving forward, not so much. He starts to scoot forward, in a gentle zigzag. Turn to the side, stay perfectly still so it doesn't roll backward, reach over and move the other wheel. After some time he makes it to his parents, watching television. *The news.*

"What, you're up?!" Su exclaims.

"That's my boy," his dad says.

"I decided if I'm going to be alive, I'm going to live. There's a thing I'm jealous of, a man with a purpose. I've never had one. Whether it hurts or helps others isn't relevant. Something to strive for, that's the point. I know what I want to do, I'm going to get out of this chair and go do it," Gnat says.

Su vets him. "What is it that you want to do?"

"Be remembered," says Gnat.

"Then you will," echoes Ju. "Your doctor called. He can get you in soon to fix your arm."

"Heard."

Until the surgery, Gnat wheels around the first floor. Stretching his arms and legs out the best he can, trying to remind himself he'll stand again. He'll play guitar. He'll travel. The surgery is routine. He deals with the intensity of the injury as he has everything else. Now it's in a splint, guaranteed to heal properly. He gets in the habit of moving as much as possible within the confines of his marred body and the house. Both of which he is trapped in. *But not eternally.*

Ima has moved back in for lack of a job that pays enough to sustain her. She enters his room, telling him to lower the volume.

"No," is his only reply.

She turns the set off and takes the remote outside, knowing he can't follow.

Knowing, or thinking? It's not that easy.

In the kitchen is a walker he hasn't used. Ju got it as the next logical step. In his wheelchair, Gnat rolls toward it. He'll use both hands, the arm in the splint can control balance, his right can do the lifting. With a bit of malice, he jumps up onto the four-cornered cane and stands up straight for the first time since being on that roof in Knighton. Using the outside edges of his feet, more like a pirate's wooden legs than an apes, he shuffles to the front door and opens it. Ima talks on the phone, she turns in shock, thinking she was alone except for an immobilized brother.

Gnat holds his splinted hand out. "Give me the remote."

"Hold on," she says into the receiver, reaching to the ground and handing it to him. "How did you...?"

"I'm not an invalid, I don't care what some *specialist* says about what I can and cannot do. That wasn't cool, what you did to me."

"It made you get up," she says, sassily.

She's smiling at him. They both start to laugh, restored.

"Go get us some food. Dad left money on the table."

"What?"

"Whatever gets us the most with what's there," he replies, shuffling to the couch, feet numbing more with each step.

The Irfa keeps turning. Eventually he runs out of movies to watch, and must revert to television with commercials. He mutes them as they come, yet the quality of his life seems to be less with them in the room. Even the programs are scripted idiotic reruns of the same ideas, done by different networks.

His dad comes home from work and asks him what's on.

"It's the same. Stopping people from using drugs, people that are extremely overweight, people hoarding possessions. It always gets to a point where if they don't stop what they're doing, the family is going to cut them out. Is that care? Is that compassion? If the person isn't willing to become part of *normalcy* according to the people around them, they are disregarded until they do. It's the people surrounding the person outside convention who are helping themselves by not having to see it anymore; they don't care about the addict or whatever it is. Who's to say it's wrong, what they are doing? It's their life, they made the choice. Just because it isn't in the confines of what usually happens doesn't make it wrong. One series is about people that don't throw anything away, not so much as trash; they are deemed sick. Another series is about people that don't throw anything away, and resell their garbage. They are collectors. It's brainwashing, every episode. Every channel. Subliminal control, conditioning viewers."

"Put on sports."

"That's rigged too!" Gnat cackles, loopy from cabin fever.

"Should we try to walk?"

"To where?" Gnat studies him.

"To the corner. It's chilly, the fresh air will be good for you."

"Alright then."

Ju stays on the side where the cars pass, making sure Gnat doesn't move into traffic. A step at a time with the walker, short hobbles, rigid movements. The brisk air *does* clear his head. The frost on his nose makes him feel alive. He thinks of a time he hiked through the night in Orrinpic with near freezing temperatures, no lamp except the light of the full moon without cloud. Stars erased, the planet circling Irfa too loud to let their calls for attention through. His nose felt this same way then.

"Will I go?" Gnat asks as they return to the house.

"Where?" Ju returns a question.

"To the wild. The mountains, the ocean. The far places nobody goes..."

"Yes," Ju states.

When they get to the house, he goes to his spot on the couch, writhing.

"You know how long that took you?" Ju yells from the basement.

"No."

"You made it a couple of ball fields in an episode of my favorite show, which I missed. Thanks, son! How fast could you run a lap at the stadium when you were eighteen?"

Gnat sighs. "Faster than one of these commercial breaks."

Ju comes in holding a can. "Don't tell your mother. Now you have something to celebrate, and a benchmark."

After everyone is asleep, Gnat is viewing episodes of a comedy from thirty spans earlier. He takes the can out from under his blanket, opening it as quietly as possible, trying not to wake anyone with the pop of the tab. He puts the can to his lips and pours the liquid down his throat. *Oh my, I missed this.* He beams, giggling with the nervous satisfaction of a teenager sneaking out of the house for the first time.

"Shut up, Gnat! Don't wake mom!" he scolds himself in a low voice.

Each visit, Dr. Pati reviews everything that's happened, not solely his arm. Every type of scan, so much radiation he'll probably die of its poisoning before he makes it to old age. Every visit there are many of the same people. Some are healing, like Gnat. Some are not. Some will not.

How many tens of millions of people have deficiencies and disabilities on Irfa that will never get better? Whether born with it, or the result of an accident. They never get to travel. Never get to leave or change what they are now. Stuck. Defenseless. Without a choice. Forgotten. Disregarded by the masses.

Many cycles pass. In the beginning most of them aided by pills, until individual cycles become boundless. He eats, he sleeps. There's no schedule. When his body gets heavy he rests. When he's ready, he rises. Appointments, physical therapy. A loss of perception occurs. The fall starts to feel as if it were spans ago, and before that, he can hardly remember what it was like to be who he was. The women, the jobs, the things he spent his time doing. *So distant.*

Battling, the chair is finally gone, then the walker. Now he has a cane, hand-carved in wood. He's weaned himself off the pills, now he only takes them if things flare up. Recently, he's started to strum his guitar. The strength of his left hand almost nonexistent the first try, it has already tripled. He will play again, as well or better than before. The doctor in Knighton was mistaken. He has driven his mother's manual-shift truck. Things are coming back; he's rounding the curve starting to make his way downhill. The hardest parts are over.

He attends the final meeting with Dr. Pati without walking aid. Dr. Pati jumps up and shakes his hand.

"Great, you look great! You've done brilliantly, never complained once, did everything I asked. What's next? Have you thought about it? You need to keep getting your movement and strength up. It will take spans to feel like your old self, if ever. Some of the pain will linger unfortunately."

Gnat answers, "There's a difference between pain, and being able to feel something that you usually don't, I've found out."

"Yes, yes. You're right."

"I don't know how to thank you, really. You returned the use of my good arm. I can play my guitar again, I can walk. I can go out there. The normal practitioner, locked in to what they've been taught, is no different than a lifeguard at the top of a slide. Only two options, go, or don't go. This symptom, this drug. That symptom, that drug. But you, the surgeon, you're a master of your art. I've seen the images from the scans. The difference in my arm from before to after is incredible. I can't believe it. I'm so grateful to you," Gnat explains, humbled.

Dr. Pati nods. "I work a *lot*. If I switched to private practice, I could be in an office somewhere making twice as much. I didn't do this for the salary, I don't need the thanks in words. You know what you patients are to me when I get you? The baby bird with the broken wing. I get to mend you, then we get here where I say okay, you are released. Go and fly again, wherever you want. Because you can. If you want to thank me, go and live your life the best way possible. That's what I want for you, Gnat. Just watch out for those banana peels, don't let them get you so down. Fly on somewhere else, yeah?"

"Yes, doctor. I'll always remember."

"Remember me, do it for you. Now get out of here, and don't come back," he pats Gnat's arm with the folder in his hand. *That's it.*

A feeling of disillusionment overtakes him at the house. Like something's waiting for him somewhere, he's missing out. He's anxious and can't relax. When he goes to his room, he's wide awake, reminiscing about Wishintown. Wanting to go back to the west coast. None of his family or friends have visited since he's been in Oia, except for a few of them for a short chat. He doesn't really want to see them anyway. What would he say? Thirty-two cycles, this part of his journey, which he didn't want to complete, before this chapter.

You can tell somebody you were incapacitated for that long. If they haven't done it, they wouldn't know. They can't possibly understand. That's mortally indefinite agony, constant pain medication can't cover up. Not being able to rest without crying your way there. Thinking everything you've ever known is gone, that you'll just have to wake up until you don't. The idea that nothing will ever be worthwhile again, life is over. No input, complete indifference. Exploring planes of consciousness not known to exist previously. Not speaking for cycles, not eating for cycles. Unable to move. Unable to get away. To get out of my own head. To have nothing but misery. A blanket of endless black ooze covering all. Seeping out of the Irfa, drowning me in the subliminal indoctrinated beliefs of people and things around me. A part of me has changed, you can't forget this. Block out the physical, that's insignificant comparatively. The ringing in my ears. The building that's burning inside. Never to be in silence again. Never to be in comfort again. Never to see the point in anyone's meaningless tasks ever again. I am ready to become what I am, ready to evolve. Ready to escape the mindlessness of things. Life on Irfa itself. It's a result of manipulation and pressure. How could any purity come from this? My reasons were sound, the execution was wrong. I did what I needed to, then. I'll find out what I have to do next.

Then a wave of euphoria, his senses that have failed him in the stop-loss of recovery return. He's at ease again, with a deep breath and sigh. He is himself. How could he have let these broken things break him? A moment of weakness mistaken for clarity. He rolls onto his side, relaxed. There's no weight, no curse or sting in his brain, no fight. The voice comes in, assuredly. *You're back.*

He's been without any aid for some cycles. Each morning, he drives Su to work and keeps her truck to run errands. He buys the groceries, cleans the house, does the cooking. His parents aren't aware to what level he has learned culinary arts, just that he's worked in hospitality. He asks his dad if he could have any meal, what would it be? Gnat will make it from scratch. There's only one thing Ju can think of.

"Chicken."

"What type? A meal, not a protein. Anything you've seen at a restaurant or on a show," he prods.

"Just some baked chicken with vegetables," Ju repeats.

Ima and Su start to laugh from the other room.

"Sure, baked chicken it is. Tomorrow for dinner." *The classic Oia diet, salted meat and burnt potatoes.*

He has a friend, Sawe, who emails him every so often from an Island off the east coast of Telaysia, Tiwi. They met the first span he went to Wishintown. She's checked on him more frequently after learning of his fall. Now that he's on his feet, she wants to come visit. She wants to see the real Omrika, the festivals, parks, caves, and fields. Who better to show her than an Oian boy? Sawe bought her ticket, he informs his family.

"So, how's the chicken?" Gnat fishes for a compliment.

Ju has a leg in his hand. "This is some good yard bird, boy," he says in an extra gruff voice, pretending to be an old hilly man. The two girls roll their eyes.

"Sawe is in for a treat, guess who is playing at the River's Bend while she's here? Velouria!" Gnat puts forward. Velouria is a punk band from his childhood, the most influential band when it comes to writing his own songs.

"Do you think she'll like that?" questions Ima.

"If not the band, the venue is the ultimate Oia experience. An outdoor amphitheater on the river, corn fields in the distance, a sunset start, sitting in the grass drinking on a blanket. Awesome," he answers.

***

Gnat picks Sawe up from the airport. She'll stay in the room next to him. He lets her settle in. Jetlag, the best of travel companions for every human.

Although she's from a culture different in every way, they get along. She's easy-going, at least when it comes to the details of monotonous activities. He takes her to parks, some farms, they go out on his father's motorcycle through the fields of endless bounty.

They get to the theme park right as it opens and stay until it closes. The roller-coasters of wood, built long ago, give him reminders of what he's been through. Gnat isn't what he used to be. He must be careful now; he's physically fragile.

They go to the international grocery store to buy the things she misses from home. They've been together for three cycles, he never gets sick of his friend. One of the few people that paid him any mind while he was down, he trusts her.

"I have a treat for you, the night before you fly home," he says excitedly.

"What's that? More drinking?" she jokes.

"No, a concert at the best venue we have to offer in Oia."

"Who is it?" she asks, intrigued.

"Velouria!"

"I don't know who that is…"

"Oh, you will. You'll be able to buy the t-shirt to prove you were there and be the envy of every person in Tiwi."

"Sounds like fun," she answers flatly.

He pushes her, "Don't be so hyped about it, you might blow a blood vessel. That's later on, anyway. First, yes, more drinking. To the Tapped Rune, we go!"

He's made her try every fast-food outlet the main street of town has to offer and she's noticed its effects.

"No more fried food, Gnat. I've gained weight since I've been here. I have a belly," she lifts her shirt, a bulge hangs out.

"We'll eat leafy greens until you go, then. After a few dozen glasses of alcohol. You are only here once! You might as well adopt the lifestyle of being a fat, drunken, stupid Omrikan in underwhelming Oia…"

"Let's go get drunk then," she giggles. "True. Why not?"

That night, she learns the difference between liquors as they take shots of every available option. Kili orders food to be delivered at the Tapped Rune. Everybody shares the cost, along with the calories.

The road to the concert venue is not perniciously curvy, but winding as it follows the level areas of the wide river it runs parallel to. The trees are thick, deciduous. Oaks and maples holding a dozen score of spans are elders in this part of the country. The tallest, oldest trees in Oia are mere saplings compared to the giants of the west. The sun has dropped to an angle that runs the rays through them as he drives, the flicker of light and its absence is projected through millions of leaves. *This must be what it is like to be traveling faster than the speed of light, beams becoming a dot matrix in black.*

The air down near the banks is rich, wet and dry simultaneously. The scent of Irfa is carried on it, dirt and organics. Mostly from the endless farms around, combined with the movement of barges transporting harvests against currents. The breezes carry allergens and the dust of grain in the humid season. It hasn't rained recently; if you look closely enough the haze of it is in every breath. The windows are down, the path is empty. Everyone uses the freeway now. Nobody has time to enjoy their surroundings any longer, there's always somewhere important to be. His arm hangs out shaped like a wing. He tilts his palm back and forth; it rises and falls. Like his mood, his desires. He checks on Sawe. She's smiling, taking in as much of this warm evening as possible. Her arm is doing the same thing as his only faster. This isn't an image he wants to forget, a perfect occasion driving by the Oia. He blinks his eyes. *Click.* Saved for the rest of his life in his memory.

"Tonight's going to be perfect," he says to her.

"It is so far," she returns.

He parks and grabs the blanket that will be their seat. As they pick a spot, he reaches up his shorts from the bottom pulling out a surprise. A pint of liquor taped to his leg to get past security, a trick used here since he was in high school. Sawe is surprised and glances around at people nearby.

"Don't worry, they do it too. Plenty of joints are going to go around once it's dark, too, just part of this place. It isn't fun to pay extortion rates for every drink. That kind of takes away from the experience, you know?" he tells her.

"First drink is mine, then." She reaches out for the bottle. They pass it between them slowly. Sawe is lying down, absorbing the sky and flies as they buzz around.

"I'll go get us some tall cans, what I brought isn't enough. You stay here," says Gnat.

"Okay, nothing light for me," she demands as he goes. *That's the way.*

He's descending the stairs to the concession, ready to enjoy the band that's gotten him through so many tough times. It's crowded, it always is here. The only escape in the city for the open-minded types that want to get away when they can. Gnat isn't paying close attention to anything as he drifts in the sea of humans. Partway down the flight, he hears someone scream.

"Hey! Pay attention! That's my foot you almost ran over! Get out of my way! Please! You are blocking the path!" the voice bellows. He sees a man. Older, tall, and balding. The latter without grace. He has on a pair of jeans barely held shut by the button, which is under immense pressure. Above his waistline, an enormous belly hangs past his legs and chest. As the man keeps yelling, Gnat notices he cares not for his teeth. They are yellow, chipped, and broken. He wears a white shirt with the words "god loves me" in black on the front. Gnat searches for the person this man attacks, then finds her.

A girl, maybe fifteen, leaving the restroom. She's in an electric wheelchair, controlled by a crippled arm. She has a breathing tube, glasses, and is genuinely terrified. She wears a Velouria t-shirt, probably her favorite. Gnat imagines how much effort it took her to get here to see them. The experience is ruined by this obese, worthless ingrate.

Gnat continues on his mission, catching another argument. At a table, a grandmother, mother, and son. The kid throws fries on the ground as his mother argues with hers.

"You said you'd take him, I have to meet up with Dini, he's only here for a couple cycles!"

The grandmother replies, "I can't, I had to pick up another shift at work. I already raised my children; I can't raise yours too. You want to shoot up with your dealer? You shouldn't have had a kid, you don't even take care of yourself..."

"What about the money you told me I could borrow?" the mother asks bitterly, "That way I can hire a babysitter and go."

"You're going to have to get a job. I'm sixty-five and still working..."

He lets the conversation trail off as he leaves earshot. In line, he browses the menu and prices, telling himself not to bother. *Just enjoy.* He's next, after a pair of girls in front of him. The clerk is a teenager, working to have cash to go out with his friends, more than likely. The patrons getting food turn on him.

"No, my friend wants water. Water is free..." the girl taunts.

The cashier answers, "Sorry, the water isn't free any longer. We have bottles for a small fee."

"Oh no," the same girl retorts, "you can't charge for water. My friend wants water. Give it to her. Water. W-A-T-T-E-R," she hollers.

A voice from behind chimes in, "Uh, that word only has one t."

"You do not need to get an attitude with her!" the partner fires.

A manager comes over, and gives them the bottle of water at no charge. *Perpetuating stupidity a drink at a time. A trifecta of morons, so much for escaping for a while.*

He politely orders four drinks, not wanting to come back. It's sunset, the opening act makes their way onto the stage. They drink, not enough to get completely trashed, he has to drive his mother's car home. He sings every word from both bands; he knows the opener also. Sawe dances. A cigarette comes around, the funny type, they both take a hit sending it forward. Afterward she buys a t-shirt and a hat. He's clear-headed, after being in the long line of traffic to exit.

"Are you a Velouria fan now?" he asks.

"For life! That was perfect. You were right!" She screams out the window, both hands up.

"AA-OO," he howls out his side, the call of a wolf, "I'm glad you got to see them, and that you came to Oia," he says to her.

"Me too, Gnat. Really, it wasn't what I expected."

"Better or worse?"

She screams out the window, again, "Much better!"

He remembers people from the night, the absolute idiocy of humans. *I can't find purpose in people, much less stand to be around them. I need to get away from the horde, the city. To the open spaces. Where can I go? More importantly, how do I get there? I'm broke. No truck. Maybe I can get a bus ticket, go to a farm. Or, just be homeless. I don't have to, though, something always gets found if you search. I'm ready to start the next chapter. I need a purpose. It's out there. The way I'll do it is by being myself, a vagabond. The only thing that comes naturally to me.*

Gnat takes Sawe to the airport the next morning, helping her get the luggage out, setting it on the ground. They hug each other, squeezing tight.

"Will I see you again?" her eyes are watering up.

"If you want to see me again, you will. When, I can't tell you. But you were there for me, I'll be here for you," he responds. "If I had to guess, it will be sooner than later."

"That's all I can hope for, then," she starts to wheel her bags into the front entrance, "Goodbye, Gnat."

"Goodbye!"

When will he meet her again? We. Shall. See.

He drops the truck off at his mother's school and *walks* to the house, recollecting not being able to.

"I'm going to remember every time I saunter the rest of my life," he says, hands pocketed, wind on his face.

II

He feels normal, as a piece in its place, not a source of pride. However, this doesn't make him bitter either. His routes are getting longer successively. Sometimes he lets Su take her vehicle and he ventures off in a random direction. Gnat found a vast stretch of grass beside a creek recently, which led to a young patch of wood. Game trails crisscross the forest, created by creatures much older than the vegetation they graze. Thoughtlessly he went into the thick of his surroundings, lording his way past the subjects, trees and flowers. He's a man, master of all, his own body included. He's done it, conquered the beast of recovery. His reward? The scratch of stiff grass on his bare feet, chilled by the dirt of Irfa. Cooling his core temperature by the science of circulation as he passes under the sustenance of the sun. The sun, in reality, the *true* ruler of this place, unbound by evolution or the history of life.

Now he'll find the opposite, the forceful and mechanical. *The human.* Thousands of tons of metal and steam scraping along silently, unable to move freely. A creation *completely* bound to the path laid out, doomed to carry whatever payload saddled along its length. Trains, in their home. A yard. The locomotive industry boomed in Nata before the great expansion westward. The terminus of the tracks still exists, along with enterprise. It's in the core of the city, and can be viewed from the surrounding hills from spots inaccessible to any form of transportation except the original. Bipedally.

The path leads on, past his high school, students inside. He recalls the drabness of state-certified curriculum. The places he ran away to as teachers rambled. That's where the abstractions originated, drawing conclusions combined with experience later on. Within the hypocrisy of that building, Gnat was caged.

Then, the ghetto. Dirty needles and trash scattered near the keystones of foundations as he passes. Buildings cut with integrity from rock, generations ago. Would those men have given the sweat of effort if they knew the final outcome? As he passes an intersection, he's offered whatever he likes. A woman, a euphoric shot in the arm, a bag of ice. Different types of bullets, to elevate or end a life...

He hears the squeal of a train braking shortly after and cuts behind the homes on a dead-end street. In the yard, a woman sits. She has a strand of rubber tubing encircling her arm, intensely focused, like a person dismantling an explosive. Poking a syringe into a found vein, it will bring her the momentary rush, which fades, bringing only the desire for another hit. Each gluttonous entry gives less until the feeling is eclipsed by a need for the substance as safe harbor from sickness. A twig breaks under his weight, they each glance at the other and return to what they are doing, separately.

Gnat climbs over a broken section of chain fence rolled up on itself, doing nothing but rusting, and heads up the incline. On the pinnacle awaits a sprawling view of Nata. Short unkempt groundcover thrives. The sky is blue, city bustling, traffic flowing robotically across the overpasses. Below, four tracks run in two directions. A fence with barbed-wire atop looms on the boundaries, taller than any human. Some cars are being loaded, most adorned with graffiti and the signs of weather endlessly punishing their exteriors. They are unstopped by whatever is encountered in their quests to deliver. Security trucks toe the line randomly keeping unwanted visitors out. The engine of the farthest track is being operated on, no steam or smoke comes from the molded exhaust that would be a nose, if it had a face. Black blood pours from the heart into a pan that would take many workers to pick up. *An oil change.*

Seated on the slope, eating, he thinks about each bite as he takes in the view. Gnat is running low on funds. A choice will have to be made. Stay in Nata and work, which is really not an option at all, or find a way to get out west. He has enough for a bus ticket or he could hitchhike. That isn't very viable on this side of the country, thumbing is taboo in Oia. In Wishintown and Sanrika, it's a common occurrence, towns are too far apart for trekking between.

As a new engine pulls in and slows to a jogging pace, the door of a car slides open on the side nearest the fence. Two people jump out onto the ground almost running in the air to match the pace of the train as they land. They stabilize and stop themselves, checking quickly for security. *The bulls.* None are present. A victory, guards in stations are known to be aggressive. There's a hole in the fence, they jump through into the woods and escape.

That's how I'll do it. I could wait right here until a train pulls in heading west. I can find the timetable, somewhere, and know when it's coming. I travel light enough; I don't need a phone. All I have to do is not get caught. I could jump off before the fences, and meet it on the other side as it speeds up to keep going.

"Hmm," he says. "I'll just go. I'll leave a note for mom and dad to find when they come home from work, saying I'll call when I get set up." *The smell of the ocean, it's been too long...*

Returning to the house, he imagines the logistics of it. Nights are frigid on a train, the opposite in the brutally hot sun. After everyone's asleep he searches for the schedules. A bag, a guitar, a man determined to source more knowledge. To find out how to turn what he has earned into meaningful substance.

He finds it. It comes through, stopping in the night, running to the coast of South Sanrika.

It comes again soon. *I start walking with weight next, I've got to get quick enough.*

He takes his pack filled with containers of water, adding more respectively with time . His legs scream at him when he lies down. It's noticeable, but bearable. He doesn't know where the stops are along the way, he'll know when he feels the train braking. A longer trip than by bus, assuredly, considering the train rolls slowly.

He's roused by his parents leaving for work. Gnat stretches and empties his bag. It has been hidden in a closet since he arrived in Oia after Knighton, waiting patiently. His clothes are rolled, muscle memory takes over in the places where the patterns are forgotten. The inside of a dry bag smells like Hipslyn's perfume, it's on his sleeping bag. *She sprayed it there, before I left her.* He pauses, then goes to the living room. On the wall hangs the painting of the sailboat. It has since before he fell, Julyen sent it by mail. He lifts it off, and turns it over. The message written remains. *A past life.* He returns to packing things in their places. Companions reunited, ready to live amongst one another again in eager humility. He writes the note to leave on the kitchen counter, folding it and keeping it safe in the pages of his journal.

In the evening, Gnat's with his parents, listening to them talk about what happened in their respective routines. He asks them if they would like to go to the chili place, it only makes sense to complete the circle of the last span. He doesn't bring anything up about the issues of Irfa, only wanting the memory of this meal. His friend from school that served them last time isn't working. He wonders if she got out from under the thumb of Fennytun. Is she living for something other than a check? *I hope you are, or are out searching for it.*

At home, before his parents go to their room he embraces each of them, holding longer than is custom for only a goodnight. Ju and

Su each let it linger, Gnat is alive and able to be himself, the most important thing for them.

"What's wrong with you?" his dad jokes.

He has to focus as much as mentally possible to not reveal the wave of tears at the gates of a dam behind his eyelids. In the sockets, the nerves, his brain, twisting his heart to shriek. He will be gone again tomorrow, to an unknown end. Every time he leaves them, he knows not when he'll return.

"The both of you, and Ima, mean so much to me. She's living her life, as I am. That doesn't mean I wouldn't be there if she asked. I don't know what I'd do without you, not only through the pain of this past span. Always. You're here for me. I know it in my pumping blood. That fact is the source of most of my strength, I never mention it..."

"We want you to find something you can wake up and enjoy," Su tells her son. "Goodnight, bug. You'll find it."

"Goodnight, Gnat," his dad fires.

He watches them turn and go down the hall, out of sight, then listens to them climb the steps. In silence, he turns a circle, studying the walls. *My prison, a part of my strength as well. The place I avoid only pushes me harder to not fail. To not become trapped.* He flicks the light switch, power desisting. He takes his clothes and puts them on top of his bag to wear again. Pulling the note from the journal, he places it on top of the pile, as to not forget. The ancient analog alarm on the desk is set. It will take a few turns of the clock to reach the hole in the chain link, the train leaves in double that. Plenty of extra time.

The buzz of the clock only gets to sing for an instant. Gnat stifles it almost as soon as it goes off to keep it from stirring anyone upstairs. He's out quickly, placing the note under his father's keys on the counter, the first to leave. No need to linger or go out a window, he opens and closes the door with perfect accuracy, not a single creak. It seems no skill is forgotten, like riding a bike. Gnat snuck out hundreds of times before he was of legal age.

He doesn't tire. This is a mission not for pleasure, only purpose. The soundless rousing of a city in the gap between phases is haunting, he sees nobody. In the absence of light, he without question would have been assaulted in some fashion by the scum. The filth of the human race is never seen during society's waking stages.

He's approaching the dead-end street again, and instead of cutting behind, he takes the path concrete grants. In front of the houses the woman from the chair with an intravenous habit stands smoking in a robe. He sees her, she does not notice him in her daze. Gnat is simply that, an insect floating through the streetlights scope, fading again into shadow. His pace has been quick, he realizes. He won't risk going in too early in case of being discovered by inspectors. Not until the engine's fires start to burn will he go. He's frozen, trying to catch any sign of life; some person, hidden, wanting to find him. As any hunter knows, time passes with haste in pursuit and anticipation. Before he even settles in, he hears the locks of a car's brakes release, then hollers in the distance. Train cars are like dominoes, the first nudges the next to move, and so on. He hears the effect of the power from the main engine cascading down the track. He feels the rumble through the ground. It starts to roll. It's creaking. Rising. Still, he waits. The pace of the iron centipede equals a man's now. He crouches at the hole in the fence, the artificial bulbs show enough for an attuned eye. The outline of the giant machine overwhelms him in the last breath before he runs. *A missed step, I'm a goner. No waking up from a train wreck.* He lunges through, his pack catches on the jagged link at the top of the hole, stopping him temporarily. He wrenches his shoulders violently, breaking loose. A car with a door open passes, he chases it.

A voice comes from behind, "Hey! Stop!"

The beam of a flashlight blinds him as he turns. A bull is locked on, Gnat is the red cape. He takes off, after a sprint of only steps, his legs start to shake in pain. The car is there, a large handle welded on its door. He turns up the tiny grade that holds a train track above standing water on either side at a gallop, reaches out with his bad arm and grasps the hold. The train is moving faster than he can now, his feet float above the rocks, skipping across as they try to pull him off. His guitar and bag are both on his back, he vaults to clench with both hands. The flashlight has stopped, he now risks falling, getting caught, and going through recovery to some extent again. In Oia. *If you survive. Now or never!* With a higher-level strength than normally possible, only to be summoned when the deepest desire of the holder is at risk, he roars and pulls himself up into the empty car. He collapses onto its floor taking the pair of paired straps off his shoulders. His hips are locked. His left arm burns, the scar tissue outweighs the healthy in his forearm forevermore. Both legs cramp to the extreme, he reaches down pulling his toes upward to bring some relief to his drained muscles. Gnat peers out. The fence has ended, the lights of the work yard are in the past. Watching the shapes of the houses and buildings as they roll by, he figures they are moving as fast as a car on a suburb's street. He turns his bag to make a pillow. He drifts casually until he can see the details of what he is not experiencing, only passing by. Morning has come. He grins. *Here we go.*

Ju turns on the bulbs in the kitchen rummaging for his keys.

"If I put them in the same place when I get home, I wouldn't have to do this. Maybe I'll build a rack," he tells himself, seeing his keys. "What's this? Another to-do list from Su, as always? It never ends, things to fix around here. We should move to a condominium, they do the landscaping, we could rest..."

He unfolds the square of parchment, his face goes blank, involuntarily he sets the keys back on the counter. He reads it once, then again. He studies the lawn, thinking of time spent with his son. Now he's at it again without a word. Ju plainly has to keep on living, wondering where Gnat has gotten off to and what he's doing. It's what he chose, what he stands by, it doesn't upset him. That doesn't imply he won't miss him though. He reads a third time, still not believing what it says.

Mom and Dad,

Time for me to move on again. I can't find purpose in the repetition people live with. There are answers I need to find before I can decide what's going to mean something to me as the spans pass. I got lost in it for a moment. I was only found again because of the two of you. I hopped a train. That old drifter's cliché. I'm headed out, to what end I am unsure. Don't worry. Remember when I got in the wheelchair for the first time? I was serious. I want to live. If I'm going to do it, it won't be for simple fleeting details. It will be with reason. When I know what that is, you'll know too-

Gnat

He sets the note down, putting it under Su's keys. Ju switches the light off. Leaving the porch, he lifts his head westward to the sky.

"You'll arrive where you're going sooner or later, we'll be here for you when you get back..."

As Ju turns out the driveway, somewhere over a boundary line, Gnat rests cross-legged in his boxcar.

***

His posture is a luxury, untold agony teaching his legs their current shape. There isn't anything on the rails to accomplish but watching things pass, and contemplate. The conductor navigates through cornfields, the only *thing* within view. Wheat or soy steal patches of Irfa, intermittently.

So many farmers put lifetimes into growing food. The people in cities have no concept. Go to a window, buy a meal. Not hungry anymore? Throw it out. It's disrespectful. That patty of beef took spans to produce. Or the milk in a slice of cheese. Someone rose every morning to gather sustenance from their herd. The various nutrition movements ravaging Omrika are ridiculous. There's no difference between eating organic food or farmed animals as far as the burden put on the environment. The scientist who began the non-modified food craze retracted what he was preaching. He told everyone he was mistaken; we can't support humans by commercially farming organic produce. There are too many people. How is it wrong to create a strain of wheat which isn't susceptible to disease? That grows in ice? That produces twice as much nutrition per stalk? It's only a negative when speaking financially, of supply and demand. When craft breweries boomed, using alternative grains, the growers couldn't keep up. The agriculture machine tried planting more than once in a season without spraying. After five seasons like this, the land became barren. It's sterile, nutrient deficient. Spent. It's only a fashion statement to eat healthy. Many retailers have been caught labeling old products as untreated and raising prices. Another example of people trying to have things both ways. There's a process to actually live sustainably. A quarter-acre of land easily grows enough to feed a family of four. If someone hunts a single deer, that will feed them through the harsh times . Fifty fish is a bonus. Half a dozen chickens eat your waste vegetables and scraps; in return you receive eggs. A goat for milk. The lowest carbon footprint available. The problem is you must tend it. There's a reason the renaissances of the past occurred every time machinery advanced. To raise a farm and animals without help from pesticides or fuel, you work whenever the sun shines. Or doesn't. Feeding, cleaning, thinning, weeding, picking, processing, packing. Art and invention are myths in this type of lifestyle. No time for thinking about how it makes you feel. You must labor. Hard. Humans aren't actually willing to sacrifice any ease to make a viable impact. It's no more than another group of labels to try to have a place and identity within society. Pat yourself on the shoulder, hold your head a little higher. The truth still exists, what you eat isn't making a difference. What's paramount is production; whether or not infrastructure's noose asphyxiates your nourishment. Names and stickers for profit on a shelf only affect public opinion, not any plausible or progressive outcome.

On the train he doesn't need to focus on the road, just absorb sights and smells. No pavement is visible, even. His current mode of transport was forged across the plains far before any highway was thought of. Gnat plays until a rhythm emerges in sync with the churning of wheels. Heavy, hard. Not fast, steady and tight. Out on the trail, exactly in his place. Where what is to come isn't known.

I left home, when I was thirteen.
Told my mother, don't cry over me.
Heard soft voices, in the trees.
Wept like a willow, that's when I learned my name.
When I learned my name.

Got a little further, each and every step.
As I got deeper
Elopement called my new name.

Screamed for mother, but nature took her place.

Felt the terror

Forever a scapegrace,

Forever a scapegrace.

Like whispers in the wood.

Voices rough like wool.

Fangs are sharp like wolves.

That's how you can tell I'm no good.

That's how you can tell I'm no good.

That's how, you can tell...

To sing is to be connected to the very air itself. His legs hang out of the open door. It must be getting late, the yellow of the rays is spiraling more toward burnt orange than white. They roll around a lumbering bend in the track and cross a river. Nothing like the Oia, much tamer, yet still wide enough to be abridged. He stares down, suspended over the drop. With the thought of slipping, immediate vertigo ensues, Gnat lies down to focus on the interior of the container.

"I've never had a fear of heights! I guess it isn't so much fear as instinct based on direct knowledge, my subconscious remembering," he says. "A river leads to a town..."

The vibration of the train changes, it's decelerating, or going to start. He takes his gear to the shadows of the car where he won't be seen.

Considerable speed *has* been shed. Before a fence starts, he sees a traffic light showing yellow. In obvious lack of knowledge about traveling this way, he adorns his luggage. If the train is to be stationed in broad-light, or something needs to be loaded, his discovery awaits. He'll do what he decided beforehand, jump out, run to the other end, and meet the train as it continues. He computes his chances of reaching the ground without injuring himself. *Not likely.* He waits, however the train still moves the same speed. He has to simply go for it, the fence approaches rapidly.

"Alright." He starts to sway like someone timing their entrance to a double-dutch jump-rope. "On three. One, two..."

Waaa. The blast of an air horn stops him.

The car jolts and rocks, almost tossing him out anyway. Something is different as he scans. *Green.* The signal was yellow, now it's green. The sound of the engine picking up revolutions carries to him. They travel down the entire length of metal fencing. No stopping here, the light meant exactly what it does for motor vehicle traffic. A simple meeting of different lines, an intersection. They caught the green to keep moving.

The locomotive does stop in cover of shadow later on. Not a city, only a depot of some sort. Maybe to refuel or pick up cargo from surrounding remote areas. There are no barriers, at most a few buildings with an access road for tractor-trailers. No task is completed, it's possibly only a regulatory break from some body of governance out of touch in an undisclosed location. As the interconnected wheels chug forward again on the hybrid track, Gnat discerns a pair of friends running through the grass. Dirty, greasy street kids. Patched jean jackets and a single bag. Not so much travelers as lost puppies, trying to find somewhere to land. They don't end up in his car, so nothing to think about. He wants them to get where they're going, like himself.

The sky is bleak, empty of everything. No alien satellites, stars, or clouds. It isn't black, or blue. The train rolls along through this incomplete snow globe, without an artificial blizzard included for someone to create. This night is devoid of duplicity, the fixation to catch and control the indomitable. In the clean contour between the meeting of sky and Irfa nothing dilutes the view. You can see the curve of the sphere he and the two others hidden elsewhere travel, the three not knowing what comes next. The slight roll of the car as they power along rocks Gnat to that other place.

He's held in a plain of rotten wheat. Blackened and feasted upon by a plague. A fire is in the distance, consuming everything. It approaches. He tries to turn and run, but is stuck. There's a weight within him, in his stomach. *Oh no, not this again...* He's pregnant with the obtuse misinterpretations of the entire human race all at once. Locked in this spot, he carries not the heaviness of the tangible Irfa on his body, but its ignorance.

As the flames get closer, he sees that they move in a wave, like the sea. A tsunami of water's opposite, not a cleansing force but incinerating. He feels the heat of it flowing toward him. He watches as the burning reaches him, ready to accept the ferocity of this externally-imposed immolation. The flames touch him, he feels nothing. Everything goes blank, the setting changes. He's in the desert of Lifeless Plain. He remembers this place. No other is around, hence its name. He tries to take a step. No. He's made of the densest form of matter here, it seems. Two planes zip past overhead. Biplanes from the past shining in the intense sun. The pistons of their engines run at the same wavelength, however ignited at different times. The pitches meet and bounce off of each other, sounding like trumpets signaling the apocalypse. It's unnatural, Gnat can't concentrate. These planes fly low, he can see who pilots them with enough detail. One is a man, the other a woman. They head toward mountains beyond the desert, not noticing Gnat as he waves. The range they approach blocks water from passing their peaks as it condenses into fog and cloud, explaining why these infertile sands exist. The drone of the opposed motors quiets as he watches them get lost in the hills, the faceless adviser residing somewhere in the canyons of his cleverness speaks to him. The voice, it's back. *Follow.*

The farms are in the past, they're encased in a wide-open grassland. Cattle dot the fields, grazing. Occasionally a house, a barn to partner it. The soil gets lighter over time, an indication of sand. Dry weeds tumble betwixt his thoughts. The rail leads into the place he dreamt of. The desert. The valley behind the Sirra Niva mountains, the tallest range in North Omrika. He has always had a certain affection for the most desolate of biomes. At first glance, lonely and uninhabited. This isn't true, everything living here is a master of survival, flourishing in the night. Gnat perches, processing from farm, to plain, to desert. This mixed container of inanimate and breathing commodities, some new, some used, is disconnecting from the shackle of civilization. Removing the distractions by only pushing forward, through whatever tempest. *As the land clears, my life is sanitizing and restoring itself. What has happened, I can live with. I don't have to live in it.*

Defined time is irrelevant. The temperature and position of shadows say the sun is at its meridian, when the main signal sounds by the hand of the conductor, who also pulls the throttle down. They are going to stop again. *Where, out here?*

An oversight. They must cross into South Omrika to reach Sanrika, breaching an international border. Which means a thorough inspection by federal agents. *The mundane details I always miss...*

There's only one thing he can do, make himself as small as possible and be still. He can't bail to the desert or grazing land, that could be cycles of travel on foot. He can't try to make a run for it once they stop in the station. So, the only virtue, as ever, is to wait.

He crouches behind his pack in the corner of the container, where no light reaches. A puff of steam sounds the final compression of the brake pads, the machine pulling unfathomable weight is pacified by the push of a button. Gnat hears men speaking South Omrikan along with the bark of a dog. *Well, that's it for me.* They are scanning, finally he can see an officer through the open door a few cars in front of him. The man is wearing a hat, a radio in his ear, and a bulletproof vest. He has a handgun strapped on each hip, semi-automatics. They can't see him. *Not yet.*

A dog starts to bark, Gnat holds his breath. He wonders if the animal can smell him from this far away. The officer becomes tense, pulls a gun, pointing it into the car. Not the one Gnat occupies, however.

"Hands, hands. Up!" he shouts. "Jump down, leave your bag."

The friends he saw earlier exit the car and are arrested immediately. Thrown to the ground, handcuffed, pulled to stand again, carried off. The glimpse of another agent taking their rucksack flashes by. None of this in full view, only parts of it as he continues to stay as still as he can. He's sure they'll return and discover him; he has no choice but to accept his fate.

The sun has visibly dropped in the sky since the boys were discovered. Gnat feels the car roll forward, then in reverse a bit. The brake has been released. Moments later, the purr of the motor starts and begins to vibrate his toes. He's dumbfounded. *Could it be?*

The train starts to move again, picking up pace as they run farther into alien land. He gives it time before hanging out the open door. He sees the outpost behind, through the heatwaves that make you wonder if something is only a mirage. He lowers and shakes his head.

"Sorry boys, it's all chance. You should have picked the caboose," he says and writes the words to a song down. He has music that he never wrote lyrics for, maybe he'll put them together. A snort of disbelief and bewilderment exits Gnat's nose as he scribbles what comes to him.

I thought I was invincible, until I turned twenty-one
My best friend found a gun.
He took that trip to town, the one that's in the clouds
Or maybe he went down.

I thought I wasn't susceptible, until I turned twenty-two
and I had fun with you.
We took all our savings out, killed the third man without a doubt
We could have been special.

Fun and hugs all around you, babe
That's what Leza used to say.
This game is hard to play, don't take the easy way
I knew to believe her.

I thought that I was free, until I turned twenty-three
The law caught up with me.
They pushed me to the ground, my brain's either lost or found
Doesn't matter now.

Fun and hugs all around you, babe
That's what Leza used to say.
This game is hard to play, don't take the easy way
I knew to believe her...
I knew to believe her....

The train rumbles along until the strain of the motor changes, coming under more load. A pencil lying in the open journal rolls out and down the length of the car. The horizon is slanted slightly. They're going up an incline, the mountains are getting closer. Still unseen, yet the lowest elevation of the lifeless valley has passed.

***

The shine of an aluminum can burns by the track. Other scraps of metal and garbage inhabit the dirt, their frequency rising. Probing, he finds a skyline. It grows closer. There's a poison tinging the oxygen. *Smoke.* It's climbing from the buildings. Then he hears it. Anger. The screams of men and women, a mob. The engine continues to hum, it delivers him to a city in turmoil. The literal furniture in the street is lit and incinerates. Many people have signs moving in orchestrated groups, chanting. Like the protestors in Knighton he doesn't know what they say, but not for lack of volume. The cause is a language barrier. An officer is being jumped, people are shattering storefront windows, looting goods and wares. A man stands with an arm raised, his projectile ready to wreak havoc on a truck parked on the roadside. It's a glass bottle filled with fuel, capped with a rag on fire. Others scuffle over a bin full of food. He doesn't know the cause, but the public is outraged. It is an all-out riot.

The train doesn't stop, somehow it seems they've grabbed a higher gear to get away from the chaos. Gnat watches as they continue with the cargo into the mountains, which can be seen across the desert now. They continue as the slant of the sky keeps increasing. He passes the time meditating. He hasn't practiced lucid dreaming since Knighton. Wandering through different states of his consciousness didn't help his outlook. Now he tries to quiet the buzz of Irfa and the ringing in his ears with slow breathing exercises, nothing more.

He's serene, the high temperature of the desert recedes as they move toward dusk. Then a sign, he can't read the corrugated metal until they pass it.

APPROACHING SOUTH OMRIKAN BORDER

"What? We didn't need to stop to cross back in? We didn't slow or stop, did we?" he questions himself. "Did I get too deep in meditating to notice? No way..."

In the foothills of the west, the lower summits easily surpass the highest elevations of Eastern Omrika. Shortly after the sign, the locomotive stops at a depot without fences again.

Gnat grabs his gear, jumping off. A road carves through the scenery over a ridge. *Was it really this easy?* He travels afresh toward the backwoods superhighway paved in gravel and broken branches. Ultimately, he meets the trail and hitches a ride in the bed of a pickup, his only company a dog, big and black. So shaggy it can hardly see from under its eyebrows, hanging down to its snout.

"You must be hot," Gnat says to him. The only response is a lick to his face. He's dropped at a gas station, solitary. The driver never said a word and tilts his cap accelerating away.

"Where am I?" he poses to the clerk, inside.

"A long walk from the main road, this is Rica Peak," the man answers, chewing an addictive leaf.

"In the Eastern Sirra Nivas?"

"Not quite. Almost. We're at the northern end of the range. You just come in?"

"Yeah, on a train," Gnat nods.

"Through South Omrika? Did you see any fighting? You're mighty brave, going there right now." He drifts off.

"I saw a riot. I didn't know the purpose?" Gnat asks, curious.

"Something about the fuel company losing its contracts to that Tiria woman and whatever she's trying to start. That's about all I know," he continues, reaching under the counter. "Here take this, read it."

He drops a newspaper on the dusty counter for Gnat, "It's old, but'll tell you the story. I've got to drain the pumps before I lock up. Gotta move you outside, unless you need to buy anything..."

"No, I'll be on my way," he says, exiting. "Thanks for the paper."

"Be seeing you."

Gnat curls the news up as he rolls down the road. After some time, he sees a nice area to build camp. By the light of the fire, he notices the paper lying next to his bag and unfurls it.

It seems the main industry in the rioting city has been mining soot-fuel since its founding. The fighting is a result of being out-bid by Tiria's new conglomeration. A business decision, plain and simple, which the people have turned in to an emotional ordeal. They call for government interference; they've lost their jobs. Much like the auto industry in Omrika, they beg for bailouts. People living standardly don't know how to deal with the negative consequences when what they're told doesn't work out, so they deflect anger to other things. In this case, stealing and robbing from neighbors to call attention to their 'plight.' Since they believe their individual lives have value, the arguments start. In opposition to Tiria, people say she's cost too many jobs on both sides, her new technology should be outlawed and regulated. The profits should be broken up and given equally to the companies suffering from her innovation. The controls they've trusted blindly all these generations have shattered and failed. It isn't fair. No concept of the notion that the pawns of industry are held in place for only a single result, to be sacrificed when people in the background can move forward safely. Tiria is forcing her hand as well, claiming she's hiring a workforce from the poorest nations of Ehfra, not Telaysia. It's been deemed progressive, posh, and inventive by the liberal media she's paid to run the stories. Telaysian, Ehfran, or South Omrikan; it's still taking advantage of weak economies and unknowing groups to maximize profits. The principle remains; payroll is ten percent of what it'd be in Omrika, the color or nationality of the employees is moot.

However, Tiria only uses the laws to her advantage, as they've been presented. The newspaper seems to be the real terrorist, filling Irfa with hate. Fear mongering as a business plan, domestically *and* internationally. Who's right, who's wrong? Whichever party plays the emotions of the masses with more finesse. What is evil? The being that thinks differently, and makes you question whether what you believe in actually holds any merit.

The people under and against this woman have made a mistake. They've trusted and held the arrangements laid out for them without earning the knowledge or conceptualizing themselves, and want those who wrote the rules to make more as long as they aren't any less comfortable. The virtue towering above the rest, for society, is ease. Tiria differs from Gnat when he was a child. She met extra growth with nurturing, finding balance. As the butterflies of Tiria's class flap toward the breeze, hers is the biggest and strongest. She made Irfa bow to her. She smiles, watching, and all she had to do was wait for the opportune moment. This, the only virtue that truly matters. *Waiting.*

He flips to the work classifieds. A lodge here in the range needs a server for hikers coming through. He tears it out and throws the rest of the editorial onto the fire. It flares up, he feels the warmth until it wastes away to embers.

The next morning, the highway is found a short trek down the dirt road, Gnat hitches to the next station. Using the payphone in the lot, he calls to inquire about the job. A voice answers, and starts to ask questions.

"Yes, I am available immediately... Yes, I have experience... I can work remotely, I've done it before... Sure, I'm nearby and can stay for a while... No, no wife, or girlfriend, or dog... Of course, I can be there soon..."

With his thumb out, someone passes and pulls over.

"Hop in, I'm going past the turnoff. You want a drink?" says a man driving the farm truck.

"If you're offering," Gnat responds, climbing in.

***

The road heading to the lodge stands in front of him. The man dropped him off and said it's a few nights sleeping alone before you get to the end. Gnat thanked him and told him to be safe, then watched him drive around a bend out of sight.

He takes a giant gulp of mountain air, tasting like cedar. *The same as Orrinpic. How many people have I come across since then? Each of them is like a breath. Inhale. Absorb whatever comes, blow out, releasing them to the atmosphere again.*

The grade isn't horrible, the first night he figures he's twenty percent of the way, and he hasn't even *heard* a combustion engine. That's alright, there's no anger in him, at least he can move on his own.

Halfway through the next morning he hears the sputter of a car behind him.

"Get in!" a voice calls from inside, "I'm headed to the lodge to drop the mail off."

The camp is only a main building with an attached patio for restaurant guests to sit outside, a bonfire pit is in front. The ground is parched, only dirt with the occasional tuft of yellow scrub. In the background, a group of trees has been cleared for hikers to sleep. Next to a lake there's a string of old campers, on a hill opposite a few

A-frames. They've been built by someone with an idea beforehand, but no practical knowledge to make it work. A woman approaches; the first thing he notices is her unclean skin full of scars. She dons a cap with a Velcro strap and large thick-rimmed glasses. She carries extra weight, not untidily, however. Her boots are perfectly clean, from the most expensive brand you can buy at a chain mountaineering store.

"You must be Gnat," she states, firmer and more masculine than her appearance should allow.

"Yes, that's me. Are you who I spoke to?"

"No, that was Berr, the lodge supervisor. I'm Tibi, the general manager. The owner, Cliim, is in town."

"Where do I put my things? I'm guessing I'll start soon?"

"Your camper is on the water. Be up at the front desk when it gets light, Berr can run you through things. It's pretty easy. Follow me," she demands unimposingly.

His trailer is vintage, white with a green stripe. The white has yellowed, the green pinstripe is dried and cracked, more purple. Inside, it has a bed, a table, and a bulb which doesn't work at night, when you'd need it. They're on diesel generator power, Tibi explains. No toilet or refrigerator, good enough, however. The view is incredible through the branches of an old growth of giant cypress trees; a glacial lake and the peaks of two mountains holding the water in, both surpass the oxygen line. For humans, of course. He sees the shape of a dinghy with a fishing pole lurching offshore. Children jump from a boulder, inadvertently scaring the fish out to the man in the boat. Hikers have set up their tents, in from the thru-hike, the Sirra Niva trail. A route from South Omrika through the range, then up through Wishintown into Montisa. Most people quit; this place is a resupply stop.

"And to grab a hearty meal," Berr told him on the phone.

North or southbound from this lodge, the next resupplies lie far enough apart to remind you how insignificant a human life is. Gnat considered this trail when he was younger, concluding it isn't a hike. Most of the path is maintained and cleared, there are shelters built along the way to sleep out of the elements. Anybody can do it, as long as they can put their screens away long enough not to career off the side of a canyon.

He starts to unpack a few things, then puts everything on the table, bag under the mattress. *No reason to get settled. How long will I be here? This isn't my place, only where I'll work for a stretch.*

Inside the lodge, a typical convenience store you would expect to find has been organized. Nothing's really needed, it's only trinkets for glamor campers retailed for double cost by the owner. Unimpressed, he finds the alcohol. A single can is the price of almost three in town, yet the more you buy the cheaper they become. By the time you buy a full case, almost half are free. Gnat thinks of the way Tibi held herself. Now this store, and the disproportionate evaluations of the products within. *I know what kind of place I ended up, the same as every other small business barely treading water for lack of knowledge from the people running it. 'But, that's the way it's been done, all these spans!* the proprietor always says.

He buys an entire case from the woman working the counter. She immediately complains about not having enough cigarette breaks during her shift.

His camper is not really that, or a trailer, he notices returning to it. It's a box with wheels. His rent? Enough to stay in the city.

He sighs. The first can goes down quickly, the second more so. Night comes early when living at elevation. The sky is hazy, overcast. The sun is pale through the sheet of dense clouds that have appeared, although if it was clear, it would already be behind the imposing summits across the lake. The tint of the atmosphere is off, you almost can't keep your eyelids completely open. It is seemingly unnatural, the color. Almost the same as before a tornado in Oia. *Surreal.* He hears someone tossing pieces of firewood behind him, up by the main lodge. *The bonfire.* Probably hikers and employees alike. *There isn't much to do other than be friends with the people you are forced to be around, remember?* He doesn't introduce himself. They're mostly hikers, he can tell by what they are talking about. Gear, how much they spent. How much their pack weighs. Most had to take vacation from salaried positions, so every leg is pre-planned. What to eat, how far they have to go. Food is sent prior to leaving and only held for a cycle so you must stay on schedule. Endless one-ups, trying to be more macho than the others in the group. More stripped down, lighter. Cheaper.

You're walking on a man-made path through the mountains instead of driving. It's a road trip on foot. You are never in danger or out of reach. Most hikers carry beacons, the helicopter is never more than a nap away. You are on the grid, registered, for anyone interested to find if they want.

A man from Southern Sanrika starts talking about surfing. The people who aren't locals come in during the best swells, getting in the way. Windows of invading cars must be broken sometimes. Or punches thrown, he explains.

Gnat finally enters. "Doesn't that defeat the point of surfing in the first place, being in tune with your surroundings?"

"Not when other people show up and ruin the vibe," he answers.

"So, your family has been in that area since the beginning of Irfa?" Gnat laughs.

"We moved there when I was a kid. It's my home," he spouts.

"So, you showed up and ruined the view for whomever was there already..." he waits for a valid response, unfulfilled.

The group continues on, one member is a solo sailor with a channel describing everything online. Gnat says nothing until the flame dies and no more logs are added. The hikers peter out. He starts to study the fire pit made of concrete laced with many pieces of volcanic glass. It's rare and has to be collected over time. Every piece is separate yet has an edge that somewhat matches the adjacent shards.

Surfing, hiking, sailing. Everyone needs to define what they're doing, define their place within whatever the activity is. In the conversation about titles and accolades, the meaning of the activity is lost. A solo sailor that broadcasts every move for the world to see? A surfer that allows no other the zen of the ocean? A hiker that misses the point of getting lost to be the fastest or make a deadline? It's inherently tart, bitter, and ignorant. Like the fireplace, what is life but wasted effort? Who cares what you do, how or why you do it, except you? Being first in a category undeniably makes you last in another.

The moon has crept out from the cover of clouds. His eyes are not focused on it, unmoving. He's voluntarily controlling them, until its shape becomes burned onto his retinas. He lowers his head to the ground. As his eyes twitch, unable to stay absolutely still, he sees the outline of the moon float across the logs. Millions of spans of evolution within him can be fooled by any bright shape drawing too much attention for too long.

***

A wake-up knock by Tibi comes, as she calls, "Breakfast with the crew, you can thank me later for the courtesy knock."

Gnat's been writing and is already dressed. Entering the hall where he'll work sit half a dozen people, most of them older men. Tibi introduces him while he nods, finding a chair. A short man comes in with a neatly-combed head, glasses, a button-down shirt with short sleeves. This is tucked into a pair of cargo pants, which are belted high above his waist, closer to his lungs.

"I'm Cliim. We have a few new people. Some that have been around aren't present, more are supposed to turn up. Now, enjoy the meal, Tibi made it. I'll be around to check on things, then gone again. Thank you everyone," he says, and leaves.

The men at his table introduce themselves as Elro, Ryi, and Sem. They point to the Omrikan military flag hanging in the store. They're veterans, as is Cliim, they explain. He helps out his fellow service members. They pay the same rent as everybody else, earn a salary, working the entirety of the season. He notices that Elro must be close to eighty, and rides an electric scooter. Both of his legs are missing.

"I think I've pretty much got this Cliim guy figured out," he tells them.

Berr shows him a very utilitarian restaurant. A ferry brings hikers across the lake from the trail, morning and night. Everything to do with the front of the house and guest relations is his responsibility. Berr tells him she'll do the next two meal services, hardly anyone is coming in on the boat. He can check out camp and get settled. A nice older woman, he thanks her and heads to the box on the water's edge where his things are.

Gnat wanders, but it isn't anything he hasn't seen. Better than Oia, no question, and he can save money. Grabbing the handle to the door, a flash of movement comes from below his trailer. A rattlesnake. It tries to strike again, hissing at him. Grabbing a shovel leaning against a shed and stepping over the snake, guarding himself with the trowel, he uses it as a guillotine to sever its head. The scream of a girl comes. He picks up the pieces of the carcass, tossing them into the weeds.

"Hey, why did you kill that snake? It didn't do anything to you," she says. "You did that for no reason. You're a murderer!"

312 | JOSEPH THOMAS WILLIG

He processes what he's bombarded by. A white girl with dreaded hair, wearing a nose ring and jacket that cost more than a paycheck for most.

"I did kill it for a reason, so it didn't kill me. It was in my area, it was attacking me." He states, trying to enter his hovel.

"You can't kill something and leave without answering for it!"

"Would it have killed me, if it bit me?"

She glares at him.

"Have you ever seen a flock of seagulls on the beach, when someone drops their food on the sand? Do they stop and divide it up? No, whoever gets it survives. That's not cruel, it's the way of things. What if I let the snake live and later tonight it went and bit a child staying here? Would that have been a tragedy?"

"Well, yes. That'd be horrible," she says.

"It's not an emotional decision-making organism, it's a poisonous product of evolution. It will take the opportunities best suited for itself. The fact that we recognize the capability of what it can do and remove it from the equation is why we *consider ourselves* more intelligent," says Gnat. "Really, I did the same thing. I didn't mali-ciously go into the forest and kill every living creature. Something entered my habitat that had the ability to hurt me, so I removed it. So I can survive. That's common sense."

"You could have left and come back later..."

Gnat continues, "No, then the immediate threat would still remain. You know how people stop birds from foraging through trash near my home?"

"How?"

"They kill one, then the rest know the consequences of trying. The risk isn't worth the reward, their life is worth more than a meal."

She puts her hand on her forehead. "I can't believe I'm hearing this! This is why I'm vegetarian."

Gnat pulls himself up into the doorway. "You know which species are honest and just, naturally, and ruthless emotionally? Plants.
They move so slow we don't realize it. Resolutely strangling each
other over spans to reach the light. If you want to make it, you've
got to fight. Nothing is guaranteed. It's not your right because
you're alive. You have to earn it. Every bite is a battle. Would you
lay down your life, so some other thing could live instead?"

She moves away, muttering, "I don't agree, that's not the way it
should be, everything should have equal opportunities..."

Everything does, chance is justice.

Later on he's drunk but avoids the fire when sundown arrives.
Ryi comes knocking at his door, a man in his late forties. He has a
gentle expression on his face, with some kind of hurt spilled over it.

"Elro said you can come down to his cabin with us for some
drinks," he says to Gnat. "If you'd like."

Gnat replies, "Yeah, alright. I'll bring mine."

"Leave it, we've got you covered," he smiles.

Elro is already drunk and has a rifle resting on his thigh. Both
legs adorn prosthetics with shoes on the plastic feet. He still rests in
the wheelchair from earlier. Sem is tall, quiet, with short hair. He
raises his glass to Gnat from the couch.

"There's only two ways you can drink in this here cabin," Elro
spits toward Gnat. "First, if you're invited. Second is if you are
drinking the hard stuff." He starts to laugh quickly, raising his voice,
like some man you'd imagine panning for gold in the past. "Other-
wise, I'm going to have to shoot you."

"I've got him covered, Elro," Ryi says, handing Gnat a glass.
"Straight up?"

Gnat grins. "The only way."

He discovers that Sem is Tibi's cousin, they grew up together.
Ryi left the service, along with his wife. He landed in the Sirra Nivas

after rambling around doing odd jobs. He stays, watching the place in the off-season. Since the road gets buried with stories of snow, a helicopter brings him supplies.

At the point Elro tries to stand up and slap Sem, Gnat bids everyone a swift goodbye. As he goes, Elro falls off his chair and loses both false legs rolling over himself, cursing his companions and their mothers. The loaded long-gun is still in his grasp, finger on the trigger.

While Gnat laughs about what he's just experienced, the pound of a fist shakes his box. He tries to see out the slatted window and screen.

"My name is Eed. I'm the cook. You know, you can't run from yourself. But sometimes, you forget who you are."

This person carries a flashlight, and in its halo on the dirt he can see the shape of a man. The man holds a backpack, dangling from his side as he enters the closest trailer. He steps inside and the pitch of darkness embraces Gnat again. His windpipe turns to lead. He can't breathe, the weight pulls him down onto his mattress.

III

Smoke wafts relentlessly above the kitchen as Gnat approaches. A glimpse of the desert dream comes to him. Where are the planes? After a fitful rest he's determined maybe they stalk him nearer than known. Behind the line a figure stirs a pot.

"Are you Eed?" Gnat interrogates.

"That's me, yes. Your neighbor and coworker. Are the hikers getting up? I start when it's still dark," Eed replies, not giving him an acknowledging glance.

"Yes. So, order from the board? I call it to you, paper checks, add the tax?"

"That's more or less the idea, you haven't told me *your* name," Eed pauses, fixing his focus upon Gnat.

Eed's irises are light blue, so watery a shade they seem to show the white behind them translucently. His skin isn't old and wrinkled, but tough. *Like hide.* He's been seared by the sun and bitten by the cold many times, tanned in a way that permeates through the layers of who he is, altering what was once fetching. His features are defined thoroughly, unblended. A long nose, a pursed mouth. The latter quieted so many times its physical form has withered. His beard is a grizzle at most. Disheveled dark hair of median length is confined under a hat. His muscles are also detailed by way of genetics, not practice. An apron covers a short-sleeved shirt, jeans, and boots. His galoshes show the distance they've wandered. There's a glimmer of femininity in the way he holds himself, a gliding caution and carefulness.

"Gnat, with a G," he responds, guessing the cook's age. *Forty-five.*

"Great to meet you, Gnat. You have experience, I presume. The door's opening, let's have a fluid service."

"Sounds like a plan," he agrees, moving to greet a hiker coming in.

Breakfast is a breeze; many guests fill the seats. Gnat handles them and clears tables while loading the dishwasher, calling orders, and keeping cups full. Eed presents plates in the window efficiently, never mixing up numbers or breaking an egg yolk. The pair work with fluidity, an observer would believe they have been running the place for spans. After the last person pays, Eed nods to Gnat.

"We'll do fine together," he says, patting Gnat's shoulder. "You know, there's a barbecue, I still have to prep. Have you ever cooked?"

"Sure thing, I can do whatever you need."

"I trust you. I'll make you some eggs. How do you take them?"

"Over-easy. Thanks."

After, he goes for a swim. The water is very clear, he and the fish at the bottom can see each other in detail. Back in the kitchen, Eed is laying ingredients on the stove pondering.

"So, what can I do?" asks Gnat.

"How about you do sides, I'll do the rest? Can you make sauce?"

"I can."

"Macaroni and cheese, corn on the cob, coleslaw?"

Gnat accepts. "How many people?"

"Fifty, with employees," says Eed, cutting open a side of beef.

"Heard."

Gnat's made cheese sauce and coleslaw, both are in the refrigerator. He stands shucking cobs of corn.

"What happens with the cooling system when the generator goes off?" he asks Eed.

"I've already said something to Cliim." He shakes his head. "It goes off, too. When I come in every morning the food is warm. When they bring the food up from the city, the van isn't chilled."

"The product goes on a drive reaching room temperature, then the fridge where it cycles through the bacteria danger-zone constantly?" says Gnat, wide-eyed.

Eed chuckles. "Exactly. People come here to eat then rebound to the trail. When they get sick, they never consider this place, only something in their pack. Perfect business practice, wouldn't you say?"

"I definitely have this Cliim guy figured out," Gnat replies.

"How long have you been out on your own, Gnat?" The cook changes the subject.

"I left home for the first time when I was eighteen."

Eed lifts his chin in curiosity. "Why did you decide to do that?"

"Originally, I was following the path laid out. The high school I attended is considered prestigious, but I never felt quite right about it. I acted out a lot, I didn't know where my place was. Not there, I knew that."

Eed prods further, "What didn't sit well?"

"The expectations," Gnat continues, "the tests, the scores, the results. It says who means something and who doesn't. Everything is standardized. *Quantified.* Value comes from what your peers perceive, not what you deem important to yourself. That gets thrown out, that's what becomes your hobby. I thought about some guys I graduated with and tried finding them on the internet. I typed in their names, and clicked on some profiles showing professional careers. It was the jobs, resumes, lists of alumni organizations, fraternities, awards. They're just trying to present as better than the next person. But everyone checks off the same list to get where they are, these things attest to nothing.

I wrote an essay in school, about the colors of our flag, the cars driving like ants in a line to achieve the false ideals the symbol represents and waves as they pass."

"And?" asks Eed.

"I still believed in learning, so I went to university to study engineering. I was always fascinated by cars, I wanted to design them. That's when I left home for the first time, not far. Still in Oia, but on my own."

"This didn't work out either?"

Gnat explains, "I found that higher learning is higher indoctrination into society. It isn't about intelligence, it's about cramming for the test, paying the tuition, and getting the degree to hang on your wall. Then the world says you're qualified. You've only locked yourself in the program. If you would have given me a job and the equations before I started, I could have done the work. These skills aren't viable unless the person behind the scenes keeps the computer on. As soon as it's turned off you are left with no knowledge of how to feed or shelter yourself."

"It seems that you already knew before you got there, why go anyway?" Eed asks, deglazing a pan. The flame jumps to the ceiling.

Gnat laughs. "I took a class, the first in the series, oral speaking. Our project was to do a presentation on anything, and give it at the end of the quarter. I chose accountability. Why do people not want to take responsibility for their actions? It is always someone else's fault. Remember that volcano exploding recently on an island off Austopia somewhere? A few dozen people died?"

"Yes," says Eed.

"In the end they tried to say the scientist reading the seismometer could have recognized an eruption was coming and saved people who knowingly went to an island with an active volcano. They knew the risks. It's no one's fault a completely random act of nature came along," Gnat rants.

"The presentation, what happened?"

"After each slideshow every student had to write down something they got from it. I used a study of worms that scientists did where they found homosexuality in a species, to give background for choice against genetics. I went on to society, how it always gives you another chance. That you never have to stand completely for what you've chosen. Whether it's actually a choice or inherent. This leads to indecisive, fickle, whiny people always waiting for a handout. You know what almost everyone wrote?"

"What's that?"

"It was cool the worms were gay." Gnat pauses. "As I inspected their faces I saw most of them were there because of predetermined definitions. Too poor, a minority, unstable. Doing what they were told by rich parents, following the footsteps of an older sibling. They won't ever understand they're the perpetuation and power source of the broken system they fight against. You can't change it by existing in its rules. I dropped out shortly after."

"Back to your parents then? Where do they live?"

"In Nata. I went there, I had no skills as defined by society. I wanted out. I thought of the military for about three breaths. I'd never fight or die for this corrupt government." Gnat drains boiling water from a pot with a grimace. The steam covers him, making him perspire. "So I said, I'll go to the beach. I ran away to F'lalasip with a few of my friends. That didn't last long, my dad had to come get me."

"You have a solid family," Eed continues. "How long did you stay in Oia?"

"A span. I ended up bouncing around, until I ended up homeless in Wai. I fished and lived in a hammock on the water. I'd go to town for temporary jobs. You'd have to go past the tourists in their gated communities to keep the indigenous people out. Inside they have restaurants, grocery stores, and movie theaters so old couples don't have to feel unsafe by actually being where they are." Gnat laughs again. "I made enough to get to the mainland. I told myself I'd learn some viable skills, so I could survive by growing my own food. I went to an intentional community, a commune. I learned what I needed, also that these people aren't progressive. They're hiding in secret, keeping things as they were in the past, unwilling to evolve. Close-minded, unenlightened. Thriving in the power of the group, not themselves singularly. I left."

"How old were you then?" Eed waits patiently.

"Twenty-three. I built a truck with solar power and got a corporate job. I made it four spans. I've only been finding more of what I don't want. There was a time when I thought I'd never find what I do want. I still might, really. I went through the process of rebuilding myself. Here I am."

"You may need some help finding what to try next?"

"I accept what comes. I don't know if more roaming is going to show me new ideas. I'm in the place where I understand what I see; I don't need to prove it to myself again. But what do I do with it?"

"We have guests seating themselves outside. Is everything ready, sous chef?" says Eed, spatula in hand.

"Already? Let me throw the macaroni in the oven, here we go."

A hungry stampede floods in and almost every person compliments the food, saying it's incredible to get something this nice so far from the city. Gnat puts on his hospitality charm, making himself and Eed a decent amount of tips. Only fair to split them, they're a team, aren't they? Halfway through service, Cliim appears as the plates start coming back.

"Hey guys, I see a lot of leftovers on these plates. The people aren't liking what you've done."

"Almost every customer has praised us," interjects Gnat. "We're giving them too much, there isn't any portion control."

"What do you mean?" Cliim puts his hands in his pockets, arching his shoulders. *Trying to make himself taller.*

"You don't have any standards of procedure. Plates are thrown together with whatever was on sale. You need utensils with measurements so every dish is the same. How do you know how much money you are making?" Gnat answers.

"Who did the macaroni, Eed?" Cliim turns to the cook.

"I did." Gnat recalls his attention.

"Eed, let's have Gnat serve from now on, no cooking," Cliim says, acting as if Gnat doesn't exist. He briskly turns and leaves, his trademark, apparently.

"Ignorance is bliss, the most encompassing saying about human life," Eed tells Gnat. "As a child, you are ignorantly joyful. As an adult, you are joyfully ignorant."

He's awestruck. "Eed! I've had that same thought!"

"I've listened to what you've done, what you've gotten from it. You've been questioning. Once you doubt everything to the point you doubt yourself, then you can start to know the truth. Skepticism is the first step to becoming a master."

Gnat doesn't reply. Service ends, the kitchen is closed, no dinner when there's a barbecue. He tries to hand half the cash to Eed.

"Keep it." Eed pushes it to Gnat's chest. "You'll need it when you leave. Why don't you come to my trailer after sunset. I'll make us supper. You can listen to my story, how does that sound?"

"I'll be there," he says without hesitation.

Later, the sun wanes. Gnat knocks on Eed's trailer.

"Come on then," he answers from within. His trailer is bigger than Gnat's. Its highlights are in red, which have kept their color better than the green of its neighbor. He also has a stove with an oven and a light that works. Gnat asks how this is possible. Old school batteries, the stove runs on gas. The cushions at the table are of a sparkly vinyl reminiscent of a roadside diner from the past.

"I've made crepes, I hope that works," he says, placing a plate in front of his guest.

"This is fine," Gnat replies. "I'm not here for the meal, as much as the company."

"Alright, I might as well jump straight in."

"I'm listening," says Gnat, taking his first bite.

"My parents owned a restaurant, in rural Nuwal," Eed starts, "I started working there at fourteen. I have some older siblings, they were out of the house ten spans before me. When I say I worked, I mean hard, along with my parents. We had no vacations, no regular time off. Most of the customers were passing through. There was a waterfall nearby. The biggest in North Omrika..."

"I've been there," adds Gnat.

"These people would tell me stories of being out and about. My friends were going on road trips when we first got permission to drive. I couldn't go, I had to help the family business. We graduated from school and everyone started going off to university. Not me, I had to stay. I became the local boy that you'd always know where to find if you wanted. I was chained to that place.

I was working with my father one shift, when he dropped over dead. He had a heart attack at fifty. Only three spans older than I am now. I was twenty-one. My mother was crushed, she sold the restaurant. I was devastated. My father spent most of his life serving people pasta and wine. I had already spent seven spans doing the same, I'd never even wanted to. I was not in control of my life, just living the way I was told. I never felt quite right. It may have been a thing that I wanted because it wasn't an option, or the stories those tourists put in my head about Irfa. I decided I wasn't going to waste my life in that town. I kissed my mother farewell and left."

"Where did you go?" Gnat asks, pushing his plate to the side.

"Everywhere. I did the same thing you have, it seems. Drifted. Worked when I wanted, slept in a tent or on someone's couch. I hitchhiked, took a bus, flew. I was completely open. Sexually. Spiritually. With drugs. I tried it all and like you said, only found more and more of what I didn't want. I'd go home, to get some peace, but never did. I knew I didn't want to be there, and I always felt silly for going as soon as I arrived."

"I hear you."

Eed carries on, "I'm sure you do. This carried on for spans. Bringing everything in to question, constantly. Myself as well. I grew tired, what was the endgame? I finally came to a conclusion. To create a philosophy, a way of life."

Gnat livens up. "You completed it? Where is it?"

"It isn't finished, it's in my head. It isn't written anywhere, although I tried. Things came up and I abandoned the notion. The idea isn't to teach someone else what to think. I wanted to give everyone the tools to be able to question things the same way I had. To make them see for themselves. If there is canon, a specific set of rules, then the system being employed always fails. That inherent desire to control others always leads to a breakdown. Someone fights back.

Putting confidence in science, math, definitions of entities we can't hold or touch, like a black hole. How is that different from giving loyalty to a king or a god? All of these institutions have been created by *us* to describe and quantify this universe. To give everything a reason for being. Why can't we put our fortitude and energy into ourselves, our experience, and not need to be given anything from outside? Is it a weakness? The need to be accepted, to belong to a group that has a common nemesis to defeat? Is it deferring the emptiness of existence we actually understand? The point is not to create another group that identifies itself as separate or above, but individuals that discern truth based on experience and knowledge. This would allow actual progress of the species."

"Everything is jaded, people only want what's handed to them regardless of the source, if it's free," Gnat says.

"Yes!" Eed exclaims. "Nothing holds value any longer, it's decaying as it's being erected. This age..."

"Of lackluster?" Gnat interjects.

"This is the age of *submission* we are entering," Eed completes. "But that's a part of it, everything becoming unoriginal and predictable. The thing you must do is recognize the patterns this society works within. Preconceived ideals. Of culture, of self. This will allow us to operate outside of its boundaries, consciously. I can only give you the basics, it isn't complete. If you want me to tell you I will. Maybe you can build something on the foundation I have poured and set."

"I will listen and learn, the weight of knowing this reality is false stupefies me..." Gnat's voice fades off to nothing.

"Tomorrow after dinner, then. Go and rest."

"Thank you for the food. I'm ready. Always. See you tomorrow." Eed nods, opening the door. "You're welcome. Goodnight."

Gnat stops and gazes, seeing the extruded dimensions of space, the varying distances of celestial bodies above. *Millions of them.* An invisible arrow shoots through an ear to his brain. The voice whispers to him, friendlier than ever. *Delineate what's in you already.*

IV

The following dusk, visibility fades at an exponential rate. Gnat picks his guitar, trying to calm down a bit from the craziness that is every restaurant on Irfa. Something diddles past his window, grabbing his attention. *A soap bubble.* Actually many, of different sizes. He moves to find the source. It's Eed, standing upwind. He blows another group of bubbles out onto the breeze, toward Gnat.

"Bubbles are beautiful, aren't they? Floating along, unknowing where they came from or of their magnificent fragility. But what forms them? Hot air. What makes them disappear? A pop. Simple and succinct. Are you ready to hear what I have to say?" he reaches into his trailer and brings a lamp to life.

"Yes," Gnat answers.

"Everything is a pattern," Eed states, when they are both settled in the booth inside. He's given Gnat a glass of water, nothing else.

"Cooking, music, school, society. People, also. If you can see the patterns, you are outside the bubble. You can guide and control any situation or conversation to whatever end you desire. You can see the difference between emotion and truth. When something happens, what is the first thing the masses grab onto? How they *feel* about it. This isn't truth, it's the opposite. A lie. When feelings fade, so does attention to the happening, the action causing the uproar. If we lived only in sanity and coherence, the past wouldn't keep repeating itself. Let's look at the patterns of society first, and how they've cascaded over the last hundred spans."

Gnat's elbows are on the tabletop, he leans forward, determined. Hushed.

"The Military-Industrial bubble, the thing that started society as we know it now. We entered two wars involving the entire Irfa. The first, Omrika had no business being a part of. The second was a necessity to sustain our way of life, creating massive amounts of production to jump start the depressed economy. This is when we started thinking we were the best. Before this, Omrika was more or less a lawless country fighting against the natives and South Omrikans. After the second war, we had a seat at Irfa's table as a superpower. Our military was the biggest and most extreme. Now we had the ability to control the flow of natural resources under the guise of spreading free enterprise and our system of government. That generation of men and women call themselves the greatest. The problem is, the name was self-administered. The issues created by them are many. A generation with stress disorders, bombs that kill millions with a single blast and leave radiation behind for millennia scarring the land, social medicine and payments running at an ever-increasing deficit, general greed and selfish policy, the ruination of education for profit. This complex still exists, it will explode and collapse in the future. Other countries will pass us, it isn't sustainable.

I mentioned education, the next festering blister growing past its effectiveness. In the beginning it was an investment in yourself. Now you are no different than a barnyard animal, living stock. An asset to the universities, government, and banking institutions who force people into roles that don't serve anyone outside what is deemed normal. This is done at great debt to the individual so they can never escape paying bills or living paycheck to paycheck. You graduate, getting a job in another city. You have to keep the job to pay your school loans. To get to the job a reliable car must be purchased. To be close to your employer you must buy a house. Which is the next thing, the housing bubble.

A house built on land bought for pennies is sold the first time. The bank supplies a mortgage, from which they profit some two hundred percent over its term. When you sell, you may break even or make a little on the principle. The bank gives out another loan on the same property, making another two hundred percent. An initial cost of land and materials of a few thousand nets millions over the course of three generations. They have convinced people they are home owners. Your landlord is simply the bank, not a person. Don't pay your bill, you'll find out if the property is really yours or not.

So, you have your job and house, at some point you want to retire right? You need to have savings to be comfortable, so you get a money manager or accountant. He puts your earnings in stocks to let it grow over time, for a fee on both sides. The boards that control speculation from the back rooms, the government and banks, let the values shoot up artificially and sell out. Then watch as it crashes. The common man suffers, the government bails out the banks who already won. The trading platform is controlled by humans and therefore could never work correctly. However, the person at the top can only feed off the ones below because of their greed, trying to be as they are. Again, this came out of the world wars which created a false sense of good times after they ended for that generation. They've depleted the system, expecting to be taken care of by the administration after retiring until they die. Living for the sake of living, not contributing, making more per span than during their careers. This has only lasted a few cycles, and is already in shambles. It isn't sustainable, not in the least. This is more or less known but people still enter it willingly. Afraid to change, a self-fulfilling destiny you can never get out from under.

What are the things we deal with now? I see three. The first is the bacterial bubble. It took a hundred thousand spans of humans existing to get to the point where we could treat infections. The advance doesn't really prove we are all that innovative. We have over-vaccinated. This has created the façade of good health. Some infections now are resistant to the drugs we've used. Soon, none of our medications will work. We will descend into ancient existence once more, where nothing but a contaminated cut costs you life or limb. Everything evolves, we are not above this.

Corporations have taken over what I call the green bubble. Not only food, which isn't any better for you or the environment, but energy sources. Electric cars create exorbitant amounts of pollution before they're ever driven. These things are simply linked to sentiment. People feel good about themselves. It doesn't change the burdens we put on the Irfa to sustain us, just where the pressure points are. We consume endlessly, whether organic vegetables or fried beef from a dumpster. To survive is to take. The ultimate act of an environmentalist would be to stop living. When does it pop? When the checks stop clearing.

The conclusion of what was given to us in the start, the Military-Industrial bubble, is what we are experiencing now. The sensitivity bubble, where people want to be congratulated and labeled for coming to terms with their apprehensions and insecurities, is beginning.

Everyone speaks out against people who operate differently than the swarm, the status quo. We will become a society of collective entities who aren't allowed to speak our minds or hold an opinion of our own, no matter how that opinion was formed. There will be no abstract thought, no one will be living. It's what the system wants, absolute deference. Every individual will exist with what they have been presented. No human will go outside of it. There will be no reason to achieve, no reason to look beyond. Eating whatever is given, passing it as soon as it's swallowed. Zombies feeding the machine. It needs humans to suffer for it to survive. People will trade liberties for a payment and the false sense of safety they have been convinced of by the top. Then, we will be completely immersed in this *Age of Submission.*

These bubbles have been created by animals. *Humans.* What templates are *they* pressed from? Limited variations of a person exist. The circumstances of life don't create more. The only thing the individual details show is how experience can bring out aspects within the types. With genetic diversity, every being, physically, can look distinct. This is why we consider ourselves unique. But even with the vast differentiation of people biologically, every trait comes from others in the past. It isn't random, you are tiny pieces of the generalized pool of genes that began the species. Things such as skin tone came from inhabiting contrasting biomes over the millennia.

The same is true of the consciousness yet the diversity isn't as grand. It is centered in ten types. These are the bases. The neural fingerprints of our species.

The user takes advantage of things that are easily changed. They find weaknesses in the ability of others, to judge and exploit them. Always seen as the superior, which is what they strive for. This ego carries them through a self-absorbed existence. These individuals don't see that they are nothing without other people's suffering holding them up. They can make it seem like they're helping you, but always make sure the biggest benefit goes to them.

The used is the victim of their surroundings. They find value in being miserable and will always take the burden. 'If it's going to get done, I have to do it.' They see value in their individuality, not the fact that they are a cog to be replaced with an exact replica when they break. The used finds meaning in life more than the others around them which allows them to be taken advantage of easily.

The clone wants to be told what to do. These people do what everyone else is doing. They don't make any choices, only do what's popular. They see themselves as progressive but cannot defend their actions with valid points, just sound bites from the world around them.

The blind will always deflect and justify. Trusting the system therefore forfeiting independence. Any decision they make can be traced to 'that's just the way it is.' Anything that comes unexpectedly isn't handled tactfully. Cut and dry, black and white. If they don't get what they want, they're the victim of some injustice. Always living in false hope that things will get better if they keep going.

The postulant thrives in self-glory, but only perpetuates their own ignorance. Grasping onto possessions, thinking this will give purpose to what they're doing. Forever in competition with some idea they never comprehend because it doesn't exist. If they live fast in flash maybe something will notice them. This is their life's goal, never querying it.

The serene goes with the flow, seemingly. They find meaning in bettering themselves, not understanding it is for nothing but personal benefit. Would be described as joyous. May try to spread this joy and don't see the feelings they cling onto for sustenance are only fictional and hollow.

The altered exist on a different level, higher or lower. They may be the ones that experience the greatest level of contentment based on the fact they do not operate in the same reality as somebody considered average. Could be that they are a link to future evolutions or downfalls along the line of coming to be what we are now. Nobody is sure, we don't study that aspect of the altered conscious, only try to find ways to bring them to standard.

The seer pierces through the patterns in some way, still existing within them. They can tell that this experiment of society has failed, but can't find an escape. Or, on a lesser level, fix it. Doomed to know all things they absorb are simply an illusion. They could find a way out, if chance allows.

The mender protects others genuinely, unaware it gives them a reason to survive. Also puts positive vibrations in the world, for notice *and* for purpose. Adores connection because something is missing from their person. Another version of the seer, they know things are amiss but don't try to live apart from it. They use emotion and always get the short end for it. They always lose parts of themselves to others, giving them openly, hoping to gain something back. Some time, somehow. The seer and the mender tread a fine line between knowledge and piousness.

Every individual finds something within themselves to be sorry about, or doubt. It's accidental. Chance. We don't create a consciousness, allow it to grow thoughts and morals, then plant it into the body it wants. Whatever you get, that's it. Live with it or don't. It will never be the way you want it to be, fairness is a childhood fantasy. If you know the way things are operating around you, clarity can be discovered."

"I could be wrong, wasn't that only nine? You told me ten," Gnat's voice cracks as he takes a drink.

"I warned you, it's incomplete. I've only told you nine because I haven't found the tenth type. I know a piece of the puzzle is missing. I've met these types in different forms, no others. Do you know which type you are?"

"I'm angry," Gnat snorts and smiles.

"You are a seer. That's why you have become angry, you can't get away from it. Have you ever had the thought 'is this it?'"

"Many times. Which are you?"

Eed sinks into his seat. "I was a seer, I let it go. I became blind, ignoring it. Not angry, downtrodden. Now I try to be serene with my quiet life."

"If you know, and do nothing about it..."

Eed raises his hand to silence Gnat. "I know, it makes me part of the problem. I've been waiting to tell someone these things again for a long time. So based on these patterns of people, we can discern why someone makes the choices they do."

"Who else have you told?" asks Gnat.

"There have been a few. Now, making choices isn't a negative thing. The stupidity is introduced when someone makes a choice, yet only understands a single side of what they are deciding. On the other hand, being so open-minded that you never take an informed stance and stick to it makes your value within the system less. The individual has no bearing on the truth, whether they believe it or not. It's still happening. You have to be strong enough to admit when you don't completely understand both viewpoints. Real understanding, which is not the same as simply comprehending the literal words of an argument. This is why people make what I call the *Societal Sacrifice,* because they are only given half of the options as they are raised and never learn to peer wider than their personal scope. It is almost the same as religion, you sell yourself out to become part of things without knowing the difference. It demands capitulation, this controller. Taxes, education, military, politics. They serve the same end, receiving and living in ideals created by men to control the weak-minded. It's a fixed game, you never so much as meet the players of the opposing team. You are bound by it before you take your first breath."

"How do you get people to stop and see both sides, letting go of anything that's ever been important to them?" Gnat continues. "Once you start school, you're really an adult. You're expected to be able to answer for yourself. You go to class, deal with interpersonal relationships, the teacher is your boss, who gives you assignments to do at home. You get your paycheck in the form of allowance.

You are new, so you aren't held accountable for your actions until you move through the ranks, then you finish school and become legal. You progressively get more on your plate, and if you fail, you repeat the step until you meet the standard set by the government. Brainwashing at its finest..."

Eed goes on, "That's why people encapsulate themselves within the bubbles we've talked about! Completing predetermined lists does not imply you're capable of higher thought, you still only know a single side. This leads to *confidence over evidence*, believing things you were taught over what you've deduced on your own through action. Nobody really respects any commandment, because as long as you bow to it there are limitless opportunities to be a part of it again.

My understanding comes out of what I have done, the consequences on either side of the path I chose. That can't be taken away. Individuals that live a life based on secondhand information from religion, media, government and peers are controlled. They are fearful, hateful of anything apart from what's been prescribed for them, consciously. But when it comes down to it we are nothing more than human."

"Laughing with someone in another country that doesn't share your language or culture. The undisputed proof of that last statement," Gnat adds.

Eed nods in agreement. "So, what of this being, that is over-confident and independent? Every individual is not equal. We want to ignore this; in turn no one recognizes reality. Every human now has a desire for a *special* existence. This leads to a loss of structure, inherently, and a lost sense of self. Some live in convention, some live in logic. The two cannot coexist. The attitudes of Irfa currently lie in personal benefit, yet as soon as someone fails they expect the whole to take care of them. It's a paradox, a logical concept powered by emotion in moments. It will never succeed.

There are two things to remember existentially, here in society. Stress is the same for everyone, whether working in business or traveling for drinking water. Everyone feels the same emotions, menial details aside. Left is left, right is right. Circumstances don't change genetic predisposition to feeling. The supremacy of our species on this planet has already been realized, whether we held it with any tenderness or not. This is the reason we focus on things like joy, there's no reason for living except existing for yourself. So, secondly, *experience without expectation*. Find value in what you have gone through and what you have learned from it, not the recognition or jealousy it brings. Live in the present, be mindful, take in the view and understand it. Not the picture you took of it. Overstimulation leads to things becoming insipid."

Gnat speaks up, "Human nature is warring. With yourself, with others. Life is nothing but struggle. We can't escape the violence of it, that is just the word we use to try and define it and assign a passionate response to it."

"Hmm," Eed responds. "Let's go to definition. First, of emotion. The situation a specific feeling arises from doesn't make a difference. Sadness is sadness, whether your dog gets sick or your grandmother does. The degree of the emotion may vary. The thing that does matter: where are the intentions of the emotion coming from? Do you find joy in a sunrise, or other's misery? What about other words? As you said, these portrayals of words and what they mean give the whole power to separate itself into smaller skirmishing pieces based on the feeling attached to them. What are these things, in reality?

Happiness doesn't exist. There is no person on this Irfa that lives in a suspended state above others, unaffected by anything but absolute joy. You are either okay with what is happening to you, or you're not. That's it.

Love is only mutual benefit, codependency, genetic instinct, and ease. Separation of couples wouldn't happen if partners were unconditionally concerned with nothing but the well-being of the other. There is always something that they get out of it, which voids the concept of giving yourself to someone from a primitive standpoint.

Faith? Only the deflection of your own ignorance, disregarding fact and reason to find value in things as they were given to you.

Justice is nothing but vengeance. Getting even, settling the score. You kill me? I kill you. Again, life isn't fair. It's random. Trying to fight against chance inherently creates more dissonance. Things happen, move on.

What is this thing, *value*, that we say so much? Individualized. Values are bought and sold on every level of human existence and are only worth what someone will pay for them. Whose fault is it that something as basic as value has been made null? When it's in a person's advantage to place blame, they place it. When it isn't in their advantage, they don't. People take what they can, fault is trying to extrude the emotion in a given situation, not what is real.

Redemption is the personification of human weakness. An acceptance that we are nothing except faulted, trying to follow this evolving animation of society. A created, fanciful reality that's failing. It's a need to allow ourselves to be animals when we want to and citizens when we need to.

Finally, truth. It exists. However not from a personal position. You can't create or conjure it. You can find it. Once you know, you can't forget or erase it. Take our scientific principles, what we call *fundamental truths*. They additionally have a built-in percentage of uncertainty. We aren't discovering new things, only pieces of what has always been. A realization of science is only such to humans. These laws of nature were here before us, and will be after us. We are a function of them. Just because our math can explain these forces to a certain point with exceptions, sometimes, doesn't mean we are an intelligent species. What we uncover is moot. It's of importance to our race, who we can put on a pedestal as *acclaimed* or *genius*. As time passes we find that everyone was incorrect. At some point, the best minds believed the Irfa was flat. Our understanding of these forces, our physical guidelines, may not be how the rest of the cosmos operate. In the future, our absolutes will be disproved again, if we make it that far. The findings still are only of consequence to people. The natural progression of things. From grunts, to screams, to syllables.

Another thing to consider, are these people really so intelligent, or willing to look outside of what they have been told? If you think of the scale of human existence, maybe a single person every few hundred spans discovers something that makes our science jump ahead. This shows one of two things. Either true intellect itself is an extremely rare attribute in human beings, so small that it's basically dispensable as a concept. Or there are many highly intelligent people too indoctrinated and afraid. This second group can also be split into further possibilities. The group that has the capacity of being revolutionary and lack drive to create a platform for themselves, or the group that thinks differently but is too meek, sticking to conventions and the hive mentality because it is more comfortable. History may simply remember the men who took a risk and stuck to their principles."

"Have you started to realize what these things argue collectively for our future?" inquires Gnat, arms crossed.

"I have a few propositions and a conclusion. Thus far, we've found that lesser-minded people are guided to believe and exist in certain things. The end result of these bubbles colliding is psycho-logical genocide. That is, the death of open thought. This part I know. My ultimate conclusion isn't sound, I have the basic idea."

"Tell me."

"The main point is that we have let go of intellect, it has been superseded by desire. There are only personal realities, individual sights and goals. As a result of this people live in comprehension they've created from, or is created amid their emotional perception of what they are. The conclusion I have now, is that *self-awareness is a biological deficiency.*"

"What can I use this for? How do I navigate the contradiction of knowing that I am aware of myself and it's only a flaw?" Gnat asks Eed.

"Feelings about happenings in life are unimportant, our species is nothing itself but a passing thought within the scale of time. Our deepest insights and reflections are juvenile. What is the baseline? *Collective relativity.* The ultimate and only true form of freedom is knowing that nothing you do will affect anything, in actuality.

"Right. I've said that legacy is generational. Nothing means nothing, we've heard that before. Doesn't it negate everything you've said?"

"No, we have been categorizing and realizing things as they have been created and named. What we are trying to get to is above and away from function and form. I'm proposing a rebirth of realizing self, not self-*worth.* Self-*meaninglessness.* Something being without meaning isn't a negative concept. Not comprehending, but *under-standing* you are nothing, that the end is obliteration of all things, you become *truly* free. Bound by a blank page. No opinion, belief, or action holds power over you. Omrika has risen and will fall. It may be the center of every political and monetary situation on Irfa now, yet it means nil. It will be vanquished and forgotten, the same as the civilizations of ancient Ehfra, or Knighton before us. If a scientist doesn't uncover something, another will. Circumstances don't create significance. Things are just happening. Awareness of yourself is what degrades truth, it makes an individual feel they have a destiny. It's a farce. There are circles to existence. Let me tell you what they are. If you can explore them, then you can manipulate them."

"Isn't manipulation a bad thing?" Gnat asks.

"Don't think of it in terms of using people, think of it as guiding them to an outcome you already know. Seeing the bubbles and patterns and living externally is an advantage. Everything is a series of circles, rings.

The smallest is the individual identity. The self-important person. Which could be one or many, a group, only processing things as they pertain to them. This is the least powerful position, with the smallest amount of influence to control any results. Even for themselves. Think of the person that hurts nothing consciously, but uses products created through slave labor overseas. They know it but don't have to deal with it, so it isn't considered.

The next biggest ring is that of emotion and convention. Or, society. An endless cycle of a world population reacting to the physical based on preconceived standardized sensitivities. It always leads to another set of poor decisions. Never progress, only repetition.

What we are discerning now is the ring of reason. We are observing things as they are, whether we agree or not. There's a circle larger than this, I haven't reached that place yet. It remains unnamed. It's a higher level of sight. If someone doesn't see the truth of reason, or the unnamed ring of a wider scope, the argument is coming from a smaller circle. If a person lives in conventional definition, the only thing they see is the importance of the system as it is currently."

"You should be *the guide* for people to see patterns they're subject to and changing minds. It's complete enough, why are you here?"

Eed sighs. "I know things others don't, or they do and haven't given it enough thought to lay it out as I have. I want to tell them, except I can't. There's a reason I am here, in this self-imposed exile. I didn't complete my thoughts; I am not willing enough. I've failed."

"You gave up without trying?"

"I did try. I knew that if I could teach another person and we could reach the largest ring together, we could start a storm. We could change the intentions humans live with, allowing an evolution of consciousness. I had a pupil who could see the patterns in people, recognize them in individuals, and change their minds more easily than I. Despite being together, we couldn't come to a conclusion. We separated; I came here. Most people believe their lives have meaning, so the system therefore does as well. Like I said, if you operate with a larger scope than society's principles, you can control them. They're transparent to you. There is no final lesson to what I've told you, not that I have found. So instead of trying to change what the structure meant to the masses, my student decided to use this vision to exist in it and gain from it personally, financially. I failed. I'll stay in these mountains until my end."

"Who is this person, Eed? Where are they now?"

"Her name is Tiria Sika."

"Wait! I know who she is, the one who..."

"Stop," Eed interrupts. "I don't want to hear about her, for the sake of my salubrity. That's enough for tonight."

"Don't be upset with me."

"I'm not, we'll speak more another time. We have to work early, and it already is," he points out the window.

It's dark, not for long. A trained eye can see that the low hanging specks of the sky are invisible. The sun is on its way.

"See you soon," Gnat says. No reply is given. He stands outside his door, staring into the emptiness.

This idea that we know the systems are wrong and we want to change them, yet the only people we see as valuable or trustworthy are the ones who have reached pinnacles set forth by it. Erasing everything is the only way to create change. Maybe us too. This species is errant and will always revert to greed and violence. What is evolution but millions of spans of trial and error? As humans, we see it as some giant unstoppable force reaching for a goal. Alas, it's no more than an explanation of chance through growth and time. Maybe he is right, maybe the fact that I'm capable of thought at all is the problem to be overcome. He hasn't put it together, he isn't capable, somehow.

He enters the trailer with an anchor pulling at him, tied off to his stomach. It is harder than ever before, denser. *What is this?*

V

Over the ensuing schedules, Eed and Gnat work without mentioning their discussion. It's busy, they've been in the weeds dealing with incoming people at every moment. A South Omrikan hiker asked for work washing dishes, his name is Nedwin. In a fashion authentic to him, Cliim pays Nedwin with dinners and a free campsite.

Gnat's been thinking of the things Eed told him since he left on the brink of that morning. Not actively, subconsciously. He's noticed glimmers of the patterns in people coming through. Not that he didn't before, however now he has a baseline to consider the inconsistencies. Just this basic foundation has removed much of the anger of his past, it's people acting how they were told to act. A girl came into the dining room with a t-shirt that read DARE TO BE YOU during one service. *We've become so suppressed that being yourself or speaking your mind is revolutionary. The age of submission is the final outcome, it's what the men behind closed doors want. Eed hit that nail on the head.*

His mind is a detonated bomb, the fallout encompassing his entire being. The defoliants of planet Irfa are exposed. He doesn't need to drown it out with alcohol, he needs to find the answers Eed hasn't. The man isn't so much a teacher as a miscarried twin lost to his own inadequacies. A peer, older, yet cut from the same cloth as he. Gnat is fading away with every breath he takes, to his gray matter, when he hears a crunch. Then, the spinning of tires in the dirt.

It's Sem, his truck is lodged on a rock at the edge of the camp-ground. He gets out, holding a gun in his hand. Gnat bolts over.

"What's going on, Sem? Are you good?"

"She found out, she left," he says drunkenly. "I was going to shoot myself, off in the woods. I got stuck."

"You don't want to do that. Why don't you let me hold that gun for you? I'll help you get off the rocks before Cliim sees."

Sem, quizzical, holds the pistol out. "Alright."

"It's probably better you hit that rock, if you would have kept going you would have been driving through a field of people in tents." Gnats takes the revolver, searching for a grin, which is de-livered. *He is the altered, I can see it in his face.* "Do you want to tell me about it?"

"Riza, she found out and caught a ride to town. She's never coming back," Sem says.

"Riza, the hiker girl that's been staying in your room? I thought you were doing okay?"

"We were, then Tibi told her. Told her..." he starts to sob be-tween words.

"Told her what?"

"That her and I have been sleeping together."

"Isn't she your cousin?"

"She is. My parents left when I was eleven, she raised me. I'm nine spans younger than her, it was just us until I signed up. When I came home it started again. I never wanted it, I do it to make her feel better. She had to sacrifice all her time for me, that didn't leave any for her to find someone."

Tibi, the user. Maybe he's altered because of her.

"It sounds like your cousin has got some jealousy issues, that doesn't mean you've got to shoot anyone. You could leave too, you know?" Gnat replies. "Forget Riza, more girls will come along. Do you have a jack? Let's free your truck."

"I do, in the bed. You're right, I can be on my own again if I want. Thanks for your help Gnat," he says with a hiccup, wiping the tears from his face.

They free the diesel easily and leave it by Gnat's camper until later.

"I'm envious of your truck, I've always wanted one like it," Gnat tells Sem as he stumbles away.

"Next drink on me, see you later."

Eed is outside under a light as Gnat returns to his metal room, giving him only an appreciative nod.

After service the next morning, he approaches Gnat in the general store.

"Follow me Gnat, I have something for you."

There's tall grass in a clearing behind a few trees, and a pile of tarps. Eed starts to remove them. It isn't only a pile of vinyl squares, but a truck under their protection. It's black, his color. Maybe his affinity for the shade comes from the absence of tint.

"I haven't started it in seasons, if you can get it to run, it's yours," Eed states.

"Why?"

"So you don't get trapped in these hills. You can do something with what I've told you. I saw you with Sem, I heard you tell him you envy his rig. Now you don't have to."

"Thank you Eed. I'll take care of it."

"Find the end of the road. You don't have to hoof it any longer. Don't be late for service." Eed smirks.

Gnat sees Nedwin leaving the employee dining room, who notices Gnat as well and jogs over.

"We have a little while, want to do a short trail?" he asks Gnat.

The circular path runs out to a waterfall which they have to themselves. They swim, letting the water punish their heads as it drops over the cliffs above. The hard stone of the mountain is perfectly smooth around the pool, roughness undone by the movement of liquid. *An aqueous solution for a solidified obstacle.* The men lay in the sun to dry like water fowl after a hunt. Not a care for anything except warmth. His skin has the smell of a chemical reaction, the rays are converting him to vitamin D. He catches a nose full, wiping the sweaty water from his eyes.

"What brought you to the trail, Nedwin?" Gnat asks, head to the side, squinting.

"Oh, that's a bit of a story."

"I'm not going anywhere." He laughs.

"I was married for eight spans. We never fought; things were normal. She told me she wanted a divorce. That I'm not exciting enough. She met another man."

"And?"

"I knew him. It turned out to be my best friend from childhood. He had been with her for five spans. He ate at my table, watched games with me, saw me all the time. He never mentioned it."

"You never really know someone, do you?" *They are all doing what's best for themselves.*

"No, I feel stupid for it," Nedwin responds. "So, after the papers were signed, I started the trail. I told her to keep everything, I didn't want it. I quit my job. I gave my car to my nephew."

"You aren't concerned with how much your pack weighs or how fast you finish the trail, I suppose?"

"Not even a thought, I'm not a hiker. I saw the trail on a show and thought about it when I signed my wife away. I'm not running.

Simply going until I find something new. I have some savings, I'll be fine."

"Things always come up, if you want them to," Gnat nods his head.

"Yeah, let's roll."

The shifts are normal, no accidents. No complaints. Actually, he hasn't gotten any since he's arrived. People are still finishing, no one needs anything else from the kitchen. Drinks are full. In the store, Berr is behind the desk.

"Can I use the computer to check my email? There's no service up here. I haven't logged in since I arrived."

"Sure," she says. "Be quick."

He logs in, nothing from home. It hasn't been long enough for his parents to worry. There is a message from Addie. His heart stops. *How long ago was that? Was it this lifetime or another?* The subject line says three words. *Help. Need money.* Gnat snorts and deletes it without reading.

In his box, Gnat sees by the light of a battery powered lantern he *borrowed* from the general store. *Apartment-sized rent for this dilapidated camper. I need to be able to see.*

He starts to think of Addie, of the story Nedwin told him. Women come and go in every man's life. Love is only a word. They use dominion and prowess to whatever end allowed. The simpler sex, males. Gnat starts, entire chords in slow triplets.

> *Solstice flings, sometimes I think*
> *Of make-believe, Dragons and Kings.*
> *Breezy trees, worms and things,*
> *Hoping to see, the sunset bring*
> *Starry night, the bugs arise,*

You look to me, joy gives us fright.

Rainy fun, Melts apart.
Frozen cold, Sun Restarts.

Flowers bloom, petals in loom,
Sometimes I think, you'll pick me.
Yes or no, the colors blow
This one's odd, don't let me go.

Rainy fun, Melts apart.
Frozen cold, Sun restarts.

Icy grip, starts to slip
Sometimes I think, love doesn't exist.

Service is an adventure the next cycle. When Eed switches his station over from breakfast, everything has gone moldy.

"Cliim and his refrigerators. Nothing but the best for his employees and guests, right?" Gnat chuckles to Eed.

As people come in there's only a single option, sloppy burger and fries. Tibi comes to call a staff meeting in the employee dining room. After they've finished the meal flung together with scraps the three of them head up to hear what the news is, uninterested.

Tibi explains revenue this cycle is higher than any other since Cliim has owned the place so he's gotten everyone a gift. It's a water bottle, the newest technology that keeps things at temperature almost indefinitely. She gives them out, each has a name tag. Neither Gnat or Nedwin receive one.

"Did you forget ours?" asks Gnat, sarcastically.

"Cliim said you haven't been here long enough."

Managed by a pair of unintelligent users, I've got to get out of here.

"What percentage of that revenue comes from the restaurant? Camping is free, nobody buys stuff in the store, it's way overpriced." He replies.

Tibi lectures the ceiling as she speaks, "It's a group effort, not a specific part of the place. Cliim made the choice, not me."

"Oh, now we aren't part of the group either?"

Eed leans over and whispers, "Let it go. You're trying to have a staring contest with someone who is blind."

"Maybe next time he'll get both of you something if it's as good," says Tibi.

Gnat stands up. "Yeah, anything else?"

"That's it for now."

He waits outside for Eed.

"Do you have some tools? I'm going to try and get the truck running then hit the highway."

"There's plenty in the back, the key is in the cup holder, the doors are unlocked. See you later?"

He assures Eed, "I'll be there."

The hood of the truck is up. The coolant is full. He tops off the battery with tap water, which isn't the best, but will do. He cleans the plugs and gaps them. He doesn't have the tool for doing this, so the edge of a knife is used. The leads are still good, no cuts or holes in the rubber. The engine has oil, transmission too. No puddles of fluid on the ground below. The clutch has pressure. The gears engage, he tests them multiple times. There is no electric air pump so the tires are filled with foot power, his pelvis aches after. It has fuel, everything is tidied up. He takes the key and turns the ignition, nothing but the click of a dead battery.

"A roll start it is," he pats the hood.

Gnat removes the concrete bricks holding the pickup in place. Gnat can't push the truck forward on his own, however the vehicle is parked on an incline. He's never tried a rolling start in reverse, but it *should* work. The clearing gives him the length of a ball field to find out, plenty of space. *If the brakes hold.* Otherwise, the vehicle is going into a tree. Or worse, the water.

He makes sure it's in neutral and the door is unlocked. Pushing the grill, he has to rock his savior from the ruts its tires have made from sitting. It starts to move, at a creep. He jogs over and takes the driver's seat. It is going, faster now. Not enough speed yet. A hand on the wheel, the other on the shifter, twisted around staring out the rear window. His left foot depresses the clutch pedal. A fifth of the distance to the end is covered. Not enough momentum. *Wait for it.* Now halfway, the speedometer has a reading. With finesse he selects the reverse gear and lets the clutch out entirely at once. A creak and a jolt as the transmission starts to turn. A sputter. A lurch. The bombination of the motor begins. It's alive. He slams the brakes; they compress with a squeal. *That will wear off once they warm up.* He shouts, puts it in first, and drives over to the trailers.

He lets it run to charge the battery as he washes his face in the lake. He turns it off and starts it three times, just to be sure. Inside he has his things on the table, he's never really unpacked so it's more organizing than anything. Service starts soon, he heads up to Tibi's office.

Gnat knocks on the doorframe; she's startled by it.

"Hey Tibi, this service will be my last. I'll be out early."

"What? Why? Is it because of the water bottle?"

"Not the water bottle itself, per se. More the principle. It's a matter of outlook. I can't work for people with no comprehension. This place is a joke, I'm over it," he states.

"I think we do a pretty good job up here, considering what it is. You are telling me I'm stupid?"

"It's not about what you think, it's about what I know. Cliim uses these people and sells the guests tainted food. And Sem, it's messed up that you did that to an impressionable young man."

Her face turns white, devoid of anything. "He told you?"

"I had to talk him out of putting a gun to his head because of it."

"When?"

"I need out of this place, it's sick. The energy is toxic," Gnat says with finality. Tibi sits in silent shock and shame as he leaves.

"The truck got going fairly easily?" Eed asks through the window.

"Ready to go, my bags are packed."

"When are you headed out?"

"When the sun rises, I told Tibi. This is my last shift with you."

Eed only grunts, putting his hand on Gnat's shoulder. "Mm."

Gnat barely slumbers, and as the idea of light starts to show itself through the windows he rises and moves onto the step under the door. He ponders in the last shards of the night. The darkness. Until there is enough sun to see, the sky is soaked in pink and blue. He throws his bags under the covered bed of the pickup. His mind out over the water in front of him and to the peaks behind the other shore. Then he notices, on the water's edge. Rats. Their fur matted and missing in spots. They're moving furiously, shrieking at one another. The carcass of a fish is the prize they fight over.

Existence serving existence. Life clamoring around for no other end but to not disappear. It's cleansing to me. The dichotomy between the sun rising and life trying to survive. This façade, the image of the sun rising as beautiful. It covers up the viciousness that is living. Which is only a word substituted for survival instinct.

In his journal, he scribbles out a poem.

Refreshed is the word that comes to mind.

In retrospect every man is dying

From the moment of conception.

So, life in itself is a deception.

A rolling hill,

A rocky road,

Lead to my more than humble abode.

I do my job.

I make a buck

And then I die.

What awful luck.

But in the scheme of horrible things

A few little truths are revealed subtly

And that's what separates me from the bees;

That's what makes me a human being

With that he pulls out his pack and places the book of thoughts inside. He removes his cash tips, counting them. *Thirty-five hundred.*

He zips it shut again, turning around. Eed strolls over.

"You didn't finish, I'm going to," says Gnat.

Eed tells him, "There may be some virtue in your singular perspective. However, you must devote yourself to the ideal, not your individual self. Become a master of only the thing. Whatever you choose, there is no going back. Live for the idea, not the state of your ego. Further the cause of understanding in a way that it will remain after you are gone. Be a piece of the whole and humbled by it. It isn't about you; it never was and never will be."

"Pain in and of itself is only a biological response of no consequence. But pain through sacrifice, then you can find some purpose through it. Capability might be the same. It's inherent, you must apply it to something to give it power. I have to do something with the truth. I've been roaming and absorbing everything so far. I need to pursue; I must actively apply what I know to life. You're right. Not my life. Life as an entity," he responds.

"If you can do what I've just said, you may find the validation of consciousness I can't."

Nedwin comes around the corner with his gear, coyly.

"I heard you are leaving Gnat. An old friend of mine has a farm in Zeon, I'm thinking I can go stay with him. Are you heading east? Can I ride along?"

Eed interrupts, "Both of you are leaving me, then?"

"You'll have Tibi to help you," Gnat jokes. "I hadn't picked a direction yet. Alright, let's get you to the farm. Throw your bag in."

"Thanks, Gnat."

"Eed, this is it. Time to bid you farewell," Gnat says, embracing him.

Eed hugs him back. "Travel safely. Don't lose sight."

Gnat gets in the pickup; it fires up like new. He shifts his focus onto Nedwin.

"I'm ready to get out of this place, it's strange," the dishwasher states.

"Oh, yes, it is."

He starts away and before the first turn he glances in the rearview mirror. Eed is standing in place, watching them go. His silhouette in that mirror is burned as a carbon copy in Gnat's memory. There's a pop somewhere inside of him, a wave of warmth ensues. *Go and find her.* The voice jumps in and echoes out.

"At least I know who she is now. When are you going to reveal who you are?" he says to the voice, barely audible.

Nedwin reaches to power the radio on. The static hurts both of their ears as he turns the knob trying to find a channel. He locates something, it is fading in and out, the signal is very weak. It's a bulletin. Gnat catches phrases over a course of instants.

"Tiria Sika... in Nuwal city... preliminary meetings... government... likely to be... may face fines or..." The station cuts out completely.

Nedwin turns the radio off. "We can try again when we get on the highway. You know, my friend will probably have some work and put you up too, if you want to hang out for a while. I can ask him when we get there."

"Thanks for the offer, but I know where I have to go. I don't like it; however sacrifices must be made."

***

They've breached the natural fortification to the ocean that is the Sirra Niva mountain range and are crossing flatland. This is a place where gusts sprint unhindered, building to be harnessed by wind farms spattered across the plains. Ostensibly random as the flick of paint from the edge of a brush, the design contained catches the most voltage possible without the giant fans having to shadow-box one another for it. Gnat swings into a fuel station that's also a gun store, a liquor mart, a fireworks depot, and a post office.

"Why don't we have these places everywhere? A single-stop man shop," Nedwin says. "What's the only thing a guy buys every time he sees them?"

"Bottle rockets and roman candles," Gnat says excitedly.

They speed down the empty desert highway burning their hard-earned pay in the form of cheap explosives. Sparks, flashes, and bangs shower out of the truck's windows. Both of them scream like children, releasing all the tensity from their job in the hills.

***

"We aren't far from the farm, we'll get there soon. I'm glad to be out of there, thanks again for bringing me," states Nedwin. "There's a rotten scent at that place. I felt stifled, it wasn't where I wanted to end up."

"I agree. I needed to leave. Cliim and Tibi are overextending their abilities. That constant toxicity, injected in your veins, soaking through you totally. At some point, the negative forces start to change the structure of your physical cells. The *weight* of it, in your bones..." says Gnat.

"This farm will do the trick."

Gnat reassures, "I have to go see someone in Nuwal city. First let's get you to balance and friends."

They bear towards the center of Zeon. Nedwin gives him directions off the remote highway. The thought crosses his mind to stay in the tranquility. Eed's words shout at him. *Don't lose sight.*

He wishes his companion luck. Nedwin grabs his rucksack and walks a dirt path, an old house awaits.

Gnat would have made an excellent long-haul driver, if he cared about such things. Navigating the wide spans cleanly, uninterrupted. He almost took the exit to Nata as he passed through Oia. He'll go when he's got things figured out. *Nobody in Nata is going anywhere.*

VI

There's a harbor in Nuwal, a port for shipping and receiving items from Ropa and Ehfra. The truck is parked near a defunct dock, his most recent makeshift home. No bothers from others come, he explores the city watching people bustle around, imagining what they're thinking as they rush.

If I don't get where I am going, the world will stop turning!

I've gotten every stop signal! The universe is against me!

Move aside, the savior is on the way to fix it!

It's noisy and never quiets. The glow of skyscrapers is too loud, you can never see the stars. You can't trust anyone, they're all trying to steal something from you. Your jewelry, your wallet, your dignity.

The blast of a foghorn at sea awakens him. Tiria Sika has a hearing at the national government headquarters.

"How could someone live in a city?" He yawns. "You only stand in lines and deal with miserly humans."

Gnat takes the short way, across the underbelly of a bridge, bringing his guitar. *Why didn't Eed come with me?* Wondering, he reaches the front steps of the building where Tiria is meeting her possible destruction. News cameras and reporters crowd the front door to bombard her. *What's she going to be like? She must be adept at manipulation, making Eed stay in the mountains. What did he not tell me?*

A song for the idea of the man, Eed, permeates him aside this orchestrated spectacle of television. The timid yet provocative person that set him on his current path, from a place people don't get found. *Or remembered.* Gnat was there with him, only moments ago. What is he doing? What's he thinking of?

He's never wrong, he's never right
He said to me, in the firelight
Happiness, is man's own plight
So make your choice, go and live the night.

He's sometimes sly, he sometimes lies.
But that's his life, no one is kind.
He slows his breath, before bed
It clears his head, of guilt and dread.

He's always smiling, he's always striving
To see the light, with a scream or a sigh.
Well open thought, is the curse of life
So make your choice, go and live the night.

Can't see through
His enlightened eyes
This boy's afterwise.

The notes ring, flowing toward the yelling of dozens. Their recorders are rolling, questions pour out. He can't decipher an entire sentence before another eclipses it. It's as if he is watching a picnic in some park. Tiria is the breadcrumb, the news agency employees are the ants. She must be headed down the steps, he can't locate her. The ball of interrogation, however, moves toward the street. Another image of nature comes to him. A flock of birds flying, a cognizant blob trying to hold its shape as it falls off the edge of a table into nothing. There's a black car on the sidewalk, he picks up his instrument and races over, standing behind the passenger door.

He is enveloped by mass hysteria instantly. Everybody is shoving their way to the front. Then she's seen, lowered face, ignoring every person. Stoically. The door is opened by someone, as she passes he leans into her ear.

"Tiria! Tiria! Eed says hello," he shouts.

She stops, turning to him. Her irises are mace, the nerves of his face are stinging. He's broken her concentration. He doesn't know, but she never thought she'd hear that name again. She enters the car, the stare ending as a forgotten folly of time.

"That can't be it," he says to himself.

The automobile starts as he prepares to watch it disappear. Then the window rolls down. Tiria hands him a business card, still no words. Somehow through the racket he hears the driver put the vehicle in gear and press the accelerator. Some of the cameramen chase after, most return to being passive and pause, disheartened. Immediately, it's over. The mistral has dissipated, volume going from violent to solely irritating. Gnat hasn't moved, he's studied the car leaving blankly, not an idea in his mind.

He remembers his hand. It's *her* card, showing no way of contacting her. Just a name. He turns it over, there's a message written in blue.

11 fifth avenue. Now.

He places it in his pocket and begins the journey. Gnat knows the way; he's been casing the city since his arrival.

A bar sits tucked under a high-rise condominium complex. It's a shady place, not so much for the setting, but the clientele that inhabit the space. Shifty glances while passing tables, low conversations barely audible to the people involved. He sees a hand rise from a table in the corner and glides in Tiria's direction. She has something the color of caramel in her glass, passing the bar he orders more of whatever the lady is drinking and continues.

Her hair is thick and has grown past her waist. It varies from bleach-tainted brown to a yellow the color of wheat. Her face is hard. You can tell she's driven and sure of herself. Her nose has a tiny curve to it, finding its end. Irises of the same color as Gnat's, hazel. They wear the same disillusionment as his. He recalls noticing this in the magazine the first time he read her name. She holds herself confidently with a rigid posture that isn't false. There's still a tranquility about her. She is covered, no cleavage revealed, her skirt goes to her knee. She's fit and smirks at him as he sits across from her. Her teeth are white, naturally. Her lips are inviting. The glow of her grasps onto him. They are connected. He can't decide if it has happened long ago when he met Eed, or as he took a seat now.

"Do you want a drink? I don't know what to call you," she says, breaking the ice. Her voice has a layer of roughness, like sandpaper, above its muliebrity.

"I've already ordered more of what you're having. My name is Gnat. How did the hearing go?"

"It's a wildcat strike," Tiria answers slyly. "They say they're going to charge me, nothing will come of it. I asked them, with what? Invention? Enterprise? The government only cares about getting their piece. It's a business, our administration. Lobbyists own politicians, who write the laws they pass. Corporations own the lobbyists. The media keeps the political parties fighting to occupy the public. Meanwhile, the agenda moves forward regardless of who wins the elections, and our rights diminish. Left, right, or center, everyone is participating in the same game.

Think of the main religions of Irfa, they all believe in the same higher power, killing each other over minuscule differences.

A supreme being would be guided by principle alone, not details. If you made the wrong choice, you would be destroyed. Removed. No reason to linger for the chance of redemption. You already proved yourself unworthy. The idea of redemption is openly recognizing your own weakness and inability to be anything other than a beast. Scrounging, scavenging, and lowly. Eed got that from me, so you know. Did he tell you that? The way he explains what words are actually covering up came from me?"

Gnat shakes his head. "No, he didn't."

"Currently I'm the center of attention. Rather than let technology guide the marketplace, we let the government dictate how and why jobs exist. We should let the jobs filter into the next generation of industry. Instead they try to sustain the past for an uninformed and inferior workforce. People are rationalizing and trying to define their own destruction, and why it's more important than the way others are doing it."

The waiter brings their alcohol, which they touch together. The rims of the containers whine. He takes a mouthful. The dryness of the liquid flows down his throat then travels up his sinuses, creating the taste of wood smoke and peat moss. *Beautiful.*

She continues, "Have you ever thought about how much of a citizen's money they take? Sure, most people pay twenty or thirty percent off the top. Then every time you buy a product, they add another tax on top of that. Most of these things, you don't want. You *need.* The registrations for your property. Insurance. Parking tickets, tolls. It's endless. I'd bet the average Omrikan gets to spend fifteen percent of their salaries on things that they want, not basic necessities or taxes. What about time? How much of that is actually yours? After sleeping, working, traveling to-and-from, shopping, cleaning and maintaining your possessions? Five percent? Following the rules, the laws, is for the docile. I know the patterns, and

I know I should use them to get as far ahead as I can. For myself. Everybody is doing exactly as I have; I'm doing it in a superior way because I accept the truth of it. Everything from who is elected in the classroom to the country, the systems controlling ballots, medicine, criminal justice, prisons, education. From how we test, manufacture, write mandates, convict individuals of crime. Every facet of society. The methodology of our institution. It's broken. People know of the absolute corruption of the world around them but still look to it for guidance and validation. The individual pieces take every advantage and break every rule they can to get ahead. Living in instinct, then placing it within a set of rules. Law. It's doomed to fail. There is nothing in my life that has come up by my doing or not, that I haven't beaten, physically or mentally." She finishes her drink, "Where is he?"

"He's exiled himself to the Sirra Nivas, because of his failure with you."

"There's something he couldn't do that I did. Do you know the story of the sword that was stuck in a boulder and whatever person could remove it would be the ruler, Gnat?"

"Yes, the strongest men tried and failed, a young boy pulled it out single-handed..."

"I figured out that that boy's destiny wasn't predetermined. It wasn't decided without his consent and thrust upon him unknowingly. You become whatever you see yourself as. The idea of being a king in the story is the boy manifesting that outcome in his own mind. He wanted out of his circumstances so he made it happen. I made my choice, not to try and find higher sight. For me it always returns to why I don't see a point. The answer is, if you can see why the rules were written, the game no longer means anything. I don't want to show that truth to anyone else, there is some level of comfort in pointlessness. Yes, I know it's only emotion. *Understanding* as I did with Eed, anything I learn, think, or do is simply for me-that's where I want to exist. I can create whatever I want to within myself without truly affecting anything else. I'm assuming he told you everything?"

"Yes," Gnat states.

"Then you'll understand. I know I mean nothing, and I am free of these restrictions the world tries to impose on me. It makes no difference what I do. *Or what they do.* I have to go, more discussions with advisors. Meet me here again?"

"I can do that."

"The drinks are on me as long as you want to sit. There's more to discuss." She gets out of the booth, stopping at the bar and pointing to Gnat as she speaks to the worker. Tiria waves and leaves.

"She's forgotten herself," he says, lifting a finger to the man at the bar. *If you can understand the pieces of the whole thoroughly, then how to affect the whole becomes more easily understood. Think of math. Taking pieces, smaller numbers, adding them up. Or taking big numbers, breaking them down. You have to fix the individual level first, the whole can never be changed unless this happens.* "How does the whole have meaning if no part of it has value?" he asks himself.

He stays at the bar until the sky darkens. He walks to his truck, six-string on his shoulder. Over the course of seemingly endless thoughts, he ponders what the connection is that he felt with Tiria. He never got a feeling like it from Eed. Is it because she's a woman? It *must* be more than that. He *knows* it is more than that. As the world turns, Gnat turns with it, imagining what will come of their next meeting.

As he re-enters the pub, Gnat finds that Tiria isn't inside. He orders something and stands sipping until it lay empty. Still no sign. A slow shift with no other customers, the barman is washing glassware.

"Hey, do you know Tiria Sika, the woman in the news right now? She comes in here sometimes? I was supposed to meet her."

The man stops, "Of course. Are you Gnat?"

"Yes, I am..." he answers suspiciously.

"Ms. Sika left a message to meet her at the private airport outside town. She's there now, waiting for you. She also said you should bring your things."

"Really? How do I get there?"

"Head north out of the city. You'll be in the fields; the single engine planes will be parked along the fence. You can't miss it," the man replies.

"Thanks," says Gnat, placing a bill on the counter, rushing out.

He starts to jog to his house, the dilapidated dock and rusty pickup. *Why is she at the airport? Where is she going? I can run!*

He navigates onto the streets of this busy metropolis. Fighting traffic, sitting at red signals, people trying to peddle stolen goods at every intersection. He gets to the highway, an escape from the concrete wasteland that is Nuwal city. Gnat isn't nervous, only relaxed in his driving position. *I'll get wherever I'm going.*

The only thing he hears is wind through the cracked driver side window. Suburbia ellipses both sides of the highway, a boy on his lawn throws a foam airplane. *A glider.* Gnat can't remember what it's like to be without care, like a child. A memory not thought of for spans appears, the best one of his life.

He and Dak, a friend he considered his brother, had been on many treks on the west coast of Omrika. The primary objective at every destination was to toss the disc. *A friz.* Both had played on a team during Gnat's last span of school and got very talented with the object. Throwing overhand, underhand, behind-the-back, through-the-legs, across-the-thumb. Never needing to talk, progressively moving farther apart. Sometimes a few, other instances thousands of passes. Hardly ever did they make a mistake.

Once, they stopped in Sanrika when the leaves began to change. They went to the beach not to swim, but toss. The spoiled citizens raised by the sea take being so close for granted, and only show up when the weather is perfect. They were alone. The tide was beyond low. The sand damp and flattened, almost as wide as a pier nearby. The disadvantage of discs, one person can throw downwind in a straight line. The other needs to throw upwind, which is much more difficult.

On this occasion, the crosswind was perfectly perpendicular to the waterline in such a way both could throw downwind. Neither Gnat nor Dak could explain it. By the climax of their separation, neither had to take more than a step to catch it. Every throw was a slow arc, floating on the breeze for eternities. At some point a Telaysian tourist asked to film them. He stood with the camera, panning between them in silence. Never in his life has Gnat felt so completely at ease except then. It was as if peace melted into emptiness. Like that boy throwing the glider, he was himself, before the disillusioning complexities of Irfa became apparent. On that beach, he felt young again.

He rejoins the present seeing the field, the planes seem to be toys in a row. He parks in the grass next to the corrugated steel of the nearest hangar and hops out, trying to determine which plane is Tiria's. Most of them are single seats, a few restored classics. Leaning out the entrance of a white jet, sleek and smooth, she appears. It has dual engines on its tail, not under the wings. He counts five windows, so maybe ten or fifteen people. *Sixteen. It would be an even number. That's no biplane...*

She returns inside. Going up to the cabin he determines no expense was spared. Burled walnut and leather envelope the floors and tables. Every edge is trimmed in chrome. Tiria is alone.

"Where are you going?" asks Gnat.

"I think it's better to leave the country until this is settled. I can negotiate remotely if I need to, no reason to risk being put in a cell while things are figured out. It's just a precaution."

"Where?"

"Austopia. I have some sites to check out, anyway. I can multi-task," she raises her eyebrows, "Do you want to come, Gnat?"

"To Austopia?"

"We are headed toward an end on the same path. Maybe that word is incorrect. *Direction.* There are more things to talk about, for you to understand. I'm leaving soon, I was only waiting to ask if you'd be my company," she explains.

"What about my truck? When do you return?"

"The truck will be fine; I'll tell the manager of the hangar it's mine. I don't know when. If you want to come back, you can. Use this jet or buy a ticket."

I have to let this play out.

"Well, let me get my bag."

He makes sure he has his passport and locks the pickup, saying goodbye to a second truck. Gnat is unsure whether he'll see it again, like the first.

"You travel with hardly anything!" she says to him.

"Only what I need, no extras. I thought you said nothing was going to happen?" he shoots back.

Tiria takes a deep breath. "The main objection people have to my way of thinking is that it's wrong. Which is ignorant. There's a difference between comprehending and understanding, correct?"

"Correct."

"If people truly understood what I am doing, what I say, the way I live, they would reject every nonsensical construct they hold on to. I told you, we're all doing exactly the same thing. My opposition is grasping onto words and ideals to deflect what's real and champion their own causes. The government will try to get the public involved emotionally, it's the only card they hold. What's the universal equalizer? The only thing that bonds differing groups of opinion? Experiencing loss. People are so ingrained they can't imagine or rationalize how others break out or rise above it. The humans respected as leaders in the world are simply stupid people who got lucky, had an opportunity, or a connection. Nobody is adding anything worthwhile to the human condition. Someone has to be at the top, which person doesn't matter. Isn't there a saying about a blind squirrel finding a nut? The common man's language has to be adopted to portray the administration's principles. Other-wise, their desired outcome is lost in a sea of pompous explanations. The commoner can only make sense of the common; convoluted definitions within for-profit education. Trying to gain the respect of peers while not understanding what's studied. Causes created to benefit the creator, not affect the plight of our race. It's the most powerful tool of our handlers when it comes to emotion, deflect-ing, justifying, or being backhanded to respond to your situation. *Conscious flight or fight.* You can either say something intelligent to enter the dialogue or you can become instinctual and protect what you believe by retreating inward. The problem is, if you're already manipulated by what you've been told, you can do nothing but defend what's inherent and indoctrinated. Which is never of sig-nificance, at most only imitated behavior. You can't change what a person thinks, they have to change it through their own deduction and experience. However, the vast majority won't go outside what is comfortable. If you don't have to see or hear about it, it isn't real. You go along with what has been done historically."

The whir of the engines starts, as Gnat waits for the conclusion of her monologue. "And?"

Tiria leans her head back. "If you can control what the morals of a society are you can control the citizens. When personal belief derives itself from cultural belief, ignorance is allowed to flourish."

The jet starts to roll to the runway and carry them to another continent. Gnat has the image of Ju, Su, and Ima in his mind. He hears his sister's giggle. *I didn't tell them...*

VII

Gnat couldn't envision a more spectacular takeoff. Every color imaginable, from shades of self-doubt in blue to the full compassion of pink and gold, they spiral in wide circles gaining elevation through the clouds. Enormous cumulus structures bring a thunderstorm to the city. However, they haven't engorged themselves on the water molecules of their surroundings deeply enough yet. Still balls of fluff, they hold the mirage of solid density. If you fall into one, will it catch you like a pillow washed and dried in a calming breeze? Or let you pass, dropping ascetically, a trusting disposition deserted to the whims of gravity? He's imbibed by the idea when something hits the floor. His gaze rolls to Tiria. Her shoes, she's taken them off, and stretched her legs to the parallel seat.

"The media throws it in the faces of the people," she says. "You want to live off the grid? They start a show about a family that already does, portraying them as unintelligent. The perception becomes only stupid people would want to do such a thing. Fast-food companies make commercials about hidden societies, the conspiracies of our time. Viewers watch, tease, and say theorists are ridiculous. Everything is forcing you into a mold, without anyone noticing. Insinuation is a powerful tool."

"What's your plan?" asks Gnat. Spreading his lower half across the seats as she has, his boots remain on. This hasn't ended.

"The only way to get ahead is to be detected and become part of the whole. You aren't going to beat the giants of industry. They've already gotten through economic depressions, wars, regulation, bailouts and scandals. The revolutions of industry and technology are over. If you can do something that decreases their revenue enough, you can affect a large portion of what's going on. Think of private food or drink producers being bought by the larger outfits, or getting your product into a mega-retailer. Then, you have the power to make a change in the market."

Gnat is surprised. "You actually *do* want to make a change for the better? Is it possible?"

She shakes her head. "It's too late. Maybe at some point I thought it was. It's like my battle right now against the smear campaigners targeting me. I gave jobs to Ehfrans instead of Telaysians. It got me the emotional loyalty of some in the marketplace, but for my company it's just the same. Where I've sourced labor is not where people usually think of cheap employees being acquired. This is somehow feared and disliked because Omrikans have this obtuse idea of loyalty to *our* economy. It's not *our* economy, it's *the* economy. It's globalized, that's not going to change. I'm using it to my benefit."

"How did you get to the point where you gave up? The same as Eed except more... actively turning against any notion of changing the consciousness of the whole?"

"At university, I wanted to change things, the same as anyone uninitiated. When I met Eed, I believed we could. I came to the conclusion that our chance for something greater is over, we sold out for personal comfort. When Eed and I put it in words and I tried to come to a conclusion, I excelled and understood fully. It was originally our greatest strength; it's become our burden. Self-awareness. This perceived destiny of everything being for us, combined with time and overpopulation. It's destroyed humans and the Irfa. Knowing what you are compared to other beings is only a detachment, not an asset. Every other animal exists in instinct. A mother leaves behind a sick child because they know, genetically, sickness and deformity weaken the gene pool. If another animal can't find food, it dies. It's only evolution and survival. Because we are aware of ourselves humans created right and wrong based on what we felt, not what we saw, infecting the environment with opinion . We not only destroyed *our* bubble, but *all* bubbles. Everything: battles, wars, rules, morals, it's based in nothing, only limited perception of purpose.

Even in the mid-ages the *value* was the condition of our species. Now the decision or mistake of a single person can become the weight for the entire society to carry, upsetting the balance. The idea of worth in a single life is farcical. We are growths, the same as a tumor, a tree, or feral dog.

Existence has become convoluted. It's always someone doing what benefits them in every example. A girl's wish is to get married and have children. It's defined as falling in love. It's *instinct*. She marries a man with wealth that can protect her and take care of her. In turn he gets to mate, which is also instinct. The same way a bull protects his cows. The continuance of his genes, that bit. Then, the man finds out that he can't have children. The woman leaves him. What we defined as love was actually codependency, mutual benefit, and instinct. As a society we use defined emotions to guide policy. This makes the policy deteriorate because it's not based in truth," Tiria finishes.

"Do you remember the man who went to war and got savagely burned, totally disfiguring him? He recovered, eventually. When he came home, his wife left him," Gnat agrees. "My sister has a friend, she got married and told her husband she wouldn't take his name until he gave her kids. How selfish is that? She let him know what it's about. That's not marriage, that's a personal-gains contract."

Tiria grins. "Do you want to get married?"

"No. I have my own ideas about words and how they've come to the point where they have open meanings. Like *marriage*: the union between a man, a woman, and a god. Any couple should be able to share financial benefits, legally. I think that's where most of the argument comes from. But religion is separate from law, that's the institution that defined the word. Forget same-sex marriages, what about a man and woman who are atheist? Should they get to be married? There has to be another word for the legal system to use to recognize the legitimacy of a couple.

What about murder? It means to end a life. What if a family is malnourishing their children and gets caught? In a world where meanings are open to interpretation, some may say that something that *would* kill someone conclusively is murder. Can you charge somebody with killing if no one has died?

What about assault? To take something by force that isn't being offered. It has spiraled too far in the media, women claiming men have accosted them. If I had to write down the number of times I've been in the same situations they describe, I've been assaulted dozens of times in my life. You're a woman in business. What's your take?"

"It's not something to put energy into, really," says Tiria. "Historically, it's been a man's world, business and entertainment. Women aren't going to get ahead by fighting it with emotional deception, they simply need to work as hard. Statistics don't show this. They work less, not as productively, and cost more to insure or replace as they raise children. Women don't actually make less than men. By the time you factor these things into the equation, it's equal. If women were truly less expensive to hire for a corporation that considers every cent, the workforce would be entirely women. Some news networks bombard you with war, death, and disease to keep you afraid of the Irfa. The others do the same with assault and sexism to make you fearful of other people and what you think. It's silly. I've seen it, men who accomplish conventionally worth-while goals are singled out, most cases are settled without anyone knowing. The women want remuneration. If that doesn't happen, they take it to the media. Trying to get noticed or using the national platform for some other gain. The networks create backlash to have something to report, then sell the movie rights on the other side to make profit, destroying reputations and careers. Stripping dignity just for a payment and a sense of self-importance or misplaced redemption over a regret. Sex is another basic need, like food, water, or shelter. It's what we were made to do, it isn't some sacred act. You aren't giving a piece of yourself away. It's nature."

"I met an elderly woman in a bus station," Gnat adds, "in Northern Oia or somewhere similar. She was maybe seventy. She held a purse tightly, worried. I sat next to her, she told me her eyelid quivers when a spirit enters her space. I bought her a drink, she gave me an extra toothbrush, I had forgotten mine. She told me the story of her oldest daughter. Some spans prior, the daughter was headed home. Four men she didn't know grabbed her, brought her to an alleyway, and took turns with her. She took the tests, finding out they had given her an immunodeficiency virus, which she died from. That, without a doubt, is assault," he stops and blows his breath out slowly. "Entering a situation willingly when parties involved might not be in control because of drugs is only personal responsibility. You made the choice to let yourself be in that state of mind, you are allowing yourself to *take* or *be taken* advantage of. No outcome is guaranteed, you can't be so naïve as to believe in the inherent goodness of others, it doesn't exist. If your boss invites you to their hotel room at night everyone knows the reason. Both sides might have thoughts of personal advantage. Does it only become an issue when someone doesn't get what they feel they've earned from the encounter?"

Tiria enters, "What about the policy makers? The government and corporations? They pass laws and mandates and take what you aren't offering. The money, the time, even your life for breaking their rules."

"I know. I didn't agree to the terms, I was born and subjected to it. We focus on physical assault, all of us are systematically assaulted every time we wake up in Omrika. In both mind and body." He stops. "Do you want to get married?"

She cackles. "After that speech? Not anymore. I went from trying to save Irfa, to seeing it isn't a possibility, to manipulating it the best I can. It never really left time for relationships."

"What about children?"

"It's the same, I did when I was young and innocent. Not after living this life. Do you, Gnat?"

"Not really, I never have. I've never gotten why it's called a miracle. As you said it's what we are biologically built to do, propagate the species. I've always noticed kids are so *smart*. It's because things haven't been defined for them yet. When they start school they're brainwashed with normalcy, taught everything works a certain way. The death of imagination is the victory of the administration, I guess. It's a mind-boggling concept to have a child. It is *completely* instinctual, the idea of living on. When a child is born in this generation's Irfa naturally and without thought, the only absolute is we come closer to our demise as a race each time it happens. We can't sustain ourselves any longer. Who would commit a life to what is coming in the future generations? No clean water, polluted air to breathe. To bring a being into suffering isn't selflessness. It's selfishness.

It's a self-fulfilling narrative. People grow up and have kids, and do everything 'for their kids.' The kids grow up, and do everything 'for *their* kids.' It's about the perpetuation of genes, not love..."

"Oh, I agree," Tiria exclaims. "People name their children after themselves, trying to live forever. When did the idea change from providing for your child, then letting them go out and discover things on their own, to *living* for them and nothing else? Is it consumerism? Boredom? Is it the ebb and flow of the times, the generations? Searching for things you were deprived of through them? There's an irony in the desire for children. I haven't had my own, no. Yet I've eaten, I've slept, I breathe. I know what it is to do the things I am meant to do organically. The emotion of having a child supersedes truth, it's another biological process. A tangible proposition of immortality. That's where a *mother's wrath* comes from. It isn't for the child specifically. Not what they do or achieve, only that they live on within another vessel. It must be protected at every cost.

I've been responsible for the lives of thousands of people. I understand the importance of imprinting on another. If we base it on only right and wrong as we've been told, no matter what you do half the people think it's incorrect anyway."

"It no more than comes down to that idea, doesn't it?" asks Gnat. "Self-awareness is an evolutionary disadvantage. A fish eats when it eats, swims, and tries to fend off predators. Plants fight for the sustenance of the sun. When they die it's a function of the cycle, there isn't a thought as to *why*. They never know the difference. Knowing the difference made us create things that don't serve anything but what we say it should. Everything can be traced to instinct; society calls it emotion. Some will survive, some will rule, some will perish. The details don't matter. The advantage within the system is to ignore it. In the end we are gone the same as every living thing."

"Play me a song, Gnat." She sighs.

He opens the case and plays a chord; the altitude has changed the tuning. He must return it to balance. He thinks of a song he hasn't played since before he left home, when he was first learning. Before things were apparent, before he had his own routines or Eed's patterns. It's slow and soft, written by an angry boy not knowing what he felt.

If you knew the places that I've known
You would see where a mind could go.
I've been to the dell of a demon's lair
Fought my way out with a lightning saber.
But you don't know
No you, don't know.

I went to the land of a thousand ghosts.
Stole my way out with a poetic rope.
But you don't know
No you, don't know.

I flew around the world on the back of a bee
Let the spirit of the land go and set me free.
But you can't see
What makes me, me.

If you knew the places that I've known.
If you knew the places that I've known.

I went to the gates just a saint and me
He said I'm stuck on the Irfa where it's easy to breed.
But you, you don't know
It's a good thing, that you don't.
O-O-O
O-o-O

"What's the story?" she asks.

"I was home in Oia. My younger sister is Ima, she was away at her private university and came home to visit. She started lecturing me about how my actions were wrong, that she knew better. The whole high-and-mighty liberal arts student speech. I told her she didn't know the real world. I got on my motorcycle and started riding. I rode the loop of a nearby highway, then wrote those words."

"Your music is very raw. Have you ever tried to pursue it?"

Gnat lowers his head. "Not hard enough. I saw what the industry is, pretty faces for profit. People release an album and are never heard from again. No names. No feeling. Everything that's recorded now is a sampled remix of a remix. The voices aren't real, the instruments are tuned and played by processors. It's become noise made by millions."

"Where is your family? What do they do?" she prods.

"In Oia, being clones. My parents and sister, I care about. My mother and father are the best people I've met, really. The rest, no connection. I don't agree with the whole idea of being kind or nice to someone because of genetic obligation."

Tiria makes eye-contact with him. "Do you feel connected to me?"

"Yes."

"Do you know what beauty is?"

"What is it, Tiria?"

"Being able to express a mental connection physically."

"Are you making an advance on me?" He throws charm at her.

"Now, why would I do that?"

"I'm not your typical intern with a business degree, I don't have a degree at all. Isn't that a prerequisite for your type?"

She moves to the seat next to him. "Usually."

An interruption blasts on the intercom from the pilot. "Ms. Sika, we'll be starting our descent and approach shortly."

"To be in Austopia?" Gnat says, stunned.

"We can travel twice the speed of a commercial airliner. Perks of the job."

"You get everything you want, don't you, Ms. Sika?"

Tiria leans in, kissing Gnat. It isn't electric. It doesn't make his stomach drop, or take his breath away. It is familiar, he feels peculiar. Comfortable.

What action could block these unstoppable forces from crumbling what we understand here and now, based on history, patterns, and conscious experience? Not the speeches and piety of a prophet or a figurehead, that would only bring strife. Argument. Anger. I can't be that. Eed missed that piece. It could only be the words of someone drowned in the bland nothingness surrounding them. The voice of a nobody, someone that understands the freedom in this designation. A human, a chance, perceiving existence as only a glimmer before it vanishes again.

Gnat comes to this realization as Tiria turns the dimmer switch for the cabin lights down. The ambience is charged with anticipation. He can only see her silhouette as she removes her jewelry...

The jet has landed, they lie on a blanket in the aisle. Taxiing to their place in a hangar, the captain gives them salutations over the speaker. They remain still, processing what happened between them. Tiria is the first to speak.

"Expanding your perception of these constructs and institutions, you'll only come to the same conclusion I have. It's not worth the energy. Stay with me, we'll exist above it and for ourselves. People think I'm arrogant, I'm not. I just understand something they don't. It happens to be the thing that makes me see everything in this existence is a joke. I recognize I am meaningless, like everyone else.

No judgments, it's the simple truth. The truth that's bigger than opinion or thought. Whether you want to believe or not, it's what we are."

"Growths on a pebble," Gnat drones, monotone.

"Yes. Think of the history of Irfa compared to the history of humans. Four billion spans, another countless number of billions until our sun collapses. We've made it a couple of hundred thousand at most? The giant reptiles ruled the land for two hundred fifty million! Self-awareness tells us this was created for us? We'll be history and another race will rule. And, another after that. Destruction follows the destructive. The wretched. The hapless. The ignorant. The unknowing. It isn't tragedy or plight. It's not foretold in some prophecy, it's not destined. It's random. It is chance, pushed along..."

"...by chaos and physics," he concludes.

"Gnat, forget finding the answer, it's for not."

For an instant, in which time is immeasurable, he stares at his hands. She's correct on some levels. Yet his fingers are long and skinny, still seeking what they have since the beginning. If he stays with her, he'll be doing the thing he's despised in every finding. *Taking the easy path.* Selling himself short for comfort. Denying the truth. Gnat studies her eyes, they have a sudden immaturity about them. He could bring her back if he took time to help her. They could figure it out together, this would be a stepping stone for him...

Don't lose sight. Eed's words. He comes to his senses, emotions so readily mask intent. As soon as they're considered, they strangle sensibility.

A touch of compunction on his tongue. *Who is this person? What are they doing?* He knows not if he is speaking of her or himself. *Eed exists in reason, not understanding the paradox of letting his feeling of failure control his actions. Tiria is the master of manipulating emotion in society, no higher. This disparity, I can see why they've failed. It's because they are still human. They have let weakness keep them from seeing.*

"I have to go," he tells her. "I can't stay, I won't. Both of you have gotten stuck. You and Eed. I know why, now. I have to find this answer, if it does nothing but kill me then so be it. I've been searching too long to settle. For you, with you, for anyone or anything. I'll stay in Austopia, but I'm leaving."

"Why have I gotten stuck?" she asks.

Gnat puts on his clothes, he ties his boots. "Because you are *human.*"

She pulls the blanket over her chest. "Where will you go?"

"Wherever my conclusion is. I'm sorry, Tiria. This ending isn't the option that leads me where I want to be."

She touches his leg. "When you find the answer, will you find me?"

"If you can be found, yes." He throws his bag around his shoulders and zips his guitar in the case, grinning. "Until then."

The last pulse of their combined energies says they both know it will never happen. He descends the steps of the plane, and, leaving the airfield, doesn't glance back.

***

Gnat feels lighter, spry. The weight is gone, that thing pulling him to the ground. His head is clear. He doesn't know why at first, then it comes to him.

The misinformation, the façade, the common courtesy is shed. The biggest abstraction of our species is the individual that does for itself, and the one that does for all. We must transcend definition itself. It's nothing but a shackle, both sides. We must rise above being human. Yes. Chaos and physics, chance. It accounts for the possibility of intelligent life evolving at some point. The scale of the universe, even as we know it is immense.

For us, unending. Infinite. Withal, the distances required to reach other places is unfathomable to our minds. Blocked to us, we aren't allowed to grow past our origin. We may or may not be alone. It's unimportant. We will never find out. Self-awareness, again, is the pitfall making us think it was made for us. Individually, along with the whole. In turn we consume everything and commit ourselves to damnation, unknowingly, before we gain the ability to rise. A greater vision of existence. It's the check. It's the evolutionary check. To keep the balance of things. What starts as your primary advantage in the beginning, allowing you to take dominion of your habitat, is also the thing that destroys you in the end. A sword with two edges. The biggest strength and weakness of a species. Self-awareness. It is the end of evolution. The failsafe of chance.

He cuts down a lane running across what seems to be a desert, guided by a corridor of conifers. The dirt is dried and cracked by the heat, forming scales that resemble the skin of a mythical creature. There's vegetation aplenty. The grass is similar to what is found in Omrika, the seeds are of a different shape, however. Skinnier, yet more robust. A small mammal scurries over the road. A miniature armadillo with no armor, short hair, and the tail of a rat. It heads into a grove of trees, palms. The pines remind him of the pictures drawn by a doctor in children's books he read growing up. Off-putting. A strange landscape, it feels surreal. Fictive.

Gnat remembers where he is. Austopia is an entire continent completely separate from any other in the middle of an ocean. It has everything the rest of Irfa does, in the sense of plants and animals. It came to be in its own fashion.

"If you don't believe in evolution, come here," Gnat says. He is well-conditioned in conscious and physical form concurrently. He's regained his confidence, in a manner of speaking. A sign reads:

NEXT TOWN NUMBAWA

"I could use the exercise. I'll have a walkabout." Gnat straightens, heading toward whatever is to be found. *Because I can.*

Numbawa is an isolated place, dry and dusty. Not kissed by the heat, scorched by it. He's stopped here to get supplies: a fishing pole, a knife, two empty journals and pens. He sends an email to his father. His salutation at the end of the message holds three syllables. *Almost there.* He'll head along the coast sleeping in the bush. Until he discovers a spot where he can finish what's been started.

The land in Austopia is tough. They lack any large predators, but as he travels he meets many insects and reptiles, all of which could kill him. He's beaten death and remains unafraid. It won't be a spider or snake that keeps him from finding it. *Whatever 'it' is.* Fresh water sources are scarce. He catches a glimpse of mist near the ocean and moves toward the coast, investigating.

A ridge above the water of a bay. A drop of twenty stories to the surface of the sea. A beach makes its way off to the right in a giant semicircle, the land touching the water is bleached and rocky. Schools of dolphins can be seen in the deep, playing and avoiding boats that troll off the coast. Gnat watches the swell of the currents across the horizon. Massive, unbroken waves rolling with the force of a raging mammoth. A man recognizes his frailty in this setting. Even the inboard diesels that push through them, designed for the task, struggle. To the left, a quarry of cliffs catches the waves that don't break in the open but cataclysmically clash with the rock. A visible lie. The water is winning the battle yet results can't be seen even in a minuscule fashion until the lives of a million men pass successively. He hauls his gear up the face of a hill behind the ridge to set up camp.

***

Gnat uses the rod to catch fish, the knife to clean his catch. He cooks over an open flame. His beard is uncut, his skin has darkened. He's skinny, he's relaxed. The sight of another person hasn't occurred except for the men that work the boats in the distance. They can't see him, though he might make out the shape of someone occasionally. Gnat is crisp, unworried, untethered. Twenty-seven moons have passed in this way. He lives with the light, sleeps in the night.

The journals and pens were purchased with intent. He has written them down, the patterns. The teachings. The things coming to fruition since meeting Eed. Not his life, he hasn't put his name on it, that isn't the idea. He will send one copy to sea, he will bury the other.

"I must bring people back to rationality!" he says, picking a journal up. "We are here now, that's all it's ever going to be. No more false hope. See what we are! *Animals surviving.* For that reason and no other. Believing things will be different, thinking there's some purpose only hinders the possibility of harmony. In the end sacrifice is the only thing that can bring change. Not talking about it. Not trying to force equality. Making a choice and sticking to it. We've seen what is being offered. There is no better or worse, only what is happening."

He puts the finished journal in a plastic bag, then another. With a palm frond he weaves the separated leaves tightly around the journal making yet another waterproof layer that can't be easily penetrated. He ties three coconuts to it, floats, and barefoot strolls toward the sandy beach.

At the water's edge he strips his clothes and starts to swim out past the cliffs, farther than dolphins hunt, until the current isn't sweeping everything to shore. Treading, he pushes the package away. The swell must be twice the height of a man. The coconuts start to retreat, to bear what fruit if any isn't known. He floats, ears underwater. It covers their ringing. The only place he hears silence, if such a thing exists. He closes his eyes, losing himself in the rise and fall of the ocean. His head comes fully up over the cresting surge. He hears a sound. *A human sound.* Turning to shore, the shape of a person waves, shouting. He begins to swim, unsure if the target is him or another. *There isn't anyone else around.*

On dry land an older man approaches him, a Mo'ti. The natives of Austopia, with skin of a copper tint and tattoos on their faces. He wears modern clothes, this isn't a shaman or a spiritual entity. However, the Mo'ti are steeped with an intrinsic insight to the land.

"Feeding time is coming for creatures in the water, the sun is past its prime. You shouldn't be wading that far out, friend," the Mo'ti tells him.

Gnat smiles. "I'll take your advice, it's too cold anyway."

"Where are you from? You don't sound Austopian."

"I'm Omrikan, from Oia. The corn fields. What about you?"

"I grew up here on the sea. Do you know how the Mo'ti say this bay was made?" he asks.

"No, how?"

"This crescent, the beach, is the mouth of a fish. The ridge there, high above us, is curved also, see?" The man points. "That's the hook of a fishing rod. The cliffs, they were the canoe where our deity sat waiting with his pole in the water. When the fish took the bait, the deity didn't know how big it was. He pulled up, it fought too hard. He left the boat and jumped to the clouds, pulling the hook and boat out, but the fish stayed on the surface of the water. It died from breathing the air and stayed where it was. The water brought the rocks, and crushed it into sand. Here we stand!"

"Interesting." Gnat nods. He notices a neon speck, hardly visible except for its mismatched color against the sand. He moves closer with arms crossed and he sees another. As his focus widens there are many, thousands float in the surf.

"What are those?" he asks the old man.

The Mo'ti points to a reef on the far end of the beach opposite the ridge Gnat occupies. It's magnificent, vibrant, and alive. Gnat sees it each sunrise from his perch.

"They become that. You stay safe."

"You too," Gnat says, already putting the pieces together internally.

Will we ever find out everything we hold on to now is false? Primitive man and his primal explanations of how things came to be. We still are that, primitive. What is the next step? The next level?

Humans are still in their larval stage. Like the coral. Floating, lost. From the smallest organism to the largest, everything is only doing what it needs to exist.

He begins the climb to his dwelling, where he watches the turning of existence.

The Irfa itself is still in its larval stage, a neon speck in the fluid. Not until you understand the function of this planet within the universe can you become integrated. It could be considered evolutionary, possibly. Irfa is no longer relevant once you know what it is. A means to an end, for life here while it exists. I must become... cerebral. I must get to the reef. To the whole.

Up the trail he finds an old metal lunchbox partly buried under a bush. He retrieves it. The chill of night has come. He strikes the knife against a flint to make sparks, to create an ember. *To start a fire.* The other journal is placed in bags and wrapped with fronds. Gnat places it in the tin box he found and shuts the latch. He begins to dig a hole in the ridge. The Irfa is hard densely packed granules of dirt and rock. He begins to breathe heavily, then sweat. Continuing until the entire length of his arm is extended to reach the bottom. The box is placed inside and covered.

"We are moving through life either stagnantly, as the dirt, or transcendently, as the sea," says the Omrikan, clapping his hands together to remove the dust. "The individuals' petty needs are the reason the Irfa is being destroyed. There are too many people, too many governmental dissolutions. I'm ready for the next plane. I know what I am. I know what we are. No more systems. No more definitions. I must elevate. What is the way out? My life as a hairless ape is finished. I'm ready to go, without anxiety or frustration. I can't change things in this time, or place. It's too far gone."

Sitting with perfect posture, he feels nimble. No hunger pangs him, although he's been without a meal for many tides. His hands tingle, he studies them. Nerves vibrating, they feel as if they are being stung by bees with electric stingers. *My totem.* He reclines, the sky's the only thing in his vision. The stars are starting to show faintly. No mist is observed. It's so clear, he couldn't possibly imagine what shape a cloud would take in this emptiness. However, it isn't empty.

"We're connected, here, also to everything we can't see. Made from the same particles. Physical form is unimportant. Eed was right, there *is* a larger circle, he let the emotion of his failure with Tiria blind him. It *took* his ability to find it."

Then he grasps what he has. *Clarity, of essence. In its true form. Not like the jump, or drugs. I've opened the connection without the substances.*

"The reason revolution fails; some group is trying to change another. The true revolution is within yourself. You are living exactly the life you want to be living. The past, the labels are only excuses, deflection of this fact. Personal beliefs, organizations, and relationships are justification for taking the easy way and not questioning everything around you endlessly.

There is no guiding light, nothing forcing you or testing you with choices. Seeing this you can rise above the curse of self-awareness.

Tiria spoke about manifesting what you need in your life. I know what I needed, the answer. I've put that intention within everything I've done. Because of this I found Eed. I found Tiria. I found the patterns, the circles, that brought me here. To clarity. Validation of myself. For myself, no other."

The buzzing runs up his arms, it's in his chest. The ringing in his ears intensifies, a wildfire runs through the membranes of his entirety. There is no weight, there is no pressure. He is a feather. Transparent. Airy.

The irrational yet quantifiable timing of my life. Always the worst moment or the best. Never normal. Always ex-curse. Stretched, like the ideas I've held on to. Because I don't try to control it, I just go. My lows are lower, my peaks are higher. I am always honest and earn another story to tell. A fiber to connect. A lesson to pass on. Again! When the situation presents itself I experience and therefore hold dear every instant of my life.

"I am... coalescent," Gnat gasps. "The tenth person. That's the name. *The coalescent...*"

Taken from and given back to the same whole. I have learned to see the connection of all things at once. There is no coming to balance as humans, it's too late for us. Our essence is tainted by greed and love of self. My intangible consciousness can only wait, the virtue that prevails across dimension. For another iteration of life, with the desire to understand. It may not even be on Irfa, that's immaterial. This isn't reincarnation, or suicide. It's broader. Higher, all-encompassing. Reincarnation is a curse to be trapped on Irfa until its demise. The flow of consciousness and knowledge within existence, that's what I have found. It's not the identity of an individual, it won't hold the memory of me. Just coalescent energy. I won't need to prove myself or learn again. The next being will already know.

Maybe these are the ones that discover things that create civilizations and push them forward. The great scientists, the artists. They became coalescent, somewhere else, in some other time. They transcended and became human. Not knowingly, the energy roamed the cosmos and filtered itself into that being, eventually. By... chance...

A strong gust comes down the ridge, blowing the flame of his fire toward the ocean. It flickers, holding on, staying alight. Gnat's permanence and senses are in a crescendo of magnetism and brilliance. The wind cuts through his core, he's becoming part of it. It moves him to stand.

"The Irfa is poisoned, yes."

The voice enters his head, screaming over the gust that remains. It has become a gale. *BUT I NO LONGER AM.*

Gnat laughs hysterically. "The voice! It's mine, it always has been..."

The turbulence pushes him forward, his hair runs in violent circles. He squints his eyes, they're almost closed. *I'm complete.*

He steps to the cliff and out. There is no plummet. Below, there is no crash, nothing sinks in the waves. The man has dematerialized, the body is no more. Memories erased, only the knowledge remains. It has dissipated into the wind. Flowing and following it to whatever end of the universe necessary. The coalescent seed of a dandelion, drifting as its harnesser had. The wisdom will plant itself somewhere. Until then, its understanding of existence is in the atmosphere. It is in the very air you breathe. *Right now.*

AFTERWARD

Alas, humans were doomed to perish as individuals and as a species. Not half a millennia passed after Gnat's consciousness reintegrated with the whole before the Irfa was unsuitable for mankind to sustain itself. Human beings are extinct, carried out by their own hand. Their neglect. Their disrespect. Their laxity in trying to comprehend balance. Even until the final members of the race died they argued over whose fault it was. Who had the answer, which of them could have handled it better.

Irfa lay damp and dormant, cleansing itself of the filth humans infected it with. Replenishing resources stripped from it entirely. With the aid of the cosmos; elements from vast distances brought in the form of meteors.

Another process proving chaos is absolution, a rock moving unhindered for twenty, fifty, ninety times as long as man existed through space untouched. Only to hit the gasses surrounding a planet causing colossal friction for the fraction of a contemplation. Flagrant vividness. Disintegration.

Eventually life starts to bubble on Irfa, then thrive. Evolution goes through the motions for its own sake.

A species rises to the top of the chain proclaiming itself intelligent. They devise a way of communicating, orchestrated grunts. Language. They transcribe these syllables visually to record. Mathematics help them define their existence with rules.

These creatures begin to explore. They find buried stone structures. The language of ancient man is deciphered. Their fossils are discovered and found to be tainted with radioactive fallout. Underground water tables are toxic, unusable, never to be clean again.

Every trace of the human has vanished except the examples they've left on how not to survive in equilibrium, but resolve in eradication. A mark was left, in the end. The endowment given to existence as a species? Ignorance.

-END-

www.ingramcontent.com/pod-product-compliance
Lightning Source LLC
Chambersburg PA
CBHW050113120726
47904CB00004B/1335